DEDICATION

For Captain USMC (Ret) and IAF (Ret) Lou Lenart, My beloved Older Brother, who one afternoon looked behind him, saw the entire Israeli Air Force, hit full throttle, took off into a setting sun, and saved a nation.

And for all the thousands of fallen and wounded, of all the wars of Israel, and those victims of the tens of thousands of terrorist attacks which have been part of Israel's life since its birth.

For Absent Friends.

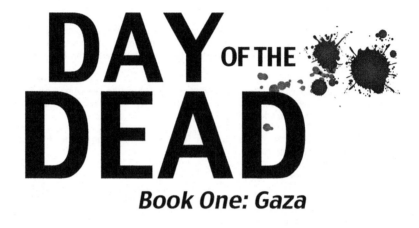

DAY OF THE DEAD

Book One: Gaza

BY:
CAPTAIN DAN GORDON
IDF (RES)

LIBERTY HILL
PUBLISHING

Day of the Dead
Book One: Gaza
by Captain Dan Gordon IDF (Res)

Printed in the United States of America.

Edited by Liberty Hill Publishing

ISBN 9781498430982

The two exceptions to the above are two very real people: Captain Lou Lenart, USMC/IAF (Ret), and Major General Doron Almog, IDF (Res). I consider both of them my Brothers, and my heroes.

In addition, Aleh Negev-Nahalat Eran Rehabilitation Village is not only a very real place, but one of the most inspirational facilities in the world. It is literally a one-of-a-kind place, that offers mentally challenged individuals, and their families, rehabilitative services, residence, hope, and unbounded love. For those looking for a worthy cause to support, please visit their website, http://aleh.org/donation-information/.

Additionally, donations can be made to Aleh Negev at the following:

JNF
7120 Hayvenhurst Avenue #200
Van Nuys,
CA 91406
or
ALEH Israel Foundation
P.O. Box 4911 New York, NY 10185
Tel: 1-866-717-0252 FREE / 917-732-2361
Fax: 212-517-3293
Email: dov@aleh-israel.org
Non-Profit ID: 30-0456686

Please designate clearly, on checks or to personnel, that any donations are to reach Aleh Negev-Nahalat Eran Rehabilitation Village.

www.libertyhillpublishing.com

ACKNOWLEDGEMENTS

I have had the honor of wearing the uniform of the Israel Defense Forces since October of 1973. I have been privileged to have served in one capacity or another in The Yom Kippur War (1973), during Operation Litani (albeit as a company sniper/squad leader in a reservist armored Infantry unit deployed in Sinai at the time - 1978), in Operation Defensive Shield (Jenin and Bethlehem - 2002), in The Second Lebanon War (Southern Lebanon/Northern Israel border - 2006), in Operation Cast Lead (Al Atatatra, Gaza, and Gaza border area - 2009), Operation Pillar of Defense (Gaza border area - 2012), and Operation Protective Edge (Gaza Border area - 2014).

I have been blessed to have served in the company of heroes.

After the war (Operation Protective Edge) in the summer of 2014, my agent, Jeff Berg, suggested that I had to do something with the accounts I had sent him and others during my service in that campaign. The subject of terrorist attack tunnels, he insisted, was a movie. The problem was, I said, that no one in Hollywood's current climate was going to make a movie in which Israeli soldiers are the good guys. Hamas, Hezbollah and a gullible, and sometimes ideologically motivated press have so vilified what is, in fact, one of the most moral fighting forces in the world, that takes more care to prevent civilian casualties than any other army on earth, that black has been turned into white, night to day, truth into a set of lies, and the victims of aggression have been portrayed as Nazis, for defending themselves against theocratic, genocidal, fascistic, imperialistic, misogynist, homophobic, racist, terrorist armies with names like ISIS, Hamas, Hezbollah, Bayt Al Maqdis, Boku Haram, Islamic Jihad, Jubhat al Nusra, and the nation of Iran, amongst others.

"So," said Jeff, "make it an American story."

"How do I do that?" I asked.

To which he replied, "You're the writer. I'm the agent. You write it, I'll sell it."

And he did. This book is now set to be a major movie. Bless you, Jeff!

In doing the research for this book, which drew upon numerous of my own experiences over the last forty years, I availed myself of the advice, counsel, and encouragement of my betters. Some people, because of their roles in the security of their nations, must remain nameless. They know who they are and how much I appreciate the help they have given me. I have been aided by numbers of retired members of various clandestine services. Again, they know who they are and I am forever grateful.

Amongst the US Military, I am particularly indebted to General Robert Magnus USMC (Ret), Former Assistant Commandant of the Marine Corps, for his advice, expertise, encouragement and unflagging friendship which, together with that of his amazing wife, Meredith, is one of the true blessings in my life. There have been only forty-eight four-star Generals in the entire history of the Marine Corps who achieved that rank while on active duty. Bob Magnus is one of them. I doubt that there has been another wife like Meredith.

Commander Richard Marcinko USN (Ret), first Commander of SEAL Team Six and Red Cell, who, many years ago, befriended me and allowed me, after many cans of adult beverages consumed in the early morning hours, to shoot his Counter-Terrorism pistol course and then afforded me the pleasure of his company in his amphibious vehicle at

Rogue Manor. His advice, humor, and wisdom have always stayed with me, and I hope I have done his spirit proud in this book.

Petty Officer First Class Harry Humphries USN (Ret) SEAL Team Two, President of Global Securities, who walked me through strategies, tactics, weapons, and procedures, and without whose expertise I could not have completed this work, and whose friendship I treasure.

Admiral Eric Olson USN (Ret) for his guidance and advice and steering me through proper procedures and channels.

Captain Lou Lenart, USMC (Ret), and IAF (Ret), for his love, friendship, advice, encouragement, inspiration, and example. Thank you, my dear "Older Brother", and my gratitude to his wonderful wife Rachel, who has graced me with her friendship as well.

Master Chief Petty Officer "T", USN (Ret), a true warrior with whom I was fortunate enough to spend many hours and Texas Longnecks.

Petty Officer First Class "B" USN (Ret) ditto, except with him it was brown liquor.

Staff Sgt. "D" US Special Forces (Ret) ditto on all counts.

In the Israeli Military, my gratitude to my "Brother", Major General (Res) Doron Almog, Founder of Aleh Negev-Nahalat Eran Rehabilitation Village, from whom I learned much more than military matters. He taught me about his son, of Blessed Memory, Eran, who, as he was for his father, has become one of my greatest teachers.

Brigadier General (Res) MK Avigdor Kahalani, one of Israel's greatest heroes, to whom the entire nation of Israel owes a debt of gratitude for reminding not only me, but an entire generation of Israeli soldiers, that one of the IDF's greatest strengths is that we have never taught our soldiers to hate.

Brigadier General Nissim Perez, for his encouragement, advice, enthusiasm for this project and, most of all, for his friendship.

Brigadier Generals (Res) Ron Kitri, Miri Eisen and MK Miri Regev, under all of whose command, I have had the pleasure and honor of serving. With special thanks to Brigadier General Regev, who okayed my battlefield promotion (against the sound advice of others, I'm sure) to Captain, and did me the honor of personally placing my Captain's bars on me after the Second Lebanon War.

To my sons, and grandson, and niece, and nephews, and grandnephews, and grandniece. No one could be prouder of you, nor love you more, nor be more grateful for your love.

To the memories of Abraham, Goddess, David, and Zaki Gordon. You gave me more love than I deserve, and I love you more than I can ever say. 'Til we meet again.

To the memory of Chanan, Mimi and Ron Greenwald, to Chaim and Vicky and Danny and Ora and Motke and Noah, and Robert, and all of *Kibbutz Ginegar*, who took me in as a schoolboy and gave me a home, that has been home to me ever since.

To the memory of Dror, my Rabbi and teacher, whom I loved as if he were one of my own sons.

To the entire Aloni clan, whom I "inherited" by being adopted by Mimi and Chanan. My beloved brother and sister and nephews, nieces and grandnephews and grandnieces and Noa. All my love. No one could want a better family, Polish *mishigas*, and all.

To the memory of Lieutenant General Motta Gur, who graced me with his friendship, regaled me with his stories, and provided a personal example.

To the memory of Lieutenant General Raful Eytan, who, from the time I was sixteen, befriended me, though I'm sure he could never quite figure out why. He was a wonderful friend to my foster parents, and shared with them, and me, the unspeakable tragedy of losing a son, and was one of Israel's greatest military leaders. More than that, however, he was one of the most soft-spoken, true *mensches* I have ever even heard of. The world is a poorer place for his absence.

To Ambassador Richard Schifter, for his very wise guidance and counsel concerning the byzantine intricacies of the United Nations Human Rights Council.

To Ambassador Michael Oren, and his wonderful wife Sally, for their love and friendship, spare bedroom, fine choice of whisky and cigars, for opening their home and hearts to me. To Michael, for being part of the Avis Recon Unit during the Second Lebanon War. We have literally been under fire together, both enemy and friendly, on numerous occasions, and there is no one with whom I'd rather have shared the privilege. Israel and the United States were both so very lucky to have you as the bridge over stormy waters.

Colonel (Res) Irit Atzmon, my former commander and dear, dear friend, a shining example of light to all who are lucky enough to know her.

Colonel Ofer Winter, Commander of one of Israel's most elite combat units, The Givati Brigade, whose contributions to the IDF's success in the last campaign are still classified, but whose inspiration and leadership and love for the soldiers under his command is absolutely unquestionable. One of the finest leaders I've ever had the privilege of knowing. You are an example to me every day.

To The Intelligence Officer, Operations Officer, and Education Officer of the Givati Brigade. No words can adequately express my gratitude for the amount of time you took answering countless questions, and receiving me as one of your own. To the Battalion Commanders, Deputy Battalion Commanders, Company Commanders, non-commissioned officers and soldiers of Givati, with whom I was so very honored and privileged to spend time, sweat with, laugh with, celebrate with, and at times, with whom I unashamedly shared tears. You are my adopted home and brothers and sisters, and *segol* is forever the most beautiful color in the world to me from now on! *Yachad, virak Yachad!*

To Lieutenant Colonel (Res) Danny Grossman, for his friendship, homemade brownies, love and hospitality and the pure joy of allowing me to share a few moments with his mother, my "girlfriend", Roz, of Blessed Memory, who lit up the room with her wit and brilliance, and who, if I was thirty years older, I would have chased around the home in my walker.

To Lieutenant Colonel (Res) Anat Berko, PhD, for her guidance and expertise regarding the inner workings of the various Islamist terrorist networks, organizations and armies, and for her true and warm friendship.

To Lieutenant Colonel Peter Lerner of The Military Spokesperson Unit, who many times, against his better judgment, allowed me the privilege of serving during the last campaign.

To Pamela Lazarus of Sar El, who, without hesitation, allowed me to serve in that wonderful organization, provided encouragement and enthusiasm for this project, and whose friendship has been one of the gifts of the last summer.

To Roni and Ditta Ninio, for their love, hospitality, spare bedroom, the affection of their dogs, and the quality of their *arak*.

To Don Ernesto, whose restaurant is more like *Ca della Nonna*, and whose food is only matched by the warmth of its owner and staff.

To my mentors, of Blessed Memory: Ya'akov Zarchi, of *Kibbutz Ginegar*, who educated generations through a personal example of what it was to be a moral human being. To Shlomo Karniel, who came to me when I was a sixteen-year-old schoolboy in Israel, and said, "I think I have bad news for you. I think you may be a writer." To Corey Allen, Don Simpson, and Michael Landon, of Blessed Memories, who taught me my craft, and graced me with their friendship.

To Mazal Nechama, who has opened so many doors for me and continues to do so, and without whose efforts and friendship none of this work would have been possible.

To Yaron Ben David, for his tireless translation efforts, and to Arnon Friedman, for his musical collaboration and hospitality.

To Shlomi and Einat Pilo, for their love, friendship and wonderful place to crash for a somewhat aged "Lone Soldier".

To my fellow officers of The International Communications Battalion of the Military Spokesperson Brigade: Lieutenant Colonel (Res) Avital Leibovitch, Lieutenant Colonel (Res) Jonathan Davis, Lieutenant Colonel (Res) Yehuda Weinrob, Lieutenant Colonel (Res) Olivier Raffovitz, Major (Res) David Baruch, Major (Res) Michael Oren, Captain (Res) Doron Schpielman, my holy brother, and Arye Green, who accomplishes more out of uniform, day in and day out, as one of Israel's most effective spokespeople.

To Sgt (Ret) Itzik Magal, my Babylonian brother, for his love and humor and teaching me to appreciate his Navajo dialect.

To Corporal (Ret) Ygal Giramberk and 1st Sgt (Ret) Carl Perkal, for forty years of love and friendship and laughter and encouragement and good food and always a place to crash.

To the entire family of The IDC Herzliyah, with whom I was privileged to work during Operation Protective Edge, to their students and dedicated faculty who have become *mishpacha* to me.

To Canadian Minister of Justice Irwin Cotler, who, together with Alan Dershowitz, are Israel's most eloquent Defenders, and who have been so encouraging to me during this last war.

To Her Honor Judge Jeanine Pirro, for steadfastly and unflinchingly standing with the people of Israel, and always on the side of Justice.

To Pastor John Hagee of CUFI, for allowing me to brief him on a daily basis during Operation Pillar of Defense, 2012.

To President Jerry Falwell of Liberty University, and Pastor Jon Falwell of Thomas Road Baptist Church, two of the most innovative leaders I have ever met, who distributed countless of my frontline blog postings to the Liberty University/Thomas Road family, throughout the war.

To Rabbis Pinchas Allouche, David Baron and Alicia Magal, for their love, support and prayers and keeping me in their, and their congregations' hearts throughout Operation Protective Edge, and for their ongoing love and friendship.

To Rob Eshman of *The Jewish Journal*, and Thomas Lifson of *American Thinker*, two of the most thoughtful and supportive editors in Journalism today. With unbridled appreciation and gratitude.

To Sara and Efraim Golan and the entire mob, who took me into their home and hearts with so much love, and have become my second family. To Shai Hermesh, of *Kibbutz Kfar Aza*, who shared his wisdom and friendship, and said to remember that his home was now mine.

To Mary Guibert, who was the inspiration for one of the characters in this book; we have shared love, laughter, tragedy, and unbelievable blessings, for over half a century.

To the memories of Tim Buckley, and Jeffrey Scott Buckley, one of whom I loved as a brother, the other as a son, both of whom were also the inspiration for characters in this book. May their memories be a blessing.

To Orna Granot who lovingly demolished every obstacle in her path, encouraging me, and this project, and making so very much of it possible, who shared her family, boundless energy, talent, drive and, most of all, loving friendship. This would not have been possible without you. *Ani asir todoth*, amongst other things.

To Sandy Price, who, during the war, became a one-woman distribution network of blogs and articles, and to whom I am so very grateful. To Helen Friedman, for her friendship and encouragement, and hooking me up with Sar El. To Judy Sirkus, for her tireless and loving encouragement. To Chris Mitchel, Jerusalem Bureau Chief of CBN, my Christian brother, with whom I have prayed and been under fire, joked and conspired. To Bodie and Brock Thoene, and Robin Handley, for years of friendship and prayers on my behalf. To Franceen Brodkin, for her constant love, support, and feedback. To Leanne Micinilio and Tye, for their friendship, and sandwiches for the road. To Sharon Markenson, the love of my youth, and Susie Congdon, for all their support, and reading the dispatches. To my sister from another mother, Suzanne DePasse, for her love, support, and for the sheer pleasure of her company. To Tera Dahl, for her friendship, integrity, and expertise on all matters Kurdish and Egyptian, and for holding my feet to the fire on certain story points.

To Steve Pressfield, for his expert encouragement and publishing advise. To Tim McKeever, my fellow writer and power lifting coach, author of *The Monk*, and the soon-to-be-published *Gum Drop House*, for constant feedback on each draft.

To my dear friends, Corby Alsbrook and Larry Boren. You were my best friends when we were in grade school, and still are.

To Zach Brutsche, for all things New Mexico, and all the Lebowski quotes.

Finally for the men and women of the Israel Defense Forces, and the US Army, Navy, Air Force, Marines, and Coast Guard, my brothers and sisters in arms, for all you do to keep us free and safe, and for the families who stand behind them, suffer and rejoice with them, and are there waiting when they return.

Excerpt from "The Coward" by Eve Merriam. From Family Circle, copyright 1946 by Yale University Press. Used by permission of Marian Reiner.

FOREWORD

Captain (Res) Dan Gordon of the IDF Spokesperson's Unit, served in Israel during the recent military operation 'Protective Edge'. We were then facing a constant barrage of attacks from some 5,000 missiles and rockets that were fired from the Gaza Strip toward heavily populated civilian areas under Israeli sovereignty. Dan took the time to visit us at Aleh Negev-Nahalat Eran – the Rehabilitation Village in the south of Israel that I founded on behalf of my beloved son, Eran, and people like him – those with intellectual and developmental disabilities. It was there, in the line of fire, that we were privileged to get to know Dan as someone who deeply loves this country – especially the disabled children here – the most vulnerable members of our society. Dan is more than a superb screenwriter; first and foremost, he is a man whose worldview encompasses patriotic, moral and humanistic values, a man who wields his pen critically to document reality with a judicious eye.

Major General (Res) Doron Almog, IDF
Founder and Chairman of Aleh Negev-Nahalat Eran
Rehabilitation Village

CHAPTER 1

July 7, 2014. 9:00 a.m., EST

T he meeting in the Oval Office was set for 9:00 a.m. sharp. Thus, Vice President Bo Fitzgerald had left the Old Executive Office Building and walked across the street to the White House, entering the West Wing lobby at precisely 8:45 a.m. He had been up since 6:00 a.m. prepping for the meeting. His ever-faithful secretary of thirty-five years, Jane Woodhall, a once-attractive woman in her late sixties, in bad need of a lifestyle lift, had made up a series of 3x5 index cards with overly-large print, so that the Vice President, always aware of the fact that, at seventy-two, he was the oldest member of the team, would not have to resort to using reading glasses. He had considered using Grecian Formula Number One to add touches of black to his already white hair, not unlike the recently appointed anchor of a cable news network who had, over the course of six months, gone from elderly white, to a sort of George Clooney, salt-and-pepper look. Vice President Fitzgerald was, however, aware that his early hair transplant, though infinitely more attractive than the bald pate it had replaced, had become the object of derision amongst right-wing radio talk show hosts. Thus, he was not about to give them more ammunition with which to take potshots against him, despite the certain knowledge that a more youthful appearance gave him a better chance against Edie Washington Howell, should he decide to run for his party's nomination two years hence.

After entering the West Wing's first floor lobby, he turned right, and then left, and made for the Vice President's ceremonial office, where he would wait until the appointed hour for the President's Briefing, which would take place in the Oval Office. At 8:55, he exited his ceremonial office, and turned right; ducking into the office of Chief of Staff Henry Clevinger, simply to make sure that the meeting was still on, and about to take place in the Oval Office. Clevinger was the equivalent of the Angel with the Fiery Sword stationed by the Almighty at the Gates of Eden, to keep Adam and Eve from returning to Paradise. But, on this particular morning, neither Clevinger nor his secretary, or "executive assistant" in the current, gender-neutral parlance of our times, was in the office.

Fitzgerald ambled down the hallway, passed the offices of various staffers, passed the Roosevelt Room on his left, and the President's Private Dining Room and Study on his right. He made a left at the Roosevelt Room, and turned right into the President's Executive Assistant's office. Valerie Jeffers, the President's E.A., looked up, smiling her condescending smile, and said, "Good morning, Mr. Vice President."

"Top of the morning to you, too, Valerie. We all set?"

"I'm sorry, sir," she said. "Didn't you get the memo?"

"Didn't you get the memo" were the words Vice President Fitzgerald had come to loathe.

No, he thought. He never got the memo! It was the latest in POTUS' unending series of slights against the older man, who had once made the dreadful mistake of calling then-Senator Rafik Mohammed Kabila "The first mainstream African-American who was articulate, bright and clean... I mean, the guy is light-skinned, with no discernible Negro dialect – unless he needs it."

Though Fitzgerald had apologized profusely, and publicly, the fact that Kabila had chosen Fitzgerald as his running mate had less to do with POTUS-Elect's acceptance of the older man's apology, and more to do with the fact that he wanted to deny the second-highest office in the land to Edie Washington Howell. He never wanted it to be said that an African American and a former First Lady were any kind of Dream Team. Indeed, Fitzgerald brought nothing to the ticket, which is why Kabila chose him. He wanted the victory to be his, and his alone. Moreover, he secretly relished the thought of humiliating everybody's affable, crazy Irish uncle for the next four years.

"The meeting has been switched to the Situation Room, Mr. Vice President. I believe they're already in session."

This, of course, added another level of humiliation to the start of Fitzgerald's morning. He exited Valerie Jeffers' office, turned right, passed the conference room, and the President's secretary, passed the press-staff offices, and the Press Corps Briefing Room, and the Press Corps Offices, thus making sure that members of the Fourth Estate saw him hurrying along, obviously late for yet *another* meeting.

This led him down into the White House basement, and yet another set of minor humiliations, as he passed through the lobby, sundried offices, the Wardroom, the Videoconference Room, the Briefing Room, the Navy Mess and Kitchen, and, finally, into the Situation Room, to which he was admitted by the Marine sentry on duty. As he entered the Situation Room, CIA Director James Francis Doherty interrupted his briefing in mid-sentence, and gave Bo Fitzgerald a smiling and understanding look.

"Morning, Bo. Glad you could make it," POTUS said drily.

"I'm sorry, Mr. President," Fitzgerald said, with as much dignity as he could muster. "Someone failed to notify me of the change in venue."

"No problem," said President Kabila. "We're just getting started. Francis, would you mind briefly bringing Bo up to speed?"

"Of course, Mr. President." As CIA Director Francis Doherty skipped through his notes, and backed up through his PowerPoint presentation, Vice President Fitzgerald quickly looked around the room. It was the full National Security team, plus one. The plus one in question was, as always, Attorney General Steadman, one of POTUS' oldest, most trusted friends and confidants.

The National Security team included National Security Advisor Deborah Wheatley, a visibly hungover and puffy-eyed Sec.Def. Dick Gaynor, the always pompously well-coiffed Secretary of State Jack O'Leary, Chairman of the Joint Chiefs, Army General Matt Tunney, CIA Director James Francis Doherty, Acting FBI Director Jack Profitt, Acting DEA Director Mrs. Graciel Esteves, and POTUS' ever-present political advisor, Mallory Mohsen.

Fitzgerald could not help but think that he'd never seen a room so full of people who had such obvious disdain for one another.

Both he and Secretary of State Jack O'Leary had run for the Presidency themselves, and both thought themselves infinitely more qualified than the former Junior Senator from Motown, who now sat in the black, high-backed leather chair at the head of the long wooden table and called the shots.

As for POTUS, he took the same opportunity, and glanced around the room, and the thought hit him, not for the first time, that, aside from Attorney General Steadman, he was the only black man in attendance in a room full of nothing but Irishmen, and Graciel Esteves, Acting Director of the DEA.

Actually, that wasn't 100% correct. POTUS had more right to call himself an Irishman than did Jack O'Leary.

POTUS' maternal grandfather was an affable, drunken WWII vet named Jim O'Callaghan.

Jack O'Leary's grandfather, after whom he was named, on the other hand, was the former Yasha Levy who, upon arrival at Ellis Island, decided to shed himself of the burden of anti-Semitism, and was reborn as Jack O'Leary.

The dumb putz *actually thought it was a step up to be an Irish Catholic*, POTUS thought to himself, and smiled ruefully.

It was not lost on him that both O'Leary and Fitzgerald concealed, in their secret heart of hearts, the ironic jealousy they both felt for the color of POTUS's skin.

If only they had been born black, POTUS knew they believed, they would have been sitting in the high-backed leather chair at the head of the wooden table themselves.

He felt a surge of righteous indignation against the key members of his own inner circle who were, indeed, not a team of rivals, but of men who harbored deep resentments and genuine loathing for one another, and their Commander in Chief.

Well, tough noogies, POTUS thought. *I won.*

CIA Director Doherty had now arranged his notes, and his PowerPoint presentation. The point of today's sudden, but in no way emergency, meeting was that a message had come in from Hamid Berzingi, the leader of the autonomous Kurdish region of Iraq. The Peshmerga, the military force of the autonomous region, had just captured a senior ISIS operative.

"You mean ISIL," POTUS interrupted.

ISIS stood for the Islamic State in Iraq and Syria. *Syria* was not a name which POTUS allowed to be tolerated in his presence, ever since its dictator, Bashar al Assad, had stepped across POTUS' hastily-declared, and ill-conceived, redline of using chemical weapons against his own people.

In the showdown between them, POTUS had blinked first.

He had absolutely no intention of revisiting that most humiliating episode of his Presidency. Thus, ISIS was always to be referred to as "ISIL", the Islamic State of Iraq and *The Levant*.

"Yes sir, Mr. President," CIA Director Doherty corrected himself. "The Peshmerga have recently captured an ISIL operative."

The operative in question, Yehyeh Al-Masri, claimed to have direct knowledge of what he said would be a mass-casualty attack against the United States heartland, carried out by ISIL, and, somehow, involving members of Mexican and South American drug cartels, as well.

The Peshmerga were evidently willing to trade Al-Masri for heavy weapons, which they desperately needed to fight off the growing threat from ISIL, whom they believed were spreading from non-Kurdish Iraq and Syria into the heart of the autonomous Kurdish region.

They were on the verge of capturing Mosul, had basically obliterated the border between Iraq and Syria, and were claiming the lands they had conquered for the Caliphate, or Islamic State, run by their charismatic leader, Abu Bakr al-Baghdadi. Baghdadi's parting words to his former American captors, upon release from his prison cell at Camp Bucca, where he had been held as a "civilian internee", were "See you in New York."

For his part, POTUS wanted no part in taking custody of an ISIL terrorist.

"I mean, if we did that, it would make *us* an ISIL target. It would give them an excuse to kidnap American personnel, to negotiate for the release of this Al-Masri. I don't want any part of that!"

Indeed, POTUS wanted no part of ISIL, nor, for that matter, anything to do with the entire Middle East, from which he had been trying to extricate the United States for the first six years of his Presidency.

"I mean, are you all new here? Do you not know that's the policy of my administration? To get us out of the Middle East, instead of finding ways to allow ourselves to be dragged back in!"

Most annoying, though POTUS did not mention it, was that POTUS would have to cut short his Fourth of July holiday. Not only because of this Peshmerga nonsense, but because the Israelis were making his life difficult for a change. Both they, and Hamas, looked as if they might begin lobbing rockets, mortars and bombs at each other again, in the wake of the kidnapping of three Israeli schoolboys somewhere in the Hebron region of the Palestinian Authority, where they had no business being in the first place, and thus no one to blame for the kidnapping of the three Israeli schoolboy settlers, but themselves.

Israeli Prime Minister Akiva "Kivi" Natanel, would, of course, have taken issue with that last comment. Indeed, Kivi Natanel, whom POTUS thought of as nothing more than a kind of redneck, Jewish, bull-headed cowboy, had the unmitigated gall to publicly upbraid President Kabila, in the Oval Office, no less, for exactly such a suggestion.

POTUS had stated, quite rightly in his own mind, that the presence of five hundred radical Jewish settlers, artificially implanted in the clearly Arab city of Hebron, with several hundred thousand Palestinians residing therein, amounted to little more than a needless provocation, and an impediment to the peace talks with the Palestinian Authority, which POTUS viewed as essential.

POTUS was indeed one of the key proponents of the theory that the Israeli-Palestinian conflict was at the heart of all of America's problems in the Middle East, and that America was paying a disproportionate price for its support of the Jewish state, and thus inflaming the passions of all its surrounding Arab neighbors.

POTUS had delivered that last observation in his usual polite, but stern, and indeed dismissive, professorial fashion. Kivi Natanel, on the other hand, had responded with ill-concealed disdain for what he charitably viewed as President Kabila's naiveté, if not his downright sympathy for Israel's enemies. This was evidenced by what he considered the massive indignity of the President of the United States bowing to a Saudi monarch. It was, Kivi Natanel reasoned, the gesture of a Moslem schoolboy, and not the President of the most powerful nation on earth.

Thus, Kivi Natanel had the effrontery to lecture the President of the United States in his own Oval Office.

"With the greatest respect, Mr. President," he said, "the five hundred Jews living in Hebron, the second-holiest city to the Jewish people after Jerusalem, can hardly be called either artificial, nor an implant. Indeed, we are the aboriginal people, not only of Hebron, but of the land of Israel. We speak the same language, Hebrew, as our forebears did four thousand years ago, we worship the same God, we read the same holy book, the Torah, that we did four thousand years ago, and any Israeli high school student can read the Dead Sea Scrolls, which were written seven hundred years before Mohammed was born, as easily as he reads the sports page in his local newspaper. If anyone is a foreign implant, it is the people whose language, religion, and culture differ completely from that of the original Canaanite inhabitants, and whose religion was born two thousand, seven hundred years after the patriarch Abraham purchased, in Hebron, the tomb for himself, his wife Sarah, Isaac, Jacob, Rachael, and Leah. These are the founders of our religion. Hebron was also the city in which King David reigned, before he came into Jerusalem, and it had a constant Jewish presence for four thousand years, until its inhabitants were massacred by their Arab neighbors in 1929, which was not only before there were any settlements in the West Bank, and any so-called occupied territories; it was before the creation of the State of Israel itself. To call Jews 'foreign occupiers', or 'artificial implants', in Hebron or Jerusalem, is like calling Frenchmen 'artificial implants' in Paris."

It was a masterful presentation, and Rafik Kabila came off looking like a child talking to a man.

To make matters worse, a photograph had been making the rounds of the internet, which featured a picture of a very stoned twenty-year-old Ralphie Sukerto, as Rafik Mohammed Kabila was then known, during his Whittier College undergraduate days. Ralphie Sukerto was smiling a stoner's sloppy grin, and sporting a kind of *Superfly*, half-assed afro.

In contrast, there was a picture of a twenty-year-old Kivi Natanel in combat fatigues, weapons belt, and an Uzi submachine gun, looking very much like an early seventies incarnation of Rambo, while serving as a lieutenant in one of Israel's most elite commando units.

The only visual contrast that put Kabila in a more negative light was the photograph of POTUS in a Styrofoam bicycle helmet, pedaling around Martha's Vineyard, compared with a photo of a bare chested Vladimir Putin, astride a snorting, galloping steed, looking like a cross between a Native American warrior-chieftain, and Genghis Khan.

Putin stripped off his shirt faster than a drunken sorority girl on Bourbon Street during Mardi Gras.

But the implication could not possibly have been clearer, especially to one who touted his street cred as a black man. Vladimir Putin and Kivi Natanel could whup Rafik Kabila's ass on the best day he'd ever had.

Now Kivi Natanel was exploiting the kidnapping of the Israeli schoolboys to launch an all-out offensive against Hamas' infrastructure on the West Bank, in what had been dubbed Operation Shuvu Achim, or, "Return Our Brothers".

POTUS rightly suspected that the operation was not so much an all-out search for the schoolboys, as a much sought-after opportunity to crack down on Hamas' growing popularity in the West Bank.

"How do we know," POTUS asked, "that this isn't just another attempt on the part of the Kurds to drag the US back into Iraq?"

"Well, we don't know it for sure, Mr. President, until we have the opportunity to evaluate the intelligence they're offering us."

"What we do know, Mr. President," interjected General Tunney, "is that ISIS is getting stronger by the day."

"ISIL," corrected National Security Advisor Wheatley, noticing her boss all but twitch like Herbert Lom reacting to the mention of Peter Sellers' Inspector Clouseau, in the *Pink Panther* movies.

"Whatever," said General Tunney, who regarded Wheatley as a rank amateur, a political hack who had no business commenting on international policy, regardless of being the President's national advisor on same. "What we do know," he said, "is that they're gobbling up territory. They're expansionist. There are reports that they've begun beheading, and crucifying, Christians, many of them children, and they make no bones about their desire to strike at the West, either. I believe, sir, we would be remiss, at the very least, if we did not seriously consider that this intelligence might just be of vital importance to our nation's security."

POTUS sat there for a bit. He hated this crap. Truly hated it. It was like the Al Pacino character in *The Godfather: Part III*. Every time he tried to get out of the morass that was the Middle East, they kept dragging him back in. That, in turn, reminded POTUS of Little Stevie Van Zandt's impersonation of Al Pacino's delivery of the same line in one of the opening episodes of *The Sopranos*. *Was that the pilot episode?* he wondered. He'd have to get someone to pull that up. He loved that show, though his wife, Jocelyne, couldn't stand it. But then, there were so many things that Jocelyne couldn't stand. She couldn't stand him filling out brackets on ESPN during March Madness. She thought it was beneath The President's dignity, which just proved that she had no real political instincts. People loved the fact that he filled out brackets; it made him an average Joe. Whereas, they couldn't stand all her organic garden crap, and taking pizzas off of school menus. I mean, he knew it played to the base of radical, organic, anti-virus-shots, upscale, Upper-West-Siders, but filling out brackets cut across party lines. He was one of the guys. He could be white, and black, at the same time. East Coast and Midwestern. SEC and PAC-12. *In fact, this year*, he thought, *Oklahoma State might just have a chance. Of course, there was always the possibility that a school like Florida Gulf Coast could come along, and spoil everything. What was that new kid Oklahoma State had?*

"Mr. President," he heard General Tunney say, pulling him out of his reverie.

"Yes," POTUS replied tersely, realizing that he had completely lost his train of thought.

"He was talking about the Israelis, Mr. President," Bo Fitzgerald said, thoroughly enjoying the opportunity to get back at POTUS for the memo that had never arrived.

"Actually," said Jack O'Leary, in his stentorian tones, "He was talking about what we do about the proposed trade for this Al-Masri character that Kurdish Prime Minister Barzini has just offered."

"Actually," said Acting FBI Director Jack Profitt, "it's Hamid Berzinji who is the Prime Minister of Iraqi Kurdistan. Barzini was Don Corleone's nemesis in *The Godfather*."

"Great movie," said a still very hungover Sec. Def. Gaynor, finally finding a point of reference in the conversation he could relate to.

"Look," said POTUS. "The most I'm willing to do is, uh... Y'o, send a team to evaluate..."

I wish he wouldn't say "y'o" like that, thought Mallory Mohsen. *It's his tell. Every time he says it, you know he's off script.* She made a mental note to send Ralphie, she was one of the few people who still thought of him as Ralphie, a memo to knock that crap off. No more "*y'o's*", no more "you knows", no more "uhs".

"...Y'o... You know, uh," said the President, "whether or not uh... This supposed intel is, uh, y'oh, you know, of any value to the US..."

"It could just be another attempt," said Bo Fitzgerald, "on the part of this Barzini character to drag the US back into Iraq."

POTUS flinched at the second *Godfather* "Barzini" reference from Crazy Uncle Bo, but let it slide.

"Well, make no mistake," he said, slipping into campaign-speak. "That is something I, under no circumstances, am willing to do. I don't care what happens to the Kurds. We are not going back into Iraq. Period."

Mallory Mohsen made another mental note to send a second memo to Ralphie, telling him not to say "period" anymore. It had too many negative connotations about the failed healthcare rollout of the previous year. People didn't need to be reminded of that, especially with the upcoming Senatorial elections within the next few months.

POTUS looked around the room. The truth was, in addition to the feeling of true personal disdain for most of the people present, POTUS deeply distrusted his military, the CIA, the FBI Counter-Terrorism unit, and the DEA, all of whom he regarded as a bunch of cowboy holdovers from a bygone era of US interventionism, intent on finding enemies everywhere so they could bolster their various budgets, at the expense of the domestic programs which he intended to be his legacy. *Damnit,* he thought, *this has got to be the summer we do immigration reform. If we lose the Senate, it's dead in the water.*

"Mr. President," said General Tunney insistently. "You were saying the most you're willing to do... Is what?"

POTUS looked around the room. It was as if the TelePrompTer in his mind had suddenly gone blank. The most he was willing to do was...

"...Appoint a team to evaluate whether or not the information that this Al-Masri has is of any use to the US, or if this is just another attempt by the Kurds to drag us into Iraq, which is something you have told us, in no uncertain terms, that you are unwilling to do." said Deborah Wheatley, proving yet again what an invaluable aide she was to Rafik Kabila.

She's kinda hot looking, too, thought President Kabila, but yielded not to the temptation to let his thoughts drift again. "Precisely," he said.

Thus, POTUS reached a decision, which many came to regard, increasingly as the Kabila Theorem:

TAKE AN ACTION, DESIGNED TO POSTPONE
A DECISION, AND APPOINT AN ESSENTIALLY
POWERLESS BODY TO DO IT.

"Okay," POTUS said. "Y'o. I want a representative from the CIA, a representative from the Defense establishment, one from the DEA, and one from FBI Counter-Intelligence." He looked around at each head of the of the various departments he had just ticked off, as if in so-doing, he had acknowledged their importance, and was acting in their interests.

"Matt, Francis, Jack, Graciel, I want you each to pick top people from your agencies. The best you have. You have this team assembled within twenty four hours. They are to travel, at my personal direction, to Kurdistan, in order to evaluate the intelligence that the Kurds are offering on this Al-Masri character."

"And who, exactly, will command this team?" asked CIA Director James Francis Doherty. This was, after all, not his first rodeo.

"No one," said POTUS, with what he hoped resembled Solomon-like wisdom. "I want a consensus opinion to be arrived at by a team of equals, with no outside pressure from anyone. And," he added, "I want them to report directly to me. With all due respect to everyone present, I don't want any one agency running this show. This is a Presidential team, not a CIA, FBI, military, or DEA team. Is that clear to everyone?"

Everyone around the room nodded.

"I need to hear that, for the record."

"Yes, sir," said CIA Director Francis Doherty.

"Clear as a bell," chimed in Acting FBI Director Profitt.

"Understood," said Acting DEA Director Mrs. Graciel Esteves.

"What, exactly, is State's role in all of this?" asked Secretary Jack O'Leary, sounding more and more like a Muppet character every time he spoke, thought POTUS. *Sam the American Eagle, that was the Muppet he sounds like!*

"I'd be happy to chair the team, Mr. President, to provide an objective point of reference." said VPOTUS. "I mean, I don't have a dog in this fight, sir. My loyalty is to you."

"Not necessary, Bo." said POTUS. "Though, of course, your loyalty is noted, and, as always, appreciated." *Clean negro, my ass*, thought POTUS. Then, he continued evenly. "Now, if there's no further business, I have a fundraiser in Beverly Hills to get to. We've got a Senate election to win. Besides, if you ask me, I'm convinced, y'o, these ISIL clowns are all-in-all nothing but a JV team of wannabes, wearing Kobe Bryant jerseys."

"Mr. President," said Jack O'Leary.

"Yes, Jack," answered POTUS impatiently.

"There are still some unanswered questions, sir."

"Of course there are." said POTUS, and left the room.

CHAPTER 2

At the same time that POTUS was reaching what he hoped was a Solomon-like decision with regard to the JV team in Kobe Bryant jerseys, two of the most dangerous ISIS terrorists in the world, Khalid Kawasme (Code Name: The Engineer), and Abdul Aziz Al-Tikriti (Code Name: *Sayef Al Islam* – The Sword of Islam) were disembarking in Egypt from what had already been a long and arduous journey. From ISIS-controlled Iraq, they had made their way into Turkey in disguises and with false papers indicating they were Sunni-Iraqi refugees driven out of their homeland by the ISIS onslaught.

In April of 2003, Turkey had instituted its new law on foreigners and international protection, relating to the status of refugees. There were already almost one million refugees from Iraq and Syria living in Turkey: three hundred thousand living inside the camps, and seven hundred thousand living outside the camps.

This, of course, made it remarkably simple for the two "refugees", who happened to be two of the most dangerous men in the world, to slip through the cracks, obtain new false papers identifying them as Jordanian textile salesmen traveling to purchase Egyptian cotton with money, new clothes, new passports, and new disguises, supplied by ISIS agents in Istanbul. Al-Tikriti and Kawasme were able to travel by train to the Turkish port of Mersin, where they were able to book passage to Nicosia, Cyprus.

From thence, outfitted with yet another set of identities, this time as Lebanese importers of licensed Egyptian antiquities, they booked separate flights to Cairo, on Cyprus Airways.

Once in Cairo, they were met by yet another of the growing network of ISIS operatives. They were outfitted with a third set of identities, this time as Kuwaiti tourists booking an eleven day/ten night, all-inclusive tour of Egyptian Sinai. Day one had them join their tour in Cairo, and proceed by air-conditioned motor coach to El Arish, in Northern Sinai, for a stay at the Palm Beach Hotel along the Mediterranean coast.

There, they paid their guide, an ISIS sympathizer, to erase any record of their ever having been part of the tour. They next rendez-voused with Sheikh Ahmed Abu Ali, a Bedouin smuggler, descended from one thousand years of Bedouin smuggler ancestors.

The Bedouins had a saying: "Allah created the *fallah*, or farmer, from the turd of a donkey. He created the Bedou from the wind." The Bedouins of Sinai recognized no national boundaries, nor held allegiances to any country. They were completely tribal in every way. Abu Ali was a member of the Hawetat, and, like virtually all Bedou, was a migrant goat herder, brigand, and smuggler.

As times changed, so did the goods which the Bedou smuggled across the Sinai desert.

In the seventies and eighties, their main stock-in-trade had been hashish.

The hashish was molded into what were referred to as "soles", because they resembled nothing so much as the sole of a shoe. These, they wrapped in plastic, and then inserted into the rectums of that reliable ship of the desert, the Bedouin camel. They were, thus, impervious to any authorities who might have the audacity to interfere with their smuggling operations. They plied the routes between Egypt, Saudi Arabia, and Gaza. From Gaza, in a remarkable, and indeed admirable show of Israeli and Palestinian cooperation, Palestinian gangs bought the hashish from the Bedouins, and in turn sold it to Israeli Jewish gangsters, who marketed the much sought-after *Nafas* to Tel Avivian hipsters. From Israel, the hashish could then be smuggled north into Lebanon, and from thence, into Europe. The crime families of the Middle East, and the Bedou of the Sinai, had no problems whatsoever in terms of peaceful, albeit criminal, coexistence.

When Hamas seized power in Gaza, in a bloody coup against the Palestinian Authority, both Israel, and Egypt's now-deposed President Mubarak, acted to isolate the terrorist group.

Thus were born the smuggling tunnels, which became Hamas' main source of income. Rather like purchasing a medallion for a taxi in New York City, Hamas sold licenses to independent contractors to dig and operate the dozens upon dozens of smuggling tunnels which ran from Egyptian-controlled Sinai into Gaza.

At first, the main stock-in-trade was weapons; AK 47s, Iranian-made rockets and, later, Libyan weapons from the arsenal of the deposed Libyan dictator, Colonel Muammar Gaddafi.

Soon, the laws of supply and demand, however, took over, and there were so many weapons in Gaza that their prices plummeted.

The tunnels, though, and their various smuggling tunnel contractors and sub-contractors, had created a new class of millionaire entrepreneurs in Gaza; the tunnel millionaire.

This, in turn, created a new demand for consumer goods.

Soon, the Bedouins were smuggling flat screen TVs, European espresso machines, and even luxury automobiles from Cairo, through the desert, through the tunnels, and into Gaza.

Car theft rings flourished in Cairo. One could order a Mercedes with a tunnel contractor, who would transmit the order to someone like Sheikh Abu Ali, who would then transmit the order to one of dozens of car theft rings in Cairo. Whatever you wanted could be had, at a discount price.

Everyone was making out like bandits, which, of course, is what the Bedouin were. The market truly flourished once Mubarak was deposed, and the Muslim Brotherhood took over.

But all good things must come to an end, and Egypt's President Mursi, who began his own *jihad* against Egypt's minorities and "Secular hedonists" who rebelled against the notion of a strict Moslem society, was overthrown, much to the chagrin of President Rafik Mohammed Kabila, who oddly viewed the Muslim Brotherhood as a moderating influence in a world of Islamic extremism.

This attitude puzzled many old-hand Arabists within the State Department, who viewed the difference between the Brotherhood, and its offshoots of Al Qaeda and Hamas, and now, ISIS, as the choice between Ted Bundy and Jeffrey Dahmer. It was true that one guy didn't eat the corpse, but both were serial killers, nonetheless.

At any rate, Egypt's military prevailed, deposed and outlawed the Muslim Brotherhood, and replaced them with former General Mahmoud Ibrahim Fahmi.

Fahmi promptly clamped down on the smuggling tunnels, ordered them flooded with sewage, and literally drowned their operatives in a sea of feces. Thus, there were now only a few tunnels still in operation.

At the same time, The Sinai Peninsula, itself, had become a kind of no-man's land. Al Qaeda offshoots had allied with Bedouin tribes, and few deadlier combinations ever existed in an already treacherous Middle East. A guerrilla war developed between the Al Qaeda-Bedouin alliance, and Fahmi's Egyptian army.

Thus, when Sheikh Abu Ali of the Hawetat tribe of Northern Sinai, was approached with the proposition of smuggling two men into Gaza, he quickly assumed that the two in question, despite their false identities, must be high-ranking ISIS operatives, since no one in their right mind wanted to be smuggled INTO Gaza, BUT terrorists.

Ideologically, he was neither for, nor against, ISIS. From that standpoint, he subscribed to the age-old Arab adage: "The enemy of my enemy is my friend."

ISIS had its sights set on Egypt's Fahmi.

Egypt's Fahmi had his sights set on Sheikh Abu Ali.

Therefore, Sheikh Abu Ali would be happy to render a service for the ISIS operatives.

For a price.

A large one.

Despite being a desert-and-sheepskin-tent-dweller, Sheikh Abu Ali possessed a satellite television, powered by state of the art, stolen solar panels. As such, he kept in touch with the news of the day, supplied by Al Jazeera. Thus, he was aware that ISIS had taken possession of numbers of Iraqi oil wells and refineries, which provided it with an income of some two to three million dollars a day. In addition, they had robbed numerous Iraqi and Syrian banks, relieving them of dinars, dollars, and gold bullion. They sold stolen antiquities on the black market for truly outrageous amounts. Yet there were always buyers.

And, added to that, was a lucrative kidnapping enterprise. In that context, the YouTube beheading videos could later be seen as strategic marketing, the likes of which a Steve Jobs would have applauded, were he, too, a terrorist.

ISIS had kidnapped literally several thousand foreigners, primarily petroleum workers, and was quietly ransoming them off to their respective countries, who were paying an additional roughly one million dollars per day.

All in all, this gave ISIS a slush fund in excess of one billion dollars, making it the wealthiest terrorist organization in history.

Thus, Sheikh Abu Ali decided to charge the same price he would have charged for a BMW, for the smuggling in of the two ISIS operatives.

Unlike what most perceived to be the custom in the Middle East, neither Al-Tikriti nor Kawasme hesitated, nor bargained. Their dream of conquest was about to become a reality. They would not quibble about price. The two devout Muslims paused in prayer. They washed their faces and their hands, their forearms up to the elbows. They passed wet hands over their heads, and washed their feet up to the ankles, in order to purify themselves. Then they offered up a prayer of thanksgiving.

The hour in which they would bring America to its knees, and displace Al Qaeda in terms of the number of Americans killed in a single attack was at hand. Allah be praised, and peace be unto his messenger!

CHAPTER 3

P OTUS' trip to Beverly Hills was to be a short one. Less than twenty-four hours. Jocelyne Kabila hated those kinds of trips. There was no time to see friends, or sights. No time to shop, even if the stores agreed to stay open privately for the First Lady, after hours. So, she opted to go to Chilmark, in Martha's Vineyard, instead, with her son and daughter. The Hamptons were more the stomping grounds of Jamie and Edie Howell, though they were equally welcomed in the Vineyard. But it was as if a secret divorce settlement had been reached between the families of the former, and current Presidents. They simply could not stand one another. Sensibly, each had agreed tacitly to stay out of the others' territory. Accordingly, the Hamptons became the province of the Howells, and the Vineyard became the retreat of choice for POTUS and FLOTUS. On those rare occasions in which FLOTUS was advised that the Howells were staying at the home of one of their East Coast literati, or West Coast glitterati friends, in the Vineyard, FLOTUS referred to the place as the Occupied Territories. Thankfully, Edie Howell had no intention of hitting the Vineyard this summer. Instead of dining on the vegan specialty of White Beans and Heirloom Grain Pilaf at The Chilmark Tavern, Edie Howell would be gazing at the Butter Cow, a life-sized sculpture of a bovine, with detailed veins bulging in the Butter Udder, while munching on deep-fried turkey legs in Iowa, trying to convince the locals she was just plain-folk, and worthy of the votes they had denied her, in her race against POTUS, six years before.

As for POTUS, he ambled out to Marine One with that strange, loose, strolling gait; a cross between faux ghetto, and movie star red carpet promenade. The ramrod-straight Marine sentry snappily saluted the Commander in Chief, and POTUS returned the salute with as much military flair as he could muster. He had, in fact, like Jamie Howell before him, practiced saluting in the mirror. It had to have that certain *je ne sais quoi*; a military bearing, yet, still, somehow, above it all, and oddly hip.

He did not pause at the top of the stair unit to wave to the entourage of press and staffers gathered on the White House lawn. It was too much of a Nixonian gesture. He contented himself instead with simply entering the helicopter. He nodded to the Marine aviators designated to pilot Marine One, who, rather than wearing flight suits, were dressed in Marine Blue Dress Charlie-Delta uniforms. Then he took the Presidential seat, and gave a brief, almost royal, wave of the hand, through the Presidential window, at the receding crowd, and then, majestically, ascended skyward.

Once airborne, Marine One was promptly joined by five identical helicopters, which began to shift in formation as a security measure, in order to obscure the location of the President. It was yet another Presidential shell game.

Within minutes, POTUS would disembark at Andrews Air Force Base, and board Air Force One. The Presidential 747 was, perhaps, along with the Marine Corps Band, the single perk which most occupants of the White House missed the most, once they were no longer in government housing.

Mallory Mohsen, who almost always accompanied POTUS on such fundraising events, was tasked this time with remaining behind, together with National Security Advisor Deborah Wheatley.

They met in Mohsen's office, just down the hallway, and significantly closer to the Oval Office than Bo Fitzgerald's ceremonial Vice Presidential digs, at the far end of the corridor. Here, Mohsen and Wheatley would spend the night, vetting all recommended personnel from each of the relevant agencies named by the President to form the powerless team which would travel to Erbil, in Iraqi Kurdistan, in order to evaluate the intelligence to be gleaned from the supposed ISIL operative, Yehyeh Al-Masri.

POTUS had two criteria for the team:

One, it had to be made up of people who were unquestionably top-flight in their respective fields, and

Two, the team itself had to be completely powerless.

Its point, after all, was to look absolutely credible on paper, while affording POTUS the opportunity to avoid making a meaningful decision.

In addition, there was a third, unspoken qualification for the makeup of the team.

It had to be both multicultural and multi-gendered. That meant, of the four members of the team; one from the FBI, one from the DEA, one from the active military, and one from the CIA, only one member could be a white male. Otherwise, there had to be a complete racial and gender balance.

Mohsen would have preferred that the CIA operative be a black female. After poring through the *curricula vitae* of various potential candidates, there did, indeed, seem to be a perfect black, female CIA operative. Sort of an African-American Valerie Plame. The problem was, she had just that morning been dispatched on assignment to Nigeria, to interview and debrief sixty-three women and girls kidnapped by Boko Haram from the Kumm Abza village in Northern Borno State on June 18.

Mohsen thought briefly about having CIA Agent Sana Johari recalled immediately, but then realized that this would surely incur the wrath of FLOTUS, who had distributed green "cause bracelets" to all White House staffers, emblazoned with the phrase "BRING BACK OUR GIRLS".

That, combined with the celebrity-packed YouTube, Twitter, Facebook, and Instagram "Bring Back Our Girls" campaign, meant that it would be more prudent for Mohsen to chew on a rusty razor blade, than to dare mess with FLOTUS' current passion *du jour*.

The only other candidate who, on paper, seemed to fit the bill was a former CIA operative turned analyst, by the name of Tera Dayton. Dayton was thirty-five years old, certainly photogenic, if not downright beautiful from her file photo, with a PhD in Near-Eastern Studies from Harvard, a Master's Degree in Conflict Resolution from Georgetown University, and, unfortunately, a Bachelor's Degree in Political Science from Liberty University, in Lynchburg, Virginia. Liberty University, having been founded by that redneck, Bible-thumping bigot, Jerry Falwell, meant that Dayton, at least, in her undergraduate years, was a Born-Again Christian. Hopefully, she had gotten over it. She was, according to her file, an expert on Middle Eastern affairs, with a specialty in counter-terrorism and Egyptian politics. Her career as a field operative had been cut short in May of 2011, when she was given medical leave for unspecified injuries suffered in a riot in Quetta, Pakistan. Since then, she had been working as an analyst in the Directorate of Intelligence, Office of Near-Eastern Analysis.

What Mohsen and Wheatley did not glean from her file was the fact that it had been altered by the legendary Clive Harriman Walker III, Deputy Director of Operations for the CIA, and a relative of both Averil Harriman and George Herbert Walker Bush, meaning his blood, in intelligence circles, was as blue as it got.

Harriman Walker III had a particular affection for Dayton. He regarded her, almost, as a surrogate daughter, and had personally recruited her while she was still pursuing her Master's Degree at Georgetown, where Harriman served as a visiting professor. He brought her into the Agency, and encouraged her to pursue her PhD at Harvard on the Agency's tab.

He was not disappointed.

Dayton combined a set of rare qualities. She was beautiful enough to make men do very foolish things in order to impress her. This was an almost indispensable quality in a female field operative. In addition, she was brilliant, with not only an almost photographic memory, but a superb analytical sense, which allowed her to connect the dots between disparate factions of little-known terrorist groups and the shadowy financial entities that backed them. In addition to this, she was utterly fearless, and a complete action junkie. She was thrilled by the adventure of it all. Finally, she possessed a religious fervor which, combined with a real sense of patriotism, meant that she would risk her life, willingly and repeatedly, in order to carry out whatever mission had been assigned to her.

In the spring of 2011, she was assigned as a paymaster working in Abbottabad, Pakistan. Working as a field operative, with the cover identity of a correspondent for a major news-gathering organization with whom the CIA had developed a long and special relationship of creating just such "legends", Dayton had developed direct evidence that the Pakistani Inter-Services Intelligence Chief, Lieutenant General Achmed Shuja Pasha, had direct information about the location of Usama bin Laden. There were, in fact, numbers of informants, whom the CIA had been paying to ferret out, and confirm, the location of bin Laden's compound in Abbottabad.

Dayton continued in her undercover role as part of the CIA-led Operation Neptune's Spear, which resulted in the assassination of Usama bin Laden by Navy SEAL Team Six, with the able assistance of the 160th Special Operations Aviation Regiment, and fellow CIA operatives, like Dayton herself.

After the death of bin Laden, Dayton was dispatched to Quetta, the provincial capital of Baluchistan Province, in central Pakistan. Quetta was known as the Fruit Garden of that country, due to the numerous and varied orchards in and around it.

It was also home to one of the CIA's leading informants, for whom Dayton acted as paymaster.

Unfortunately, it was also base of operations for Jamiat Ulema-e-Islam in Quetta, an offshoot of Al Qaeda, whose members took to the streets, rioting at the news of bin Laden's demise at the hands of SEAL Team Six.

When they saw Tera Dayton making her way back to the three-star Quetta Serena Hotel, at the corner of Zarghun and Concilgin Roads, the crowd of frenzied men surrounded her taxi, and pulled her from it. They did not see in her a CIA agent. They simply saw a blond-haired, blue-eyed woman, who was obviously somehow connected with the Great Satan, America, which had just killed The Sheikh, Usama bin Laden.

Clinging to her "legend", Tera flashed her press credentials, and said, "Journalist!" first in English, and then, "*lekhaki!*" which meant "writer" in Urdu.

"*Lekhaki!*" The men shouted derisively at her.

"*Kafir!*" They shouted at her in Arabic, meaning "infidel", and they began pulling at her.

They ripped off her head scarf, and tore at her long-sleeved blouse, which she had worn in keeping with the customs of modesty.

They ripped off its buttons.

They tore it away from her, as she screamed, shouting, *"Limaadhaa?"* "Why", in Arabic.

The frenzied men, laughing and lustful now, mocked her accent, and shouted back at her, *"limaadhaa, limaadhaa!"*, and she recognized the Arabic word for "whore", *"sharmuta!"* as they tore her brassiere away from her body.

She tried to cover her breasts with her hands, as one of the men spat on her, and another hit her with his fist.

Suddenly, a red slash of pain tore through her head as first one rock struck her, and then another, and she felt their hands ripping away at her long skirt, and then, at her underwear.

At first, she struggled to remain conscious, but then began to pray for another blow to the head, that would render her mercifully unable to see, or think, or feel. But, no such blow to her head followed. Only fists pummeling her body, and the knife held to her throat as she was carried into one of the fabled orchards of Quetta, the Fruit Basket of Baluchistan.

There, she was raped, and beaten, again and again and again, sodomized, forced to orally copulate, spat upon, as they laughed, and cursed, and lusted.

All the while, she prayed for death that never came.

She prayed to her Lord and Savior to be saved. And salvation never came.

She prayed for an end to the seemingly endless pain and humiliation and terror, until their fury and lust were spent, and, with parting kicks, and spittle, and saying she was lucky they did not behead her as they had the American journalist, Daniel Pearl, or cut out her tongue, they left her naked and bleeding, in the fragrant orchard, staring up at a merciless heaven, in a growing pool of her own blood.

She did not remember how she made it back to the hotel; whether alone, or with the kindness of a stranger, whether naked, or clothed. Indeed, she did not remember the hotel. Her first real memory was of being in a hospital room, with the sounds of Urdu swirling around her, and the kindly face of Clive Harriman Walker III looking down at her, tears filling his eyes, trying to smile bravely.

Tera Dayton, however, neither smiled, nor cried.

She simply stared at the ceiling.

Abandoning her "legend" completely, Clive Harriman Walker III had a team of ten CIA operatives, all of them former SEALs, enter the hospital with weapons drawn. They took Tera Dayton, as gently and lovingly as only comrades in arms can, and took her, in an armored SUV, to a waiting chartered jet. There, CIA medical personnel tended to her on the flight back to Rhein-Main Air Force Base, just outside Frankfurt, Germany. Harriman Walker III insisted there be no debriefing there. He stayed with her every day at the base's hospital where she was checked for AIDS, and other STDs, until, gradually, she began to speak once again, in the deadened voice of the truly traumatized.

He brought in DVDs of whole seasons of *Seinfeld*, which had been her favorite show.

She watched blankly the neuroses-filled antics of Jerry, George, Kramer, and Newman, until the episode in which Elaine's boss forces her to go see *The English Patient*, and Elaine bursts out in the middle of the movie, "Quit telling your stupid story about the desert, and just *die* already! DIE!"

And then, Tera began to laugh; quietly at first, a chuckle, and then raucously, until, in the midst of the uncontrollable laughter, she was sobbing.

Within three months, however, back in the United States, and with her iron-like self-discipline, she willed herself back into the world of the living. At least, seemingly so. She was wise enough to know that she could no longer be a field operative, that she could no longer depend upon her nerves holding steady, that she could no longer find herself in a sea of Middle Eastern men without the growing and over-powering sense of total panic. But, still, she had that wonderful analytical mind, and the ability to connect the dots. Clive Harriman Walker III had her transferred to the Directorate of Intelligence, Office of Middle Eastern Analysis, and, to all outside appearances, she thrived there. There was, of course, the nickname she earned amongst her male colleagues: she was the Ice Queen, the beautiful, but unapproachable, woman. What they didn't know, was how hard she struggled to keep from falling apart any time a man touched her arm. What they didn't know, was that her sense of shame prevented her even from discussing her trauma with her pastor. There was no question that she would not seek a CIA psychiatrist. That, she rightly feared, could jeopardize, if not end, her career entirely, and her career was the only thing she had left to hold her together. And so, she began to drink herself to sleep each night with a secret flask of vodka.

She lived with the quiet terror, shame, and guilt that only a Born-Again Christian, living in sin and denial can know.

The irony, of course, was that Mallory Mohsen, looking at her file, pronounced that Tera Dayton was a perfect fit for the team.

Force Master Chief Petty Officer Darwin Washburn was the next to be picked by Wheatley and Mohsen. He was an anomaly in the Navy SEAL Teams.

He was black.

He had been in the Teams twenty years, and was referred to as a "Bull Frog". As Senior Enlisted Advisor to the Commander of Naval Special Warfare Command, he was widely regarded as the top enlisted authority on SpecOps capabilities in the US Military. His journey into the world of Naval Special Warfare Operations was an odd one, to say the least.

A native of Atlantic Avenue, near 4th Street, in Southeast Washington, DC, which consistently made the list of twenty-five most dangerous neighborhoods in America, the then twelve-year-old Darwin Washburn, Jr, had been watching Al Campanis being interviewed by Ted Koppel on the fortieth anniversary of Jackie Robinson's Major League Baseball debut. As Washburn recalled it, Koppel had asked the Dodgers' General Manager why it was there were no black General Managers in Major League Baseball. Campanis said that it was because they didn't have the necessities to be a General Manager. Sort of like the fact that blacks couldn't swim, because they didn't have the buoyancy.

It was at that point that Darwin Washburn, Jr. said bad things about Campanis' mother, and told the televised image to perform a physically impossible act.

The next day, seething with anger, he presented himself at the local YMCA, announced his decision to become a Navy SEAL, and demanded to be taught how to swim.

Extraordinarily strong, and a gifted athlete, Washburn was, within one year, participating in, and winning, YMCA swim meets across the country. He balanced those activities with mastering the necessary survival skills one needed in order to stay alive on some of the meanest streets in America.

He dropped out of high school, got his GED, and never forgot his dream of becoming a Navy SEAL.

It was at that point in time that his cousin Darren, who had done time in a federal penitentiary for selling drugs across state lines, had told him about a guy he had met in the pen, a former Navy commander of SEAL Team Six, named Mark Dicek. Dicek had spent thirty years in the Navy, and had founded and commanded its most elite special ops team. He had, since his release from prison, written a *New York Times* best seller called *Rogue Operator*, and now ran a counterterrorism training school in Virginia. Darwin's cousin, Darren, had the address and provided an introduction to his former cellmate, Commander Mark Dicek, winner of the Silver Star, Legion of Merit, and Bronze Star with Valor Device and three gold stars.

Washburn made his way through the Virginia countryside to Dicek's home *cum* counterterrorism school, whimsically named Rogue Manor.

As he drove up the winding path to the large ramshackle home, he saw the hand-lettered sign, which read:

ROGUE MANOR
TRESPASSERS WILL BE SHOT
SURVIVORS WILL BE SHOT AGAIN

Armed with an appointment and letter of introduction, Washburn felt he was on safe ground.

At 8:00 that morning, he rang the doorbell of the aforementioned, imposing, Rogue Manor.

The door opened to reveal one of the largest and most intimidating white men Washburn had ever seen in his life. Dicek had black hair, down to his shoulders, and a bushy biker's beard, and looked as if he could punch a hole in your chest, and rip out your still-beating heart.

"Mr. Dicek," Washburn said, trying not to let his eighteen-year-old voice crack.

"Yeah," said Dicek.

"I'm Darwin Washburn."

"What's that supposed to mean?" said the former Navy SEAL, and convicted federal felon.

"I'm Darren Washburn's cousin? He said he wrote you about me?"

"Oh, yeah, yeah, yeah," said Dicek. "Come on in, kid, have a seat. You're the one who wants to be in the Teams."

"The Teams?" Washburn said.

"You want to be a Navy SEAL. A Sea-Air-Land Warrior. That's what we call 'Being In The Teams'," said Dicek, with ill-concealed disgust and impatience.

"Yes, Sir," Darwin answered.

"And why, exactly, is that?" asked the Rogue Special Operator.

"Because Al Campanis said black people can't swim."

"Can they?" Dicek asked.

"I can," Washburn said, looking Dicek straight in the eyes.

"So, why don't you take that up with Campanis? What are you busting my balls for?"

"Campanis can't help me become a SEAL, Sir."

Dicek just looked at him.

"You want a beer, Derek?"

"Darwin, Sir."

"Darwin," said Dicek,. "You want a beer?"

"Are you having one, Sir?"

"Oh, hell yeah," said Dicek, pulling out a sixteen-ounce can of Colt .45 Malt Liquor. "Wanna brewski?"

"Damn straight," said Washburn.

"Then crack a goldie on me, kid," Dicek said, and tossed him a can.

Three six-packs later, Darwin Washburn was completely blitzed, and Mark Dicek was as steady as a rock.

"Would you like to try to shoot my counterinsurgency course?" Dicek asked.

"You have a counter'surgency course?"

"Absolutely", Dicek said. "Come with me, kid, let's see what you're made of."

So saying, Mark Dicek led a none-too-steady Darwin Washburn through the woods, up a rise, into a full-scale, special ops counterinsurgency course. Mark's number two, Harry Andrews, was running some trainees through the course of pop-up targets. These were men who wanted to find work as independent contractors in foreign lands, where the US government did not like to have uniformed American personnel. Most were veterans of police departments, or various units of the military.

"Clear the course," Dicek said to Andrews. "We have a distinguished visitor. A close, personal friend of Al Campanis, who is about to demonstrate his prowess with the firearm of his choice." Dicek turned to Washburn. "What would you like, Derek?" he said.

"Darwin, Sir," said Washburn.

"…A .45, or a Glock 9mm?" said Dicek, ignoring Washburn's correction of his given name.

"Uh…" said Darwin.

"I don't have an 'Uh'," said Dicek. "I've got a .45, or a Glock 9mm."

"Glock," said Darwin.

"Give my man a Glock," said Mark Dicek to Harry Andrews.

Now, there were three things in life which Darwin Washburn knew how to do really well. One was swim. One was shoot a Glock 9mm. And the other would win him the affections, if not downright admiration, of numbers of women around the world – including, but not limited to, his soon-to-be wife, LaDonna.

"The course is simplicity, itself," Dicek explained. "There will be a series of rooms, which you will have to clear. Various and sundried targets will pop up. Some will be of bad guys; others will be of terrified hostages. You can, if you'd like, shoot them all, just to be on the safe side, but that would reveal an undiscerning eye. In addition, this is a timed course. There are fifty-three targets, which you will be expected to shoot. Each magazine contains seventeen rounds of ammunition, and you will be given four to complete the course. Here is your weapon. Here are the spare clips. You will commence at Mr. Andrews' command. Go with God, my son."

Andrews counted down from five, clicked a stopwatch, and a very drunken Darwin Washburn entered the first of twenty different scenario rooms, each of which would contain a number of "Bad Guy" pop-up targets.

There is an old saying amongst Olympic trap shooters. Olympic trap is one of the most demanding of all shooting events. The saying is, "shoot with your eyes, not with the gun." What it means is you must learn to be an instinctive shooter, if you are to survive. Unlike the art of the sniper, it is not a matter of careful aim and fire in between heartbeats to minimize gun movement. It is fire in motion. It is run and gun, with the weapon sweeping from target to target. Aim is important, of course, but it must be intuitive, and not studied, for while you are studying, your opponent will be shooting, and you will be dead.

Had Darwin Washburn been stone-cold sober, he probably would have done poorly on the demanding course. But, it was as if the alcohol liberated him from all hesitation and thought processes, and allowed him to shoot almost out of his subconscious, in a completely instinctual manner.

He aced the course.

All fifty three targets, dead center-mass.

And he had done so in near-record time.

"By god!" Dicek bellowed. "Did you pukes see what this child of the ghetto just did? Screw Al Campanis, and the horse he rode in on!"

He crossed over to Darwin Washburn, and relieved him of the 9mm and spent clips. He did not congratulate Darwin, did not pat him on the back, nor award him a certificate of merit. He simply said, "Derek, would you like to drive my amphibious vehicle?"

"Do you have an amphibious vehicle, sir?" Washburn asked.

"Well, sure," said Dicek, as if that were a foregone conclusion.

Dicek led Washburn to his amphibious vehicle, which he joyously piloted through the marshy land, the long way back to Rogue Manor, where Mark Dicek, founder and first commander of SEAL Team Six, personally wrote out a workout regimen for Darwin Washburn, whom he continued to call "Derek" for the next twenty years. One year later, Darwin Washburn had a golden trident pinned to his Dress Whites.

By the time he was selected by Mohsen and Wheatley, he had spent almost twenty years in the Teams.

Raul Peña was thirty-two years of age, a New Mexico born-and-raised DEA agent. He was movie star handsome, completely fearless, and a total action junkie, which trait, would spark an immediate attraction to Tera Dayton. This would, in turn, be noted with a good deal of disapproval by Darwin Washburn, who, like any sailor, realized that women were trouble aboard ship, especially with guys like Peña around.

What neither he, nor Tera Dayton, nor Deborah Wheatley, nor Mallory Mohsen knew, however, was that Peña possessed a secret which, like Washburn's fixation on Al Campanis, had led Raul Peña to become a deep-cover DEA agent.

Like many New Mexico-born natives, Peña was raised speaking a peculiar dialect of Spanish that dated back to the time of the Conquistadors, from which many native-born New Mexicans were, in fact, descended. Thus, in order to blend in with the thugs of the cartels in Old Mexico, Peña had to, in effect, learn what was, for him, an almost foreign language.

But, then, in a sense, there was nothing new in that.

For Raul Peña had been a spy his entire life.

So had his parents.

And their parents before them.

At an early age, Peña became painfully aware that there was something different about his family. They were raised in the tiny Northern New Mexico village of Abiquiu, about an hour north of Santa Fe, and around thirty miles south of the equally small village of Chama, and eighteen miles south of Ghost Ranch. It had a rugged beauty not unlike that of the Red Rock country of Sedona, Arizona. It was, in fact, that beauty, which drew to it the famous painter, Georgia O'Keefe, who immortalized the landscape locals called *Plaza Blanca*, the White Place.

Abiquiu was a village of only some two hundred souls, ninety percent of whom were Hispanic. In such a place as that, everyone knew each other's business. Everyone knew what color underwear you had, and how, and when, it was soiled.

Gossip in such a place is not only a unifying factor, but a ruling one. Ancient communities have ancient superstitions. And Abiquiu was nothing, if not ancient, tracing the roots of most of its inhabitants back to the very first Spanish explorers of North America.

The superstitions ran the gamut of all provincial and long-isolated communities.

"Beware of this one; her grandmother was a *bruja,* a witch!"

"Beware of that; he has *mal de ojo,* the evil eye!"

"Beware of those, because, somehow, they are not like us. Somehow, they are different." And, being different, they are to be feared. And, being feared, they are to be despised.

So it was with the family of Raul Peña.

They had odd customs.

Like virtually everyone else in their village, they were Catholic. Indeed, the adobe church in the center of town dominated the village and its life, physically, socially and spiritually. Every Sunday, virtually the entire village filled the pews of the seemingly unassuming edifice. Mass and Sacrament were as much a part of the fabric of life as bread and water. And Peña's family dutifully attended.

Yet, there were things about them that set them apart from their neighbors. Peña's *Abuelita,* Sara, lit candles on Friday nights.

When someone died in their family, they covered the mirrors.

Unlike their neighbors, they refrained from eating pork.

And, one day a year, in the early autumn, they fasted.

All of these things were done in secret, hidden from their neighbors' prying eyes, and never explained to their children.

Still, they were felt by all the other villagers in Abiquiu, and thus, the Peñas were shunned.

The daughters of the village were warned away from the sons of the Peña family.

Then, on Raul's fifteenth birthday, his *Abuelita,* Sara, suffered a fatal heart attack. As she was dying, she called her children and grandchildren around her. It was time to reveal the family secret, just as it had been revealed to her upon the death of her *Abuela,* Raquel.

They were Jews.

More specifically, *Cripto Judíos,* Hidden Jews. Their family had escaped the Spanish Inquisition, by traveling with the Conquistadors to the New World. Anything, even a wild land full of untamed savages, was preferable to the rack, or being burnt at the stake.

But the Inquisition had followed them from the Old World, to the New, and its officers set up their hunt for *Los Moranos,* those Jews who, on the surface, had converted to Catholicism, but continued secretly to follow the religion of Moses. And so, those hidden Jews, those *Cripto Judíos*, pushed Northward into New Mexico, and tried to blend in, and secrecy became, not just a part of their religion, and their life, but the very core of it. It was not that they were living a lie, it was that, like spies, or DEA Agents posing to be drug runners, they were living undercover. It was the perfect training ground for a secret agent.

Indeed, Peña had dreamed of becoming a CIA operative, not unlike Tera Dayton, but that was something which was reserved for college boys, and college was not something within Raul Peña's reach. His family lived below the poverty line, and then there was something else, as well. The nearest medium-sized town to Abiquiu was Española. It was where you went for groceries, or the coin-op laundry, and was known as the Low-Rider Capital of New Mexico. If Harvard and Yale were the recruiting grounds for the CIA, then Española was the fertile soil in which future DEA agents were hatched. Raul Peña vowed to get as far away from Abiquiu as was humanly possible, and the DEA was the low-rider that would take him there.

He, too, had Wheatley and Moseley's stamp of approval.

Now, all they needed was a white guy.

They did not need just any white guy. They needed a pliable one. One who could be counted on if the *fahzool* hit the fan, to dutifully clean it up. To take one for the team. To manage whatever cover-up became necessary. And cover-ups, in government work, were almost always necessary.

Clint McKeever was a fifty-year-old Irish, lapsed Catholic, FBI counter-terrorist senior Special Agent. His identical twin, Bud McKeever, was also an FBI counter-terrorist agent. But, it was Clint whose career had outpaced that of his nine-minutes-younger brother. His career had taken off not so much because of the cases that he had successfully cracked. His career had taken off, because he was the Bureau's go-to guy when it came to covering for the foul-ups and conspiracies, the bureaucratic mishandlings, and sometimes just plain incompetence, which had cost thousands of people their lives, and weighed down heavily on the conscience of Clint McKeever.

In the opening hours of the Oklahoma City bombing, for instance, two suspects were identified, and composite drawings were made of them. The drawings were widely disseminated through the press, and on local and national television news programs. The two suspects pictured in the composite drawings were labeled "John Doe Number One", and "John Doe Number Two."

John Doe Number One bore a striking resemblance to the man who would shortly be arrested for what was, at the time, the worst terrorist attack ever perpetrated on American soil. He was tall, Anglo-Saxon in appearance, with a long, thin face, and a crew cut, and his composite drawing was so exact that no one had a problem matching it with Timothy McVeigh.

John Doe Number Two, on the other hand, was short, stocky, dark-skinned, with a roundish face, jet-black hair, and appeared to be of Hispanic, Filipino, or Middle Eastern extraction.

Indeed, within one day of the Oklahoma City Bombing, the FBI had taken statements from no less than Twenty-four witnesses, who had seen John Doe Number One, Timothy McVeigh, in the company of the man they recognized from the composite drawing, who appeared to be of Mexican, Filipino, or Middle Eastern origin, and who was called, John Doe Number Two.

The witnesses placed John Doe Number One and John Doe Number Two, together, in Oklahoma City the night before the bombing, the morning of the bombing, on the way to, at the scene of, and fleeing from the Murrah Federal Building. In fact, two separate witnesses had seen John Does Number One and Two exiting the Ryder truck minutes before it exploded, killing 168 people, and injuring 680 others. Nineteen of the victims were children, and three were pregnant women. The victims ranged in age from three months, to seventy-three years.

McVeigh had been arrested within ninety minutes of the explosion. He had been stopped by an Oklahoma State Trooper for driving without a license plate. The Trooper then noticed the weapon sitting on the seat next to him, and McVeigh was arrested for unlawfully carrying same. The VIN number of the Ryder truck was recovered, which led to the agency from which the truck had been rented, and quickly linked Timothy McVeigh, and a Kansas farmer named Terry Nichols, to the bombing.

There was only one problem. While Timothy McVeigh was an exact match for John Doe Number One, Terry Nichols looked nothing at all like the composite drawing of John Doe Number Two. He was tall, where John Doe Number Two was short. His hair was thinning, where John Doe Number Two's was thick and black. Nichols wore glasses. John Doe Two did not. Nichols was white-complected, whereas John Doe Number Two was dark-skinned. Terry Nichols was the quintessential WASP, and John Doe Two was either Mexican, Filipino, or Middle Eastern.

To make matters worse, the night manager and handyman at a motel some ten minutes outside of Oklahoma City clearly recognized Timothy McVeigh, and John Doe Number Two, as being in the presence of six other, clearly Middle Eastern, men.

Indeed, a gas station attendant vividly recalled John Doe Number Two pulling up in a Ryder truck, and in a thick, Middle Eastern accent, demanding fifty dollars' worth of diesel fuel, which he paid for in cash. The service station employee told John Doe Number Two that he would certainly sell him the diesel fuel, but that the Ryder truck that John Doe number two was driving did not take diesel; it took unleaded gasoline. John Doe Number Two angrily demanded the fifty dollars' worth of diesel. The gas station attendant turned on the pump, and watched as John Doe Number Two opened up the back of the truck, and pumped the diesel fuel not into the gas tank, but into waiting fifty gallon drums.

The bomb, which exploded the Ryder truck and the Murrah Building, was composed of ammonium nitrate and diesel fuel.

Clearly, the Justice Department had a problem.

They had arrested two white suspects, and neither of them matched the description of the man twenty-four witnesses had placed in the company of Timothy McVeigh in Oklahoma City.

They had two solutions to their quandary, from which to choose. They could either say that they had caught two white guys, but that up to six Middle Eastern terrorists had gotten away, and thus, they had failed to catch the perpetrators of the worst terrorist attack in the history of the United States, or they could declare victory, and say the two white guys had acted alone.

As for John Doe Number Two, that was a mistake.

There was no John Doe Number Two.

He had never existed.

The person they chose to institute the cover up, to make John Doe Number Two disappear, to dissuade or discredit witnesses, and, in one case, to destroy the career of a brother FBI agent, who was not willing to comply with the cover up, was none other than Clint McKeever.

It would not be McKeever's first cover up, and, God help him, it would not be his last. Thus, McKeever, too, became a secret drunk.

But as far as Wheatley and Mohsen were concerned, Clint McKeever was, as well, a perfect fit for the team.

The irony, of course, was they had just put together a team of some of the most deeply flawed individuals imaginable.

While National Security Advisor Deborah Wheatley, and Senior Political Advisor Mallory Mohsen were putting together a team, which, technically, did not exist, to vet intelligence from a source POTUS was determined to ignore, in order to postpone a decision the President was loathe to make, Major Dani Kahan, a forty-four-year-old, American born, Israeli raised, IDF intelligence officer, assigned to the elite Givati Brigade, was scouring the rugged hillsides of the Judean Desert, near the ancient Biblical city of Hebron. He and his men were part of the massive effort to locate the three Israeli schoolboys who had been kidnapped a little over two weeks before.

They were searching near the village of Halhul, just north of Hebron. Kahan saw something which, to his trained eye, simply didn't look right. He had with him an Israeli Army Bedouin tracker. He nodded in the direction of a small rise.

"Khaled," he said to the tracker. "What do you think?"

Khaled took one look at the place Dani indicated, saw plants that looked out of place, and moved them away, revealing a small pile of rocks that seemed hastily arranged.

Slowly and carefully, Khaled and Dani Kahan approached the scene, looking for tripwires of possible booby traps. It was certainly not out of the question that Hamas, which was the prime suspect in the boys' abduction, would arrange what looked like a hastily-dug grave, and then lace it with IEDs, which would blow apart the torsos of any Israeli forces not professional enough to detect them. So, Dani and Khaled moved slowly and methodically, telling the rest of their men to take up defensive positions, in case this were an IED, coupled with an ambush. The Bedouin tracker saw no signs of tripwires, while Dani removed a probe from his sixty-pound pack, and began carefully inserting it every few inches, looking for pressure plates of improvised explosive devices that could kill them both. When both he, and the tracker, were satisfied that no such devices were to be found, they began slowly removing the rocks. Then, they saw the maggots. And then, the decomposing skulls of the teenage boys, each of whom had been shot numerous times in the backs of their heads.

Dani radioed in the information, and, within minutes, agents of Israel's Shin Bet, or, Security Services, the domestic counterpart to Israel's vaunted Mossad, were on the scene.

For the past two weeks, a frantic manhunt, one of the largest in the history of the Israeli army, had been conducted throughout the West Bank, in search of the three missing boys.

In truth, however, it was not so much a search for the boys, as it was both a search for their bodies, and a chance to break up Hamas' infrastructure throughout the West Bank.

In 2005, Israel had withdrawn all of its troops, and uprooted all of its settlements, in a unilateral move to end its occupation of the Gaza Strip. It left the area to the troops of the Palestine Authority, in what had become known as "the Gaza First Policy". The notion initiated by Israel's ultra-right-wing Prime Minister, Ariel Sharon, was enthusiastically embraced by Israel's left-wing parties. The idea was, if disengagement, and the end of the occupation could work first in Gaza, it could be a template for the end of the occupation in the West Bank, and the creation of a Palestinian State, living side by side, and in peace with Israel.

Unfortunately, this turned out to be a pipe dream. In short order, Hamas, an offshoot of the Muslim Brotherhood, that was dedicated to reestablishing the Islamic Caliphate of a thousand years before, seized power, in a bloody coup, from their secular rivals of the Fatah Party.

They machine gunned almost two hundred of them, lined them up against walls, and gunned them down, blindfolded and bound them, and pushed them to their deaths from high-rise buildings, and shot the kneecaps off those whom they did not murder. For Hamas, the destruction of Israel was simply a stepping stone to the establishment of the Islamic State. For Hamas, it was not the West Bank that was occupied territory, nor even Tel Aviv. For Hamas, *Spain* was occupied territory. And now, they were rising to power in the West Bank, as well.

Thus, Prime Minister Kivi Natanel seized upon the kidnapping of the three Israeli schoolboys, as an opportunity to uproot Hamas from the West Bank, arresting some four hundred Hamas operatives in the process. Hamas, in turn, had begun launching rockets against Israel, from Gaza, and tensions were already at a fever pitch.

Now, the bodies of the three murdered boys had been found, and identified, and their families notified of their deaths.

The Jews of Israel, like their biblical counterparts, were a stiff-necked and quarrelsome people, almost always at each-other's throats; secular against religious, left wing against right wing, Jews of Middle Eastern origin against Jews of European origin. But, for over two weeks, the country was united in anxiety and prayer for the missing schoolboys.

And now, they were united in grief, and rage.

Prime Minister Natanel called an emergency session of his security cabinet, and spoke to the press before it began.

"This evening," he said, "members of our security forces found three bodies, and all the signs indicate that they are the bodies of our three kidnapped youngsters."

There were audible gasps among the members of the press, as the rumors that had begun to circulate were confirmed by the Prime Minister.

"Hamas is responsible," he said, "and Hamas will pay. These boys were kidnapped, and murdered in cold blood by human animals. Satan, himself, has not yet invented the vengeance for the blood of a child."

All across the country, there were spontaneous outpourings of grief. Memorial candles were lit in the square named after slain Prime Minister Yizhak Rabin. Israel's left-wing, ninety-year-old president summed up the country's emotions, by saying, "All of Israel bows its head today, in grief..."

At the conclusion of the meeting of Israel's security cabinet, the Prime Minister, without hesitation, gave the green light to the targeted assassination of seven Hamas leaders, via an airstrike, to be carried out by the Israel Air Force, on targets in the Gazan village of Khan Younis. They had real-time, actionable intelligence, and, unlike POTUS, no committee was formed to verify it. They knew where the operatives were, and they were going to kill them.

At Netivim air base the call came in from the "Pit", the main war room in the Kirya, Israel's version of the Pentagon. The call was for two air crews to be scrambled immediately. They would be flying two F15I Ra'am aircraft. These were the two-seater, Israeli-modified versions of the American F15 Strike Eagle.

Unlike the Americans, the Israelis could not afford a fighter plane designed as a designated bomber or interceptor. Its planes had to be both unbeatable in a dogfight and able to bomb the eyes out of a snake at altitude. The Israeli version could not only rule the skies with eight air to air missiles. But the Israelis, not wanting to place all their faith in Buck Rogers technology, had also insisted upon a twenty millimeter Gatling gun, which could fire a hundred rounds per second. In addition the F15I could also carry a full load of bombs, with a navigator to guide each precision guided weapon to its target, be it a few minutes away in Gaza, or in the Ayatollah's bathtub, in Iran.

Kadosh Mintz, Chief of Staff of the Israel Defense Forces, took his seat in the war room, as did Kobi Golan, The Defense Minister, and Major General Rahm Efron, Commander of The Israel Air Force. They would all sign off on the final decision to hit the target, which in this case consisted of seven senior Hamas operatives, meeting in what they thought of as a safe-house, in Gaza.

The green light was given to start engines.

When eyes on the site indicated no civilians were present, a second green light was given for takeoff.

The lead pilot switched from Tower to Tactical Controller and within minutes both planes were over their targets. The navigator in Eshkol 1, the lead aircraft, keyed the mike on the squadron radio and gave the code word, "Hammer", indicating she had ID'd her target, and was illuminating it with the laser designator in her LITENING targeting pod.

In addition, an IAF Heron Unmanned Aerial Vehicle hovered above the target, sweeping its sensors in search of any tell-tale signs of uninvolved civilians.

None present.

Still good to go.

As they approached the target, both Eshkol One, and Eshkol Two, signaled the Controller that each had locked on to their targets. As the range to target on the Multi-Functional Heads-Up Displays counted down, each navigator said the silent prayer that all pilots have prayed since the days of Chuck Yeager. "Dear Lord, please don't let me screw up!"

The Controllers relayed their final status reports and clearance requests to the "Pit". Then the Chief of Staff of The Israel Defense Forces and the Commander of the Air Force looked at their monitors one last time, consulted with their aides, and then gave the final okays.

The code word "Anvil" was flashed to Eshkol One and Two, and the pilots pressed the "pickle" button on their joysticks, each releasing their four 500-pound bombs, as a new countdown began. The "Time To Go Until Impact" was displayed on the Heads-Up MFD. Each navigator held their cursor on the precise spot of their target, hoping there would be no last minute call that civilians were present, meaning they would have to "drag" the bomb off target to harmlessly explode in a pre-designated open area.

No last minute abort order came in.

The countdowns flashed Zero.

Then, the screens filled with blinding light and smoke, as the first four bombs hit their targets, followed by four more precision-guided weapons from the second F-15I. And seven Hamas senior leaders had an opportunity to see if the seventy-two almond-eyed virgins thing was true or not, as the air crews turned for home.

Within an hour, CNN was reporting the bombing, Israel was confirming that it had carried out the targeted assassination of seven terrorist commanders, and Hamas was declaiming yet another genocidal attack on the helpless Palestinian people.

But for Dani Kahan, it was not as simple as the usual Hamas *Kabuki* dance of victimhood. Hamas, he knew, was brutal, genocidal, imperialistic, theocratic, and fascistic, but they were not irrational. There was always a logic to what they did, and how they did it, and when they did it.

If they knew anything at all about Israel, it was that children were its soft spot. Hamas' founder, Sheikh Ahmed Yassin, before the Israel Defense Force had arranged for him to meet his very own seventy-two almond-eyed virgins in Paradise, had summed up Hamas' extremely accurate differentiation between themselves, and the Israelis:

"The Israelis," he said, "love life more than any other people on earth. We worship death."

And of all the lives that Israelis loved, it was the lives of their children that meant the most to them. It was absolutely Israel's weak spot. They could not tolerate casualties, especially the deaths of children. And, since everyone's son or daughter served in the military, they were casualty-averse even when it came to the Israeli Army. How much more so, then, when it came to the lives of schoolboys?

No one needed to instruct Dani in this basic truth. He knew it in the marrow of his bones. It visited him each sleepless night, in the nightmare visions of his son and ex-wife being blown apart in a pizza parlor in Jerusalem, in 2001.

So, why would Hamas kidnap, and immediately kill, three schoolboys, knowing full well that Israel's response would be a vengeance that not even Satan had yet created?

Kidnapping, in the Middle East, was a way of life. One kidnapped hostages to gain the release of one's own hostages. Thus, Hamas had kidnapped a nineteen-year-old Israeli soldier, named Gilad Shalit. And so high was the price that Israel put on the lives of its sons and daughters, that it released one thousand captured Hamas terrorists, for the release of one kidnapped Israeli soldier.

In 2006, at the end of the Second Lebanon War, Israel had released hundreds of convicted terrorists, simply for the bodies of two slain Israeli soldiers, which had been spirited away by Hezbollah operatives for precisely such a trade.

Knowing all that, why would Hamas not kidnap, and hold, the three schoolboys, and then demand the release of three thousand imprisoned terrorists? If one nineteen-year-old soldier yielded a thousand returned prisoners, what could they not then get for three imprisoned schoolboys?

It made no sense. The only sense it could possibly make was if the object of the kidnappings and murders was not for the release of hostages, but to initiate a war.

And why would Hamas initiate a war against a technologically superior force like the IDF, unless they thought they possessed some new secret weapon, some surprise, which they believed would allow them to win it?

As Dani Kahan was sharing those musings with no one but himself, Khaled Kawasme, The Engineer, and Abdul Aziz Al-Tikriti, the Sword of Islam, the two most dangerous ISIS terrorists in the world, were meeting in Gaza with the leader of the military wing of Hamas, Yasser Darwish. They were celebrating the discovery of the bodies of the Israeli schoolboys, and indeed, the Israeli air strike which would provide them the public relations excuse for a new war.

Now, it would begin, both for Hamas, and for ISIS.

For Hamas, the Divine Victory against the Zionist Occupier was at hand.

And, for ISIS, the final countdown to the attack that would supplant 9/11 as the most catastrophic blow against the Great Satan of America had finally begun.

CHAPTER 4

amas' main command and control bunker, unlike the supposed safe house, which proved to be less than safe for the now dead Hamas commanders, was absolutely impervious to Israeli air attack. This was so for two reasons. The first was that it was located deep underground, with a five story building on top of it.

The second reason was that the five story building in question was, in fact, a hospital.

The great irony, which almost always brought a smile to the lips of Yasser Darwish, was that it was the Israelis themselves who had built the beginnings of the complex of bunkers beneath Building #2 of Gaza's Shifa Hospital. They had done so in 1983, in order to create an underground operating theater and patient facilities which would be impervious to Palestinian terrorist attacks, or resistance actions, depending on what side of the suicide bomb you happened to find yourself. All this was at the height of the Israeli occupation, when the hospital was meant to treat not only Palestinian civilians, but to provide immediate care for severely wounded Israeli soldiers, as well.

Hamas, after having gunned down their Fatah rivals during their coup in 2007, engaged in one of their first acts of civic improvement: a major construction project at Shifa Hospital. None of it had anything to do with patient care. Instead, they enlarged the original Israeli underground facility, and built a huge command and control bunker, as well as luxurious, secure living spaces in which all of the Hamas elite could hide comfortably in times of the wars they were planning to initiate against Israel.

There was a very conscious decision, on the other hand, not to provide shelters for ordinary Gazans above ground.

This became part of what was later referred to, even amongst themselves, as "The Dead Baby" strategy.

The modern "Dead Baby Strategy" was born in 2002, during Israel's Operation Defensive Shield, in the West Bank. This full-scale reoccupation of the West Bank came in response to a wave of suicide bombings during the Second Intifada, culminating in what the Jews called, "The Passover Massacre".

The "Passover Massacre" was a modest affair, as our more contemporary massacres go. Still, it killed a respectable number of the Zionist enemy. A Palestinian suicide bomber, Abdel-Basset Odeh, disguised as a religious Jewish woman, detonated himself at a Passover Seder, at the Park Hotel in the Israeli seaside town of Netanya. Thirty Israelis were killed during the holiday celebration, and another 140 wounded.

Some of the victims were Holocaust survivors.

Those killed ranged from twenty years of age, to ninety.

Numbers of married couples were killed together, which was either a blessing, or a curse, depending upon one's point of view. All, however, agreed that the father who was killed alongside his daughter, could only be seen as a tragedy.

Israel responded to the "Passover Massacre" by re-occupying the West Bank, especially the refugee camp in Jenin, which proudly called itself "The Suicide Bombing Capital of the world".

Dani Kahan, who'd returned from Hawaii to become the Intel Officer for the reserve Paratroop Battalion that went into Jenin, vividly recalled the posters that lined the walls of the small town of cinderblock houses, which was still referred to as a refugee camp, conjuring up images of long gone tents and soup kitchens, some half a century after its founding, and the tent city's demise.

At first, he thought the posters that lined the walls of Jenin were for cheesy Arabic action films. Each one featured a Palestinian warrior with a Rambo headband, crossed bandoliers, and an AK 47. But the posters that were on and inside virtually every home, were not of young Palestinian would-be Stallones or Schwarzeneggers. They were all suicide bombers whom, it was fervently hoped for in Jenin, were now enjoying the favors of the seventy-two promised virgins.

These holy "martyrs" were responsible for killing some one thousand Israelis, including Dani's ex-wife and nine-year-old son, who had been ripped to shreds by sixty nails that tore through his body, two of which lodged in his brain, which turned out, Dani supposed, to be some sort of blessing, because his son was burned over sixty percent of his body as well. Unfortunately, his ex-wife, Anat, a sweet girl, whose only fault that day was in succumbing to her son's desire for a slice of pizza, lingered to watch her child die in front of her, before she succumbed to her own wounds.

The perpetrator of the suicide bombing was the twenty-five year old son of the wealthiest restaurant owner in the city of Jenin, which bordered the camp. His name decorated every home in the area referred to as the refugee camp. Ahmed Ahmal Al Shukeri was their favorite son.

Al Shukeri was escorted to the restaurant by an attractive, twenty-year-old Hamas activist, who disguised herself as an Israeli college student. Her name was Leila Dahlan. She was one of the one thousand terrorists released in exchange for Gilad Shalit. After her release, she gave an interview on Al Jazeera, in which she stated that she had made her escape from the scene of the bombing by taking an Arab bus near the Damascus gate of the Old City of Jerusalem.

The driver had the radio on, she said. As the first news reports of the suicide bombing came on, everyone started congratulating each other. "They didn't even know each other, yet they were exchanging greetings, you know, as if our football team had just won a championship. When I heard the first reports and they said only three had been killed I was grief-stricken, but as the death toll rose to eight, I couldn't hide my smile. And when they said fifteen were killed, I said, 'Allah be praised'."

No matter how much he drank, Dani could never stop hearing her voice in his head from that interview, after she was released. And in Jenin, in 2002, everywhere he looked, he saw the Rambo pose of the heroic martyr, who had ripped his tender young son's body to shreds.

The battle to clean the terrorists out of Jenin was a difficult one. Twenty-three Israelis were killed and fifty-two Palestinians, of which over forty were wearing combat boots and had weapons next to them.

It was a battle the terrorists had prepared for, well in advance. Indeed, in retrospect, Dani suspected the suicide bombing in Netanya was carried out precisely to suck the Israelis into "The Suicide Bombing Capital of The World" in order to grind up the Israeli troops they knew would be brought in to retake the terrorist enclave.

The refugee camp had been largely evacuated of civilians before the Israeli forces arrived. After that, almost every room of every house in the center of the rabbit warren of streets that made up the "camp" was booby trapped. To that generation of terrorists' credit, the "Dead Baby Strategy" had not yet become a matter of doctrine. Indeed, when compared to today's breed of terrorist, they appeared almost quaint in their adherence to a certain ethical creed, which dictated that they first evacuated their civilians from the battlefield they had prepared, in which they intended to defeat the Zionist forces.

Now, in almost any Western army in the world, to say nothing of the armies of non-Western countries, when you have an area that has been clearly identified as a terrorist enclave, and in fact bills itself, proudly, as the Suicide Bombing Capital of the World, you flatten it.

You can do that in a variety of ways, all of which are, more or less, equally effective. You can bomb it out of existence, either with air assets, or heavy artillery, or you can bring in tanks. Usually you do all three, which is euphemistically referred to as "softening the target", before you send in light infantry to mop up what's left.

But Israel, even in 2002, knew it had to play by a different set of rules, knew that it would be judged as a war criminal for the exact actions carried out by the armies of those who would judge her.

Thus there was no "softening" of the target. No air strikes. No bombardment of 155 mm howitzers, and no tanks. This was not entirely done out of public relations, nor for humanitarian concerns. There was a certain amount of hubris or arrogance involved, as well. Israel had been going after wanted terrorists in the West Bank and Gaza for years. These operations were seen as "policing" actions, rather than war. Israeli special operators staged raids on an ongoing basis in the West Bank, surrounding the houses of "wanted" men, and arresting, or killing them, should they be foolish enough to offer resistance.

There was a difference, the Israelis reasoned, between terrorists and armies. They had contempt for the former, and respect for the latter's abilities. What they had not yet imagined was the hybrid that was now in its embryonic stages; a terrorist army.

Thus, without softening up the target, they sent light infantry into the Jenin Refugee Camp. As an intelligence officer, Dani blamed himself for part of the hubris. But that was only part of the sin of which he was guilty.

He wanted revenge.

He wanted, personally, to kill the men who had sent Al Shukeri and Dahlan into Jerusalem, and murdered his ex-wife and nine-year-old son. The words of King David's lament after the death of his son rang incessantly in his brain. *O Absalom, my son, my son, would that I had died in your place, my son, Absalom, my son, my son!*

And, not having died in his place, Dani would now kill, to avenge him, instead.

As many as he could.

He prayed for it.

There is a Rabbinic tale, that says hatred is like holding boiling water in your hands, hoping to find the person you want to throw it on.

It ends up burning you, instead.

So it was in Jenin. Through a combination of disdain, underestimating the enemy, hubris, and a desire for revenge, Israel sent in a reservist battalion of paratroopers. Thirty- five and forty-year-old married men, some with pot bellies, some who hadn't trained in far too long a time, without softening the target, they sent them, marching like idiots, into the Suicide Bombing Capital of The World, the "refugee camp" in Jenin.

They knew the names of the terrorists they were after. This would be an arrest operation like hundreds of others before it. They entered the city of Jenin in Armored Personal Carriers, and like nineteenth century dragoons who rode horses to the scenes of battle and then DISMOUNTED, and fought on foot, they went walking into the terrorist army's lair.

Contrary to what had actually happened, Dani and other senior intel officers assumed the camp was still heavily populated with civilians. This was another reason for sending in light infantry and working slowly, house by house. They were seeking to avoid large-scale civilian casualties, which they were sure would occur if they deployed artillery and armor.

Ironically, after the battle you could see that not even a flowerpot was out of place on the porches of the suburban homes of the city of Jenin, outside the camp. The Israelis had parked their Armored Personnel Carriers, dismounted, and not so much as touched a one of those houses, because they knew that none of the men they were looking for were inside of them. The terrorists they were after were in the "camp".

There was a main road that skirted the camp and then made a sharp right turn into an alleyway, which lead into the heart of it. They had no idea it was, in fact, neither a camp, nor a city, but a meticulously prepared battlefield.

A D9 armored Caterpillar bulldozer was sent in to widen the alleyway to clear a pathway for tanks or APCs if that became necessary, and to detonate any booby traps which might be present. It was accompanied by an Israeli-made Merkava III tank.

As the Reserve Battalion Intel officer, Dani rode in the armored cabin of the D9, pointing out the way from the map he had been issued in the briefing the night before. Suddenly, they were taking fire from every rooftop. At first, it was the ping of M16s and AK 47s against their armor, then heavy machine gun fire, and then anti-tank rockets.

"Go, go go!" Dani shouted at the driver and radioed back to battalion, "We're taking fire from the rooftops! This is a trap!"

The Reserve Battalion Commander, Lieutenant Colonel Oded Zamir, turned to his Air Force close air support liaison officer. Dani was shouting that they needed an F-15 strike. But in the Kirya, the decision was made against anything that could create that much collateral damage. They dispatched AH-1 Cobra helicopters, instead, to take out the Palestinians' rooftop positions with precision wire-guided missiles.

By the time the D9 and Merkava III had penetrated almost two kilometers into the heart of the camp, widening the alleyway, and then withdrawn, Dani counted 115 detonations of IED booby traps.

Back at the battalion forward command post, Dani said they were marching into a disaster. They had to go in, in force, in tanks and armored personnel carriers, and not on foot. If they didn't want to use tanks and refused to simply flatten the houses from which they were under fire, they should hit the corner of the house with a D9 bulldozer, knock down a wall, and then jam up in an APC and dismount paratroopers straight into the opening, instead of marching them through the alley-ways of the camp, where they'd be ground up like sausage.

"I'm not going to be tried for giving the order to kill a bunch of civilians!" Zamir shouted back at him. "You think CNN isn't going to be all over this? I guarantee you, there's some army lawyer in the Kirya right now, opening cases. It's just a question of who they're going to file against first. And I'm not going to be the one, because you're afraid of a bunch of guys with headbands and Kalashnikovs!"

"I'm the battalion intelligence officer," Dani said, fighting down the bile he felt rising from his gut, "and I am putting in writing my official assessment and recommendation. You want to give the order to go in on foot? You can bear responsibility for that, too! You're more afraid of a commission of inquiry than you are of getting your own people killed!"

"Who the hell do you think you're talking to?" Zamir said, the spittle flying into Dani's face, "You come waltzing in here from Hawaii, and just because they killed your kid you want a massacre?! Huh?! You think you can't be brought up on charges, Kahan? You think you can't be relieved?"

"Go to hell!" Dani said, and stormed out of the tent. But Zamir followed after him.

"I'm giving you an order, Kahan!" Refuse it and I'll court martial you, right here, on the spot! You turn to me, and stand at attention!"

Dani turned to him, not sure if he would stand at attention, or kill him. He wasn't thinking about a court martial, or prison time. He was contemplating murder. His hand slipped onto his M4 as if straightening it in its sling. He indiscernibly thumbed the safety up to semi-auto. All he had to do now was pull back the action, and chamber a round. He edged his left hand toward the action of the M4 as if adjusting its weight, and smiled softly.

Zamir eyed him. "You want to be a hero?" he said, "Tomorrow, at 06:00 hours, Company B goes in, as briefed, and you go in with them as Intelligence Officer. Now you salute and say, 'Yes, Commander', or we can start the court martial, for refusing a direct order in time of war, right now."

Dani looked at him a long time. Men were going to die tomorrow. He could be with them or not. But this idiot was sending them to their deaths, and suddenly, death didn't seem like such a bad idea to Dani Kahan.

"Yes, Commander," he said, smiled more broadly, saluted, and left.

At 06:00 hours the next morning, B Company entered the camp on foot.

From his observation post inside one of the cinderblock houses halfway down the alley, Awad Hamadi, Deputy Commander of the Palestinian Forces in Jenin, could hardly believe his eyes. The arrogant, Zionist pig fools, were actually WALKING into the camp! No tanks. No APCs. Nothing. Just out for a stroll on a spring morning...

After the Israelis had widened the alleyway the day before with the D9, he had prepared his men to escape. There was no way their preparations could defeat the Israeli tanks and helicopters. But now they were actually entering on foot. He sent the ten-year-old boy runner, Daoud, to pass along the order to remain in position.

The Israelis were in for a surprise.

As B Company turned right into the alleyway, with weapons at the ready, the paratroopers eyed the windows of the cinderblock homes, and rooftops, swinging their weapons this way and that, on the alert for would be snipers.

There was a deadly quiet to the place.

That was the first thing Dani noticed.

It was quiet because all the civilians had been warned this would be the scene of the battle and ninety percent of them, if not more, had already gone to take refuge with relatives outside of Jenin. The only ones staying in the heart of the camp were those who, quite bravely, said, they would live and die alongside the fighters. There were a few children who, like Daoud, would serve as runners, and several women who had agreed to martyrdom.

As B Company rounded the right turn into the camp, Dani, as intel officer, was with the point man. It was Dani's job to lead them, with the newly marked up maps they had gotten at the company briefing earlier, to the addresses of the "wanted" terrorists. They had up-to-date, actionable intelligence, Zamir had assured them.

There weren't the usual smells of an Arab village, Dani remembered later. No smells of charcoal fires, or of coffee with cardamom, no sounds of livestock, dogs, or children.

Down the alleyway, Daoud had passed the word to the Palestinian cohorts, who were all thanking Allah for the gift they were about to be given.

As the Israeli paratroop company neared the wall of the third home on the left, in the alley, nineteen-year-old Mahmoud Zouabi held the cell phone Awad Hamadi had issued him.

He wiped the perspiration from his palms. He felt the beads of sweat, stinging, dripping into his eyes from his forehead, as the Israelis slowly advanced downhill, through the alleyway. He recognized one of the Israelis in front. He had seen him in the cabin of the D9 bull-dozer, leading the way for the tank, the day before. *Too bad he is up front*, Mahmoud thought.

Buried inside the wall of the third house on the left in the alley, were five kilograms of explosives, wired to six propane gas tanks. With incredible discipline and sweat streaming down his face now, despite the springtime morning chill, Mahmoud waited until the first third of the company had passed the house, thus assuring that the main body of soldiers would be exposed to the full force of the bomb blast.

Then he whispered, "Allahu Akhbar!", and pressed "send".

The shock wave from the blast blew Dani across the street and into the wall of the building opposite him. Blood was streaming from his right ear. He couldn't feel the right side of his face and he could hear nothing but the high pitched ringing in his ears. He fought not to lose consciousness and clear his head, but the ringing wouldn't stop. Suddenly he was aware of the pain ripping through his left shoulder just below the protective covering of his flak jacket. He smelled cordite and blood. He looked back where his men had patrolled just moments before, and saw one of his friends, Yair Levy, cut in half, his entrails, red and ghostly pale at the same time, spilling out of his body. The sounds gradually began to override the ringing; men screaming, gun-fire, more explosions of grenades, as he felt someone grab his flak jacket and pull him inside a doorway, just as machine gun fire stitched its way down the alley, where he had been lying, trying to clear the ringing from his head. His pal Chaimkeh, built like a bear, had dragged him with one hand, while firing his M4 with the other, to the sudden relative safety of the doorway.

Dani saw at least a dozen, maybe more of his men strewn, broken and bloodied, some still writhing, others staring blankly to the heavens, dead or dying, in an alley of blood that flowed downhill toward him.

Then he heard the woman shout "Allahu Akhbar!"

He wheeled his M4 instinctively, and he and Chaimkeh shot at the same moment. Chaimkeh had hit her in the head, but Dani's shot hit her center mass and detonated the suicide belt. He felt the heat of the blast searing his skin, the shrapnel whizzing past him, the door behind him blown open from the force of the blast, the burning pain in his leg and saw Chaimkeh blown backward, blood streaming, and brains showing, from where his forehead had been only a moment before.

Suddenly he heard footsteps rushing downstairs toward him from inside the cinderblock house. He pulled a grenade out of the upper pouch of his combat vest, pulled the pin, though the pain now in his left shoulder was almost unbearable. He let the "spoon" fly off the M26A1 grenade, thus igniting its fuse. He counted to three in order to let the fuse burn down, so whoever was coming down those stairs to kill him, wouldn't have time to pick the grenade up and throw it back outside at him. He threw it inside the doorway and dodged back against the wall for cover.

The grenade exploded two seconds later, just inside the house, and he heard the screams. Then he thumbed the safety on the M4 to full automatic, led with the gun, and ducked inside the doorway, spraying a long burst into what was left of the four terrorists' dead and dying, ripped bodies, flowing blood, staring, some of them, with that same vacant look of the dead Israelis outside. Chaimkeh no longer had eyes with which to see. His skull had been blown open from the middle of his face to his helmet, offering an obscene view of his brains blown apart by the shrapnel.

Dani looked across the street and there on the wall opposite him saw the heroic pose of Ahmed Ahmal Al Shukeri, and swore he would not die today, not in front of Shukeri's Rambo gaze. Not today.

He had emptied his clip on the now-dead terrorists, but had a second clip duct taped to it, separated by a plastic wedge to allow it to slide into the weapon unobstructed. The second clip was upside down, so all he had to do was thumb the release, reverse the magazine and snap the action, chambering a new round. He kept the safety on "full auto" and led with the weapon, pointing it around the corner of the doorway, down the alleyway, and firing off a short burst to give himself cover as he ran across the street. Just as he made his dash, a kid, probably not more than fifteen, jumped from a doorway into the middle of the alley, and threw a grenade at Dani. It bounced between Dani and the doorway, so that if Dani had jumped back into the house with the dead terrorists, it would still have blown him apart.

So he did something insane.

The boy didn't have a weapon on him. His only weapon had been the grenade, and not having had Dani's experience in combat, he had not let the fuse ignite before throwing it. Thus there was time for Dani to save his life. Had he picked up the grenade and thrown it back at the kid, the fragmentation would still have gotten him. He might have had the satisfaction of knowing the kid would die with him, but he had already sworn not to die today beneath Al Shukeri's heroic gaze.

So Dani charged the kid, grabbed him and spun him around, and used the kid for a shield. The kid was looking into Dani's eyes in disbelief and terror as the grenade exploded.

It detonated with a blinding flash and the fragments tore through the kid as Dani looked into his eyes, heard him scream, and felt him twitch into his death dance, and dropped him.

Dani ran and dove into the open courtyard of the second house in the alley, where what was left of the company had sheltered. The company commander, Captain Benji Shiloach, was dead. The radio was destroyed. Those men still able to fight were struggling up the stairs, fighting room to room and setting off yet more booby traps. But they all knew they had to reach the rooftop if they were to survive the onslaught of Palestinians who now began advancing on their position, raining fire down on them from every direction.

The firefight went on for almost three hours, until they were finally rescued by a company of regular army special operators.

Zamir, meanwhile, had ordered in the D9 bulldozers and Armored Personnel Carriers, and they were doing exactly what Dani had laid out for him the day before.

The bulldozers led the way, punching an opening through the wall of whatever house the terrorists were using for cover. Then the D9 hit reverse and an APC jammed right up to the newly created hole and disgorged its fighters.

The Palestinians withdrew further into the center of the camp, and now, when they came up to a structure, Zamir had orders given over the loudspeaker for those inside to surrender. He gave them five minutes and then gave the order to bulldoze the house. If they came out and surrendered, they were taken prisoner. If not, they could stay in the house and be bulldozed along with it.

It's hard to outrun a bomb, but pretty easy to outrun a bulldozer, so in terms of the way in which one could destroy the center of a town, it was without doubt, the most humane method.

Slowly, methodically, the Israelis bulldozed an area the size of a football field.

The Palestinians, seeing the bulldozers, almost without exception surrendered.

Dani was evacuated to Tel Hashomer hospital.

He had shrapnel in his left leg and shoulder, a torn rotator cuff, a broken collarbone, and a punctured right ear drum.

From that day on, he was determined never to underestimate the enemy again.

The battle of Jenin was over.

The Palestinians had fought bravely.

So had the Israelis.

But the PR battle was just beginning.

For, if the Jews had started this war because of the "Passover Massacre", both Hamas and the PLO were determined to one-up them, and have a massacre of their own.

The Jenin Massacre!

Arafat began referring to the camp as Jeningrad!

Eyewitnesses swore that the Israelis had lined up whole families, and machine gunned them, killing at least five hundred people, and then shoving their corpses, Nazi-style, into a ditch that they hastily covered over with dirt shoveled in by a bulldozer. The entire world jumped on the story. The Jews had committed an horrific atrocity, "The Jenin Massacre"!

The UN promptly sent a representative to investigate the Israeli-committed slaughter of innocents. UN envoy Terje Roed-Larson, on his first day in Jenin, called it the worst war crime since Bosnia. Tearful widows wailed before the cameras about dead husbands and sons, mothers and fathers, buried in the mass grave that the Israelis had hastily dug, to mask their Hitlerian, barbaric act.

Dani watched it all on CNN, in his hospital room, in amazement. And, ironically, while the PLO and Hamas media spinners were bemoaning the "Jenin Massacre" in English, their newspapers were bragging, in Arabic, about the fact that they had killed scores of Israeli paratroopers, in a Divine Victory, while only losing a few dozen martyred warriors, themselves!

Israel demanded an investigation. It demanded that the UN find the mass grave and show the bodies of the slaughtered five hundred victims of "the worst war crime since Bosnia".

A month later the UN issued its report which was carried in two-inch columns on the back pages of every newspaper that had screamed, in doomsday headlines, about Israel's massacre of hundreds of innocent Palestinian civilians.

The result of the UN investigation?

Fifty-two Palestinians killed in a battle, which claimed the lives of twenty-three Israeli soldiers. Of the fifty-two dead Palestinians, some forty were military aged men, wearing combat boots.

No mass grave.

No hundreds of corpses of whole families slaughtered together.

No questions asked of the "eyewitnesses" who, weeping copious tears, recounted their tales of horror.

Nothing.

It was all a lie.

And it didn't matter.

The "Jenin Massacre" was now part of the narrative of Jewish atrocities and Palestinian victimization.

And the "Dead Baby Strategy" was born. It thus became Hamas, The PLO and Hezbollah's doctrine to carry out acts of terrorism, while making sure they wore, always, the mantle of victimhood.

One would not exist without the other.

To insure that there were dead babies to show an all-too-willing press, which followed the age-old dictum, "If it bleeds, it leads", part of the doctrine entailed firing rockets and mortars from within schools and mosques, even from within UN schools, or at the very least, next to civilian houses.

The calculus was a simple one.

Fire a rocket next to a school or home.

If it kills an Israeli, that's a victory.

If the Israelis fire back, and kill Palestinians, that's a bigger victory.

If you fire a rocket, and kill an Israeli, and then they fire back and kill Palestinians, that's the biggest victory of all!

Terrorism, wearing the mantle of victimhood.

In the Second Lebanon War, Hezbollah brought the Dead Baby Strategy to a level of macabre perfection. Because not all reporters could get to the scene of an Israeli bomb attack at the same time, Hezbollah had crews "dig up" the dead babies and then race them to a waiting ambulance, which took off with sirens screaming, for the benefit of whatever news crews were on hand.

Then, when those crews left, they reburied the corpses of the dead babies, and waited for the next news crew to arrive, then dug them up again, and raced them once more to the waiting ambulances, which dutifully sped off with sirens screaming. And each tableau was accompanied by wailing women, shocked at the just-discovered remains of their loved ones, murdered by the Nazi-like Jews...

In one instance, they dug up, reburied, and rediscovered the same corpses for a half dozen different news crews. The fact that some of the dead babies were dug up in the morning, and then rediscovered at night, made no difference.

And when there were no dead babies, they staged funerals of martyrs wrapped in white sheets for the news crews. And when the crews got their footage of the tragic burial processions, and left, the corpses, magically, came to life, and got off their funeral biers. The fact that an Israeli surveillance drone actually filmed a supposed corpse magically resurrected, after the western camera crew left, and distributed the footage via YouTube mattered not a whit.

There was one narrative, and one only.

Israelis bombed, and Palestinian babies died.

The only Western reporter who resisted the "Dead Baby Strategy" during the Second Lebanon War was, as Dani recalled, Anderson Cooper. He was reporting from Beirut, and Hezbollah offered him the same faked footage his colleagues were gobbling up, and Cooper, not yet the rock star he would later become, refused, and left Beirut to cover the war from Israel. Dani referred to him as the Righteous Gentile.

However, it was that same "Dead Baby Strategy" which Dani so bemoaned from his hospital room, after the "Jenin Massacre" of 2002, which was about to save Israel from the greatest catastrophe in its history.

In Gaza, as Yasser Darwish now explained his original plan to Khaled Kawasme and Abdul Aziz Al-Tikriti, in the comfort of the underground lounge in the Hamas elite living space, below Shifa hospital, an aide brought cups of freshly-pulled Italian espresso for the three of them.

Darwish lamented the "Dead Baby Strategy", which had won out over his original concept.

He sipped the espresso, which he preferred now to the thick Turkish coffee with cardamom, which had been such a fixture in their culture before the advent of the wonderful Italian machines with their individual pods. So convenient.

"What was the original plan?" Al-Tikriti asked.

"During the Jews' holiday of Rosh Hashanah," Darwish explained, "my original plan called for infiltrating between five hundred and a thousand Hamas fighters, each armed with anti-tank missiles, machine guns, grenades, plastic handcuffs, and tranquilizers. The Jews always send the majority of their soldiers home for their so-called High Holidays."

This was how Egypt and Syria launched their surprise attack on Yom Kippur, forty years earlier. All along the border with Gaza, thousands of Jews, in little agricultural villages, with communal dining halls, would be eating the holiday meal. Some of the dining halls held up to eight hundred people.

"Can you imagine it, Brothers?" Darwish said, "We could have killed thousands and taken hundreds hostage."

Al-Tikriti stared at him in disbelief, "What do you mean 'could have'? Why don't you? It's perfect!"

"Money," Darwish said, shaking his head at the lost opportunity to implement a plan, which was his life's work, five years in the making.

Hamas' benefactor had been Iran. But Iran, being a Shiite country, was backing Bashar Al Assad's Shia government in their civil war against the Syrian Sunnis.

Hamas was a Sunni organization. And thus, they withdrew their support of Iran, for the latter having participated in the slaughter of over 100,000 of their fellow Sunni Moslems.

Iran, in turn, cut off all financial support to Hamas.

"Then," said Darwish, "that Jew-loving pig, Abbas," which was how he always referred to the PLO President of the Palestine Authority on the West Bank, "that Jew loving pig Abbas cuts off our money as well! All of a sudden, we can't pay forty thousand of our bureaucrats... Or our fighters!"

"But," said Al-Tikriti, "What about Qatar? They have promised to pay you. They are Sunni, just as we are."

"Yes, but that's the problem, my Brother," Darwish said, leaning back in his leather wing chair and lighting up his *nargilah*, which he always enjoyed with the Italian espresso. "The political leadership is afraid that if we carry out the Rosh Hashanah attack without warning, and the Qataris support us, they will become pariahs. They will lose the Americans, the Saudis, the Emirates, the Jew-loving pig Egyptians; everyone will turn against them. The Qataris are like immoral women, worse than whores. They want to lie in everyone's bed. So the political leadership says, 'We cannot do the Rosh Hashanah plan. We have to go back to our doctrine. Make the Jews attack us, show the dead babies, and then we can attack their civilians with our Divine weapon', and we say, 'what choice do we have?'

"Do we have F-15s?

"No!

"Tanks?

"No!

"So, we must use the other means that we have planned, my brother, for five years, and which the Jews will never see coming in a million years."

"Money!" said Al-Tikriti derisively. "That is why the first thing we did was to take the oil wells in Iraq, and rob their banks, and steal and sell their antiquities. You cannot be a true warrior of Allah, if you have to suck at the tit of the Qataris!"

"If only we had known you sooner, brother," Darwish said, passing the *nargilah* to Al-Tikriti, "we would have been free of the political leadership, AND the Qataris."

"Timing," said Kawasme. "Everything is timing."

Al-Tikriti took a deep drag of the fragrant smoke of the *nargilah* into his lungs and exhaled languorously. "If," he said, "this weapon of Divine Victory is as you have described it, you won't need the charity of the Qataris."

"It is, my brother," said Darwish. So saying, he finished his espresso, glanced at his Patek Philippe watch, politely excused himself, and entered Hamas' main command and control bunker. There he gave the final order to proceed with the launching of over a hundred rockets at the Zionist entity.

Some were fired from next to Shifa Hospital, some from next to the Is Al A Din Mosque, others next to a hotel housing foreign journalists, while others were fired from next to Wafa hospital, and still others from next to the Shati Refugee Camp. Almost all were fired from pre-pre-pared underground sites, as they had learned to do from Hezbollah, in Lebanon. And almost all were fired from within the densely populated civilian neighborhoods and suburbs of Gaza City. Let the Jews fire back all they wanted. Whether the rockets hit their marks or not was of little importance. The "Dead Baby Strategy" always hit its bull's eye: the foreign press.

And with that, the third war between Hamas and Israel, in five years, began.

But this one, Darwish knew, would be different.

This one, *Insh Allah*, unlike Jenin, or the Second Lebanon War, or the wars of 2009 and 2012, THIS war, would bring the Zionists to their knees.

And as one hundred rockets fired off toward Israel, Tera Dayton, Darwin Washburn, Raul Peña and Clint McKeever were all landing in Iraqi Kurdistan to see whether ISIL, and its operatives, now safely ensconced beneath Shifa Hospital in Gaza, were indeed just the JV team in Kobe Bryant jerseys, or not.

CHAPTER 5

F orce Master Chief Petty Officer Darwin Washburn, Papa SEAL to those in the Teams, was cranky.

And anyone who knew Papa SEAL knew that was not a good thing.

Washburn was not a gregarious man, by nature. Indeed, he might be thought of as taciturn. But he could be engaging, on occasion. Though not what most would describe as charming, he could nonetheless, if in the proper mood, what others with perhaps a more nuanced eye, even be described as "convivial".

He loved that word.

He liked the sound of it.

It was a word that sounded as if Morgan Freeman were saying it.

Convivial.

It sounded Southern, and somehow, to him, black. And it bespoke power and maturity. Indeed, gravitas.

He liked to roll the word "convivial" around in his mind, and then swirl it in his mouth before saying it.

It was rather like the cognac he had come to enjoy, with fine Cuban cigars, while sitting in some Godforsaken, third-world, dung-hole, fleabag establishment with his fellow Frogs, who had, nonetheless, managed to find a way to secret, amongst their belongings, some of the more refined pleasures in life.

The young Frogs just liked to guzzle their brew, belch, and then bellow for more.

But the crustier older guys, like Papa SEAL, had learned to appreciate a thing or two. And he had certainly been exposed to some of the finer things, as rewards, under the wise and masterful tutelage of former

Commander, and federal felon, Mark Dicek. Two of those things to which Papa SEAL's own personal Obi-Wan Kenobi had exposed him were the Hoyo de Monterey Double Corona cigar, and Delamain Très Vénérable Cognac de Grande Champagne.

The inhaling, and imbibing, of those two of the more pleasurable fruits of earthly Paradise put Force Master Chief Petty Officer Darwin Washburn in a decidedly convivial mood.

He would lean back his six-foot–five-inch, two-hundred-seventy-five pound frame, stretch languorously (which was another word he had grown to love), and feel the way Morgan Freeman's honeyed, Southern-hewn, black voice sounded. Convivial.

On the other hand, if you packed Force Master Chief Petty Officer Darwin Washburn's six-foot–five-inch, two-hundred-seventy-five pound frame into the coach seat of a commercial jetliner, and flew his sorry ass sixteen and a half hours to Frankfurt, Germany, gave him a four hour layover, and then stuck that same six foot–five-inch, two-hundred-seventy-five pound frame into ANOTHER mother-jumping coach seat, and flew him ANOTHER four and a half hours to Cairo, and THEN, instead of letting him enjoy some of the epicurean pleasures for which the Cairenes were justifiably famous, kept him in the airport for ANOTHER four hour layover, only to cram him into ANOTHER coach seat, for the two and a half hour Egypt Air flight to Erbil, Iraqi Kurdistan, thus totaling almost thirty-two hours of travel time, with squealing, puking babies, and the general malodorous flotsam and jetsam of international coach class travel, Force Master Chief Petty Officer Darwin Washburn could be downright cranky.

And what was the justification for inflicting this commercial air pilgrimage on Washburn, Dayton, Peña and McKeever, all of whom had been flown separately, but on equally torturous, yet different, routes and airliners?

It was because that limp-dingussed, bunghole, pathetic imitation of a supposedly black man in the White House did not want it to appear as if the United States of America was, in any way, militarily involved in the current collapse of the Iraqi army, or defending against the rise of the Islamic Caliphate, at the expense of Iraqis and Syrians, Shias, Kurds, Christians, Yezidis and Turkomen. All of which meant that, instead of cutting a six-foot–five-inch, two-hundred-seventy-five pound brother a break, and letting him fly in a US Military transport where, once at cruising altitude, he could actually stretch out on his gear and sleep, President Rafik Kabila, in order to camouflage the true nature of their mission, had them all fly separately, on commercial flights… Coach! For thirty-two hours!

And then, thought Papa SEAL, *the ignorant fool might have asked himself what kind of camouflage there is for a six-foot–five-inch, two-hundred-seventy-five pound black man flying to Erbil Kurdistan?! Could Kabila be so totally and completely clueless, as to believe that there would be ANYONE in Cairo International Airport, who wouldn't immediately know that the ONLY reason a six-foot–five-inch, two-hundred-seventy-five pound black man could POSSIBLY be flying to Erbil, Kurdistan, was because he was, in fact, US FREAKING MILITARY???!!!!*

HUH??!!!

Do you think??!!!

"I mean, I'm just sayin', ya know?" said Papa SEAL to Clint McKeever who, at six-foot-three and two-eighty-five, was equally cranky.

"This woman from Abuja or somethin'," complained Peña, "with like five kids, an' all of 'em, ya know, with snot runnin' down their faces… Ya know? Her kid spits up on me! I coulda got Ebola or some-thin'. *Dios Mío*, man. *Dios Mío*."

The only one who wasn't complaining was Tera Dayton.

The four of them were jammed together, with their all their gear, in a 1984 Toyota minivan, which had picked them up at Erbil International Airport.

The airport itself was about the size of Lynchburg Regional Airport/Preston Glenn Field, in Virginia, which was where Tera used to fly in and out of when she took her bachelor's degree in PoliSci at Liberty University.

She listened to the three men complaining like fifth graders. "Are we there yet? Huh? How much longer? Are we there yet?"

She loved being in Erbil. She loved the Middle East in general, and Egypt and Kurdistan in particular; loved their people and their language, the customs, the food, the smells of the *souk*, the deter-mination, in the best of them, to build something new and different.

They were America's best friends in the Arab Middle East, and the US, under President Kabila, was doing everything humanly possible to turn them into enemies. That was probably why she went out of her way, as an American, to let them know that not everyone from her country felt that way.

Peña looked at her sitting up front with the driver, chatting away in Arabic.

This Chica *speaks Arabic like a freakin' Arab*, he thought, *and she is hot*, 'Mano! Esta mujer está caliente, *Bro*. He kept looking at her neck, hoping she'd turn around, but so far she was the ice maiden.

Tera Dayton could feel him looking at her, could almost hear his thoughts, knew the dialogue running through his brain, and wanted to turn around and bash his face in! She wanted to shout, I have a PhD from Harvard, you low-rider bozo, and you're lookin' at me like I'm a twenty dollar hooker in Tijuana!

But she just sat in the passenger seat listening to Hamoudi, their Peshmerga driver, talk about "The Situation", as she watched the skyline of Erbil appear suddenly out of the brown and barren desert landscape.

High-rises were going up everywhere, almost as if this was Shanghai, instead of Iraq.

"Dude, I never knew this place was so modern, man!" Peña said looking at the steel and glass office buildings and apartment houses, white and gleaming in the Middle Eastern sunlight, against a cloudless, cobalt, blue sky.

"Yes," said Hamoudi, "Very modern. Very much money in Erbil, before *DAEESH*."

"*DAEESH*?" asked McKeever.

Great, Tera thought. *The FBI counter terrorism expert doesn't even know what Islamic State is called in Arabic.*

She turned around to him.

¡Muy Caliente! Peña thought when she turned around, her blond hair framing a close to Grace Kelly perfect face. Though of course, Peña didn't have a clue as to who Grace Kelly was. But, had he ever seen a picture of her, he would have thought she was hot, just like Tera Dayton.

"The Islamic State in Iraq and Syria," Tera said, trying not to say it through gritted teeth, "In Arabic, is '*DAEESH*'. Short for *Dawlat al–Islamiya fi al Iraq was Sham*."

"She speak Arabic good!" said Hamoudi appreciatively, as they passed the sign for KFC, at the Abu Shahab Mall.

"I don't think we're allowed to say 'Syria'," said McKeever, ever the loyal Washington toady.

"Syria," said Papa SEAL. "There. I said it. Hey, you guys got KFC here?"

"Yes, yes," said Hamoudi. "But, it not Kentucky Fry Chicken. It stand for Kurdish Fried Chicken. But very tasty, very crunchy. You like we stop?"

"I LOVE we stop!" Papa SEAL said. "I'm hungry, man! I couldn't eat any of that crap on the plane."

"Yeah *'mano*, this baby spit up Ebola on me, you know?"

"I actually don't mind airplane food," McKeever said.

"That's because you're in the FBI, *hermano*," said Peña. "None of you guys know how to eat."

"The corrupt ones do." said Papa SEAL.

"Shouldn't we be getting to where we're supposed to go?" Tera said

"We'll get there, Baby Sister. You're like what, five–three? Well I'm six-foot five, and six foot four of me doesn't have any food in it."

The Abu Shahab Mall had an Italian restaurant, a Lebanese restaurant, the KFC, and a branch of the original Abu Shahab restaurant, referred to by the locals as "Abu's Kebabs". That's where Tera wanted to eat, extolling the virtues of the indigenous cuisine, but Papa SEAL was the hungriest, so KFC it was.

"This is really crispy!" said Papa SEAL, gobbling a fried chicken leg in one bite, "I mean, it doesn't have the Colonel's seventeen herbs and spices, and it's not as good as Popeye's, Church's, or Chick-fil-A, but it's really crispy!"

"It's eleven herbs and spices," McKeever said softly, ever a stickler for precision. It was as if a dangling participle, or an incorrect fact, constituted verbal litter hanging in the air of conversation, which McKeever felt obliged to recycle.

"I like it a little more *caliente*," Peña said, looking at Tera, and licking the KFC off his finger.

Tera looked away and felt ill. "I've got to go to the ladies' room," she said, and got up and left...

"That salad bar is pretty good, too! And the hummus," McKeever said. "Very impressive place. First rate!"

The patrons were mainly expats, Westerners like themselves. They worked for the big oil companies, though with the rise of ISIS, most of the oil companies were cutting their staff down to skeleton crews.

Tera came back from the restroom as Papa SEAL and the others were finishing their meal.

"Weren't you hungry?" Papa SEAL asked Tera, as he looked at her plate.

"Not very," Tera said. "I'm actually anxious to get going."

"And why's that?" Papa SEAL asked.

"So we can talk to this ISIS informant they've got. I mean, that's what we're here for, isn't it?!" Tera was getting a bit cranky herself.

"Well," said Papa SEAL, "I'm gonna get me a little more Kurdish Fried Chicken, and try that salad bar. Besides, that'll give our Peshmerga friends a little more time to torture the guy before we get there."

He turned to Hamoudi, "I mean you guys DON'T Mirandize the ISIS guys, do you?"

"Oh, no, sir. Definitely not," said Hamoudi, who had no idea what Mirandizing was, but thought it prudent to deny to the American, that they would ever consider doing such a thing.

And, indeed, while Papa SEAL cruised the salad bar and tried the yogurt and cucumber dip, which Hamoudi highly recommended, and the stuffed grape leaves and naan bread, Colonel Adan Zahawi of the Kurdish Security Forces, or KSF Intelligence Unit, was grinding his bootheel into the face of Yehyeh Al-Masri, who lay naked - except for a Depends diaper - on the bare floor of the interrogation cell beneath Daniel's Church, a two hour drive from Erbil into an arid and rocky desert landscape.

The interrogation cell smelled like torture chambers everywhere: a noxious mixture of feces, urine, blood, and sweat; a smell of fear, of abject, "cry for Mama" terror.

Al-Masri had been interrogated almost non-stop for ten days by Colonel Zahawi , who saw in him his country's only real chance to get the equipment they would need to keep *DAEESH* from slaughtering them all. Now that the Iraqi army had fled like cowards in the field, and given up their billions of dollars' worth of modern heavy military equipment to the Caliphate's terrorist army, there was a very real threat of genocide, not only for the Kurds, but all others whom *DAEESH* regarded as infidels, polytheists or apostates. Just thinking of those tanks and humvees, recoilless rifles and howitzers, made Zahawai grind his boot heel into the open burn wound on the side of Al-Masri's face even harder. By now, he was fairly certain that Al-Masri had given up all that he had to give. He had methodically tested the veracity of his intelligence in every way possible.

Zahawi was not unskilled in his profession, having been trained at the wrong end of a torture session conducted by some of Saddam Hussein's best, or worst, depending upon which end of the torture session one found oneself.

Zahawi would never do to another human being what had been done to him by Saddam's fiends. But he knew how to apply pressure. Not that he enjoyed it, because he did not. But this was now a war of survival, and no, he would neither Mirandize Al-Masri, nor allow him to lawyer up. The most slack he would cut the *DAEESH* terrorist was the Depends diaper, because the man had soiled himself repeatedly under Zahawi's stern questioning.

Meanwhile, Tera, Peña, Washburn, and McKeever were making slow and painful progress in their 1984 Toyota minivan. The temperature was forty-three degrees Celsius, roughly 109 degrees Fahrenheit.

"But it's a dry heat," Tera said, trying to remain cheerful, though the air conditioner in the minivan was broken, and the hot air blowing in through the open windows, from the desert outside, was like a blast furnace.

"Who cares?" said Peña, no longer caring whether he made a good impression on Tera or not. "*Demasiado caliente, Chica.*"

"Don't call me Chica, please. Okay?" said Tera. "I'd really appreciate it."

There was a deadly silence in the car.

Hamoudi was self-conscious, because of the broken air conditioner. He tried to lighten the atmosphere, by inquiring whether their lunch had been satisfactory.

"First rate!" said McKeever.

"Wasn't no Popeye's, but you done good, my brother," Papa SEAL said, leaning over, and giving Hamoudi a friendly pat on the shoulder.

Hamoudi basked in the black man's compliment, and brotherly love.

"First rate!" McKeever said.

"Did you also try the chips?" Hamoudi asked.

"Chips?" said Peña. "I didn't see any chips. I woulda liked some chips. I like those barbecue ones, or the onion dip ones, ya know?"

"You're talking about *potato* chips." McKeever said.

"Right," said Peña, "Isn't that what he's talkin' about?"

"*He's* talking about *chips*," McKeever said, emphasizing the noun.

"Yeah, and I didn't SEE any," said Peña, emphasizing the verb.

"When he says chips, he means french fries," Tera said, and immediately regretted having joined the conversation.

"They call potato chips french fries?" Peña asked not only incredulously, but almost as if he was offended by the notion.

"No," said McKeever, "What you call french fries, they call chips."

"And I call 'em freedom fries!" said Papa SEAL, "It's like fish and chips," he said, beginning to be annoyed at Peña's provincialism.

"Yeah?" said Peña, as if aware of the fact that he was stepping onto a linguistic IED.

"Well," said McKeever, "Fish and chips are fish and french fries."

"What is french fry?" Hamoudi asked.

"The British call what the Americans call 'french fries', chips," said Tera, praying the conversation would come to an end.

It did for about five seconds.

"Okay," said Peña. "It's like that Tarentello movie."

"What?" asked Papa SEAL.

"He means Tarantino," Tera all but hissed.

"Isn't that what I just said?" asked Peña, getting really ticked off himself, now.

"No," said McKeever. "You said Tarentello."

"But you knew what I meant right?" Peña demanded. "SHE knew what I meant!"

"We ALL knew what you meant, my brother," Papa SEAL said, trying to chill things out.

"Great movie," McKeever said. "First rate dialogue."

Why doesn't he leave it alone, Tera thought.

"Yeah," said Peña. "That's the whole chips and french fry thing. I get that. 'Cause that guy said, 'Hey, you know what they call a Big Mac in France? They call it a Royal with cheese."

There was silence, and Tera was praying to her Lord and Savior that McKeever would ignore it, though by now she knew that was impossible.

"Actually," said McKeever softly, "It was a Quarter-Pounder."

"What was a Quarter-Pounder?" asked Peña.

"What you called a Big Mac," said Papa SEAL, shaking his head.

"He said they called a Quarter Pounder a Big Mac in France?!" demanded Peña. "That is bull, man! He said they called it a Royal." Peña said definitively, and then added as an afterthought, "With cheese!"

"Actually..." said McKeever

"Just leave it alone," Tera begged.

But McKeever ignored her.

"The line was," he said, "'You know what they call a Quarter-Pounder with Cheese in France? A ROYALE with cheese.' It wasn't a Big Mac. It was a Quarter-Pounder. And it wasn't a royal. It was a ROYALE."

Silence.

"You SURE about that?" asked Peña, as if he could actually be mollified now.

"Positive," said McKeever.

"Okay... Maybe I was wrong. I can admit a mistake."

"Thank you, Jesus," Papa SEAL said.

Silence. But it wasn't over. Tera knew it wasn't over. It would never be over. They'd ride forever through a 109 degrees Fahrenheit desert, trapped in an air conditioner-less Toyota Minivan. *This is Jean Paul Sartre on wheels*, she thought.

"'Cause, what they got in France," Peña said, "is centigrams. Right? So it couldn't be a Quarter-Pounder. 'Cause they don't have pounds. So that's why they called it a Royale."

"Precisely," said McKeever.

"Thank you, O Lord," Tera whispered.

Silence... Silence... Silence.

"So, how many centigrams would that be?" Peña asked. "You know, if they called it a Centigramer, instead of a Quarter-Pounder?"

"Pull the car over, please," Tera said urgently to Hamoudi.

"You are going to be sick, madame?" Hamoudi asked.

"It's, like, two point two pounds to the key, so that'd be…" Peña said, trying to do the math.

"Pull the car over!" Tera said, and Hamoudi complied.

"So, a half a key is one point one pounds…" Peña continued calculating.

Tera opened the door and walked briskly fifty meters into the desert and began to scream. "AHHHHHHHHHHHHHHHHHHHHHHHHHHHHHHHHHHHH!!!!!!"

"Dude, what's wrong with her?" Peña asked.

"Roughly 193 centigrams," McKeever said.

Two hours later, they arrived at the torture chamber.

"Do you know what you're going to ask him, Master Chief?" Tera asked Papa SEAL, just before they got out of the minivan

"Say what?" he asked.

"The informant," she said. "Have you prepared your part of the interrogation?"

"Oh…" said Papa SEAL. "Yeah. I'm gonna ask him what they call a Quarter-Pounder in France."

Peña high fived him.

Tera felt ill.

I hate them all, she thought.

"So," said Hamoudi, "Here, we have arrived. Daniel's Church."

Daniel's Church was actually a low hill, or a mound that rose, like the hump on a dowager's back, out of the arid, rocky, lunar-looking desert landscape. The stones and rocks reflected the 109 degrees of desert heat back up into their faces. If there had indeed once been a church there, it was long since destroyed. There was the mound, or low hill, the ruins of a wall, which may indeed have once belonged to a modest church, and there was a squat, square, cement block house, that really wasn't a house, at all. It was the air raid shelter–like entrance to a series of steps that led underground. The entrance itself was concealed and protected by stacked sandbags meant to shield against artillery or sniper fire. There were three Peshmerga soldiers wearing olive drab, camouflaged uniforms. Papa SEAL quickly noted their shiny green helmets had no camo netting, thus making them a perfect target for anyone with a sniper's weapon and a halfway-decent scope. Those helmets were not going to stop a Barrett M82 fifty-caliber sniper slug. *Ah, well*, he thought. *Ah, well.*

"So, why do they call this Daniel's Church?" McKeever asked.

"Because," said Hamoudi. "This is the Church of the Prophet Daniel, Peace be upon him. You know? Daniel, from miracle of the Den of The Lion?"

"Daniel in the Bible?" McKeever asked.

"Yes, sir. Exactly so," said Hamoudi.

"And, this is where he's buried."

"No, no buried here. This is just his church."

"Then, why do they call it his church?" McKeever, ever wanting to be precise, asked.

"Because it *is* Daniel's church. He has builded this church."

"That's not possible," McKeever said.

"Very possible," said Hamoudi, his own anger and frustration growing. "Daniel's Church, because Daniel has builded his church in this place. Therefore, it is called 'Daniel's Church'."

"But, the Prophet Daniel lived during the Babylonian exile," said McKeever.

"Just so," said Hamoudi. "Iraq and Babylonia, same thing, my dear sir."

"Precisely," said McKeever, pedantically. "But, the Babylonian exile was six hundred years before the birth of Christ, and, therefore, there were no Christians at the time that Daniel was alive. So, how could he have built a church?"

"It is another miracle," Hamoudi said, ending the conversation.

Just then, the tall and imposing, professional-looking Lieutenant Colonel Adan Zahawi emerged from behind the sandbagged entrance to the underground fortress Hamoudi referred to as Daniel's Church. He looked cursorily at the four Americans, and immediately spotted a brother military man in Papa SEAL.

He crossed over to him.

"Commander Stone?" he asked Washburn. Each of them had been given a *nom de guerre* for this trip. Also, it had been decided not to inform Lieutenant Colonel Zahawi that the United States was sending a Force Master Chief Petty Officer, instead of an officer of equal rank. All throughout the Middle East, officers of every military service looked down upon enlisted men. In this case, it didn't matter that the one person most properly suited to determine Special Ops capabilities and limitations HAD to be the Force Master Chief Petty Officer, and, therefore, top enlisted man in the Naval Special Warfare Command, instead of a mere, run-of-the-mill Commander, which was the equivalent of Zahawi's KSF Lieutenant Colonel's rank.

"That's right." said Washburn.

"Lieutenant Colonel Adan Zahawi, at your service."

The two military men saluted one another.

Washburn made the introductions. "May I introduce Doctor Susan Price, Mr. John Buckley, and Mr. Ray Martel."

"Let me guess," said Zahawi, looking at each, in the order of their introduction. "Although, none of those are your real names. Dr. Price is of the CIA, Mr. Buckley of FBI Counter-Terrorism, and Mr. Martel of the DEA."

"Actually," said Washburn, "We're all from the Department of Agriculture."

Zahawi laughed charmingly. "Right this way, Gentlemen and Lady," he said. He began to lead them past the sandbags and down the steps, into the place known as Daniel's Church.

At first, it was pleasantly cooler, as they descended the steps into this ancient underground edifice. *It's not inconceivable*, thought Tera, *that this had been a church. With the Moslem conquest spreading out of the Arabian peninsula, it would have made sense for seventh or eighth century Christians to build their church below ground, rather than above, and to be able to be sealed off from any invading force. So here we are, hundreds, if not more than a thousand, years later, with the building once again being used to protect its inhabitants from those who wished to convert by the Sword of Islam.*

As they descended, Zahawi told them that the underground fortress contained over two hundred rooms. Modernity had shown its face through electricity, supplied by a gasoline generator, and running water. Other than that, it was as if they were stepping back into an age of barbarism, which, of course, they were.

Tera assumed that the information they were about to receive would be of a lone underwear bomber, or a lone shoe bomber, or perhaps someone who intended to plant a pressure cooker bomb in Times Square. It certainly would be easy enough for a lone terrorist to plant explosives in a car bomb, and go to Vegas, hand the keys to the valet, and detonate it via cell phone, thereby killing dozens, if not hundreds. There was even the possibility of an Oklahoma City-type truck bomb that could take out an entire building. She had prepared a list of questions and memorized them. She felt confident that she was up to the task at hand.

And then the smell of the interrogation cells hit them like a sledgehammer. Tera gagged, and struggled to maintain her composure. Peña went silent. He had spent time in such a room as this in Cartegena, when his cover had seemingly been blown, and was only saved at the last moment, from certain death, by the timely intervention of the Brigada Anti Narcoticos of the Colombian army.

Washburn, on the other hand, had been in many such rooms. But he was always the one asking the questions, instead of being subject to "enhanced interrogation", sometimes by US forces, and more often, by those of our allies in the war against terror, who did not believe in Presidential findings, or Miranda warnings, either. He had a developed a technique or two of his own along the way, as well.

Zahawi led them down a low-ceilinged corridor. Christians of the seventh century were decidedly shorter than Washburn and McKeever, who had to crouch, as did Zahawi. They zigged and zagged, passed rooms with men who moaned and screamed behind closed doors, until they came into a small, monk-like cell illuminated by a single light bulb.

Yehyeh Al-Masri had been cleaned up for the occasion. He wore a loose fitting robe, and a fresh Depends diaper. But the smell on him was still enough to turn Tera's stomach.

"He speaks English," Zahawai said. Then he turned to Al-Masri, and said one word. "Talk."

"All I know..." Al-Masri began softly.

"Louder," Zahawi said.

"All I know," Al-Masri said, in a louder voice, "is that there is going to be a mass casualty attack in the US, carried out by *DAEESH*. It will involve Mexican or South American Drug Cartels. And, it has been planned, and will be carried out, by Khaled Kawasme and Abdul Aziz Al-Tikriti."

"Who are they?" asked Peña.

Tera shook her head in disgust. The whole point of an interrogation was to make the suspect think you knew everything he knew. Before Al-Masri could answer, she looked at Peña and said, "They are to 2014 what Usama bin Laden was to 2001."

Peña, realizing he had just stepped in it, simply said, "Got it."

"You know more," Zahawi said, bitch-slapping Al-Masri on the back of his skull.

"Yes, yes," said Al-Masri, bowing his head as if to avoid another blow. "They are both in Gaza, right now."

"Gaza?" Tera asked. "They're coordinating this with Hamas?"

"I don't know coordinating. But they must to meet with Hamas," he said, "And they are there now with Yasser Darwish…"

"More," said Zahawi.

"Yes. I have given to this man," Al Masri said, looking at Zahawi, "the address of the apartment they will be staying in, where there is an underground bunker."

"When you say 'mass casualty', how many people are you talking about?" asked Papa SEAL. "I mean is this a car bomb, truck bomb, what?"

"That I don't know. I swear it! But the numbers…they are talking of killing thousands."

"Thousands?!" Tera asked, incredulously.

"Thousands," Al-Masri said, then added, "But I don't know if it is bomb, or truck, or car, or what, or how."

"And they're going to be in some kind of apartment with a bunker, in Gaza?" asked Washburn.

"Yes," said Al-Masri.

"Why aren't they going to be in the complex under Shifa hospital?" Washburn asked. Tera was impressed with the SEAL's knowledge.

"Because, there is something, I don't know what, but something, they want to observe more closely. This I know because we don't use cell phone now or internet. They are afraid of NSA, and so if we have for them a message, we must to know where they are, because we will smuggle in a runner, and he will give to them this message. So, no NSA. And my job... I was responsible for these messengers. So I know the address of where they will be."

"And they actually believe they can kill thousands..." said McKeever.

"Yes."

"What drug cartels? What are the names of the cartels or the contacts in Mexico or South America?" Peña asked.

"This, I do not know," said Al-Masri. "There is different department, different brother for to communicate in Mexico or South America... This is not me. I do not know."

Zahawi bitch-slapped Al-Masri again, across the face. "Tell them about the hostages," he commanded.

Al-Masri nodded, and instinctively moved his head to avoid another blow. "Yes. There will be hostages. They will kill thousands, and maybe take hundred, two hundred hostage."

There was complete silence in the room, as that sentence sank in on the four Americans.

Finally, Papa SEAL broke the silence. "Civilian or military hostages?" Washburn asked.

"They will take civilians. Womens and childrens."

"And..." said Zahawi, raising his hand to strike again, but it was unnecessary. Al-Masri held nothing back.

"And all these womens and childrens hostages...." he said. "Some, they will cut off their heads, and some, they will put in cages, and burn them alive."

"Say that again," said Tera, unable to conceal her shock, unable to fight down the feeling rising up in her off being surrounded in Quetta by the men who raped her, and said she was lucky they did not cut off her head, as they had done to the American journalist before her.

"They will cut off the heads of these womens and childrens... Or, burn them in the cages," said Al-Masri, "and then they will put it on internet, on the YouTube, for all the Americans to see. And then, they will know there is no power that can save them."

CHAPTER 6

I t was the third day, of the third Hamas-Israeli war, in five years, although Israel wasn't calling it a war. The Israeli government rarely used the term "War", not out of public relations concerns, but because it had economic implications which, in a down year, could be disastrous in the very difficult budget negotiations that Kivi Natanel was facing with his new Coalition partner, from what he derisively referred to – in private – as "The Cottage Cheese Party".

The year before, there had been a consumer revolt over the high price of cottage cheese, a staple of the Israeli diet. It was sort of an Israeli version of the Occupy Wall Street movement, except they wanted to Occupy the Dairy Case. At any rate, out of that consumer revolt, there grew up a new political party, called the New Future Party, centered around a telegenic former newscaster, named Yaron Kochavi. Kochavi had ridden a wave of populism into enough Parliamentary power to force Kivi Natanel to bring him into the coalition, as Finance Minister.

Kochavi had then brazenly given an interview on Israel's most popular television news program, predicting that, in the coming elections, he would become Israel's next Prime Minister.

Of course, this was nothing new in Israeli politics.

The Foreign Minister, a barrel-chested Russian immigrant named Menasheh Leibovitch, from the Israel First Party, which, not coincidentally, was mainly made up of Russian immigrants, of whom there were some 1.2 million, out of Israel's total population of eight million, had predicted that he, too, would become Israel's next Prime Minister, after the next round of elections.

Added to that was the fact that Natanel knew that his Defense Minister, Justice Minister, and Interior Minister also intended to replace him, and you had not a Team of Rivals, but a shark tank at feeding time.

The reason each Israeli government, and, especially, the current government of Kivi Natanel, was reluctant to use the term "War" was the fact that, legally, in Israel, once something was called a "War", as opposed to a "Campaign", or an "Operation" (which were supposedly more localized in their scope), it triggered a higher rate of compensation for all Israeli civilians who suffered property damage in the conflict. Up until the Second Lebanon War, that had not been much of an issue.

The Second Lebanon War, however, introduced a new type of conflict; one waged, not by a State Actor, but a terrorist army. A State Actor, like Egypt, Syria, or Jordan, waged conventional war, with conventional armies, which met on the field of battle and tried to impose their will upon their adversary, by defeating that adversary's military force, thus resulting in the attainment of whatever political objective was the cause of the conflict in the first place.

Non-State Actors, however, like Hamas, Hezbollah, ISIS, and, to a lesser extent, Al Qaeda, formed what Dani referred to as terrorist armies. Their objective was not necessarily to defeat an army, but to inflict mass civilian casualties and property damage, by literally bypassing Israel's clearly superior military force, in order to hit its population centers. This was done by means of short, and increasingly longer-range rockets. These rockets could be launched by remote control, from underground sites, and literally flew over Israel's army, and struck at Israel's home front.

Thus, in 2006, Hezbollah ushered in this new type, and era, of terrorist warfare aimed not at defeating one's military rival, but terrorizing their civilian population, despite all the actions of their military.

When Israel responded to these rocket attacks, the Non-State Actor, like Hezbollah and Hamas, employed the "Dead Baby Strategy".

The Non-State Actor fired rockets at Israeli civilians, from positions next to Palestinian, or, in the case of Hezbollah, Lebanese, civilians. Thus, when Israel struck back, there was inevitable collateral damage, and a parade of dead babies, with which to turn the world's media and therefore populations and ultimately, governments, against Israel for its "disproportionate response".

According to this new reality, Israel had a right to defend itself, as long as it was buried in the sand up to its neck, and could not effectively strike back at those who were attacking it.

In the 2006 war, Hezbollah launched four thousand rockets at Israel's Northern communities, inflicting heavy property damage. Because the government employed the term "Second Lebanon War", the amount of money it had to pay out for Israeli civilian property compensation was significantly higher than would have been paid, if the conflict were simply called an "Operation".

To deal with this new reality, of both the "Dead Baby Strategy", and Israeli loss of life and property, for which the government had to provide compensation payments, Israel devised three new strategies.

First, it set up an entire unit, whose sole job was to warn Arab civilians in areas which Israel was about to attack, that Israel was, in fact, about to attack those areas. And, thus, for the sake of their own lives, those civilians were advised to flee to safety. Israel did this, first by dropping leaflets a day or two in advance, warning of an attack. Then, it took to the emerging social media, as well as the growing cell phone market, and actually began calling the cell phones of every civilian in the area it was about to attack, with a recorded message – in Arabic – stating that an attack was imminent.

Israel then sent out text messages to virtually all the cell phone owners in the area they were about to attack, stating that the attack would be within a matter of hours, if not minutes.

Finally, it developed a strategy of first dropping what, in essence, were large firecrackers, non-lethal explosive charges, onto the roofs of buildings that would be attacked within the next five minutes. This became known as "Knocking". It was the last warning to the inhabitants of a building to flee for their lives. All this was done in an effort to minimize civilian casualties as much as humanly possible, and was remarkably effective.

Israel had the lowest civilian-to-combatant casualty ratio in the history of warfare.

By comparison, American forces bombing Bosnia and Kosovo, for instance, killed four civilians for every combatant, and that was regarded as an acceptable and indeed, humane ratio since previously, the ratio had been has high as ten to one.

Israel had gotten the ratio of civilian-to-combatant casualties down to one to one.

And it didn't matter.

One image of a mother wailing over a dead child spoke louder than all the statistical evidence in the world.

Stalin had put it best when he said, "A million deaths is a statistic. One death is a tragedy."

Thus, the "Dead Baby Strategy" inspired protest marches, and denunciations, throughout the world, while the Non-State Actor continued to rain rockets down on Israel's civilian population.

Here, Israel actually became a victim of its own success. It designed a remarkable anti-missile interceptor system, called "Iron Dome", which was effective in shooting down ninety percent of the terrorist rockets aimed at Israel's civilian population centers. Once it was implemented, the difference between Israeli and Palestinian casualty figures became even more pronounced. The aggressor, thus, wore the mantle of victimhood, and the press, pursuing a single narrative, became as complicit as any enabler of child or spousal abuse.

This was so, despite the fact that Iron Dome saved not only Israeli civilian lives, but Palestinian civilian lives as well, since in 2012, for instance, it obviated the need for an Israeli ground operation.

In that campaign, known as Pillar of Defense, when Hamas once again rained down thousands of rockets on Israel's civilian population centers, Iron Dome was so successful that Israel had no need to launch a ground invasion to suppress the rocket fire. It could simply hit Hamas from the air, until Hamas calculated that it had incurred enough destruction to claim genocide, and receive billions in aid to rebuild all that the Zionist, Nazi-like aggressors had destroyed in their barbaric attacks against the helpless Palestinian people.

Hamas then stole the money, enriching its coffers, and decided to make an ingenious use of the building materials it had received, in order to create a new Divine Victory Weapon, to be used against Israel in the next war, for which they were already preparing.

When Israel imposed a quarantine on Gaza, Hamas said, "What are you afraid of? Do you think we can build rockets out of cement and steel? These are the things we need, to rebuild the schools, and mosques, and hospitals, and baby clinics, which the Zionists so wantonly destroyed."

It was pure genius, and the Western democracies were in no mood to be confused with facts.

They had, after all, seen the pictures.

As for the high cost of compensating its own citizens for property damage, due to Hamas or Hezbollah rockets, Israel employed a third strategy for purely domestic use. It simply stopped calling the conflicts "Wars".

They were now "Operations" and, as such, triggered lower compensation payments for Israeli civilian property damage. Otherwise, the country may well have gone bankrupt. Thus, the past two wars with Hamas were called "Operation Cast Lead" (2009), and "Operation Pillar of Defense" (2012). And, the current conflict of the summer of 2014, was called "Operation Protective Edge".

On this third day, of the third war with Hamas in five years, Major Dani Kahan was driving back from an intelligence briefing in the Kirya, to the Southern headquarters of the Givati Brigade, to which he had recently succeeded in getting himself assigned.

After his throw-down with Lieutenant Colonel Zamir in 2002, Dani had been officially reprimanded, and Zamir had been promoted to full Colonel, and became a brigade commander, as opposed to battalion commander. Dani earned the reputation of being not a prescient intelligence officer, but a malcontent troublemaker. In short, Zamir had juice, and Dani was pulp.

Accordingly, in the 2006 Second Lebanon War, Dani, who was by then a reservist, was not called up to serve as an intelligence officer at all. Indeed, he was being completely sidelined. Not knowing whether he would be called to service in the Hezbollah-initiated conflict, and refusing to simply sit it out, Dani traveled, from his home in Tel Aviv, north to Haifa, where rockets were falling on a daily basis. He checked into an inexpensive hotel, called The Nof. He brought with him his uniform and a pair of work gloves. If he could figure out a way to get them to call him up, he had the uniform handy. And, if not, he would simply put on the gloves, and go to work where necessary, clearing rubble.

Once he was in The Nof Hotel, he began calling every person he knew in the military intelligence branch, trying to get them to activate him as a reservist. But, Zamir had put the word out, and Dani was poison. Finally, he threw his last Hail Mary pass: he knew a guy named Shlomi, who had once served in Military Intelligence, and was now in the Military Spokesperson Unit. Shlomi's office was in the Kirya, in Tel Aviv.

"Shlomi," Dani said over the phone. "You've gotta get me into this war."

"No way," said Shlomi. "What am I gonna do with you?"

"I'm an intelligence officer. I'm a native English speaker. I've given hundreds of briefings. I know how to talk to the press. You don't have anybody with my level of expertise. I'm a natural fit for you guys!"

"Your area of expertise is Gaza, not Lebanon. That's the first thing."

"I can get up to speed on Hezbollah, and you know it."

"I don't have the budget for another reservist."

"So, find the budget!"

"Dani, stop being a *nudnik*. If I don't have the budget for another reservist, I don't have the budget! End of story."

"Then, let me just volunteer to help out... As a civilian! I don't care. I cannot sit out this war."

"All right," said Shlomi. "Let me tell you what. We've set up a Northern command post, in Haifa, in the basement of The Nof Hotel. Maybe they'll let you serve coffee. I don't know. The commander is Lieutenant Colonel Ohad Rafaeli."

"The Nof Hotel," said Dani, brightening. "Got it."

So saying, Dani put on his uniform, and strolled down to the basement of The Nof Hotel, in which he was already in residence. The commander of the Military Spokesperson Unit's Northern Command Post, Lieutenant Colonel Rafaeli, was busy speaking on the phone to the head of the AP.

Dani entered, and because the Israel Defense Forces are notoriously informal, he didn't salute; just poured himself a cup of coffee, and nodded at Rafaeli, who waved him off until he'd finished his conversation.

When Rafaeli hung up, Dani said, "Ohad?"

"Yes?" said Rafaeli.

Dani stuck out his hand. "Dani Kahan. I just spoke to Shlomi, in the Kirya."

"Okay. So?"

"So... I'm in."

"In what?" said Rafaeli, thumbing through his daily briefing notes.

"I'm in the unit."

Rafaeli looked up at him. "What unit?"

"This unit," said Dani, as if talking to a child. "I'm an intelligence officer, I'm a native English speaker, I've got a ton of experience giving briefings, and I've just talked to Shlomi, and Shlomi said, 'Go see Ohad', and here I am. I'm in! I just need to check out a flak jacket, a helmet, and a weapon. I just need you to tell me where to go, and what to do, and I'm there. Easy."

Rafaeli just looked at him. "I have no idea what you're talking about."

"I'm in!"

"You're not in anything," Rafaeli said.

"I just talked to Shlomi."

"So, go back and talk to Shlomi!" said Rafaeli. "I don't care. Shlomi doesn't run this unit, I do. Shlomi's in the Kirya, I'm here. Go to the Kirya. I'm busy."

"Ohad," Dani said, smiling, as if he was Rafaeli's new best friend. "We both know how cheap the Israeli Army is, right?"

"So?" said Rafaeli.

"So, there's no way that the Israeli Army would rent me a room in this hotel, unless I was actually in the unit that's headquartered in this hotel, right?"

"Right. And, I didn't rent you one, so you're not here. So, go bother somebody else."

"Give me two minutes, and come with me. The worst that could happen, you'll waste two minutes."

Rafaeli sighed, and went upstairs with Dani. Dani crossed to the front desk, and said hello to Yossi, the front desk manager, who had checked him in earlier.

"Hi, Yossi. Could I have my key, please?"

"Certainly," Yossi said, and handed Dani his key.

Dani turned to Rafaeli, and dangled the key in front of him.

Rafaeli just shrugged, and said, "Okay. I guess you're in. You'd think Shlomi would have had the courtesy to call me, and tell me what's going on."

"Well," said Dani. "He's busy, you're busy… Everybody's busy. The main thing is, like you said, I'm in."

Dani checked out a helmet, flak jacket, a trusty old Israeli-made Galil assault rifle with collapsible stock, instead of the more upscale American M4s, and began serving in the rotation, giving press briefings to English-speaking correspondents.

When the command post moved from Haifa up to the Lebanese border, he moved with them. They were temporarily billeted in one of the border *Kibbutzim*, so there was no hotel to check into. He simply grabbed a mattress and a couple of blankets, and made some of the best friends of his life.

The Military Spokesperson Unit had some of the most extraordinary brainpower of any endeavor in which Dani had ever participated. One guy, Gal Alon, was a world-famous historian. Another was a Professor Emeritus of French literature. Yet another guy was a high-tech startup king. One guy was a bank manager, another ran one of the leading archaeological sites in the world. There was a female full Colonel, named Yehudit, who managed a four billion dollar charitable foundation. There was guy, a former *kibbutznik*, who somehow, had become a fairly successful screenwriter in the United States, and had shown up during the first week of the war in an Avis Rent-A-Car, and simply followed the group North. They even had one billionaire in the unit, who had offices around the world, and flew in on his Gulfstream, put on a uniform, checked out a helmet, flak jacket, and M16, and lined up for mess with everyone else. Almost all of the guys were in their late forties, or early fifties; well past the age of regular reservists, and all were volunteers.

On the night of July 26, 2006, they were gathered at the end of a long day, near the Avivim crossroad on the Lebanese border. It was around ten thirty at night, and the adrenaline was still pumping. Most of them had been under rocket fire repeatedly throughout the day, and now they were smoking cigarettes and drinking coffee, waiting to see if, at that time of night, there was anything left to do.

What few people realized was that, in the opening two weeks of the war, Israel was outnumbered on the ground by Hezbollah. It was probably one of Israel's worst wartime governments. The Prime Minister at the time was a real estate lawyer, who would later be sentenced to prison. The Defense Minister was a former labor leader, whose sole military experience was having been a sergeant in an armored infantry unit, twenty years before. And, for the first time in Israel's history, the Chief of Staff was the former head of the Israeli Air Force, and thus had no experience whatsoever commanding ground forces. During the first three days of the war, the Air Force had performed wonderfully, taking out Hezbollah's Command and Control center in Beirut, and virtually all of their long-range rockets. After that, however, no one seemed to have a clue as to what to do. Outside of the volunteers in the Military Spokesman Unit, almost no reservists had been called up. Thus, facing Hezbollah, on the Lebanese border, Israel had a bit of Regular Army paratroopers, a bit of the Golani Brigade, a bit of Combat Engineers, and the normal Northern Garrisons of the Regular Army. They were, in fact, outnumbered by Hezbollah on the ground almost two to one, and there seemed to be no rhyme, nor reason, to anything in the ground campaign.

Forces were sent in to take territory one day, and withdrawn the next.

The Chief of Staff, being an Air Force officer, was far more comfortable deploying Israel's air assets than managing its ground forces. The main objective seemed to be not victory over the terrorists, but limiting casualties to Israeli soldiers, and that was about to go horribly wrong.

Thus, on that particular night, an officer appeared at the Avivim junction, and said that a battle was taking place inside Lebanon, in a village called Bint Jbeil. Units from the Golani Brigade were taking heavy casualties. Evidently, their commander had chosen to lead not from the ground, but from a distant war room, and, because of the hilly terrain, kept losing contact with his ground forces. It was chaos. One Israeli helicopter had been lost, and Hezbollah had so many Sagger anti-tank missiles that they were firing them like rifle rounds. Dani had just dodged two fired at him and two Bedouin trackers while taking an

American camera crew onto a rise to film the action that day. The officer approached the eight middle-aged men from the Military Spokesman Unit, and said that helicopters couldn't land to evacuate the wounded, because of heavy Ground-to-Air Missile fire. They were looking for every available soldier to go in, and act as a covering force to evacuate the wounded. Would these guys volunteer?

Without a word, each man picked up his flak jacket, weapon, and helmet, and loaded extra clips into the pouches of their combat vests. They had only one slight problem: they had no vehicle of any kind, other than the Kia that the guy from LA had rented from Avis, and driven to the front. Thus, the eight of them piled in, rolled down their windows, pointed their weapons out both sides of the vehicle, turned off the lights, and, following a sketched-out map the officer had hastily drawn, drove into Lebanon. The LA guy drove the car down into a *wadi*, or ravine, to try and keep them down below Hezbollah's sight-line. There were flares going off everywhere, and they knew that they were not being set off by the Israeli forces. Hezbollah knew they were out there, and was hunting for them. They could hear the staccato bursts of automatic weapons, and occasional explosions of grenades. These weren't the sounds of war, but of light infantry. There was no artillery, no air support, nothing but semi-automatic and machine gun fire, grenades, and Hezbollah-fired Sagger antitank missiles. They drove as noiselessly as possible, all the while looking at the hand-drawn map. The LA guy, who was, after all, a movie guy, whispered to Dani, "Remember that scene in *Full Metal Jacket*, where the guys are somewhere in Vietnam, and surrounded by the Viet Cong and North Vietnamese, and the squad leader's looking at the map, saying 'I don't know where we are, man'?! I mean, the guy's almost crying, saying 'I don't know where we are, man! Where the hell are we?!' Remember that scene?"

"Yeah," whispered Dani.

"Well," said the LA guy. "That's the scene we're in right now, and there's nobody to cut to another location. We are so totally and completely screwed, dude. These guys aren't where they're supposed to be. You know the ambulances that we're supposed to protect? They're not where they're supposed to be. Or, we're not where *we're* supposed to be. The only people who are where they're supposed to be, are

Hezbollah, man! We are in the middle of freakin' Hezbollah land! In an Avis Rent-a-Car!"

As noiselessly as possible, they got out of the car. Suddenly, Dani heard the unbelievably loud bleepBLOOP chirp of the rental car's doors being locked. He turned on the LA guy, and hissed at him in a whisper, "What, are you afraid Hezbollah's gonna *steal your car?!*"

"You're right. You're right. I'm sorry, I'm so sorry! Just habit, man, I mean, you know, LA."

"We're not in LA !" said Dani.

"Got it, got it," the LA guy said, "No more LA."

They fanned out down the ravine, trying to see if they could make out anything that looked remotely like an Israeli ambulance, or soldiers carrying stretchers of the wounded.

Nothing.

Just the sounds of gunfire, and the flares overhead, that meant Hezbollah was hunting for them.

And then, there was the sound of a Katyusha landing somewhere behind them.

They waited another long hour. And, finally, the LA guy said, "Here's the deal. My car, my rules. We're outta here. Either the guys we were supposed to hook up with are dead, or they got out without us. But, either way, our ass is hanging out here, all by its lonesome."

They all looked at one another, and they all knew that, as much as they hated to admit it, the LA guy was right. They made their way back to the Kia, which now bore the marks of shrapnel from the Katyusha that had landed behind them.

"Dude, man," said the LA guy. "I do not have insurance for this!"

"Look at it like this," Dani told him. "You probably won't live long enough to check the car back in, anyway."

"True dat," said the LA guy, and, as quietly as they could, they got back into the Avis rental car and, weapons pointed out of the windows, drove back across the border, into Israel.

At Avivim, it was probably now around two or three o'clock in the morning. None of them could even think about going to sleep. The adrenaline was still pumping through their systems, like steroids through Lance Armstrong. Then, the same officer appeared out of the darkness. He told them that the ambulance had, indeed, gotten out by itself with the wounded, under cover of darkness. But, now they needed to evacuate the dead. Would they be willing to go back in?

Once again, without a word, all eight of them picked up their gear, and piled back into the Avis Rent-a-Car.

Dani had never been prouder of a group of guys in his life.

By now, the LA guy knew how to navigate the ravine. And, this time, they hooked up with the kids from Golani. There was an ambulance, with four or five dead boys. The flares were still going off, and Hezbollah was still hunting for them. There were occasional tracers shot off overhead, across the ravine, which was keeping them out of Hezbollah's line of sight. They fanned out around the ambulance, taking covering positions, as several more bodies were loaded in. Then, they loaded back into the Kia, and led the ambulance down through the ravine route, until it could hook up to a route three kilometers away that would lead them down to Rambam Hospital, in Haifa.

They gained a certain notoriety as the "Avis Recon Unit".

That, however, was a double-edged sword, because it brought the men of the Avis Recon Unit, including Dani Kahan, to the attention of Shlomi, in the Kirya. And, *fahzool* running downhill, that brought to the attention of Lieutenant Colonel Ohad Rafaeli the fact that Dani Kahan was officially *not* in the army. Indeed, Rafaeli discovered, Dani had never actually been called up. Rafaeli ordered Dani to report to him, at once, at their new forward command post at *Kibbutz Sassa*.

"You lied to me!" Rafaeli shouted at Dani.

Dani feigned a shocked expression. "Me?!"

"No, me! Yes, you! You lied to me! And, now you're going to be court martialed! Zamir was right about you. You're nothing but a troublemaker!"

"Ohad," Dani said.

"Don't call me 'Ohad'. Call me Lieutenant Colonel Rafaeli! And get ready to be court martialed!"

"How can I be court martialed, if I'm not in the army?" Dani asked, in wide-eyed "innocence".

It was, for Lieutenant Colonel Rafaeli, a Homer Simpson, "D'oh!" moment.

"Okay," said Rafaeli, through gritted teeth. "Then, get ready to be arrested by the police for impersonating a soldier!"

"Ohad, my brother…"

"I'm not your brother."

"My friend," said Dani.

"I'm not your friend, either," Rafaeli said. "I'm your worst nightmare. Now, give me your helmet, flak jacket, and weapon, and *take off that uniform.*"

"I don't have any other clothes to wear."

"Then get ready to be arrested in your underwear!"

"Ohad," said Dani, "I know you're upset, but you need to think this through. I'm saying this for your own good."

"*My* own good?" said Rafaeli. "Don't worry about what's good for me. You need to start worrying about what's good for you, like what you're going to do for the next three years, while you're in prison!"

"Ohad," said Dani. "I might be in a little bit of trouble. But, if you press charges, you're going to be in a LOT of trouble."

"*Azoy,*" said Rafaeli, employing the Yiddish term for, "is that so", even though Rafaeli's family was from Turkey.

"Yeah. *Azoy.*" Dani said. "I've been on CNN, Fox, ABC, NBC, CBS, the BBC, and Christian Broadcasting Network, representing the Israeli army…"

"And, that's why you're going to go to prison."

"No, no, no, my brother. That's why you are in deep *caca.* I've represented the Israel Defense Forces on every major television network in the world. I've gone into Lebanon, twice, as part of a combat unit, in, I might add, an Avis Rent-a-Car. And, all of that was under your command. And now, you want to tell everyone that it was all while I was a civilian… Under your orders? Who signed off on my paperwork? Ohad, the worst mistake you could make for your career, and I'm telling you this as your friend and your brother, is report me to the police. In fact, the only thing you can do to actually *save* yourself at this late stage of the game, is to make sure that I get officially called up as a reservist, under your command. Then, we just backdate the paperwork, and, instead of being the idiot who let a civilian represent the IDF on television, and go into Lebanon, you're a hero, and all my good work reflects nothing but honor on my commander, and friend, and brother."

"I hate you, Kahan," said Rafaeli.

"No you don't," said Dani. "You just think you do."

"No, I really hate you."

"Well, then," said Dani calmly. "There's an answer for that, too. When this war is over, just see that I'm transferred back into Military Intelligence, and you'll never have to hear from me again."

And that was how Major Dani Kahan got back into the Israel Defense Force.

It was symptomatic of the whole war: total chaos, and yet, somehow, it had worked.

Dani's personal situation had worked out because of pure, unmitigated *chutzpah*, and BS.

The military campaign had worked out, primarily because of the effectiveness of the Air Force. The irony was that, what Israel thought of as a failure hit Hezbollah so hard, it had kept the Northern Border quiet for eight years thereafter. It was one of the longest periods of quiet ever achieved in that area by any military campaign.

But, for Dani, the great lesson of that war was the end of what had been called the "Rust Theory". Hezbollah had been acquiring thousands upon thousands of missiles and rockets, and all the experts in the Israeli military said that Hezbollah would never launch them. They were simply using them as some kind of status symbol, and possibly to rake off some skim. But, the rockets, according to all the experts in Israeli military intelligence, would just sit there and rust, never to be used.

And now, on this third day, of the third Israel/Hamas war in five years, it was déjà vu all over again. Dani's nemesis, Zamir, had retired as a Brigadier General in 2009. And, after a disastrous affair in Hawaii with the most beautiful woman he had ever seen – who was truly psychotic, and evil, and now in prison for the murder of her ex-husband, whose body had never been found – Dani had come back to Israel, and reenlisted. With Zamir gone, Dani was back as a combat intelligence officer, assigned to the elite Givati Brigade, on the Gaza border. He was driving there now from Tel Aviv, nearing the city of Ashkelon. One drove with the window down, so you could hear the air raid siren, and with the radio on, so one could hear the code red alert, which meant that if you were driving, especially where he was now, near Ashkelon in the South, you had less than thirty seconds to pull the car over to the side of the road, and take shelter from the incoming rocket attacks from Gaza.

He had just been to a briefing in the Kirya, where the conventional wisdom was that the present conflict would be an exact replica of 2012.

2012's Operation Pillar of Defense had lasted eight days. Hamas had fired around 1,500 rockets, and Iron Dome had intercepted eighty-five percent of them, completely obviating the need for a ground operation. After eight days, Hamas agreed to an unwritten ceasefire, and shook down the international community for billions more in reconstruction aid. This summer's campaign, the experts believed, would be exactly the same. Seven to ten days, they'll shoot their rockets, we'll intercept them, they'll accuse us of genocide, and the international community will cough up billions – which they'll steal.

Indeed, the "Three Ks" – Prime Minister Kivi Natanel, Defense Minister Kobi Golan, and Chief of Staff Lieutenant General Kadosh Mintz, were offering Hamas a way out, on a daily basis. "Calm will be answered with calm," they kept saying. Which was another way of saying, "Stop shooting, and we'll stop shooting, too."

The Kabila administration was pushing for a ceasefire.

Secretary of State Jack O'Leary was trying to give Qatar and Turkey a role as peacemakers. The Egyptians wanted no part of it, saying they were the only game in town. And, Kivi Natanel kept saying, "Let somebody offer us a ceasefire, and we'll take it!"

And, all the while, Hamas kept firing rockets, at roughly 100 to 120 a day, and the experts said there wasn't a thing to worry about. "Eight to ten days, then it's over. Just like before."

And the more they said it, the more Dani Kahan wasn't buying it. Hamas had to get some sort of Divine Victory out of this war, otherwise they would be overthrown from within.

In 2012, they were the unchallenged rulers of Gaza. Today, however, Islamic Jihad, Al Qaeda, and even ISIS, had forces in Gaza, who would act to overthrow Hamas if they didn't deliver some kind of victory that would give them, at the very least, street cred. They had to pull off some kind of indisputably successful terrorist attack, in order to proclaim their Divine Victory. In 2012, they had played the card of "We withstood the Zionist onslaught, and we're still here. Therefore, we're victorious!"

They couldn't use that one again; their own people wouldn't swallow it. They had to be able to show something that would be worth the misery they were bringing down on the heads of their own people. Their rocket fire wasn't doing it, and they were already being criticized from within.

Yasser Darwish had been asked publicly why the Hamas rocket fire wasn't inflicting more damage on the Israelis. Not wanting to give Iron Dome the credit, he said, "We fire the rockets. We aim them properly. But, their God blows them away."

Just as Dani was ruminating on Darwish's explanation, the air raid siren went off, and the car radio said, "CODE RED IN ASHKELON. CODE RED IN ASHKELON."

Dani swerved to the side of the road, and jumped out of the car. There was no shelter nearby, not even a low retaining wall behind which to take cover. Up above, he could see four rockets arcing toward him.

Not more than twenty feet in front of him was a religious couple, who had also pulled over to the side of the road. The husband had his arm around his wife, sheltering her, and he also saw the four rockets heading toward them. In a loud, unshakable voice, he began reciting the 121st Psalm.

"I will lift up mine eyes unto the mountains, from whence cometh my help.

"My help cometh from the Lord, who made the heavens and the earth."

And, the minute the man said "My help cometh from the Lord", BOOM! Like Mighty Mouse, four Iron Dome interceptors swooped in, and blew the rockets from the sky!

"Amen!" Dani shouted to the religious guy, who turned around and smiled.

And then, Dani got back in his car, and drove south to Givati headquarters, by the Gaza border. He would be under three more rocket attacks by the time he arrived, by which time he had memorized the 121st Psalm. *It's like chicken soup*, he thought. *It couldn't hurt.*

By the time Dani had arrived at Givati Headquarters, the President had convened the meeting of his National Security Cabinet in the Oval Office. The Vice President walked in, just as James Francis Doherty, head of the CIA, was beginning his presentation.

"Sorry, Mr. President," said a visibly irritated Bo Fitzgerald. "But, this is really intolerable! I want to know why I don't receive the memos as to where these meetings are being held! I went to the Situation Room, and..."

"Hey, Bo," said POTUS, as if he were talking to a homie. "No harm, no foul, y'know? Francis was just getting started."

"I would really appreciate it, Mr. President, if someone on your staff would see to it as their mission in life that I am apprised of the time and location of..."

"Absolutely, Bo," said POTUS, and turned to Mallory Mohsen. "Mallory, can somebody on your staff..."

"Absolutely, Mr. President," said Mallory, fighting as hard as she could to suppress a smile.

What an insufferable SOB, thought Fitzgerald. Mallory Mohsen hated him. She wouldn't spit on him if his guts were on fire. *And that's who he's telling to make sure that I stay in the loop?* From that point on, Bo Fitzgerald did not hear a word that the Director of the CIA was saying. He listened only to his own interior monologue, listing all the slights he had been made to suffer under this administration.

"The initial reports that we've received from our team in the field," said Director Doherty, "indicate that this Al-Masri character believes there is going to be a mass-casualty attack against the United States of America, carried out by ISIS."

"ISIL," Deborah Wheatley corrected the Director, who ignored her.

"...In cooperation with Hamas and, either a Mexican or South American drug cartel. The Kurds believe they have given us valuable intelligence and, of course, if it pans out, they have, indeed. And, they're expecting a *quid pro quo* in the form of equipment, with which to defend themselves against..." he looked at Wheatley, and said, distinctly, "*ISIL*."

But, Bo Fitzgerald wasn't the only one tuning out CIA Director Doherty that morning. POTUS, himself, was in a foul mood. The fundraiser in LA had gone well. In fact, it had gone wonderfully. But, there had been hell to pay for it on the home front. He had raised a total of five million dollars, a good deal of it at the home of Glynnis Petrov, a beautiful, forty-something actress who had recently "consciously separated" from her rock star Brit husband, and relocated, with her two children, Peach and Mohandas, to her hometown of Beverly Hills. Glynnis was the daughter of Barry Petrov, a gifted - and thoroughly likable - television writer, and his wife, the equally gifted - and thoroughly likeable – actress, Sybil Donner. Glynnis herself was second-generation Hollywood royalty, having been named for her grandmother's best friend, Glynnis Johns. Glynnis the younger was beautiful, cultured, well-educated, and progressive. She spoke three languages, and had graduated from one of America's more prestigious universities. All of which, one would have assumed, would have prepared her to introduce the President of the United States to her $35,000-a-plate guests with the dignity and grace befitting the occasion, her own upbringing, and place in the industry, and the high office of the Presidency of the United States of America. Instead, she gushed like a Valley tween with a backstage pass to a Justin Bieber concert.

"You are so handsome," she said breathlessly, "that I just can't speak properly! This is just like, this, really, really, *really* profound honor, because I am one of your biggest fans – if not the biggest! And have been, since the inception of your campaign. And, I just think it would be wonderful if we could give this man all of the power he needs, to pass the things he needs to pass."

FLOTUS, who had chosen not to accompany the President to Beverly Hills, did not take kindly to the attention publicly lavished upon her husband by the mother of Peach and Mohandas. Indeed, FLOTUS had found it necessary to go off on the campaign trail, herself, without so much as a word of "Hello" or "Farewell" to the President. Indeed, he began referring to her, in his own mind, as Sasquatch, so rare and fleeting were her sightings of late in the White House. And, it wasn't as if she had done so badly by marrying him, y'know what I mean? She was FLOTUS! I mean, it wasn't as if he was Jamie Howell, diddling a White House intern in the butler's pantry off the Oval office with one of JFK's cigars! And besides, FLOTUS was the one who wanted the White House even more than he did. The truth was, unlike most modern Presidents, Rafik Kabila, the former Ralphie Sukerto, had not lusted like, let us say, a Richard Nixon or a Jamie Howell, to become President of the United States. The only thing he had lusted after, as a child, was an identity. Any identity. He had a black father, whom he had never known. He was raised by white Midwesterners, in a community in which he was the only black. And, he didn't even sound black! He actually had to go to movies, like *Superfly*, to try and develop an African-American dialect. The only time he had truly felt at home, and comfortable in his own skin, was in Malaysia. His mother had never been home; she was always off getting a degree, or protesting something, and just as he was starting to feel like he fit in, somewhere in the sixth grade, his mother married Hamed Sukerto, and hauled his ass off to Kuala Lampur.

Ironically, it initiated the, up until then, happiest period of his life. While his mother worked night and day on getting her PhD, Hamid Sukerto became the father he never knew. Ralphie adored the man. And, what's more, in Malaysia, he looked like pretty much everyone else. A young, thin, barefoot, brown boy, who reveled in the attention his stepfather lavished upon him... Until they got divorced, and his mother shipped him back to his Midwestern grandparents. If ever a kid had emotional whiplash, it was Ralphie Sukerto. Was he black, or white, Malaysian, or American? The truth was, he was nobody's child, and all he wanted was to belong... Somewhere. Anywhere. He was, in the words of one of his Jewish college friends, *nischt a yid, nischt a goy.* Neither a Jew, nor a Gentile; neither fish, nor fowl. Indeed, he had been in love with a white girl, whose family accepted and welcomed him. He knew, in fact, that because of their liberal, Upper-West-Side views, they saw him as a bit of a catch. He could almost hear them saying the words which Bo Fitzgerald would later use, "a bright, clean, articulate negro." He was their trophy, the living proof of their noble tolerance. They could be the Tracy and Hepburn to his Sidney Poitier, and he hated it. And that's when he jumped ship, and moved to Motown.

The truth was, he was just as happy being a law professor as anything else. Not, mind you, because he loved teaching the law, which bored him almost as much as Bo Fitzgerald did, but it afforded him the adulation of his students, who gushed over him just like Glynnis, mother of Peach and Mohandas, which was all he'd ever really wanted.

His identity was neither black, nor white. It was above them both. His identity was coolness. He was the epitome of cool. Jamie Howell wasn't cool before he was President. He was a chubby Southern white boy, married to a smart, homely girl with thick glasses, and more ambition than he had. He *became* cool by becoming President, but that wasn't the case with Rafik Kabila. He was *always* cool. In fact, the Presidency became *cool* because of *him!* And, that was why he liked being around movie stars. None of them had any real identity, either. They were all just really cool. And he was the coolest of them all. He was cooler than Sinatra. Cooler than Elvis. Cooler than Mick.

"Mr. President," he heard James Francis Doherty say insistently, which snapped him out of his reverie.

"What?" said POTUS.

"We need a decision about what to do regarding the intel from this Al-Masri character."

"Y'o, uh, y'know, Francis. I'm sure if you were President of the United States, instead of me, y'know, you'd shoot first, and aim later, make a decision just like that," he said, snapping his fingers. "But, I'm a bit more deliberative than that, Francis. I think the people of this country deserve for me to be a bit more deliberative..."

He has completely lost focus again, thought Mallory Mohsen.

"That's why," continued POTUS, "I'd like the input of all my advisors. Deborah?" he said, looking at Wheatley, knowing he could count on her to discretely let him know what they were talking about.

"Well," said his National Security Advisor, "I think you've already put an excellent plan into place. Under your leadership, we've sent a diverse team of experts to evaluate what this Al-Masri had to say. They've indicated that there are ISIL operatives in Gaza, and we have an address, which is actionable intelligence."

"Absolutely," said POTUS.

"So, are you suggesting," said General Tunney, "that the military prepare an option to intercept these terrorists? I mean, I think that's what the Director has been asking for. We just need you to sign off on it, Sir."

"I don't think that's what the President is saying at all," said Deborah Wheatley.

"That's the last thing we need," said Mallory Mohsen. "Something goes wrong, and we've got Benghazi all over again."

"I think the President's plan is a sound one. Now, all we have to do is follow up on it."

"Which means what?" said General Tunney. "Pardon me if I sound a little bit dense on this, but I'm not aware of any plan here."

"Well," said Deborah Wheatley. "I think the Israelis are presenting us with an opportunity. If they do, indeed, carry out a ground incursion into Gaza, the President has appointed a diverse team of experts to accompany them into Gaza City, while they do a snatch-and-grab of the bad guys."

"No Presidential finding?" asked the CIA Director.

"No need for one," said Wheatley. "It's an Israeli operation."

"Exactly," said the President.

"The Israelis do the snatch-and-grab." said Wheatley. "Their security services do the interrogation. The team that the President has put in place provides the questions, and listens to the answers. We don't have to lead from the front on this one. The Israelis owe us. Let's see them do some heavy lifting."

There was silence in the room, as everyone seemed to nod in agreement.

"Any questions?" asked POTUS.

"No, Sir," was the answer that echoed around the room.

"Good," said the President of the United States, "problem solved."

CHAPTER 7

n Israel, just as the President of the United States was proclaiming "problem solved", three ultra-religious Jewish brothers had, what for them, was a much more difficult problem, or as they would have put it, *tsuris*, than the one which National Security Advisor Deborah Wheatley had just dealt with for the President of the United States.

The three Jewish brothers in question, Yehezkel, Pinni, and Srulik Feigenboim, had a *Matzah* factory in Bnei Brak. It wasn't the smallest *Matzah* factory, and it wasn't the largest *Matzah* factory. It was a nice, little, modest *Matzah* factory, of normal proportions, and humble aspirations. It made a living. They specialized in making what is called *Matzah Shmura*, an über-kosher Passover *Matzah*, which must be watched over, from the first moment the seeds are planted, by religious Jews who follow all of the biblical strictures. The wheat, in addition, has to be harvested before the sheaves have completely dried out. For, once the wheat is completely dry, it does not draw water from the ground. Then, if it should, perchance, become wet because of rainfall, or improper storage, it might accidentally ferment, which would make it completely unsuitable, and no longer kosher for Passover. It would become, in a word, *chometz*, heaven forbid. Indeed, the wheat kernels have to be carefully examined, to make sure that the grain is not sprouting. In addition, there is the biblical prohibition, which dictates that the harvesting of the fields not include the edges thereof, which are left for the poor. But, most important for Yehezkel, Pinni, and Srulik Feigenboim, was the fact that the land on which the wheat was planted be allowed to lie fallow every seventh year, in keeping with the Lord's commandments.

2015, or the Jewish year 5776, would be just such a sabbatical year, known in Hebrew as *Shnat Shmita*. That meant that, in 2015, the *Shnat Shmita* in question, there would be no harvest with which to make *Matzah Shmura*.

That, in turn, meant that the Feigenboim brothers had to find a field of green wheat, planted by religious Jews, following all the biblical strictures, which could be harvested now, and stored for two years.

There was an additional, and darker problem, however. Reb Moishe Yankel Haimovitch.

And who, you might ask, was Reb Moishe Yankel Haimovitch?

Reb Moishe Yankel Haimovitch was the son of Reb Yisrael Ben Shmuel Dov Haimovitch, of Blessed Memory, founder of the Haimovitch *Matzah Shmura* Factory of Jerusalem.

Did I say founder of the Haimovitch *Matzah Shmura* Factory of Jerusalem? I should have said, Haimovtich *Matzah Shmura EMPIRE* of Jerusalem.

Indeed, Reb Moishe Yankel Haimovitch was to *Matzah Shmura* what Vladimir Putin was to Russia.

This is not to say that he rode bare-chested on a fiery steed. But, the man, where *Matzah Shmura* was concerned, was nothing less than a Cossack in a *Hassid's* clothing. As far as *Matzah Shmura* was concerned, he was Genghis Khan in a *shtreimel*.

Because the year 2015 would be a sabbatical year for the earth, or, *Shnat Shmita*, it will be remembered that whoever would make *Matzah Shmura*, would have to find a field of green wheat, planted by religious Jews, in accordance with all biblical and Talmudic strictures, which could be harvested now, while the wheat was still green, and stored for two years.

Whoever couldn't find such a field of said green wheat, which could be stored for two years, would, in two years, be out of the *Matzah Shmura* business.

And, Reb Moishe Yankel Haimovitch, the ISIS of *Matzah Shmura* makers, had cornered the market on suitable green wheat.

Yehezkel, Srulik and Pinni Feigenboim first traveled from Bnei Brak southeast, to Beit Shemesh, some nineteen kilometers to the west of the Holy City of Jerusalem. Beit Shemesh had been known, since the days of the Bible, for the quality of its bountiful wheat harvests.

Indeed, in the Bible, when the Ark of the Lord is being returned from the Philistine territory, in order to remove the plague which the Holy One of Israel, Blessed be He, had visited upon the Philistines, the Ark is put onto a cart, and taken up to Beit Shemesh, where it is recorded, in First Samuel 6:13, "Now, the people of Beit Shemesh were harvesting their wheat in the valley, when they looked up and saw the Ark, and they rejoiced at the sight."

Thus, if the wheat of Beit Shemesh was good enough in the eyes of the Lord, Blessed be He, to be the resting place of the Ark of the Covenant, how much better was it, then, for the Feigenboim Brothers' Matzah Factory, of Bnei Brak?

Accordingly, the Feigenboim brothers set out to purchase as much green wheat as possible from the fertile, and biblical, fields of Beit Shemesh. But, when they arrived, they found that Reb Moishe Yankel Haimovitch had already bought up every sheaf of green wheat to be had in the valley.

Srulik Feigenboim turned to his brothers, and quoted the Scriptures. "As it says in Jeremiah," he said, "They have sown wheat, and reaped thorns. They have strained themselves, to no profit, but be ashamed of your harvest, because of the fierce anger of the Lord."

He didn't actually say, "The Lord", because religious Jews refer to the Lord as "*Hashem*". So, what he actually said, was, "Be ashamed of your harvest, because of the fierce anger of *Hashem*."

"Srulik," said his brother, Pinni. "Don't exaggerate. There's no fierce anger. They didn't harvest thorns. Reb Moishe Yankel simply got up earlier this morning, and bought all the wheat."

"*Azoy?*" said Srulik.

"*Azoy.*" answered his brother.

"And what about the *Gemara?*"

"What about the the *Gemara*?" asked Pinni.

"Lo," said Srulik, "'He that stealeth *a seah* of wheat, and soweth it in a field, it were right that it not come up to be harvested'."

"He didn't steal. He bought."

"Notwithstanding," continued Srulik, "The fools that deal corruptly will have to pay a penalty."

"Penalty, shmenalty," said Pinni. "We need wheat."

"Aha!" said Srulik. "Judges 6:11. 'Gideon was beating out wheat in the wine press, in order to save it from the Midianites!'"

And, where was Gideon? In Ophra. And, where was Ophra? Near the Valley of Jezreel. So, the brothers Feigenboim, with the Bible as their guide, headed North, to the Valley of Jezreel. And what, you might ask, did they find in the Valley of Jezreel? Reb Moishe Yankel Haimovitch, who had just bought up all the wheat in the valley.

They searched high. They searched low. And, wherever they searched, they found not green wheat, but the Tatar-like conquest of Reb Moishe Yankel Haimovitch, the *Matzah Shmura* King.

Then, Srulik turned to his brethren, and said, "Judges 15."

Pinni and Yehezkel turned toward one another.

"Of course!" Pinni said.

"Judges 15, verse one," said Yehezkel. "Why didn't we think of it before?"

"The main thing," said Srulik, "is that we've thought of it now."

And what, is in Judges 15, verse one? "But, it came to pass after a while, in the time of the wheat harvest, that Shimshon (Samson) visited his wife."

And where did Samson hang out? Near the land of the Philistines, from which the word "Palestinians" is derived. In other words, in Gaza.

Thus, the brothers Feigenboim traveled south, from Tel Aviv, to the Yad Mordechai Junction, where they turned left, toward the direction of the agricultural villages on the border with Gaza. As they passed the junction, they heard the air raid sirens, and the radio alert, which said, "CODE RED AT YAD MORDECHAI. CODE RED AT YAD MORDECHAI." They swerved their car over to the side of the road, and took cover in one of the many reinforced concrete bomb shelters that dotted the highway. Iron Dome tracks rockets, and intercepts them only if they are going into populated areas. If they are going to fall in unpopulated areas, they simply let them drop. Unfortunately for the brothers Feigenboim, they found themselves next to a large, empty field, in an unpopulated area. The salvo of rockets hit a few hundred meters away, and, though their car was riddled with shrapnel, the shelter in which they had taken cover, and the Holy One of Israel, blessed be His name, kept them from harm. They offered up a prayer of thanksgiving, and got back into their now shrapnel-riddled Peugot, and continued down the highway, until they arrived at the Eshkol Junction, where they turned right, and proceeded to their biblically-inspired destination: the religious *Kibbutz* called *Kfar Shimshon*, which meant, in English, "The Village of Samson". There, next to the *Kibbutz*, and running straight up to the border fence of Hamas-ruled Gaza, was a huge field of five-foot-tall, tender, young, perfectly green and Kosher wheat.

The Feigenboim brothers turned right, into the entrance of *Kfar Shimshon*. What they didn't know, because they were not of a technical mindset, and had never served in the Army, was that this *Kibbutz*, and others like it that sat directly on the border with Gaza, were some of the few places in Israel not protected by the Iron Dome Missile Defense System. This was so, because Iron Dome needs at least three miles in which to intercept its target, and these *Kibbutzim* were less than one mile from the missile launching sites of Hamas. Had they known it, however, they would have rejoiced, instead of despairing, because Reb Moishe Yankel Haimovitch may have been many things, including the *Matzah Shmura* tsar. But one of the things he was not, was brave. And, thus, there was no way in Creation that he would travel to *Kfar Shimshon*, because of its vulnerability to Hamas' rockets.

The Feigenboim brothers had just found their wheat field.

While the Feigenboim brothers were feasting their eyes on the living salvation of their *Matzah Shmura* factory in Bnei Brak, Tera, Washburn, Peña and McKeever were boarding EgyptAir's flight 741 from Cairo to Larnaca International Airport, in Cyprus. The flight arrived on schedule, at 5:30 p.m. And, as seemed to be the case with all flights that had been arranged for them by the White House, instead of the military, or the CIA, there was a five-hour layover. They then boarded Cyprus Airways Flight 428 from Larnaca at 10:45 p.m. and touched down one hour later, at Israel's Ben Gurion Airport.

Thus, a flight which should have taken them less than half an hour, gate-to-gate, in a US military transport, took close to eight hours of travel time.

Ben Gurion Airport is a marvel of modern convenience and efficiency. And, within less than half an hour, they had retrieved their bags, cleared passport control and customs, and passed into the main reception hall, to be greeted by Major Dani Kahan, of the IDF, who suffered the indignity of having to hold up a sign, like a taxi driver, that read, "Doctor Susan Price, and Party". It was Tera who spotted the sign first.

"There he is," she said.

But Papa SEAL, Force Master Chief Petty Officer Darwin Washburn, was already quickly walking toward Dani Kahan, whom he swept up in a bear hug, and with whom he exchanged high fives, and said, "Dan the Man! What it is, my brother?"

"Hey, Papa," Dani said. "Nobody told me it was gonna be you!"

"Who'd you *think* they would send?" asked Washburn, smiling.

"I don't know," said Dani. "They told me they were sending somebody good."

"Nah," said Papa SEAL. "All those guys were busy, so they had to send me, instead."

"Major Kahan?"

Dani looked up into the almost perfect, Grace Kelly-like face of Tera Dayton. *If it's possible to be smitten in one look*, Dani thought to himself, *color me smitten.*

"Please, Dear Lord," said Dani. "Tell me you're with him!"

"Actually," said Tera, smiling, "it's the other way around. He's with me."

"You're Doctor Susan Price?" Dani said, sticking out his hand.

Tera took it, and said, "Pleasure to meet you, Major."

"Dani, please," said Dani Kahan, holding her hand just a beat or two longer than necessary, "so, what's your real name?"

Tera slowly, but firmly, removed her hand from Dani's friendly grasp. "Susan Price, Major," she said.

"Right," said Dani. "And, Washburn, over here, is actually Navy Commander Stone?"

Tera just looked at him.

"We've worked together on joint exercises," Washburn said. "He's been to my home, and I've been to what he laughingly refers to as his home. Though, as I recall, it was your basic futon-and-card-table-with-a-microwave."

"I believe in minimalist décor," said Dani.

"Dani Kahan, Tera Dayton, of the CIA. The PhD part is real, though," Washburn said.

"I'm sure every part is real."

Tera bristled immediately. "Why don't we keep this on a professional footing, Major."

"You bet, Tera," Dani said, and then stuck out his hand to McKeever, "Hi. Dani Kahan."

"Clint McKeever, FBI Counter-Terrorism."

"Good to meet you," said Dani, then turned to Raul Peña, who had been eying the way this Kahan guy was looking at Tera Dayton.

"Raul Peña, DEA," Peña said, and stuck out his hand.

"Good grip," Dani said, looking into Peña's eyes, as the latter squeezed as hard as he could. "You guys hungry?"

"You bet," said Washburn.

"Is there anything open? It's past eleven o'clock," said McKeever.

"My friends, welcome to Tel Aviv. War, or no war, the ice cream stands stay open until three o'clock in the morning. New York is a provincial village, compared to this town."

"Yeah?" said Peña. "What you guys got here?"

"You name it," said Dani. "Whatever you feel like. Italian. French. Sushi. Chinese. Brazilian, Middle-Eastern Fusion. Whatever you want, it's here. "

"What's that place you took me to before, with like the nine thousand salads, and the kebabs, and the hummus, and all that?" Washburn asked.

"Itzik Ha Gadol, in Old Jaffa," said Dani.

"That's the place!" said Washburn.

Dani piled the Americans and all their gear into his SUV, and headed out of Ben Gurion Airport, into the heart of Tel Aviv, driving north along the Ayalon Highway, which cut through the heart of one of the most exciting cities on earth. Skyscrapers lit up the night, and, as they pulled off and turned left on Derech Hashalom, they passed the lit-up Azrieli Towers, reminiscent of an I.M. Pei work of art.

Though it was past midnight, the streets were full of young people, as they passed the main drags of Ibn Gvirol and Dizengoff Streets.

"Damn," said Peña. "You guys got some hot-lookin' women here, '*mano*!"

"Most beautiful women in the world," Dani said, then looked at Tera, and smiled. She looked away. Peña, however, was unabashedly enthralled. There were young women soldiers, who had tailored their regulation-issued Army pants into the equivalent of hip-hugging skinny jeans. There were golden-haired girls with olive complexions, and raven-haired beauties, black women in miniskirts, and disco queens with stiletto heels, and the skimpiest of skimpy black dresses. They walked with a kind of panache unlike women in any other part of the world. There was a brashness, a confidence to them, and a ferocious appetite for life. They laughed, and chatted on cell phones, flirted with boys, gossiped with each other, sat out in cafes, and boogied in all-night discos. And this was a country at war.

As if to prove the point, the air raid sirens went off just as they hit the intersection at Dizengoff Street.

Just as the other drivers did, Dani pulled the SUV off to the curb, and ushered his American guests into an all-night Brazilian steakhouse jammed with young people, and waiters carrying skewers of succulent beef and chicken. All the patrons got up, still engaged in their conversations, most still holding their drinks, one or two with skewers of juicy steak that made Washburn's mouth water, and made their way to the safe room, or air raid shelter, of the eatery.

"No need to rush. We've got close to sixty seconds in Tel Aviv, so, no need to panic." Dani said, looking at Tera.

"Major," Tera said, looking at him with some of the coldest blue eyes he'd ever seen. "This is neither my first rodeo, nor first rocket attack."

"Good to know... Not your virgin outing, then," he said, and smiled.

Four M75 rockets, launched from sites next to the Is al a Din Mosque in Gaza, arced north, toward Tel Aviv.

The first veered westward, north of Ashkelon, and exploded harmlessly in the Mediterranean.

The second lost power, and fell short, exploding, ironically, next to Shifa Hospital, where Abdul Aziz Al-Tikriti and Khaled Kawasme were just being taken by their host, Yasser Darwish, to view what they had come so far to see.

Darwish saw the rocket first, breaking off its path and coming toward them.

"Back! Back! Back into the hospital!" he shouted, and the trio dove into the shelter, as the rocket impacted just to the south of the hospital. The shrapnel killed an ambulance attendant, who was smoking a cigarette next to his vehicle.

The third rocket landed in the courtyard of Al Shati Refugee Camp, and killed ten children, wounding close to fifty others.

The fourth rocket arced straight toward downtown Tel Aviv. The Iron Dome battery to the south of the city tracked its route, calculated the winds aloft, and dispatched an interceptor.

Inside the Brazilian steakhouse, people were pressed up one against the other, in the small reinforced concrete room. The crowd, pushing together, was laughing and talking. There were no signs of panic, or even fear. It was a party, with just the slightest undercurrent of tension. The slightest acknowledgement that, with bad luck, one's life could end tonight. All the more reason to party that much harder. To enjoy each drink, each bite, each stolen kiss, each caress, each body pushed up, one against the other, as Tera Dayton found herself pushed up now, against the body of Dani Kahan. He looked down at her with just the slightest smile.

Normally, if one could call anything normal during the last few days, he would have made a slight, subtle, but definite move on her, just to test the waters, as it were. But, hard as she tried not to show it, he could see the panic rising in her eyes.

"Are you okay?" he said, touching her shoulder, not trying to come on to her, but out of genuine concern.

She threw his hand off her skin.

"I'm fine," she said.

"It'll be over in a second," he said. "We're okay in here."

"I said I'm fine!" she said.

But, he could see the tiny beads of sweat forming on her forehead.

"Hey, no problem," he said.

Just then, there was a loud **BOOM**, as the Israeli interceptor took out the incoming M75 rocket that would have killed scores, if not hundreds, had it followed the path of its arc into downtown Tel Aviv.

"Iron Dome," Dani said, smiling proudly.

"Thank the Lord for that!" McKeever said.

"Amen." Tera said, softly.

Peña crossed himself.

And Washburn said, "Thank you, Jesus."

"Actually," said Dani, "you can also thank Rafael Defense Systems, Israel Aerospace Industries, and the Congress of the United States of America, bless their hearts and souls."

"Why aren't people getting out of here yet?"

"I don't know," said Peña, looking down at the olive-complected, black-haired beauty that was smiling up at him. "Not so bad in here, if you ask me."

"You have to wait a minute or two, to see if there's going to be another rocket, and also, because there might be shrapnel falling."

By now, Tera's forehead glistened with sweat.

Slowly, the crowd, still laughing and talking, went back outside to their drinks and dinners, their cell phones and flirtations.

In the Shati Refugee Camp, children were screaming, bleeding, dying, writhing in pain. Desperate parents were crying out to Allah for mercy, and cursing the Israelis, and the ones who had watched the arc of the rocket, and knew that it came from within Gaza, instead of from without, cursed Hamas, and Yasser Darwish, as well.

In Shifa Hospital, Darwish, Al-Tikriti, and Kawasme exited into the warm Mediterranean night.

"Israeli air strike?" Al-Tikriti asked.

"No," said Darwish. "One of ours, falling short. Nothing to be done. Come, my brothers. Now, we'll see what will soon make it all worthwhile. The rockets are nothing. An illusionist's hocus-pocus. But, now, I will show you the *real* magic."

In Tel Aviv, Dani, Peña, Washburn and McKeever walked out of the restaurant full of smiling, beautiful, youthful Israelis, for whom not a dent had been put into the party of that particular night. People got back into their cars, and simply continued on their drives, as midnight revellers lined up once more at the ice cream or falafel stands, or sipped their espressos in sidewalk cafes, and young lovers walked hand-in-hand through nighttime Tel Aviv.

"Amazing people," said McKeever. "Can you imagine something like that happening in Manhattan, or LA?"

"Yeah. One punk sniper in the trunk of a car shut down all of DC," said Washburn.

"Tel Aviv," said Dani Kahan. "Party never stops." But, looking at Tera Dayton, he could see that, for some reason, the party, for her, had stopped some time ago.

He drove down to Ha Yarkon Street, the main beachfront street, with its pedestrian promenade, and impromptu restaurants all along the beach. During the daytime, the restaurants had deck chairs out on the sand. At sunset, they pulled them in, and put couches and low coffee tables out in their place, on the Mediterranean shore, and the entire beach, from the discos in the north, down to Old Jaffa, one of the most ancient, constantly inhabited port cities on earth, with the high-rise luxury hotels behind them, the whole shoreline, was one big party. Bands playing, people singing, lovers dancing in the sand.

"Man," said Washburn. "You guys know how to do up a war."

"Don't let it fool you," Dani said. "Hamas isn't done with us, yet. Not by a long shot."

"Hey," said Peña. "With that Iron Dome you got, they can fire as many rockets as they want. You guys just keep boogyin'."

"It's not necessarily their rockets I'm afraid of," said Dani.

"What are you afraid of, Major?" Tera asked, as they drove through the velvety Mediterranean night, with the lights of the high-rise hotels on their left, and the almost gaslight charm of the *tavernas* of Old Jaffa before them.

"The rockets were the surprise they had in store for us in 2009, with longer range rockets in 2012," said Dani. "So, we came up with Iron Dome. But, that's an answer to the surprises of the last war. What worries me are the surprises that they have in store for us in this one."

As Dani pulled the SUV past the ancient Ottoman clock tower that was the centerpiece of the charming old Mediterranean port of Jaffa, Yasser Darwish drove through the *Sha'jaiya* suburb of Gaza, toward Al-Wafa Hospital.

In the distance, Israeli F15Is were hitting targets at the northern end of the Gaza strip. Al-Tikriti and Kawasme watched the explosions light up the nighttime sky, followed by the billows of black smoke, and secondary explosions, meaning the Israelis had just hit a rocket storage facility, or an ammo dump. Al-Tikriti cursed the mothers that bore the Zionist pigs, but Darwish just laughed.

"Calmly, my brother. All of that is just more hocus-pocus. Now, we go to see the surprise we have in store for them!"

He parked the BMW 745il, for which he had placed an order with Sheikh Abu Ali, who had personally transmitted it to the car theft ring in Cairo.

Darwish loved the car.

"Truly," he said, "it is the Ultimate Driving Machine." Then, he led the two men down the alley, to the sandbagged entrance of Al-Wafa Hospital.

A uniformed Hamas sentry saluted the military commander of all Hamas forces in Gaza, and opened the door for these most important visitors. Darwish led his two guests through the corridors of Al-Wafa Hospital, passed children being brought in on stretchers and gurneys, screaming and bleeding, from the Al Shati Refugee Camp. Their mothers and fathers were wailing, and imploring *Allah il Rahman*, Allah the Merciful, to let their children live, and to kill the murderers who had turned their lives into a living hell.

Darwish turned left, into an area of the hospital that was suddenly devoid of screaming parents, dying children, or desperate doctors trying to save them. Here, there were nothing but Hamas fighters. They came to a set of stairs guarded by yet another Hamas sentry, who snapped to attention, and saluted smartly, as he saw Darwish approach. They descended the stairs, into a dimly lit corridor that ran through the basement of the hospital, to yet another set of stairs protected by a sandbagged entrance, and yet more sentries. This set of stairs led down, almost a hundred feet beneath the hospital, until Darwish turned to his guests, and smiled.

"Thirty meters beneath the hospital, my brothers. Completely impervious to Israeli air attack. Cannot be seen by their surveillance. Not by their drones. Not by their satellites. Not by their observation balloons. Invisible."

He walked to the far end of the corridor, where there was a sandbagged machine gun nest, manned by half a dozen Hamas fighters. Whatever lay behind that sandbagged entrance was obviously the jewel in the crown.

The men saluted. Darwish returned their salute, and opened a heavy iron door. Just inside the door, there was a ladder that led down a reinforced concrete silo, into a network of forty underground tunnels, all of them built with reinforced concrete and steel, with air conditioning, and electrical cables running along the ceilings, wide enough to accommodate an army of infantry, tall enough so that none of them had to crouch as they walked along the pre-lit pathway. Here and there, Hamas workers were widening sections of the tunnels.

Some of the construction projects had already been completed, revealing their true purpose, which was not to widen the tunnels, per se, but to make holding cells. Underground prisons.

"Here, my brothers, you can see," said Darwish, "we are making the cells that will hold the hostages. Hundreds of them. And, what will the Israelis do? How will they know where they are? How will they find them? It was in such cells as these that we held Gilad Shalit, for five years."

"Amazing!" said Kawasme.

"Beautiful!" said Al-Tikriti. "And, we are how far beneath the earth?"

"One hundred feet down," said Darwish. "And these prisoners, we will not hold for five years, I promise you. We will issue our demands and, if they are not met, the Israelis can watch their women and children pay the price, as *our* women and children have been made to pay the price."

"Praise be to Allah," Al-Tikriti said.

Darwish led the two ISIS terrorists over a mile and a half through the tunnel, until they came to its end, where a long ladder reached up, and up, and up.

They spoke in hushed tones now. "Now," said Darwish, "we are literally under the feet of the Zionist enemy."

"We are in Israel?!" Al-Tikriti asked.

"Yes, my brother," Darwish answered, smiling, with tears of joy in his eyes. "This tunnel comes up no more than two hundred meters away from one of their children's houses, in one of their villages. Another tunnel comes up in the dining hall of one of their *Kibbutzim*, where six hundred people take their meal at once. Can you imagine the bloody surprise we will give them?"

"It is more than I ever dreamed of!" said Al-Tikriti. "More than I imagined. More than I prayed for."

In Old Jaffa, Dani, Washburn, Tera, McKeever, and Peña sat at a long table, in Izhik Ha Gadol's restaurant. In front of them were twenty eight different types of salad: *babaganoush*, rosemary potatoes, *matbucha*, red beets, spicy Moroccan carrots, *falafel, hummus* with pine nuts, *tahini*, grilled Portobello mushrooms with tomatoes and onions, huge, fresh-baked *laffa* bread topped with olive oil, garlic, and *za'atar*; skewers of marinated chicken thighs, and lamb kebabs, all of it washed down with very drinkable Yarden Cabernet-Sauvignon.

"So this is a country at war, huh?" said Washburn.

"No," said Dani. "This is a country asleep... Just like your country."

And, as Dani and his American counterparts feasted upon Mediterranean delicacies, Abdul Aziz Al-Tikriti returned from his own underground excursion into Israel. Though he was less than fifty miles from Tel Aviv's nightlife, Al-Tikriti had partaken of no delicacies, no salads, no late-night ice cream. He had gone not on any stroll along the promenade skirting Tel Aviv's beaches.

For him, however, his journey had been of far greater importance. Indeed, only his pilgrimage to Mecca had meant more to him than the one and a half mile, underground walk he had just taken into the heart of the Zionist entity. Upon their return to the apartment, and the underground bunker adjoining the networks of terrorist attack tunnels which Darwish had made available to them in the *Sha'jaiya* suburb of Gaza, Al-Tikriti and Kawasme offered up a prayer of thanksgiving to Allah the Merciful. Then, Al-Tikriti sent a coded radio signal to a counterpart in London, to arrange for the transfer of one hundred million dollars into an escrow account for Hamas, in return for the Divine Victory that ISIS was about to enjoy, by carrying out the greatest terrorist attack in history. Not against the Little Satan of Israel, but the Great Satan of the United States of America.

CHAPTER 8

D ani picked up Tera, Washburn, McKeever, and Peña the next morning at 07:00 hours from the US embassy, where they were being billeted. The embassy sat on Ha Yarkon Street, the main beach road that wound from the Port, in North Tel Aviv down to the Old City of Jaffa, the scene of their feast the night before.

As they piled into Dani's SUV, Dani could see Tera's red-rimmed eyes.

Either she cries herself to sleep, or drinks herself to sleep, he thought. *Takes one to know one.*

They drove south, from the rear entrance of the Embassy, along the beach, past the morning joggers and bike riders, and early morning swimmers along the Mediterranean. In the distance, Jaffa shone like an image out of Lawrence of Arabia, in stark contrast to the ultra-modern high-rise hotels and condos that lined the shore. Tel Aviv was one of the only cities Washburn had ever been to where, no matter where you were, even in the heart of the business district, you were no more than twenty minutes from the beach. *It's an amazing place*, he thought. *It's got a New York nervous energy buzz, and yet everything is kicked back and Mediterranean, at the same time.*

And the women! Peña thought. He had never seen so many hot looking women in one place. He and Washburn had gone pub crawling after the dinner the night before, and Peña couldn't believe how each girl was more beautiful than the one before. And they all partied like *Latinas*!

Peña felt weird about the place.

He knew he was a Jew.

That's what his grandmother had told him on her deathbed. *"Somos Judíos."*

He hated those two words.

They were the brand that made him different and despised, from the time he was a child in his tiny backwater New Mexico village. It was the reason people looked at the Peñas as if they were somehow foul, foreign; a malignant, cancerous implant that might have been here for five hundred years, and might be there another five hundred years, but would never belong.

And it wasn't just the looks.

He still had nightmares about it.

He was eight years old and some of the kids in his class had older brothers who went to school with his older brother Josue, which was Spanish for Joshua. And they wanted to know why his family never ate pork. No *chorizo*, no *carne adobada*, the red chile and pork stew that was a staple, no *posole rojo*. Why did they light candles all the time on Friday? It wasn't just because their mother thought it was pretty, like they said, and hey man, EVERYBODY ate *carnitas* or pulled pork! But not the Peñas. So, *¿Que pasa con eso, 'mano?"*

When he was in third grade, he heard the words *"perro judío"*, "Jew dog" and he looked around to see what they were talking about, and saw that they were all looking at him.

One day, some of the kids from his class followed him home.

They had on *Dia de los Muertos nagual* masks. Those were the masks they wore when *La Mascarada*, on *Dia de los Muertos*, was danced. The Day of the Dead. The masks were skulls with horrible teeth. They hid the faces of the boys who followed him up the dirt path to the hill where his house was. He started to run and they threw stones and then ran after him and he tripped and they held his arms. Others held his legs. They pulled his pants down and then his underpants and he was screaming and crying and they laughed at his Jew cock, because most of the kids from his village were uncircumcised and one of them grabbed a pencil, he had nightmares of it still to this day, and this kid grabbed his penis and jammed the pencil up his cock, and he screamed and cried and bled and they laughed and maybe got scared from the blood, and after a while they ran too, and he remembered he peed in his pants and how it burned, and, when he got home, his *Abuelita* held him, and cried with him too.

She put him in a warm bath and the bleeding stopped. His mother wanted to take him to the doctor, but his father didn't want any trouble. Not with the police, not with the neighbors, like if you just ignored it man, they wouldn't do it again, like somehow it was what they knew would happen sooner or later and his *maricón* ol' man never did a thing, man, never did a thing. And that's when he decided it would never happen to him again. He knew who one of the kids was, knew him from his sneakers that were ripped on the side, and he didn't say a word, just came up behind him at school with a piece of pipe, and hit him as hard as he could in the head with it and hit him again, would have killed the kid if they hadn't pulled him off. They didn't send him to juvenile detention hall, because they said he was too young, but they expelled him from school, which was just fine with him. They stuck him in a school "for troubled youth", which was just fine, too, and he made a point of eating *carnitas*, and *chorizo*. Hell, he would have eaten a pig raw to prove he wasn't a Jew dog, and if anybody looked at him crosseyed, from that time on, he hit them first and then asked questions later, and when he started hanging with the low-riders, he knew he could be a gangbanger, or DEA, and wanted the DEA, man. He wanted a badge and a gun and POWER, and he never wanted to hear another thing about Jews again as long as he lived.

And here he was, in a whole country full of them.

And the women were hot.

And the guys, and the girls, for that matter, were all in the army and they all had guns.

And Raul Peña didn't know whether to laugh or cry. Didn't know whether to say, "Hey, I'm one of you too!", or do everything humanly possible to hide the fact that he was. Didn't know if he was at home, or in hell. And though he didn't know the phrase, it would have fit him as much as it did POTUS. *Nischt a Yid, Nischt a Goy.*

All he knew was, for whatever reason, he didn't feel like a stranger here. And that scared him most of all.

"So, you think there's going to be a ground campaign?" Tera Dayton asked Dani as they drove south from Tel Aviv, toward the border with Gaza.

"You want the conventional wisdom, or what I think?"

"I heard they called up reserves," Washburn said as they drove down the Ayalon Highway.

The radio played softly, and then a female voice came on and said, *"Tzeva Adom Bi Machlef La Guardia"*.

Dani and all the other drivers started pulling off to the right.

"Wazzup?" asked Peña.

"Code Red at La Guardia interchange. That's us. Out of the car." They all piled out of the SUV and crouched next to the retaining wall. Two rockets came arcing in from the south. Very quietly, in Hebrew, Dani recited *"Esah einay el ha harim...* I will lift up my eyes to the mountains, from whence cometh my help. My help cometh from the...."

And he was shocked to hear Tera Dayton reciting the Psalm in English.

"My help cometh from the Lord..."

"That made the heavens and the earth." Dani finished, and smiled at her.

"He will not suffer thy foot to be moved," she said. "He that keepeth thee will not slumber," she recited from memory.

"Hineh Lo Yanum vi lo Yishahn shomer Yisrael," Dani recited.

"What's that mean?" McKeever asked.

"Behold," said Tera. "He that keepeth Israel shall neither slumber, nor sleep."

Just then two Iron Dome interceptors took out the rockets arcing above them toward the center of the city.

"One hundred twenty first psalm," Tera said.

"Damn..." said Peña, "That's a good one to know."

And then, the other drivers got back into their cars, and continued on their way.

"Amazing people," said McKeever. "Can't get over it. Rockets come sailing in, and they just shine it on."

"We've had practice," Dani said.

They got back into the SUV.

"This is the really dangerous part," Dani said.

"What's that?" Tera asked.

"Driving in Israel. The rockets are nothing. It's the Israeli drivers you have to be afraid of."

He pulled back out into traffic, and they continued south.

After a second, McKeever, who just couldn't stand the thought of an uncompleted sentence, or thought, turned to Washburn and said, "So, you say they called up reserves."

"That's what I heard," said Papa SEAL.

"The government okayed the call-up of forty thousand reservists. That means they're authorized to call up that many, but, so far, I think it's maybe just four or five thousand."

"So does that mean you guys are going into Gaza in a ground campaign?" Tera asked.

"Depends," said Dani.

"On what?" asked Papa SEAL.

It was, after all, the reason the Americans were here. They had all discussed it the night before. Dani had received orders all the way from the Chief of Staff in the Kirya. This was top priority. If there was a ground incursion, the Americans would go in with the Givati Recon Unit and do a snatch and grab of two targets in the *Sha'jaiya* neighborhood of Gaza. When he had asked who the targets were, he was told that information was not available to him yet. *Obviously*, he thought, *they aren't Hamas. We're doing a favor for the Americans, so their President won't have to get his hands dirty*. More than likely, they were going to grab some Al Qaeda higher ups, who had smuggled themselves into Gaza from Sinai, probably to get away from the Egyptians who were doing a great job taking them on. Maybe the Americans had already tried a snatch and grab in Sinai that had failed, though he doubted it. More than likely, the Americans had pressed the Egyptians just the way they were pressing the Israelis now, and whoever they were after had gotten away, and gotten themselves into Gaza. He knew there were elements of Al Qaeda there now, together with Bayit Al Maqdis, and assorted other Jihadis. He'd even heard there were elements of ISIS in Gaza. Whoever it was, he knew Israel owed the Americans big time for helping fund the Iron Dome system that had just so routinely saved their lives.

"So, what's it depend on?" McKeever asked.

"Well," said Dani, "two things, as far as I can see. What war we're fighting... And what war Hamas is fighting."

"What do you mean? You're both fighting the same war, aren't ya?" Peña asked.

"Not necessarily," Dani said, "So far, WE'RE fighting the last war. I don't know yet what war Hamas is fighting. That's what bothers me."

"Probably the reserve call up is just to apply pressure on Hamas to get them to agree to a cease fire," Tera said.

"Is that what the CIA thinks?"

"That's what I think," said Tera, "Just like in 2012."

"You guys called up reserves then, right?" asked Washburn. "And then Hamas saw you were serious, and there was a cease fire."

"That was 2012, all right," Dani said. "And that's probably why we're doing it again. Like I said, so far we're fighting the last war."

"And what makes you think Hamas will act any differently this time? Their rockets certainly aren't having any effect."

"You guys killed how many of them rag-heads so far?" Peña asked. "Over a hundred, right?"

"One hundred twenty–nine was the last thing I heard this morning, before I picked you guys up."

"And how many Israelis they killed so far?" Peña asked, almost joyously. "Zip, right?"

"So far," said Dani.

"So," said Peña, "the score is, Jews: One twenty nine, Arabs: nothin'... I'd say ol' Kivi Natanel and the boys are doin' okay."

You could hear the joy in Peña's voice. The notion that Jews were kicking serious tail, despite his best efforts, made him smile at his own secret past.

"So, why are you worried?" Tera asked.

"Because, they wanted this war too much. They killed three school-boys to get it started. They know as much about Iron Dome as we do. They knew up front their rockets weren't going to put a dent in our day."

"And they also knew you'd bomb them, and they'd say Gaza had to be rebuilt, and the world would pony up a few billion," Tera said.

"Which they'd steal," said Washburn. "So, why not do it?"

"Because, they've got to have a Divine Victory. And money won't do it for them."

"A couple billion would do it for me, *'mano*."

"What WILL do it for them?" Tera asked.

"Dead Jews," said Dani. "Lots of 'em."

"Well," said McKeever. "With Iron Dome, I don't think you have a lot to worry about."

"Rockets, shmockets!" Pini Feigenboim told Yair Hermesh.

"*Azoy?*" said Yair Hermesh.

Yair Hermesh was the Secretary of *Kibbutz Kfar Shimshon*, on the Gaza border, and the Feigenboim brothers had just offered to buy up all their wheat.

"On one condition," said Pini.

"So, *nu*… What's the condition?" Yair had asked as they sat in the dining hall of the *kibbutz*, and sipped glasses of hot, sweet tea with their lunch. There were perhaps fifty *kibbutzniks* in the dining hall with them.

"The condition," said Pini's brother, Srulik, "is that you harvest the whole crop now."

Just then, the air raid alarm sounded. It was a loud buzz, but even before it sounded, Yair's cellphone app sounded its own alarm. Amazing! Rocket attacks had created a new Israeli startup, which marketed rocket alerts apps for smartphones! There were now three different apps being marketed, and they all were wired to the national alert system and showed, in real-time, where the rocket was heading.

"Quickly!" said Yair. "We have less than eight seconds!"

There was a reinforced concrete safe-room just down a short flight of steps that led to the basement of the dining hall where the bathrooms were located. There were two sets of stairs, and the fifty-odd *kibbutzniks* used both of them to get out of harm's way. Yair and the Feigenboim brothers had just barely made it down the steps, when there was a deafening roar, and the earth shook, as three Qassam rockets slammed, one into the side of the dining hall, and two more into the lawn leading up to the dining hall… The area in front of the glass doors to the dining hall had been blocked off with concrete blast shields, as had the windows. Moreover, a year earlier, they had built reinforced concrete shells over the dining hall, and over the school, kindergarten, and day care centers. But a direct hit was a direct hit, and it got your attention.

Yair excused himself, and got on his radio. The *kibbutz* had its own security team, and its own first responders. Because it was an older *kibbutz*, most of the supposed security force were in their sixties. Yair left his guests in the dining hall and went out to inspect the damage. Walls could always be repaired. Thank the Lord no one was hurt. And the truth was, it wasn't the rockets he feared, even though they were too close to the border to be protected by Iron Dome. It was the mortar rounds. There was no warning for them. No sirens, no phone app, no code red, no nothing. Just the shriek, which, if you heard at all, gave you a second, to a second and a half, to flatten yourself and pray. And unlike the Qassam rockets, which the Palestinians just pointed and shot, hoping they would hit something, the mortars were remarkably accurate weapons. You could aim them and hit exactly what you were after, and with Google Earth, the terrorists just popped an image of the *kibbutz* up on their laptops, and zeroed in, mainly on the kindergartens and day care centers. The point was to sow as much terror as possible, and the way they did that was to go after the children.

On closer inspection, Yair, in fact, found that what had hit the dining hall wasn't a Qassam at all. The three Qassams that had been fired had hit down the road. These were 120 millimeter mortar rounds. And they had hit what they were aiming for: the dining hall, at lunch time.

Yair returned to his guests, who inquired politely if everyone was all right, to which Yair replied, "Yes," and they answered, "Blessed be His Name."

"Now," said Yair. "Where were we?"

"We want to buy your whole wheat crop," Pinni Feigenboim said.

"Everything," said his brother Srulik.

"The whole lot of it," said Yehezkel.

"On one condition," said Pini.

"The wheat isn't harvested 'til mid-September. We're in the middle of July, and already you're giving me conditions?" Yair asked.

"That's the condition," said Pinni.

"What's the condition?" asked Yair.

"It has to be harvested right now."

"The whole wheat crop." said Yehzkel.

"All of it," said Srulik.

"You're *Mishugah*! Crazy!" Yair exclaimed. "There are rockets falling everywhere, and he wants to harvest wheat!"

To which Pini Feigenboim had said, "Rockets, shmockets!'

And what about the mortars?" said Yair.

"Mortars, shmorters!" said Yehezkel.

And Srulik explained that this was the only field of green wheat, planted according to biblical strictures, which Moishe Yankel Haimovitch had not snatched up.

"Moreover," said Pini, "Every day that it's not harvested is another day it can't be stored!"

"We'll be out of business!" said Srulik.

"And, what if one of those rockets or mortars hits your wheat field when it starts to ripen? It will all burn up! You'll lose it all," said Yehezkel.

"And, what if the army goes in with tanks, into Gaza?" said Pini. "You think they couldn't come right through your field, if they had to?"

"And, it's not as if you're not in danger already," Pini reminded him. "Here you are, having a nice lunch, sipping a glass of tea, and those *choleras* are shooting at you!"

"We'll give you the same price you would have gotten in September. You won't have to irrigate, or cultivate, for over two months."

"It'll have to be put to a vote," said Yair.

"So?" said Pini. "Somebody said it shouldn't be put to a vote? Vote in good health, *gezunter heit*!"

The truth was, they had blast shields up all along the border with Gaza, to prevent the sniper fire which had plagued them for years. So, the terrorists couldn't see what was happening on the other side. And, the truth was, anyone just walking along the pathways of the *kibbutz* was in as much danger as anyone could be in already. And, the truth was, what the older brother had said was also correct. Nobody knew how long this could go on, and every day the wheat ripened, it was that much more susceptible to being set on fire by a rocket or mortar anyway. And it wasn't as if they weren't milking the cows three times a day. They were already doing that, and changing irrigation pipes, and, the truth was, the chief landscaper on the *kibbutz*, a total *mishugenner*, was still mowing the lawn!

They put it to a vote, and, more to symbolically stick their thumb in Hamas' eye, and show them their Qassams and mortars couldn't keep them from farming... They agreed! Rockets, shmockets!

The Feigenboim brothers offered up a prayer to the Holy One of Israel, who had kept them in life, sustained them and brought them to this time. Then they spit three times so as to ward off the evil eye. *Tphew, tphew, tphew!*

Dani pulled up in his SUV to a nondescript base. The sentry, who was in full combat gear, with a ceramic flak jacket, combat harness, and Micro-Tavor assault rifle, looked at Dani's ID, exchanged a few words in Hebrew, and waved him through.

"Anyone ever salute in this army of yours?" Peña asked.

"Once a year," Dani said. "On Independence day... I think. It's been so long, who can remember? I always get a kick out of going up to Kuneitra, to the UN crossing into the Syrian Golan. They've got a bunch of Austrian soldiers up there, and those guys damn near knock themselves out they salute so hard... *Jawohl, Herr Major!* And they whack themselves on the sides of their heads, and I'm like, 'Yeah, right, whazzup?'"

Nineteen and twenty-year-old boy and girl soldiers were walking to their various posts, all of them with an M4 or a Tavor slung over their neck and shoulder, and all of them in flak jackets.

"I've got flak jackets and helmets for everybody in the back," Dani said. "Put 'em on. We're in mortar range here."

The four Americans stepped around to the rear of the SUV, popped the hatch-back, and pulled out flak jackets and helmets. Dani took his Micro-Tavor, slung it over his neck and shoulder, and led them to a nondescript cinderblock building.

In the distance they could see an observation balloon that looked like a dirigible, tethered to a stanchion, giving it a view of Gaza just across the border fence, not more than a few hundred meters away. Suddenly, there was a shriek-like whistle. Unlike in the movies, a mortar round sound doesn't get softer the closer it is to landing. It gets louder, and whooshes as it shrieks. Dani grabbed Tera, and shouted, "Down!" He didn't shout "incoming," which he always thought was a pretty dumb thing to shout anyway, since it sure as hell wasn't "out-going" when it blew up. Plus, all his military terms he knew in Hebrew instead of English. So he grabbed her, and flattened her and put his body over hers. Peña, Washburn, and McKeever hit the deck, and they all felt the earth shake. Mortars were usually fired in groups, which meant if there was a first one, there were likely to be a second, and third as well.

The first mortar exploded just inside the compound, and no one seemed to be hit.

"Damn!" Peña said. "I gotta learn me that psalm."

"Let's go!" Dani said and they all raced in a crouch to the low cin-derblock building with the reinforced concrete roof and concrete blast shields all around it, as there was another whoosh and shriek and thud just inside the gate. Dani looked back at the sentry who had just waved them through. He flashed a thumbs up, and shook his head as if to say, "Too close!"

"Everybody good?" Dani asked.

Peña, Washburn, and McKeever all nodded. This was another day in the park for Papa SEAL.

"I really don't need you throwing yourself on top of me like that," Tera said to Dani.

"Oh, gee," Dani said. "You're welcome."

He just looked at her. She was trembling, but he had a feeling it wasn't from the mortar.

"Right this way, my dears," he said, and took them into the cinder-block building that sat behind the concrete blast shields and under the reinforced concrete roof.

It was cool inside, and there was the low hum of air conditioners. A few dozen nineteen and twenty-year-old girls sat in front of banks of television monitors, staring intently at the screens. Their M4s were at their feet on the floor in front of them, within easy reach, and their flak jackets were slung over the backs of their chairs. Occasionally one or another would zoom in on something on-screen with a joystick, to check out whatever had looked suspicious. There was no conversation. No joking. These girls were all business.

"This place is the eyes of the State, along the Gaza border," Dani said.

Each monitor gave a different view. Some were from observation balloons like the one they had seen tethered near the border, others were from drones flying overhead, some of them armed with hell-fire missiles, and others were from ground level. And one was from a vehicle on patrol, and the fish eye camera lens was controlled with a joystick, operated by a dark-haired, pony tailed girl, who looked all of eighteen.

Dani crossed over to a twenty-one year old female Lieutenant named Irit, who was in command of this shift. She was beautiful and black, an Ethiopian Jew, and looked as if she could just as easily have been a runway model. Tall, and slim, and elegant.

"How's it look?" Dani asked, in Hebrew.

"Like a war," Irit said.

"Don't be smart," Dani said, smiling at her.

"What? You want me to be stupid like your *freichot*?" *Freichot* was an old school bit of slang for a skank.

"Me?" Dani said. "With *freichot*?"

Irit just looked at him. The truth was, there was a real attraction between these two, but Dani drew the line at twenty-year-olds... Actually, if the girl was thirty, she generally made him feel like he was on social security. Still... If she had father issues she needed to work out... At any rate he and Irit enjoyed an easy, flirtatious relationship that never stepped over the line, and neither of them let the flirt last more than a few seconds, especially when Irit was on duty.

"No signs of anything?" Dani asked.

"Nothing, other than, you know, a rocket launching team here, or mortar team there. They're harvesting wheat in *Kfar Shimshon*."

"That doesn't make any sense," Dani said, "Wheat harvest isn't 'til September."

"*Shnat Shmita*," Irit said. "They sold the whole crop to some religious *Matzah* makers from Bnei Brak."

"And you know this because...?"

"I know it because I'm a Jew, and not a Tel Avivi socialist, former *kibbutznik* atheist barbarian, like some people I know. My grandfather told me that's how we used to farm in Ethiopia."

"And your Grandfather told you they were from Bnei Brak?"

"No. The Secretary of the *kibbutz* told me that, when I called over there to see what was going on. *Mishugaim!* Crazy people."

"The Lord takes care of fools and drunks," Dani said.

"Thank God, you're safe then. On both counts," Irit said, and they both smiled. Then Dani's look changed as he watched the monitors.

"They're going to try a terrorist attack. I'm telling you."

"You've BEEN telling me."

"All right, so I'm telling you again... You and your girls are the only thing between us and disaster. They have to have a Divine Victory. And the more they make noises like they want a cease-fire, the more I know they're going to attack..."

"My girls are the best," Irit said.

"Somewhere, across that border, there's some Hamasnik saying, 'My guys are the best.' We can't have disdain for them."

"Dani," Irit said, "I know. Okay? I know, and my girls know."

Dani gave her a one-armed hug.

He crossed back over to the Americans, "I'm telling ya," he said, "There's something we're not seeing."

"How come there's nothin' but girls in this unit?" Peña asked.

"Because guys don't have the same powers of concentration," Dani said, then he looked at Tera with the slightest smile, "They keep thinking about sex."

Peña decided he couldn't stand this guy.

"What's that monitor over there?' Tera asked pointing at the one that looked like it was mounted on a vehicle, and yet it was clear that the camera was being operated by the pony-tailed, four-foot-eleven, ninety-two pound girl sitting at the console, whose name was Tamar.

"That," said Dani, "is a camera mounted on a robot vehicle. We've got a couple of them. They cruise the border fence, and there's no danger to any crew this way. Not from snipers or IEDs. Couple of them even have mounted thirty caliber machine guns."

Another nineteen year old slip of a thing, named Orna, was zooming in on her monitor, which showed an aerial view of the border from one of the many observation balloons they had seen earlier. Each girl there was glued to her screen. *Maybe Irit's right*, Dani thought, and then prayed that she was.

Dani was making his rounds as an intel officer, but he also wanted to show the Americans both what he was proud of, and what they were up against. It was clear that he loved the army, and its eighteen to twenty-two-year-old conscript soldiers, as well as the older reservists.

"Come on," he said. "I'll show you some of our bad boys."

"You have any kids?" McKeever asked.

Washburn shot him a look, but it was too late.

"One," Dani said.

"Oh, yeah? What's he do?" McKeever asked, totally oblivious to the way Papa SEAL was trying to signal him to shut up.

"Not much," Dani said.

"I got a kid like that," McKeever said, sighing at the burden. "Doesn't have a clue. How old is he?"

"What?" Dani asked.

"Your son..." McKeever said, "How old is he?"

"He would have been twenty-two... Just getting out of the army about now. He was killed when he was nine."

"Geez, I'm so sorry," McKeever said. "I didn't... How..?"

"I can't really talk about it. Ya know?" Dani answered quietly, his voice, despite himself, suddenly hoarse. "I mean, honestly. It's been thirteen years, but uh...." Dani grimaced, unconsciously. "Part of the reason I love these kids so much... They could be mine."

"Half of 'em probably are," Papa SEAL said, whacking Dani on the shoulder to change the subject and get rid of the funk in the room.

But Dani didn't smile. And Tera, for the first time, stopped resenting him, and saw in him a pain as great as her own, and perhaps worse, she thought.

Just then, there was the thump of another mortar round outside, and another, and another.

"Just another day at the office," said Washburn.

"You bet," said Dani.

When the mortars stopped falling, they climbed back into the SUV, and Dani took them over to the Givati Quick Response post, home of Samson's Foxes Recon.

These were his bad boys, and he was as proud as any papa of these twenty-year-old fighters. These were the best of the best. They were mounted on dune buggies that could do eighty miles an hour. No armor of any kind. Their job was to respond to the first indication that terrorists had penetrated the border fence. And in this part of the world, the border fence might only be a few hundred meters away from a *kibbutz* dining hall, or kindergarten. In this part of the world, they didn't have minutes to respond. They had seconds.

And all day long, Dani went from post to post, exhorting each unit to be especially alert.

In the White House, the "Dead Baby Strategy" was already having an effect.

CNN, it seemed, had the dead babies on a loop. Dani, from his days of dealing with the press in the Second Lebanon War, could write their reports for them. In fact, most of them already had their narratives down before they even landed in the Middle East. There were those who were simply rabidly anti-Israel, from an ideological point of view. They were mainly the Europeans, and the Israelis reminded them, so they thought, of themselves, white colonial Europeans exploiting and murdering downtrodden brown-skinned people. It didn't have to be any more complicated than that.

Others were just stupid.

He remembered one female co-host of a major network morning news show. She had gotten the plum assignment of putting on cargo pants and a safari jacket, and leaving the studio in Manhattan for the battlefield. Dani had been her escort officer. As a former intel officer, he was trying to give her as much background and understanding of the current situation as possible, and, though he admitted he was biased, as an Israeli soldier, he thought he was doing a decent job of giving her an objective overview and analysis. He mistakenly thought that might be useful to a journalist.

He took her to an artillery battery that was opposite a Hezbollah force in Southern Lebanon, which was raining down rockets on all of the north of Israel. She asked if she could interview one of the soldiers. Dani told her to pick any one she liked. Almost all of them spoke some English and he would translate if necessary. She walked up to a thirty-two-year-old reservist, who had just been called up, and had left a nine-months-pregnant wife, and a two-year-old baby girl at home, in order to defend his country from some of the most ruthless terrorists on earth, with whom Israel had no quarrel whatsoever, since Israel had long since withdrawn completely from Lebanon. Hezbollah was an Iranian-backed, Shia Lebanese terrorist organization that had killed thousands of its fellow Lebanese, and over two hundred US Marines. They were hardly the "brown-skinned masses" oppressed by the white Colonialist/Zionist Occupier of their native land. They were the proxy military arm of a theocratic Iranian regime bent on reestablishing a Persian empire, at the expense of their Sunni Arab neighbors.

The morning news host stuck her microphone in the Reservist's face and her first question was, "How does it feel to know you're murdering innocent women and children?"

The reservist, whose name was Avi, looked at Dani, and asked, "is she crazy, or anti-semitic?"

"I have no idea," Dani said.

Dani confronted her, and asked if she knew of any incident in the current conflict, in which Israeli artillery, let alone this particular battery, had killed innocent women and children.

"No," she said, "Not yet. But that's what always happens. You guys drop your bombs and what have you, and innocent Palestinian babies are killed."

"First of all," said Dani, "the people we're fighting are Lebanese."

"Right," she said. "Lebanese Palestinians."

There was just no way to change the narrative, or challenge it with facts about who initiated the conflict, and, in this case, who was even in the conflict. The narrative was, "Israelis drop their bombs and what have you, and Palestinian babies are killed."

Thus, the "Dead Baby Strategy" proved its efficacy, once again. There were protest marches throughout Europe, which quickly morphed from "Free, Free Palestine!" to "Hamas, Hamas, Jews to the gas!" It mattered not a whit that neither Hamas, nor the Palestinians, were involved in the current conflict.

Now, eight years and two wars later, in this summer of 2014, POTUS wanted this war with Hamas to come to an end. Two hundred Palestinians had already been killed, and only one Israeli, who had been killed by a mortar round that morning. He was a civilian who had come down south to hand out chocolate bars to the troops. Two hundred to one! How was that proportional? Huh? Let alone fair? So POTUS had told Kivi Natanel, in a blunt phone call, that he wanted it to be over.

"Mr. President," said Kivi, "They began this by murdering three of our schoolboys..."

"And then your people murdered a Palestinian teenager! So, you know..."

"Yes, that's true and we caught the murderers, and arrested them, and they'll stand trial for murder. The head of Hamas said, 'Blessed be the hands of the kidnappers', and then they launched over a hundred rockets at us, violating a cease-fire that we've upheld for over a year and a half."

"Look, Kivi," said POTUS. "The images are awful, and it has to end. The United States pays a very high price for supporting your policies, which are at the heart of all our troubles in the Middle East, from which I have been trying to extricate my country for six years. And you're not making it any easier for me!"

Kivi couldn't believe this guy. This wasn't about the Middle East, and it wasn't about Israelis and Palestinians, it was about HIM. "Mr. President," he said, "with the greatest respect, the entire Middle East is in flames, and it has nothing to do with Israel."

"Your settlement policies are inflaming the whole region!"

"Mr. President, that's absurd. You had a revolt in Algeria. It was about the cost of living. There was a revolt in Syria. It was against Bashar Al Assad, and has nothing to do with Israel. Your government helped topple Muammar Gaddafi, over whom I shed no tears, but then you left chaos, and now it's a hotbed of terrorism, and his weapons are smuggled into Gaza, and being fired against my people. You've got a Sunni versus Shia religious war throughout the Middle East that has nothing to do with Jews or Israel! Now you've got ISIS on the rise, about to strike into the heart of Iraq, and possibly even against your country, and we're more than willing to do our part to help you with that sir, and so are the Egyptians. But none of that has to do with settlements, or Israel, in any way. The only way it relates to Israel, is they want to finish us off, as a stepping stone to hitting the United States! And we're the guys who want to help you, Mr. President. And so are the Egyptians. We face the same enemy. We're on the same side. Surely you can see that."

"I see pictures of dead Palestinian babies, Kivi, and I'm telling you I want a cease fire. Now Jack O'Leary is trying to get the Qataris and the Turks to act as honest brokers here and..."

"Honest brokers!? The Qataris are BANKROLLING the terrorists! And Turkey is led by the biggest Jew-hater since Hitler and, may I just ask sir, what exactly has Turkey done for the United States lately, aside from refusing to allow you to fly over their country to attack Saddam Hussein, after you gave them billions of dollars worth of aid?"

"Kivi, you're missing the point. I'm not debating you. There are no cameras rolling in the Oval Office, so you can lecture and embarrass me. I'm TELLING you. You want replacement parts? You want funding for your Iron Dome? I want a cease fire and I want it now!" and he hung up.

When Jack O'Leary came to Egypt's President Fahmi, and said he wanted the Qataris and the Turks involved in brokering a cease fire, Fahmi basically told him to pound sand. Egypt was the only game in town.

Fahmi announced he was putting forward a cease fire proposal that would call for a cessation of all hostilities.

"But," said O'Leary, "Hamas wants to have an airport and a sea port, and wants the borders between Gaza and Egypt opened. I mean, you've shut them in worse than the Israelis! And I believe this is an opportunity to..."

"Mr. Secretary," said President Fahmi, "Your President, your government, backed the head of the Moslem Brotherhood, who started his own personal jihad against the Egyptian people. We, of the military, stepped in, and stopped him. Hamas are his allies. Why would I open the door to the man who wants to murder me? Why would I give him a sea port to smuggle in weapons, when I've spent a year flooding his tunnels to stop him from smuggling in weapons, which they want to use against EGYPT!? Here is the cease-fire proposal. Cease... Fire...

That's the proposal. After that, after all the killing has stopped on both sides, anything anyone wants to discuss, can be discussed. But first, Cease... Fire... Without the Qataris. Without the Turks. Hamas speaks Arabic, after all. So do I. Neither of us speak Turkish."

And thus, Jack O'Leary, who, only moments before had had images of a Nobel Peace Prize dancing his head like sugar plum fairies, opted for Plan B.

He went to the Qataris and the Turks, told them about Fahmi's proposal and then said, "You be the guarantors. Hamas won't speak directly to the Israelis. They don't recognize them. So you go and say you talked to Hamas, which I'm sure you can do, and tell Hamas they don't have to say a thing. That way they save their dignity. They're not agreeing to anything regarding the cease fire, but you are guaranteeing it. Now whether Fahmi likes it or not, you're in."

"Yes," said the President of Turkey, "And then, of course, so are you."

At seven that evening Egypt put forward its cease fire proposal, seven days after the conflict began, and Kivi Natanel held a thirty minute cabinet meeting, and basically informed his cabinet that the three Ks - Kivi, his Minister of Defense, Kobi Golan and Chief of Staff, Kadosh Mintz - were taking the deal. By eight o'clock that night, Israel announced it had accepted the cease fire proposal that would go into effect at 9:00 a.m. the following morning.

By ten o'clock that evening, Hamas had still not announced whether they would accept the cease fire, but the Qataris and the Turks had assured Jack O'Leary, who enjoyed, to no end, sticking it to Egypt's President Fahmi, that the Turks and Qataris were now the guarantors of the Cease Fire.

Indeed there was a lull in the rocket fire out of Gaza, and Israel, accordingly, ceased its aerial and artillery bombardment.

In *Kfar Shimshon*, the Feigenboim brothers sprang for renting every bit of equipment form the neighboring *kibbutzim*, and, by the head-lights of the tractors, they worked all night long to complete the wheat harvest, because, as Pini Feigenboim so eloquently put it, "Cease-Fire, shmeese-fire. Let's finish it while they've stopped shooting. Who knows what those *choleras* will do tomorrow?!"

In the Givati dining hall Tera Dayton said, "Eight days, just like 2012," and she smiled at that know-it-all Dani Kahan.

Jack O'Leary, for his part, began mulling over the main themes of his acceptance speech for the Oslo ceremony of the Nobel Peace Prize presentation, while in Washington, POTUS wished he could light up a doobie, but contended himself with a tumbler of scotch and some *Classic Hoops* on ESPN.

"Guess we're not going to get to do that snatch-and-grab, after all," Washburn said to Dani.

"Did you hear a fat lady sing yet?" Dani asked.

"No, but she's running scales backstage," said McKeever.

And Peña thought it was too bad it was all over, 'cause he thought he might have stood a chance with the Ice Maiden after all.

In *Kfar Shimshon*, as the sun came up, the last of the wheat was harvested, leaving the edges of the field uncut, in keeping with the biblical injunction to save the gleanings for the poor.

The Feigenboim brothers prayed the *Shacharit*, or morning prayers, and offered special prayers of thanksgiving, for having been delivered from the hand of Hamas and Reb Moishe Yankel Haimovitch.

But Dani wasn't buying any of it. He had made the rounds that night, between the observation unit and the Givati Recon patrols. "Keep your eyes open," he said. "They're not done with us yet."

The Cease-Fire was to take effect at 9:00 a.m.

All across the front, commanders were preparing to give the stand-down orders to their troops.

At 8:30 a.m., instead of finally announcing they had accepted the cease fire, Hamas launched an opening salvo of forty rockets, in what was to be the deadliest onslaught of the eight day old war. They used their long range Fajr 5 and M75 rockets to hit Jerusalem. The fact that the rockets fell harmlessly into an open field and caused no damage didn't matter to the Palestinians who were dancing in the streets. Hamas had not only NOT given in, they had shown they could hit Al Kuds, Jerusalem itself. They hit as far north as Hadera. All across Israel the sirens wailed and Israelis ran to their shelters. They even managed to hit within spitting distance of Ben Gurion airport. And when they did that, POTUS had the FAA issue an advisory against any flights landing in Israel's national airport, just to show Kivi Natanel who was boss. The Europeans quickly followed suit, and Israel found itself cut off by air from the rest of the world. Just like the Yezidis on top of Mount Sinjar.

"Guess you were right," said Tera Dayton.

"This is nothing," Dani said. "This is the magician's sleight of hand. They're coming to get us."

He raced back to the observation unit and exhorted the girls once again. The nation's fate was on their shoulders. Then, he consulted with the Brigade Commander, Moti Dagan, who agreed with him that an attack was imminent, and dispatched him to the Givati Recon Unit, Samson's Foxes, and told them to be ready to move at a moment's notice. They needed to be mounted up, in harness, locked and loaded and ready to fight. The rockets were nothing. The real attack was coming. He just couldn't see from where.

"If there is an attack, these are gonna be your trigger pullers?" Washburn asked.

"You bet," Dani answered.

"And you're gonna be mounted up with these guys?"

"Affirmative on that, too."

"Then check me out a weapon bro, 'cause I'm gonna be with you."

"You're an American observer who, from what I gather, isn't even here… Unless I'm mistaken."

"If we're not here, there shouldn't be any problem giving us weapons," said Tera. "Look," she continued. "If this whole thing is going to be some kind of joint Hamas/ISIS operation, then it could be a dress rehearsal for whatever they've got in mind for us. We need to be there."

"Absolutely," said Peña.

Dani looked at all four of them. "Washburn, yes. He's a professional, and we've been on joint exercises. He knows how we move and we know how he moves."

"We're all professionals," Tera said.

"Wrong profession. It's not open to discussion. Brother Washburn can mount up with the Recon team, and you guys can take your choice of being in the observation unit or the war room. Your call."

Washburn checked out an M4, more comfortable with that than the Tavor MTAR 21, or Micro-Tavor. Dani took Tera and McKeever to the war room, and introduced them to Colonel Moti Dagan, the Brigade Commander, who had already been told by the Chief of Staff, personally, that the Americans were to have carte blanche, while Peña went back to the all-girl observation unit.

Dani, meanwhile took, Papa SEAL over to Givati's Samson's Foxes Recon Unit. The unit was divided up into three-man teams, each team mounted up on an All Desert Raider dune buggy. The buggies were rigged so that each fighter had a quick release mount for his weapon, which provided stability of fire while in motion. There would be one fighter standing up in the middle, above the roll bar. He's the one who would be decapitated if the thing flipped. He had his Negev 7 5.56mm light machine gun clipped into the quick release pivot mount. The fighter riding shotgun and the driver each had quick-release side mounts, as well, for their Micro-Tavors. Thus, the driver, steering one handed, could still provide additional firepower to the target, while the fighter riding shotgun, and the one up top, could provide more accurate fire toward whatever enemy force they faced.

All the teams were mounted, in full battle harness, ceramic vests, weapons checked and checked again, radios tested, headsets on.

Dani and Washburn both suited up. Ceramic vests first, and then tactical combat harness on top of that.

In the front there were four ammo pouches, each with two clips, with fast load separators, so you could release one magazine and slip the other into the receiver, without having to go into another pouch for a second clip.

There were two smaller pouches on the upper right hand side for M26 grenades.

The left-side pouch held the first aid kit, and, in back, the upper pouch held the communications package, complete with tactical bone-construction headset that fed to a boom, with a large-button, push-to-talk mic.

Dani and Washington slipped the headsets on last, and then their helmets. To finish it off, each helmet was topped off with the Israeli-made *Mitsnefet*, which gave the helmet an irregular shape, to make it more difficult for snipers to spot.

On his left leg, Dani wore his map pouch, and on his right leg an Israeli version of the Serpa hard drop leg holster, which Dani had purchased himself for his Glock 9mm, and then spray-painted olive drab, from the original mud color, to go with the rest of his uniform.

The back rear pouch on the tactical vest was usually for food.

But in addition to the few cans of tuna, Danny tossed in six extra M26 grenades, and two smoke grenades. To the right side of that pouch, he mounted his Camelbak hydration pack. In addition, he shoved in pairs of plastic handcuffs and a prisoner hood, together with a few yards of flannel, usually used for weapons cleaning, but which could be used for blindfolds as well.

"You planning on taking that many prisoners?" Washburn asked, as he saw Dani load in the handcuffs, hood and flannel.

"Ya never know," said Dani.

"That's the difference between trigger-pullers and intel guys," Papa said. "You wanna talk to 'em."

Within a few minutes both of them were completely suited up, sweating already in the humid Gaza summer heat. They checked the tactical computer each three man team had, as well as the individual iPad-like, real time tactical tablets, and GPS nav systems. In that way each team could input intel gained on the scene, in real time, and share it simultaneously, with the main Brigade War Room, each unit in the field, as well as air and naval assets.

Both of them pulled the mags out of their weapons, cleared them, cocked eight times and fired "dry" into the air, and then reinserted the magazines into the receivers, checked the safeties, again, and then, again.

The Micro-Tavor was an amazing weapon, the best tactical assault rifle Dani had ever fired. It had a laser sight, and as long as you placed the red dot dead center, through the eyepiece, and then put it on your target, you couldn't miss. It was lightweight, stable, with a front pivot grip enabling you to fire effectively while charging forward. It was perfect for close-quarters, and crazy effective at ranges that belied its compact size. It had a muzzle flash suppressor and could be mounted with a silencer. Its 5.56 ammo could put a serious dent in a Jihadi's day, and provide a copper-jacketed implant that would enable immediate communication with the recipient's creator, or the much promised almond-eyed, raven-haired virgins.

It was completely instinctive. On the right side of the weapon, just above the trigger, was the magazine release. Take your finger off the trigger, push the release, and the mag slipped out easily. The safety/single fire switch was on the left side of the weapon. You thumbed it up to fire and down to safety. There was no automatic fire on it, because the IDF, in its wisdom, decided they didn't need it. The thought, Dani supposed, was that any kind of a marksman was far more accurate in single fire mode, and you could still generate a good rate of fire with the Micro Tavor.

Still there were times, when, shooting from the hip and charging forward, you wanted to be able to let off a few short bursts at the bad guys, who, with their trusty AK 47s, ripped through clips like Rambo.

Dani packed in two extra batteries for the laser sight, and checked the backup iron sight once again.

He wished he had time to go to a range and zero in the sight, just in case the usual jostling around had gotten it out of whack. But he knew they could be deep in the *fahzool* any minute. And at the same time they could be here for hours.

The kids of the Recon Unit pulled out boxes of combat rations. Each one had an individual can of tuna. They finished that, and then used the tin as a plate for the canned corn, olives, stuffed date leaves and pickles that came with the combat rations. And, because they were basically kids, there was bread and chocolate spread.

An Ethiopian kid, a Second Lieutenant, took several of the empty tuna tins with the olive oil still in the bottom, and stuffed them with toilet paper, and then lit them up. The tuna and olive oil turned them into mini burners. He put four of them inside the cardboard combat rations carton and used that to boil water for the thick Turkish coffee with cardamom that he sweetened with heaping spoonsful of sugar, and offered up for his guys.

If I was in New York right now, instead of on the Gaza border awaiting a Hamas terrorist attack, Dani thought, *I could be at the*

Trattoria Del Arte, and Brendan, the maître d', would be taking care of me, offering up a properly chilled glass of Prosecco. Or, I might be at the Veau D'Or, sipping an ice cold rosé brought to me by Cathy, the beautiful owner of the place. And, even though it was mid-July, I'd start with onion soup, which was the best outside of the Pied du Couchon in Paris. Then, perhaps, I'd have the monkfish, sautéed in white wine, lemon, and butter. The perfect, leisurely repast for a delightful summer's day. Instead, he opened up a tin of tuna, and swallowed a brackish swig of warm water from his hydration pack.

Then they checked their weapons again... And again.

Waiting, waiting, waiting.

At 13:00 hours, in the basement entrance to the network of tunnels beneath Al Wafa Hospital, Yasser Darwish met with the thirteen commandos of the Al Aksa Martyr's Brigades.

These were his most elite troops. The Delta Force of Hamas.

Each man was armed with a Yassin RPG, a local version of the Soviet RPG2. Each one of those could take down a row of Israeli houses.

In addition to the RPGs, each man had a Kalashnikov, a full complement of grenades, thousands of rounds of ammunition, hundreds of pairs of plastic handcuffs, and dozens of tranquilizer shots. And each one of them was wearing Israeli army fatigues, so anyone seeing them, at first, in the *kibbutz* they were about to attack, would assume they were Israeli soldiers... There to protect them.

It was almost too easy.

Abdul Aziz Al-Tikriti witnessed the scene with tears in his eyes, as did Khaled Kawasme.

"Today," Darwish said to his men, "You will bring the Jews to their knees, and they will beg for mercy! But there will be no mercy! *Allahu Akhbar!*" he proclaimed.

"*Allahu Akhbar!*" they shouted back, again and again. "*Allahu Akhbar! Allahu Akhbar!!*"

The cells were ready for the hostages they would drag back through the tunnels, into Gaza.

At exactly 2:15 p.m., Darwish gave the order to attack.

Al-Tikriti took his leave of Kawasme, who would stay behind to witness the operation, and learn whatever lessons there were to be learned. Al-Tikriti would not be there with him.

This was merely a dress rehearsal for what he would inflict on America.

The elite Hamas terrorist team made its way down the main attack tunnel.

They were timing their action for the exact moment when *Kibbutz* parents would be picking their children up from the day care centers, with their reinforced concrete roofs. Where they were safe from Hamas' rockets...

With luck, they might be able to take whole families hostage, and kill and maim the others.

They made their way one and a half miles from Al Wafa hospital to the end of the tunnel, one and a half kilometers inside Israel's 1967 border. At exactly 2:55, they would blow open the last foot of earth that separated them from the Zionist enemy.

This would be the fulfillment of the Hamas Charter, the fulfillment of the Promise of Allah, when Muslims would kill the Jews, who would hide behind the rocks and trees until the rocks and trees cried out, "O Muslim, there is a Jew hiding behind me! Come and kill him!"

This time it would not be martyrdom.

This time it would be victory!

At 2:55, Ahmed A Rahman Mahdi, who had helped plan and execute the kidnapping of Gilad Shalit, set off the small C4 charge that blew away the last bit of earth.

They emerged from the darkness of the tunnels, into the blazing sunlight of *Kibbutz Kfar Shimshon*, ninja-rolled into position... And then looked up in terror!

Where was the wheat field that was meant to be their camouflage?! Where was the field of five-foot-tall green wheat that was supposed to make them invisible for the last five hundred meters until they reached the day care center of the *kibbutz*?!

"*Ya' Allah!*" Ahmed a Rahman cried out in pain and anger and anguish.

The Jews' God had made their wheat field had disappear!

CHAPTER 9

Orna Arieli was the nineteen-year-old conscript who saw them first.

She had completed her *"Tazpit"* observer training course only three months before, and she was the most girly girl in the unit. Her pants were tailored to a more shapely fit than the other girls. She never appeared without makeup, and at least a little eye shadow, and when on leave she never wore combat boots, but delicate-looking gold-banded sandals that set off the green nail polish on her toes. She had yet to adapt to army food. She was pampered, and some would even say spoiled; a typical *"Tsfonebonit"*, a derogatory term applied to the rich girls who lived in the trendier high-rises of Northern Tel Aviv. Her father owned a high-tech startup and she was an uncanny lookalike for Lindsay Lohan, with blond hair and hazel eyes and a figure that never failed to attract attention in her "skinny" army pants. She had a new BMW 228i that daddy had bought her when she graduated high school, and she knew the lyrics to every Beyoncé and Lady Gaga song ever recorded.

She was, in short, the most unlikely of heroes. She was a 2014 version of Goldie Hawn in *Private Benjamin*. But, at 3:00 in the afternoon of July 17th, 2014, she saved Israel from the greatest catastrophe in its history.

Her monitor showed the image from the observation balloon above the border area adjacent to *Kibbutz Kfar Shimshon*.

Had she been checking her nails, or daydreaming about her boyfriend, or allowing her mind to wander to any of the myriad things which consume nineteen year old girls the world over, it is likely that hundreds of men, women and children would have been killed, wounded, taken hostage, and dragged back through the tunnels into underground cells in Gaza, and the State of Israel would have been brought crashing down to its knees.

But, like every other girl in her unit, whether from European background, Yemenite, Moroccan or African, whether olive skinned, black, or fair, whether from the development towns of Kiryat Gat, or the orthodox neighborhoods of Jerusalem, from city or *kibbutz*, from the ocean view high-rises of North Tel Aviv, to the dusty little town of Afula in the Jezreel Valley, whether drop-dead gorgeous, or plain, all of them knew they were, indeed, the eyes of the State, on the border with some of the most vicious and capable terrorists in the world. They believed what Dani had told them, and what, basically, every Israeli soldier has been inculcated to believe; that the fate of their nation, and their people, rested on their shoulders, personally, individually, ultimately theirs.

So instead of checking her nails, or thinking about the text that Idan, that really cute boy who was in flight school, had sent her that morning, or if he was really serious about her, or liked that other girl, who thought she was as hot as Bar Rafaeli or something, instead of letting her thoughts drift to any of that, she sat like a mongoose in front of her monitor, and watched the earth open up, and, like a scene out of *The Night of The Living Dead*, she saw zombies rise up out of their graves.

Except this wasn't a movie, and these "zombies" had assault rifles, and ninja-rolled into what had been a wheat field just the day before.

They looked around in shock, anger and anguish. And without a second's hesitation, she hit the "All Quarters" alarm.

Irit was already at her side as they counted six, no... Ten, no... Thirteen terrorists sprouting up from the empty wheat field, clutching their AK 47s, only five hundred meters away from the children's house at *Kibbutz Kfar Shimshon*, where parents had just arrived to pick up their preschoolers and kindergarteners.

"Terrorist attack!" she called out, as she hit the alarm.

The alarm sounded simultaneously in the war room at Givati Brigade headquarters, in Sedot Daniel Air base near Tel Aviv, home of the 422 UAV "Drone" Squadron, in Ad Halom Air base, home of the 607 AH-64 Apache helicopter squadron, in Air Force Headquarters in

Tel Aviv, in Negba air base, near Beer Sheva, home of the 399th Fighter Squadron, and with every team of Samson's Foxes, the Givati Recon Battalion, stretched out, all along the Gaza border.

At the same time, the image and GPS coordinates appeared on the screens of each relevant air and ground asset, and on the field laptops of each of the Recon teams, mounted up, in harness, locked and loaded, and waiting for exactly this moment.

In the Brigade war room, Colonel Moti Dagan activated a system that called up the closest aerial asset, which in this case was one of the new Rodef UAVs which, at that moment, was patrolling the southern sector of the border.

The Rodef was capable of over forty hours of continuous patrol with a full payload that included laser targeting, infrared and visible light surveillance, line-of-sight data link, and satellite relay, and could operate at 35,000 feet with a maximum speed of one hundred and fifty knots.

Most importantly, it was armed with two hellfire missiles.

It had just fired one of those missiles at a Hamas rocket launching crew, and taken them out.

It had only one left.

Now, it was tasked with taking out the thirteen terrorists who had just been spotted by Orna Arieli.

The drone pilot, Itai Zarchi, and Sensor Operator, Lior Nesher, switched their surveillance cameras to the new coordinates.

"We have eyes on target," Nesher announced to Moti Dagan, the Brigade Commander, who was now in charge of the intercept operation.

Samson's Foxes Recon Team "B", which Dani and Washburn had attached themselves to, was given the order to roll. The four "All Desert Raider" three-man dune buggies roared out at eighty miles an hour, racing for *Kibbutz Kfar Shimshon*.

On the ground, Ahmed A Rahman Mahdi, who was leading the thirteen-man Hamas terrorist unit, realized in an instant that the Israelis had, by now, spotted them, and both air and ground assets were already being activated to destroy them.

How could the wheat field have disappeared?!

It was here!

Their target, the *Kibbutz* day care center, was still five hundred meters away.

They had to kill at least some of the Jews before they were intercepted!

They had to get close enough to take a shot with an RPG.

To maximize his chances to inflict the most harm on the Zionist enemy, he would split his team. Three of his men would set up to take RPG shots, and the other ten would charge the Jews, in two groups of five each. If the Jews sent a drone, he knew it had only two missiles.

Some of them would, at least, get close enough to inflict death upon the Jews...

This is what they had trained to accomplish for over a year.

What had happened to the wheat field!? *Ya' Allah!*

In The Givati war room, Colonel Dagan gave the UAV crew the command, "Execute."

"Copy," said Zarchi. He spoke in that flat, calm pilot's voice, but he could see the terrorists running toward the children's house and day care center, and he knew there were parents there right now, with toddlers in their arms the age of his own son Dror, and they were completely unaware that they were seconds away from death.

"Master arm," he said to his Sensor Operator.

Both he, and Nesher, saw the terrorists running toward the day care center.

In the *Kibbutz*, the code red alert sounded.

There was no separate signal for terrorist ground attack. The parents, thinking a rocket attack was imminent, ran with their children back into the day care center, not knowing that they were making themselves a perfect target for the terrorists, now racing toward them.

Nesher and Zarchi saw three of the terrorists setting up to take a shot with their RPGs, and the remaining terrorists split into two groups, who were each charging the day care center.

"Paint the RPGs," Zarchi said, making a split-second decision to hit the RPG team with the only missile they had left.

"Copy," said Nesher and "painted" the three RPG shooters with the laser sensor.

"Sensor ready," he said.

"Copy. Five seconds to release... Four... Three... Two... One. Weapons away!" Zarchi said, pressing the "pickle" on the joystick.

The countdown to impact display started to tick off.

"Ten seconds to impact," Zarchi said, his mouth gone dry.

Too long!

The terrorists would get their shot off before the hellfire missile could take them out.

"Come on, come on!" said Nesher, as he watched the three terrorists shoulder and aim their RPGs.

In the war room, Moti Dagan had already keyed Dani's Recon team. "How far away are you?"

Dani and the other Recon members knew almost every cactus along the border. They could navigate this area in their sleep, and now, over the terrain, which had slowed them to sixty miles an hour, Lieutenant Yossi Cohen, technically the commander of the teams, answered back. "One thousand meters."

"Fire your weapons now! Make all the noise you can!"

Yossi didn't ask why or question the order. He knew it was probably just to buy time. He knew that the terrorists now were only seconds away from killing the women and children who were their targets.

For Dani Kahan, this was his worst nightmare all over again. His son and ex-wife sitting in the pizza place in Jerusalem and the suicide bomber putting his thumb on the detonator button, and not a thing he could do about it.

Yossi gave the order to fire, and, though there was no target of any kind, all four dune buggies began firing their Micro-Tavor assault rifles AND Negev 7 light machine guns toward the border.

The three bazooka operators heard the gunfire, and paused just long enough to look around and see where it was coming from.

Zarchi counted down. "Five... Four... Three... Two... One. Impact!"

He saw the screen go white with the flash of the explosion.

On the ground, the three terrorists screamed as their flesh burned and shrapnel ripped through their bodies, incinerating and eviscerating them at once.

Ahmed A Rahman Mahdi heard the whoosh of the hellfire missile, and then the explosion. He turned around and saw three of his men, and part of his dream of victory, go up in white-hot shrapnel, fire and smoke, and, as he paused and turned, his men did as well.

Dani could see him now, as his dune buggy jumped a berm and crashed down onto the northern end of the wheat field, on a line of trajectory that would put them between the terrorists, and the mothers and fathers racing into the day care center that would be their death trap, unless Dani and his Recon team intercepted the Hamas cell bent on murdering them. He could see Achmed A Rahman Mahdi, pause and turn to look at the smoke rising from the burning corpses of three of his men, who were only a second late in firing their bazookas.

Then, A Rahman Mahdi turned to his men, and shouted, "*Allahu Akhbar!*" God is great! And he motioned them to follow him, as he raced toward the Jews.

Dani saw him, and knew he was their leader, and a good one at that.

Like an Israeli officer, he was saying, "After me!" He wasn't panicked by the hellfire missile, which, for all he knew, was a prelude to a second missile that would incinerate him as well. He had a mission in which he fervently believed: to kill Jews. And he was determined to accomplish it.

Everything slowed down for Dani, as had happened before for him in combat. It was as if he had time to think, to reflect, to go out and have a falafel, and take a nap and still have time in the next few seconds to accomplish HIS mission.

When he was a kid on the *kibbutz*, his stepfather had given him a book, in English, about the Texas Rangers. In it, he read the story of Jack Coffee Hays, who, at twenty-three, became the Captain of the most important Ranger station in all of Texas during their ongoing war against the Comanche in the early 1840's.

The Comanche were the only Native Americans who had not only stopped white expansion on the American continent, they had actually pushed it back. They were the most feared warriors in North America. They had defeated the greatest European Imperial Army since Rome, and pushed them back into Mexico. They did so by being absolutely the most brutal warriors on earth. They were as feared by other Native American tribes as they were by the whites.

In battle, they killed all the men, and kidnapped the women and children. They made the women their slaves, and if a child was too young to be "converted" into being a Comanche, they killed him on the spot, usually in front of the child's mother, whom they repeatedly brutalized and raped.

The dreaded Apache were in Arizona, because they had fled from the Comanche in Texas.

The Comanche warriors were the finest light horse cavalry in the world. They were technologically superior to the whites, who, at the time, had only single-shot Kentucky rifles and single-shot pistols, and bowie knives with which to fight the feared Comanche braves.

The whites rode to battle, and then dismounted and fought.

The Comanche fought on horseback, and could shoot twenty arrows from beneath the neck of a galloping pony in the time it took the dismounted whites to reload a Kentucky long gun.

All that changed, when twenty-three-year-old Jack Coffee Hays walked into a darkened warehouse, and saw a crate of the only working Colt .32 revolvers in the world.

A twenty-six-year-old snake oil salesman named Samuel Colt had invented them, and sold one thousand of them to the US Army, who thought them useless, and, in turn, sold them to the "Navy" of the Republic of Texas, for twenty five cents on the dollar. The Texas "Navy", consisting of three sailing ships, likewise, could find no use for them, and forgot about them.

Jack Coffee Hays saw them, and knew he had just won the war.

He outfitted each of his Rangers with two of the five-shot revolvers.

He drilled them in firing the weapons on horseback, at close range, until they were expert.

Then, like Gideon in the Bible, he chose a small force, only seventeen men, and went out in search of a Comanche war party. He encountered a group of almost one hundred Comanche warriors... And charged them.

He had told his men, who were actually boys, whose average age was eighteen, that they each had ten shots, and were each to pick out ten targets. But the Comanche, he knew, were superstitious. If their leader fell in battle, they assumed it was because he had bad medicine, and they lost heart. So he told each of his men that their first target should be the chief of the War Party. When he gave the order to charge, he yelled out what became a legendary battle cry, in Texas Ranger lore.

"Crowd 'em, boys!" he shouted. "Powder burn 'em!"

The usual tactics of the Dune Buggy Recon teams were to advance toward the enemy, and then dismount the dune buggy, utilizing the quick release from the pivot mount, so that each soldier then took his Micro-Tavor and advanced on foot.

But, seeing the terrorists running toward the men and women who raced back toward the day care center with their children in their arms, Dani yelled what was an incomprehensible sentence to all but Darwin Washburn, to whom he had told the story of Jack Coffee Hays, on a joint-training exercise, when they first met.

"Crowd 'em, boys!" he yelled, and raced his dune buggy directly at Ahmed A Rahman Mahdi.

Washburn, who was up top, opened up with his Negev 7, while Dani and Gabi Katzin, who was riding shotgun, opened up with their Micro-Tavors.

A Rahman Mahdi heard the gunfire, and saw Dani's dune buggy racing directly toward him, and, in his own slowed-down world, moment of reflection, he thought he could die, being shot in the back by these Jews, or forget about his mission, forget about the women and children he had come to kill, turn and face his enemy, and do his best to kill as many of them as possible before his own death, which he knew, now, was only moments away.

Thus, he stopped, turned toward Dani's dune buggy, assumed a rifleman's kneeling position, and took aim at Darwin Washburn, who, at six-foot-five, and standing upright in the dune buggy, was the easiest target.

He gave the order to his men, who turned, and saw the dune buggy bearing down upon them, as well.

Three of the other men in his group of five did not have the same heroic fervor of their leader. They chose neither to engage the oncoming dune buggy, nor to wait for the next missile strike, nor to continue toward the day care center.

Instead, they turned and began running back toward the tunnel, rightly assuming that the Recon force would ignore them, to deal first with those who were still a threat to the Jews.

"Cowards!" A Rahman Mahdi shouted at them, and in that moment, he gave Dani a chance to begin zig-zagging slightly in his course.

When Mahdi turned back, Dani was already zig-zagging toward him, causing Washburn's body to gyrate in the opposite direction.

A Rahman Mahdi laid down a long burst from his AK 47.

The 7.62x39mm hollowpoint slugs were pinging into the dune buggy that bounced and zig-zagged along its way, closing with Mahdi and Mahmoud Zouabi, who had chosen to remain with his commander.

One of the rounds ripped into Gabi Katzin, literally tearing the left side of his face away, and shattering his eye socket. He let go of his weapon and screamed in agony, as Washburn continued to lay down short bursts of fire, and Dani fired off single shots that danced all around their targets.

The two sets of adversaries continued firing at each other, as the distance between them raced to close itself. One of the hollow points exploded into Washburn's ceramic vest, throwing him back against his harness. Another hit the top of Dani's helmet. As the dune buggy continued toward them at almost fifty miles an hour, bouncing up and down over the wheat field, Mahmoud Zouabi lost his nerve, and ran as well. But Ahmed A Rahman Mahdi got to his feet, still firing up to the end, yelling, *"Allahu Akhbar!"* as Dani slammed the dune buggy into him, sending him flying.

Dani jammed his feet down on the brakes, and Washburn righted himself, slipped the Negev 7 light machine gun from its quick-release pivot, dismounted, aimed, and fired at Mahdi, who was struggling to get to his feet.

The short burst from the Negev 7 ripped straight into Mahdi's face, below the helmet.

It was the kind of shot only a Navy SEAL could make two seconds after he'd dismounted from a gyrating dune buggy.

The other dune buggies had raced to put themselves between the remaining terrorists and the parents, who huddled with their children in in the day care center. Two of those terrorists immediately broke and ran back toward the tunnels.

The Recon team ignored them and concentrated on those who were still a threat, and not running away. They dismounted, taking their weapons from the quick release mounts. Chaim Dovrat, a young Lieutenant, pulled an M26 grenade out of his combat vest, pulled the pin, let the spoon fly, threw it, yelled "*Rimon!*" which meant "grenade" in Hebrew, and he and his men flattened on the ground.

The grenade hit a few feet away from the other group of three remaining terrorists, who had now flattened themselves on the ground as well, and were firing at the Givati Recon team. The grenade exploded, spraying the terrorists with shrapnel, but because they were prone, it did little damage. It did, however, do exactly what grenades are meant to do. It kept the enemy's heads down and gave Dovrat and his men time to charge, firing as they went.

Two of the Givati Recon fighters went down, with the rest continuing to fire.

Dani and Washburn now engaged them from their flank, choosing their targets carefully, Dani centering the red laser dot first on one terrorist's head, and then another, as Washburn slowed and sighted with his Negev 7, and carefully issued death from the barrel of his weapon as well. Inside of thirty seconds, the battle was over.

Eight terrorists were dead and five had run back to the tunnel entrance and disappeared inside. One Givati soldier, Gabi Katzin, was dead, and three others wounded.

With the attacking force neutralized, they now divided into two groups of four, one, with Dani, stayed next to the dead terrorists, to make sure they were, indeed, dead, and no longer a threat, and to begin slowly and carefully searching their bodies for documents and IDs.

The other team raced back toward the tunnel exit point, into which the remaining terrorists had disappeared. Technically, Dani was not in command of this unit. He was the intelligence officer who had more or less forced himself upon them. The commander of the team was the twenty-two-year-old Lieutenant Yossi Cohen. He had instructed Dani to stay with the downed terrorists, while he and his team pursued those left.

Dani was turning over the body of Ahmed A Rahman Mahdi, and beginning slowly and carefully to search through his pockets. He saw the mini-cam attached to Mahdi's helmet.

They had recorded the battle, probably meaning to post the Divine Victory attack on the internet.

Then, out of the corner of his eye Dani saw Yossi, adrenaline pumping, start to go down into the tunnel itself.

Dani stood up and shouted, "No! Toss in a grenade first!" The grenade would have blown any booby traps.

But he was too late. Dani heard the explosion. Yossi was literally blown in half by the IED the terrorists had left, in order to cover their escape into the tunnel, and back into Gaza. The upper half of his torso lay, now, in the barren wheat field, where all had suddenly become so quiet.

At the Al Wafa Hospital bunker, the five surviving terrorists told the story of what had happened to a shocked and disbelieving Darwish.

When the first of the group, Mustafa Abadi, told Darwish that the wheat field had disappeared, Darwish bitch slapped him and called him a lying coward of a dog, and cursed the mother who bore him. He pulled out his pistol and was ready to shoot the traitor on the spot, when the others implored him, saying that it was true! The wheat field, meant to hide them, meant to assure the success of their mission, had completely disappeared!

Later, sitting alone in his command bunker, Darwish watched the video from their helmet cams. He watched in horror, as they emerged from the darkness of the tunnel into the blazing sunlight, and saw that, indeed, it was true.

The Jews' wheat field had disappeared!

"Their God!" he called out, in a mixture of fury and despair. "Their God!"

As for Abdul Aziz Al-Tikriti, the moment he heard about the failed attack, he made for the smuggling tunnel that would take him out of Gaza, and into the waiting arms of Sheikh Abu Ali, who would smuggle him back into Cairo.

Now he knew the Israelis would open the gates of hell upon Gaza.

But that was Hamas' problem.

Not his, and not ISIS'.

His mission here was now complete, and, for America, he knew, there would be no wheat field, nor any God, that could save them.

CHAPTER 10

D ani, and the remaining members of Recon Team B of the Samson's Foxes Reconnaissance Battalion, were soon joined by other members of the Givati Brigade, including Colonel Moti Dagan, who personally came to the scene to oversee all three phases of the continuing operation; identification and removal of the dead - and all their body parts - together with medics of the IDF Medical Corps, and Military Chaplaincy, identification and examination of the dead terrorists and their effects, and the hunt for any remaining terrorists who may still have been at large in the area. This last phase called for all the residents of the *kibbutzim* along the border with Gaza to shut themselves into their safe rooms, until further notice. Dani took it upon himself to personally inform the residents of *Kibbutz Kfar Shimshon*.

For him, these *kibbutzniks* were not just farmers who lived in little agricultural villages, they were family. Indeed, in most ways, they were the only family he had ever known while growing up.

Dani was born in America, in 1970, the second child of Miriam Palikoff and Charles Timothy O'Bannion. Charlie O'Bannion was a minor folk-rock star in the late sixties. When his mother and father were in high school together, in Anaheim, California, Miriam became pregnant. Her parents, seeing her college career vanish before their eyes, wanted her to get an abortion. Instead, she and Charlie ran away. Charlie was seventeen, Miriam sixteen. If Charlie had been eighteen, Miriam's parents would have filed charges of statutory rape. Instead, they reluctantly consented to the marriage they were sure would ruin their daughter's life. It was as sad a little wedding as anyone in attendance could remember. It was clear that Charlie felt trapped, and Miriam disgraced. But, they were young, and in love, and were sure that, somehow, like every hokey teenage ballad, "Going to the chapel, and gonna get married" would make everything turn out all right. Charlie, who just wanted to play rock 'n roll, got a job in a restaurant bussing tables, and dutifully enrolled in classes at Fullerton Junior College. They lived in a sad little apartment, in a sad little complex, until Dani's older brother, David, was born.

And then, Charlie got his big break.

A sleazy agent named Bernie Rosen had heard him on Hootenanny Night at The Troubadour. That landed him a record deal with Elektra, and a tour to New York. And that, in turn, got him the tour to England.

In the first year of David's life, Charlie was at home a total of three months.

The marriage, if one wanted to call it that, lasted until 1970, when Dani was born. Dani was a mistake, and the final nail in the coffin of Charlie and Miriam's union. They got divorced, and Dani had vague memories of having once spent a week with his father, and his new live-in girlfriend, when Dani was five years of age. He remembered being told not to touch his father's guitar.

Miriam, meanwhile, soldiered bravely on, and, with her parents' help, began attending UCLA part-time. It took her six years to graduate with a BA in English. And it was during that time that she met a young Israeli, named Amit Kahan, who was getting his BA in English Literature.

Amit was from a *kibbutz* in the Valley of Jezreel, but not, by any means, the image of the tanned, strong, *sabra kibbutznik*.

He was pale, and wore glasses, was bookish by nature, more of a poet than a farmer. Indeed, it was the poet in him which attracted Miriam. He had spent only two years in the Army, instead of the customary three, having been discharged when he was diagnosed with leukemia.

Originally, he had gone to Los Angeles for treatment and, once he was in full remission, began attending classes at UCLA.

He was already a published author in Israel, having achieved some minor success, and was even being compared, by some, to a sort of lesser version of Israel's foremost young *kibbutznik* author, Amos Oz.

He was twenty-one, and Miram was twenty-seven, with two children, eleven year-old David, and five-year-old Dani, but they were madly in love. Amit would later tell Dani that, in fact, Dani was part of the reason that he had fallen so deeply in love with Miriam. He and the boy bonded immediately, and Amit, whose own father was killed in the 1956 Sinai Campaign, and who, because of the aggressive cancer treatments, was now sterile, saw in Miriam and her children the ready-made family he never had. For Miriam's middle-class, Orange County, Jewish parents, it was a double disaster: first, a rock star, then a *kibbutznik*!

But, Miriam was of age, and she and Amit were in love, and, in the summer of 1976, they came back to *Kibbutz Ginegar*, in the Valley of Jezreel, and were married. It was a big, raucous *kibbutz* wedding, and Miriam and her children were embraced by the entire community as one of their own.

Dani loved every second of it, and his brother, David, hated it. There was no question that Dani made the adjustment easier because he was so young, whereas, for David, being uprooted from his friends, from American television, and plunked down into a farm that smelled of cow manure and fertilizer, in the middle of nowhere, with only one black and white TV station, was a living hell on earth. A year later, Charlie O'Bannion OD'd on heroin, and Amit formally adopted both boys, and their last name became Kahan, instead of O'Bannion.

But, David continued to be miserable, never having made the adjustment to *kibbutz* life, and, with Miriam's parents' encouragement, it was decided that he would return to California, and live with his grandparents during the school year, and return to Israel each summer to be with Miriam, Dani, and Amit.

The summers shrank, from three months, to two, to one month, and, by the time David was fifteen, to a tense two week period. He hated the *kibbutz*, he hated his stepfather, he hated being away from his friends, and finally, he asked to change his name to that of his grandparents, and so he became David Palikoff.

Thus, Dani became a *de facto* only child, for whom Amit was the only father he'd ever known.

Amit possessed a kind of calm, which Dani had never seen in any other human being. When Dani was old enough, when he was thirteen or fourteen, he asked Amit about it, and about why, as a twenty-one-year-old, Amit had been so eager to take on the responsibilities of marriage and children.

Amit sighed, and told him a story.

He asked Dani if he remembered when Sadat had come to Jerusalem. It was 1977, and Dani was six years old, and had just recently come to Israel, but he did, indeed, remember the excitement. They were spending the weekend with Amit's cousin, in a little farming village off the main road to Jerusalem, called Neve Ilan. He remembered being glued to the television set as Sadat's plane landed in Tel Aviv. He remembered the adults smiling, and shaking their heads, at the miracle of it, and some of them choking back tears as, first, the Israeli Air Force Band played the Egyptian national anthem, and then the Israeli national anthem, *Hatikva*, which meant "The Hope". They watched as Anwar El Sadat, the President of Egypt, stood at attention, saluting the flag and anthem of the Jewish State, only four years after the Yom Kippur War, which, many of them thought, would be the end of the Jewish State.

He remembered them all going out spontaneously to their gardens and ripping up flowers and going out to the highway called Bab El Wad, which during the 1948 War of Liberation was a deathtrap for the Jewish convoys bringing food to a cut-off Jerusalem. The convoys ran the gauntlet of Arab villages that poured down murderous fire on them as they crept up the steep two lane road to the Holy City which most of them never saw, because Bab El Wad became the grave from which they never rose.

There were still burnt-out armored cars along the highway as a memorial to those who fell trying to lift the Arab siege of Israel's ancient capital.

And now, the President of Egypt was coming up that same road, past those burnt-out armored car memorials to his former enemies, to make peace.

And so they all went out to the highway, and threw flowers out onto the road, and offered up bouquets to the motorcade.

Later, Sadat said that when he saw those simple villagers with their flowers, he knew peace with Israel was possible. *Only four years earlier*, Dani thought now, *they were ready to annihilate us.*

The Yom Kippur War, for Dani's stepfather's generation, was the most traumatic event of their lives.

They had gone from the euphoric victory of the Six Day War, in 1967, to Israel's own Pearl Harbor, and moments of horror and despair, which even the great Moshe Dayan believed had brought the Third Commonwealth of Israel to extinction.

Amit had been in boot camp when the war broke out. He had been a soldier for only three days, barely enough time to learn how to fire and take apart an Uzi, let alone an FN assault rifle.

Suddenly, everything went to the front, to the soldiers on the line. Uniforms, combat boots, weapons. They were reduced to training with World War I Czech Mausers. Amit's group of draftees had not yet even been issued dogtags.

Within three weeks, however, at the horrific cost of almost three thousand men killed in twenty-one days, the Israel Defense Forces turned an assault that had looked like utter defeat, into victory.

In the south, under Arik Sharon, they had crossed the Suez Canal, and encircled the Egyptian Third Army.

In the north, they had not only taken the Golan Heights back from the Syrians, but had pushed to within forty kilometers of Damascus, in an area that was referred to as "The Bulge".

In addition to facing the Syrian Army, which, at the beginning of the war had outnumbered them by almost eight to one, they had faced elements of the Jordanian Army, and a forty-thousand-man Iraqi Expeditionary Force, which had joined the fight on the Syrian side, as well.

By the third week of the war, a cease-fire was imminent, but the reservists, who had fought nonstop for three weeks, were on the verge of total exhaustion. Someone in the General Staff got the bright idea, then, to bring raw recruits up to the front, to stand guard duty over the armored encampments, and thus allow the exhausted reservists some much-needed sleep.

"A soldier on guard duty," Amit explained, "has one real function: it is to die loudly. You are there to get shot. Maybe you'll shoot back, maybe you won't shoot back, but the main thing is, someone will shoot you, and that will wake up the real soldiers. So, we were sent up there to do guard duty. Israel wasn't going to push any further into Syria, and the real fighters needed to rest. And, for us, it was very exciting. We were at the front. We were soldiers, now. We were fighters!

"Some fighters!" Amit said ruefully, smiled, and shook his head.

He spoke in such a quiet voice, in a tone that Dani had never heard before, as if he were about to impart to his stepson the single, most valuable lesson he had learned in life. Dani listened without saying a word, not asking a question, waiting through Amit's long, awful silence, as he seemed to look inward, remembering something at once terrible, and of immense importance.

"Then, on the night of October twenty-third or twenty-fourth, I really don't remember, our regimental Sergeant-Major came in. His name was Shimshon, Samson, and he was a really big guy. He was a paratrooper, you know, red boots. Red beret. A real warrior. And, everyone could see by his look that whatever he was about to say was very serious. He said we had received intelligence reports that, the next day, at sunrise, when the sun was in our eyes, that the Syrians and Iraqis would counterattack all along The Bulge. With the addition of the Iraqi forces, we would be outnumbered by a factor of ten to one. He said that the General Staff had decided not to bring up reinforcements, because we didn't want it to look in any way to the Americans, on satellite photos, that we were, at all, provoking the attack. Why? Because we needed the Americans to resupply us. Without those supplies, we would be dead. So, it wasn't just a military question, it was a political question. It wasn't just 'can we win the battle?', it was 'what will the Americans think?' And, so the Americans wouldn't think that we'd provoked the attack, or that, God forbid, we were getting ready to attack ourselves, it was decided that no reinforcements would be brought up, and we would have to blunt the attack only with the forces that we had available. Which now included us. We had been in the Army a little over three weeks. What I'm telling you is still a major secret. No one talks about it. It was a big *fashlah*. A big, catastrophic mistake, that no one has admitted to this day, and they probably never will. We had just gotten American LOW antitank rockets. They looked like a tube you would put a poster in. They were used one time, and you threw them away. Very simple to operate. You cocked it by pulling it apart, and an iron sight popped up, you pointed it, looked through the sight, there was a button on top that you squeezed, and you fired the rocket, and you threw it away. Because they had almost eight times more tanks than we did, we were split into tank hunter units, three men in each unit, and we loaded up with these LOW rockets. And, that night, we prepared to go into battle.

"We loaded extra clips for the FNs, and we practiced with the dummy LOW rocket, cocking and pressing the button. We never got to actually fire one. We were told to dig in, and camouflage our positions, and our Sergeant-Major said, 'Your job is to take as long dying as possible, and to take as many Iraqi tanks with you as you can. But, you have to hold out for at least two hours. That will give time for the reinforcements to get up to the Line.'

"Then somebody, I don't remember who, raised his hand, and said, 'Sergeant-Major, I have a question.'

"'OK,' said Shimshon. 'What's the question?'

"'Well,' said the soldier, 'we don't have any dogtags yet. What should we do?'

"And Shimshon looked him, and said, 'take a piece of cardboard, write your name and serial number on it, tie it to a bootlace, put it around your neck, and pray to God you don't burn to death, so your mother will have something to identify your body with.'

"All that night, we prepared, then we went down to the Line, dug in, and tried to camouflage our positions. We had three lines of defense, and the idea was, the minute the Iraqis start to move toward us, get off a shot, then run like hell, with the rest of the rockets, to a second camouflaged position, because the minute you shot, they would bracket you. So, you shoot, run like hell, try to get off another shot, then you run like hell again. And Shimshon said, 'If the man beside you falls, you don't have time to take care of him. You run, and get another shot. And, if the next man falls, you don't have time to take care of him, either. You run, and get off another shot. No matter what happens, you keep firing, you keep fighting. You never stop.'

"And I saw men... Well, not men, boys, pee in their pants, and cry and some of them actually hid, and when Shimshon found them, he said, 'I'll get a jeep and get you out of here,' and a few of them actually left, and the rest of us stayed. And, I tell you Dani, I had no doubt that, the next morning, I would be dead. And, it didn't really frighten me. Not because I'm brave, because I'm not. It was actually kind of... Calm.

Because, everything was so simple. There was absolutely nothing in life to do, except shoot, run like hell, and try to get another shot off. It's all I thought about. That's all I wanted to do. Because, we knew. It wasn't a joke. Our country's fate was on our shoulders. So, we shoot, we run like hell, we cock another one of the *fercocktah* rockets, the iron sight pops up, aim, press the button on top, run like hell. There was nothing more in life. You didn't have to worry about college, girl-friends, grades, marriage... Nothing. All of your life will be lived out by tomorrow morning. And, for some reason, maybe I'm stupid, that seemed calming to me, somehow.

"Now, mind you, I hadn't yet seen a corpse. I hadn't yet seen a body, charred to the bone, still smoking, that a second ago was your friend and now looked like something you'd burned at a barbecue. If I had, I wouldn't have been so calm, I guarantee you."

Amit was quiet again for a long time, and Dani finally had to ask, "And then what happened?"

In a voice, barely above a whisper, Amit said, "It was still dark, and we could smell the Turkish coffee they were beginning to make. We could smell the smoke from their tobacco, and, in that pre-dawn light, we could see them pulling the camouflage netting off their tanks. And then, nothing."

"What do you mean?"

"I mean, nothing! Nothing happened. The sun came up. It was in our eyes. They didn't get into their tanks. They didn't start their engines. We heard their voices. We stayed there for maybe five hours like that, dug into our positions. No one speaks. You can't make a sound, you can't move, because you don't want them to see you. If you have to pee, you pee in your pants. Five hours, maybe six, I don't know. And then, we see them get into their tanks, and we think, 'Okay, here it comes!', they start their engines, and they keep the turrets pointed at us, but the tanks turn around, and they leave. That was it! They were gone. And, an hour later, the word comes down the Line, 'it's over'. Sadat has accepted a cease fire, and with Egypt out of the war, the Syrians have decided to quit, too! In the south the fighting went on a bit, but for us it was over!

"And, a few years later, Kissinger gives an interview, and he explains what happened. He explains why I'm alive, telling you this story today. That night, he calls Sadat. While we're digging in to cam- ouflage our positions, and putting rounds into magazines, and training with rockets, Kissinger is on the phone with Sadat, and says 'Golda Meir', who was Prime Minister of Israel at the time, 'has gone as far as she can go. She is not going to give any more. If you accept a cease fire now, I can preserve your military gains, and you'll begin to get the Sinai back. But, if you don't accept a cease fire, the war will go on, and the Israelis will destroy your Egyptian Third Army, and it'll be a repeat of of the defeat of 1967.' And, Kissinger says, Sadat did the one thing Kissinger never expected of him. Kissinger said, 'Any other leader would have replied, *'let me talk to my advisors, and I'll bet back to you in the morning'.'*

"If he'd done that, then I would be dead. The war would have gone on. The Syrians and Iraqis would have attacked, and I would never have had the great pleasure of being your father, and your mother's husband.

"But with Egypt out of the war, Assad of Syria didn't have any choice. *If Egypt has quit*, he decided, *that's it. The Israelis will transfer forces from Sinai and their Air Force and maybe I'll lose Damascus for my trouble*. So he quit, too. And when he quit, the Iraqis got disgusted and ordered their troops to come home immediately. That's what saved us. That's why I'm alive today and why you're in Israel. Look how life works, huh? You want to know why you're on a *kibbutz* today? Because Anwar Sadat knew how to make a decision."

"And then, a year or so after the war, I got sick. But, because I had faced death once already before, it wasn't a stranger to me. It wasn't a friend, mind you, but the monster in the closet wasn't quite as fero- cious, and I said to myself, 'if the Iraqis couldn't burn me alive, and if this cancer doesn't kill me, I am going to meet the girl of my dreams, and have a family.' And, here you are!"

Less than a year after that conversation, the leukemia came back, and, this time, unlike when the Iraqis were opposite him, and unlike the first bout of leukemia, the Angel of Death did not pass over Amit Kahan's house a third time.

And, a year after that, Dani's mother, Miriam, was killed in a car accident on the highway between Afula and Haifa.

Dani's grandparents wanted him to come home, to Anaheim, but he said, "I'm already home."

And the *kibbutz*, the little farming village of *Ginegar*, arranged a kind of O. Henry miracle. There was a couple who were old enough to be Dani's grandparents, whose only son had been killed in '73, in the Yom Kippur War.

They were parents without a son, and Dani was a son without parents.

And so, at the age of sixteen, Dani had his third family.

Two wonderful people, Chanan and Mimi, who loved him as much as any parents ever loved any child, who lived to see him get married, and have a son of his own, to whom they were *Saba* and *Savta*, Grandma and Grandpa.

And God, in his mercy, spared them the sadness and horror of outliving their nine-year-old grandson.

Both had been lifelong smokers, and both were dead of cancer before they turned sixty-five.

So much sadness, Dani thought, *for such a small country*.

So, the truth was, Israel, the *kibbutz*, and the Army were the only family Dani had, which is why he personally went to Yair Hermesh, the secretary of *Kfar Shimshon*, and told him that the residents would have to close themselves in their safe rooms until they knew there were no further terrorists out there. But, he wanted to promise them, he wanted to make sure that each and every one of them knew, that his soldiers, and all of the soldiers of the Israel Defense Forces, were putting themselves, and their lives between the residents of *Kfar Shimshon*, and those who would do them harm. Because they, and all Israel, were family.

This wasn't Afghanistan, and it wasn't Iraq, and it wasn't Vietnam.

It was no foreign land.

It was their home, and they would defend it with their lives.

Yair Hermesh shook Dani's hand, patted him on the shoulder, and said, "Once the all-clear is given, if any of your boys or girls need a place to shower, or take a nap, or want a hot meal, you know this *kibbutz* is their home, right? If they need their uniforms washed, clean underwear, whatever, we're their home. We're their families."

And Dani remembered a story that Chanan, his third father, had told him.

Chanan was a seventeen-year-old boy in the Jewish Brigade of the British Army in World War Two. The Jewish Brigade was made up of Jewish boys and girls from what was then British Mandatory Palestine.

When WWII ended, the Jewish Agency, the Jewish self government of the still unborn Jewish state, tasked the boys of the Jewish Brigade with going through occupied Europe to find out how many Jews were still alive, because no one yet knew the extent of the catastrophe that was the Holocaust.

They picked four enlisted men, and one officer, a twenty-six-year-old Captain named Hoter Ishai, to go throughout Europe to find out how many of the Jewish people were alive, and how many were dead. Between them, they spoke every language of eastern and western Europe. Chanan was their driver.

They were the first into the concentration camps, and then the DP camps. And because the unit flash on their shoulders was a yellow Star of David against a blue and white Israeli flag, word spread, there were JEWISH SOLDIERS!

For the living-skeleton survivors, this was a miracle. Jews with uniforms and weapons, who could fight to defend themselves, not be slaughtered like sheep. Thousands lined up to kiss the Star of David on their Jeep, and kiss the insignia they wore.

Hoter Ishai got up on the Jeep and addressed them in Yiddish. He said, "We're going to set up tables and each one of these soldiers speaks your language. You need to tell us what village you're from, what city and how many are left alive so we know how to help you."

And one of the camp survivors angrily said, "You're wasting your time! You want to know how many are left? You don't have to set up any tables! I can tell you! No one is left! Only what you see here. No towns, no villages, no cities, no Rabbis or teachers or friends, no mothers, no fathers, no brothers, no families! Nothing! So you have your answer! You can leave now and make your report! No one is left."

And twenty-six-year-old Hoter Ishai said, "You say you have no mothers, no fathers, no sisters or brothers, no families… We are Jewish soldiers from the Land of Israel, and WE will be your mothers and WE will be your fathers and we will be your sisters and your brothers and we will bring you home to *Eretz Yisrael*."

And here it was, almost seventy years later, and Jewish soldiers were now being told by these farmers, whatever you need , WE are YOUR family. We are YOUR mothers and YOUR fathers and YOUR sisters and YOUR brothers. And, we are YOUR home.

"I'll make sure to tell them that," Dani said, turning away suddenly, as if he had some urgent business to attend to, and fighting back his own emotions.

And, too, he knew that this was just the beginning of something awful, not the end.

He knew that this was just one tunnel, and they had others, and they would use them.

He knew Hamas wanted nothing less than what Hitler did, their annihilation.

And, he knew that, by tonight, they would be going into Gaza.

It was exactly what Hamas wanted them to do.

They were waiting for them.

Just like Jenin.

Just like Lebanon.

Just like Yom Kippur, and every other war the Jewish state had to fight simply to stay alive in this tiny patch of land, in what had become, of late, an ever-increasingly Islamist sea.

They'd be going into hell.

CHAPTER 11

I n Jerusalem, Kivi Natanel convened his security cabinet. It consisted of his Defense Minister, Kobi Golan, his Finance Minister, Yaron Kochavi, the Interior Minister, Binyamin "Benny" Dan, his Justice Minister, Ruti Lavi, and the Foreign Minister, Menasheh Leibovitch.

Each one of them wanted to displace Natanel as Prime Minister.

In addition to the members of his government, Lieutenant General Kadosh Mintz, the Chief of Staff, was there, as were Menachem Yizraeli, the head of Shin Bet, Israel's Internal Security Service, Major General Amichai Granot, head of Military Intelligence, and Ephraim *"Froikeh"* Yaffe, head of the Mossad.

The Prime Minister opened the meeting without preliminaries. "Because of this new element, of this terrorist tunnel attack – and the devil only knows how many more of these tunnels they have – there is no choice now, but to launch a full-scale ground incursion into Gaza."

"Finally!" said Benny Dan, throwing his arms out wide, as if, at last, he had been vindicated.

"And this time," shouted Menasheh Leibovitch, "WE CRUSH THEM!" And, for emphasis, the barrel-chested Russian smashed his fist down on the table.

"Menasheh," said Kivi Natanel wearily, "this isn't Russia, you're not Kruschev, and you don't need to bang on the table with your shoe to make your point."

"Who used a shoe?!" said Leibovitch. "Who said anything about shoes!"

"And, it's about time somebody banged a table in one of these meetings," said Benny Dan. "The Arabs only understand one thing, and that's force!"

"And, when we don't use it," said Leibovitch, "they see it as weakness."

"And they're right!" said Benny Dan, pointing his finger at Kivi Natanel.

"Well, what kind of choice have we given them?" Ruti Lavi said. "We had a chance to open negotiations, and we spit in their faces!"

"Nobody spit in their faces," Kivi said.

"We *should* have spit in their faces!" said Leibovitch, banging the table for emphasis once again. "You think Abbas is a 'Partner for Peace'? He's a Partner for Hamas!"

"He's denounced Hamas!" said Ruti Lavi.

"He denounces them out of one side of his mouth," said Benny Dan, "and he praises them out of the other."

"He cut off their money. You can't say he didn't do that," said Yaron Kochavi.

"Oh!" said Leibovitch. "The television commentator finally comments!"

"You want a comment?" said the still telegenic Kochavi. "If we had a Foreign Minister who wasn't an international pariah, we wouldn't be in the shape, diplomatically, that we are in today!"

"It's time to stop talking about diplomacy, and start acting!" Leibovitch shouted.

"The nation's chief diplomat just said 'We should stop talking about diplomacy!'," said Ruti Lavi, looking around the room, as if she were the only sane person left on earth.

"Anybody else have a contribution to make to this colloquium?" Kivi asked.

"Colloquium, shmolloquium!" said Leibovitch. "It's time to crush them once, and for all!"

"And then what?" asked Defense Minister Kobi Golan.

"What do you mean, 'And then what?'" Leibovitch demanded.

"I mean," said Kobi Golan, "and then... What?"

Kobi Golan was a former *kibbutznik*, and a former Chief of Staff, perhaps the most successful Chief of Staff in Israel's history. At first

blush, it would seem that nobody could argue with his military credentials. But, there was a story about a conversation that David Ben Gurion
had with JFK, in which the American President said that Ben Gurion's
job was a relatively simple one, compared to his. Ben Gurion, after all,
was the head of a nation of, at that time, of only two and a half million
people, whereas JFK had to lead a nation of almost 190 million people.

"Yes," said Ben Gurion. "But, all of my two and a half million are
generals."

So, it was now in the meeting of the Israeli Security Cabinet, when
former Lieutenant General, and current Defense Minister Kobi Golan
said, "And then... What?", that Foreign Minister Menasheh Leibovitch,
who had never spent a day in the Army himself, said, "What do you
mean, 'and then what'? Then they'll be dead, that's what! *Kebini maht!*"

"And, when they're dead," asked Kobi Golan, "who will take their
place? ISIS? They're waiting in line. Islamic Jihad? Al Qaeda? You
think any one of them is going to be an improvement over Hamas?"

"*We'll* take their place!" Benny Dan declared.

"We should never have left in the first place!" Leibovitch said, and
Kivi Natanel grabbed his cup of coffee, so that Leibovitch's fist hitting
the table wouldn't cause it to spill once again.

"And then, we'll be stuck in a guerrilla war that will slowly grind
us up for the next ten years. And, by the way, this operation, which
you can't wait to launch, of crushing Hamas, will take us between
six months and a year. House-to-house fighting. Room-to-room. How
many Israeli casualties do we project?" Kobi asked the Chief of Staff,
Kadosh Mintz.

"Thousands," said Lieutenant General Mintz. "Maybe more.
And, that's killed, not killed and wounded. And tens of thousands of
Palestinians."

"And, before we'd finished the operation," said *Froikeh* Yaffe, head
of the Mossad, "The world would force a cease-fire on us. The EU
would impose sanctions, worse than what they had on South Africa,
and we'd lose our closest ally, the United States of America."

"*Pize'domaht!*" Leibovitch mumbled under his breath, "That's
what I say to the EU, and to that Malaysian in the White House."

"Good," said Kivi Natanel, "I see we're all in agreement, then."

He looked around the room at each of them one at a time. "Now, let me tell you what we're going to do. And, anyone who wishes to take a principled stand by resigning from this government is welcome to do so, because I have parties lined up who are willing and eager to take your places. Minister Leibovitch, you think the Labor Party wouldn't be only too happy to have the Foreign Ministry? Minister Dan, you think the religious parties wouldn't jump at the chance to have the Ministry of the Interior? Try me."

The truth was, it was all a formality. The Three Ks – Kivi Natanel, Kobi Golan, and Lieutenant General Kadosh Mintz – had already decided what the country's path would be.

"We will go in with a full ground incursion, but our objectives will be limited. We are not going in to wipe out Hamas, we are going in to deal, first of all, with these terrorist tunnels. Find them, blow them up, destroy them. Second of all, we're going to hit Hamas hard enough, so that they raise a white flag, and they don't even think of attacking us for a period of five, six, seven years."

"That's it?" demanded Benny Dan. "That's what you're going to buy with the blood of our sons? 'Five, six, seven years'?!"

"Yes," said Kivi Natanel, evenly. "With as little of the blood of our sons as can be shed, I want to buy as long a period of quiet as is possible. I want to hit Hamas hard enough so they won't be a military threat to Israel for years, but I want to leave them strong enough to fend off ISIS, or Islamic Jihad, or Al Qaeda."

It's so easy for these back-seat Generals to grandstand, he thought. *None of them has to give the order. None of them has to think about tomorrow, or the day after or the year after or ten years after.* This wasn't about one campaign. It was about the survival of the Jewish State.

"You've set up be a very delicate balancing act," said Yaron Kochavi.

"President Kabila isn't going to give us enough time to accomplish such a nuanced feat," said Ruti Lavi, with as much scorn as she could muster

"We're all cognizant of that, Ruti," said Kivi Natanel. "On the other hand, we're about to do President Kabila a very big favor. We're going to send in the Givati Recon Battalion to do a snatch-and-grab of two of the most dangerous ISIS terrorists in the world. He'll give us a little more time, in exchange for that."

"*Kebini maht,*" muttered Leibovitch.

"And, with that bit of eloquence," said Kivi Natanel, "I believe this meeting of the Security Cabinet is adjourned."

"We're coming with you," said Tera Dayton.

She, Peña, and McKeever were standing opposite Dani Kahan and Washburn at the Givati Assembly Point. Members of the Recon unit were checking equipment, cleaning rifles, loading extra magazines and grenades into their combat vests, and doing all the thousand and one little tasks that combat soldiers do before entering the war zone.

They had time to eat a last meal, and so had broken out combat rations; once again, the cans of tuna and canned corn, stuffed grape leaves, olives, and chocolate spread for bread. Like little kids at school, they vied for the chocolate spread.

The Ethiopian Lieutenant once again took the empty cans of tuna, and filled them with toilet paper, and then lit them, turned them into burners, and made Turkish coffee for his men.

"I said, we're coming with you," Tera repeated to Dani Kahan.

"Actually, you're not. End of discussion," said Dani.

"Uh, look," said McKeever. "We're all part of this operation."

"Every one of us, '*mano,* and you don't pull that military crap on me, 'cause I don't take orders from you."

"Oh, that's where you're wrong... '*Mano,*" said Dani Kahan. "You *do* take orders from me. My ball, my rules. This is for soldiers, not spies, not FBI agents, not DEA guys. Combat soldiers. End of story."

"Actually," said Tera. "We take our orders from the President of the United States of America. And, if you like, we can put in a call to him right now, and then he can put in a call to your Prime Minister, who will, in turn, put in a call to your Chief of Staff, and, my guess is, you will find yourself with a brand new orifice, from which you can blow your particular brand of smoke all day long."

Dani just stared at her.

"Try me," said Tera, not blinking.

"You go, *chica,*" said Peña.

"Do not," Tera said to Peña. "Ever. Call me *'chica'*. Again." Then she turned back to Dani. "Repeat, Major. Try me."

Oh, baby, thought Dani, *you have no idea how much I'd love to try you.*

"Papa," said Dani to Washburn. "You know I'm right, man. These people have never seen anything like what we're gonna be up against when we get in there. All they're gonna do is wind up getting themselves killed, or wind up getting one of us killed."

Washburn looked at Peña, McKeever, and Tera. "I hate to say it... But, he's right," Washburn said.

"I hate to say it, but we're going with you. End of story," said Tera.

"Look," said McKeever, in that Washington, DC, "I'm only here to help" voice, "We've *got* to be a part of this. We've *got* to go in with you."

"Actually, you don't," Dani said.

"Actually, we do," said McKeever.

"*Oye*," said Peña. "Let's say we go in there. There's a firefight. The bad guys get killed. There's intel on the ground that has to do with the cartels. Do you know how to interpret it? Do you know if it's something we need to take with us or leave behind? Do you know what questions to ask if the guy is still alive, and can only answer just one thing? No, you don't. Because, that's not your area of expertise, *'Mano*. That's mine."

"Each one of us has something to contribute, here," McKeever said, smiling that Washington smile.

"Bottom line," Tera said, "We're going in with you. So, check us out some flak jackets, helmets, weapons. The whole deal."

Dani turned to Washburn. "Papa, let's just cut the crap, and order them to stay put? How 'bout it?"

"I can't," said Papa SEAL.

"Of course you can! Just say, 'No deal. That's an order.'"

"No can do, Dani."

"Why not?!" demanded Dani.

"Because," said Force Master Chief Petty Officer Darwin Washburn, "I'm not in command."

"You're kidding me! Well, then, who is?" said Dani, looking from one to the other.

"No one," said Tera.

"Kabila Theorem," said Washburn. "If no one is in charge, no one can make a decision."

Dani just scratched his head. "Turgeman!" Dani shouted out to his regimental Sergeant-Major.

Rafi Turgeman was every inch the Combat Regimental Sergeant-Major. He was the guy who gets things done. In Hebrew, Dani said, "Check these tourists out with helmets, combat vests, M4's, and uniforms."

"Is this a joke?"

"Not a funny one. They're our gift from the President of the United States."

Dani turned back to Tera, Peña and McKeever. "This will be urban warfare. 360 degree warfare. You got a ticket to ride? Fair enough. You're gonna ride. But, I'm not about to risk any one of my men to save you. And, if the President of the United States doesn't like that, he can check out a helmet, a combat vest and a weapon, and hump a sixty pound pack, and then we can talk about it.

"No one's going to need to save us," said Tera.

"Every one of us has been in a gunfight," Peña said.

"This isn't gonna be a gunfight. You're gonna wish it was. Just, stay low, follow my commands, and do not get in the way. Whether you get killed, or not, is none of my business."

Dani turned to walk away.

Tera, ever the practical one, said, "We don't have any dogtags. Can you get us some?"

"Take a piece of cardboard," Dani said. "Put your name on it, put it on a bootlace, and put it around your neck. Then, pray to God you don't burn to death, so there's something for your mother to identify."

"I don't have a mother," Tera said, jutting her jaw out at him. "My parents are both dead."

"No problem, then." said Dani, "Forget the cardboard."

CHAPTER 12

A t 20:45 hours that night, Colonel Moti Dagan came on the Brigade radio net, addressing the soldiers and commanders of the Givati Brigade.

"We have been granted a great privilege to serve, in this Brigade, at this time. History has chosen us to be on the cuting edge of the war against the Terrorist enemy. As it says in the Book of Joshua, chapter thirteen, verse three, this is 'The one of Gaza who curses and defames the God of Israel.' Let us prepare ourselves for this moment, when we accept this mission with a sense of urgency and complete humility, and with a readiness to put ourselves in danger, or give up our lives, if need be, to protect our families, our homes and our nation.

"Let us do everything we can to fulfill our mission, to cut the enemy down, and remove the terror from the people of Israel. Our credo is, 'We do not return before the mission is complete.' But know as well that we will do everything humanly possible, utilize every means at our disposal, and expend every effort required, in order to bring each and every one of you home in peace...

"I am relying on each of you to do your duty in the spirit of the Jewish warriors who came before us, in the time of our forefathers. I lift up my eyes to the heavens, and say with you, *Shema Yisrael Adoshem Elokeinu, Adoshem Echad*!" May the Lord God of Israel bring success in our mission!

"In the name of the fighters of the Israel Defense Force and the warriors of the Givati Brigade, know that, as the Bible says, 'The Lord your God goes out with you to do battle with your enemies for you, and to save you.' And let us say Amen!"

After that, Israel opened up the gates of hell.

And so did Hamas.

The Israel Defense Force hit Hamas with a barrage from a dozen batteries of M-109A5 155mm howitzers, scores of Merkava IV tanks firing 120mm cannon, and air and naval strikes.

Hamas answered back with Qassam, Grad, Fajr 5 and M75, short, medium, and long-range rockets, and 120mm mortars. Everything that everybody had, they threw at one another in a belching orgy of violence that lit up the sky in orange bursts of flame and thunder, that shook the ground as if it was one huge volcano about to erupt, in the midst of an earthquake and storm of brimstone.

Dani thought of the song *Fire and Rain,* and thought, *Oh Sweet Baby James, you child, you demented, poor precocious child. You've seen nothing, if you were not here tonight.* All the normal trappings of civilization are loosened on such a night. Any pretense at humanity is stripped away. Thunder and fire, flame and white-hot, murderous steel are the only languages belched across the night-time sky, as men in machines, and men waiting for them in tunnels, did everything humanly possible to kill one another, to rip each other's bodies apart, to burn their flesh, incinerate and tear them limb from limb. There are no beasts so vicious as war. No animals so ferocious. No maniac so insane.

The Israelis used artillery and air strikes to get the enemy to keep his head down.

But this time, Hamas' head was not only down, it was underground.

They were ghosts.

They had learned from Hezbollah and Iran and the North Koreans. And they had been attentive students.

An attacking force advances, hoping to overwhelm.

Hamas, underground, was invisible, waiting to devour.

The battlefield was theirs, meticulously planned for this night of murder. If they had been cheated out of part of their Divine Victory during the afternoon, they would reclaim it all, in the night.

For five years they had dug not only a network of terrorist attack tunnels leading into Israel, but a network of tunnels *within* Gaza, meant to chew up the advancing Israeli forces.

185

Once the Israelis entered the *Sha'jaiya* neighborhood, every street, every alleyway, was booby trapped, coiled like a snake and ready to strke.

The Hamas fighters were in underground tunnels. Through periscopes, or with lookouts, they would watch the advancing Israelis. Each hundred meters or so, there was a different waypoint, which was numbered, with an IED buried beneath the road, or burrowed into the wall of a building. Sometimes, there were both. When a tank or Armored Personnel Carrier passed waypoint number one, a Hamas fighter in an underground tunnel, touched a wire to a control board and detonated the IED at waypoint number one.

Then, another team would pop up from another tunnel and fire RPG2s or Sagger anti-tank missiles.

Yet another team would be standing by to pop up from yet another tunnel, machine guns blazing, to kill and kidnap whatever flaming soul emerged from the fiery deathtrap they had just created.

That was the plan.

The Israeli plan was no less brutal. Lay down a curtain of fire, meant to keep them in their tunnels as you advance, and, when they pop up, spot them with the drone you have flying overhead, providing real-time intel to each advancing unit before the Hamasniks fire, and then take them out with machine gun or cannon fire.

The entire invading Israeli force had one objective. Find the tunnels and blow them up, and hit Hamas so hard they would not be a military threat for another year, or two, or six, if they were lucky.

No one had any illusions. There were no wars to end all wars for Israel.

Hamas could publicly commit itself to a war of annihilation, in fact, of genocide.

It was, indeed, what the world expected, from Hamas and ISIS, Al Qaeda, and Hezbollah.

Israel, on the other hand had to observe the "Rules of Warfare", and then some. They went to lengths no other Western army had ever imagined. They dropped leaflets, warning residents to flee. They literally phoned and sent text messages, saying, "Run for your lives, the Israel Defense Forces are coming."

Israel, at least, had to pretend to blush in the presence of the naked pornography of war.

But there was one tiny Israeli force that had a totally different objective than all the others.

They were to make their way to number 37 Street of the Martyr, in the southeast section of *Sha'jaiya*, and snatch-and-grab two high-value ISIS terrorists, at the behest of the President of the United States of America.

Dani, Washburn, McKeever, Peña, and Tera were crammed into an Israeli Nagmachon Armored Personnel Carrier. It was a heavy, rumbling beast built on a British Centurion Tank chassis. It had no real firepower. Just a couple MAG 7.62 machine guns and mounts and ports for personal weapons. But, what it lacked in firepower, it made up for in underbelly and side armor. It wasn't impervious to IEDs or anti-tank missiles, but pretty darn close. In addition, it had a raised superstructure - almost like the wheelhouse of a tug boat – except, it was armor-plated, and had bulletproof windows that provided close to a 360-degree view. The superstructure was called "The Doghouse", and the commander of the vehicle, and Dani, stood up in it now. Dani piloted the way from the briefing maps, and GPS coordinates, and satellite photos, as well as the ongoing intel from the Heron drone overhead, that would accompany them throughout the entire operation.

In his map and battle plan carrier, there was an aerial photo of the *Sha'jaiya* neighborhood. On top of that was a clear plastic overlay, which showed the known, and suspected, Hamas positions. There was a second clear plastic overlay on top of that, which showed the route they would take to their target, as well as possible alternate routes should their way be blocked. In addition, each Israeli unit's area of operation was clearly marked as well, to avoid friendly fire casualties.

Most importantly, they had real-time intelligence that said the two terrorists had been seen going into the house at number 37 Street of the Martyr. Of course, that real-time intelligence came from a Palestinian, who just as easily could have been luring Dani and the team into a death trap. There was always that chance.

Peña, Washburn, McKeever, and Tera were stuffed down into the belly of the beast with the ten-man Givati crew. The Nagmachon was only built for a ten-man crew, plus driver and commander. But

Dani was unwilling to lose four Givati soldiers to make room for the Americans. So, they laid atop one another, unable to move, jammed up against the soldiers in their ceramic body armor, helmets, tactical vests, radios, with their weapons slung across their shoulders... It was boiling hot, and smelled of sweat and fear and diesel and grease. Tera was doing everything humanly possible to keep from throwing up, from screaming, from throwing off her helmet and begging them to go back, get her out, not away from the Hamas machine gun-fire and rockets that exploded into the sides of their armor, but from the pressed-up flesh, pushing in against her, throwing her into a panic.

When you are in the belly of such a beast, you are in a sensory deprivation chamber. Except, instead of quiet, it is deafening. There is the roar of the engine, and the treads ripping into asphalt, the enemy machine gun fire pinging into armor, the thunderous explosion of RPG rounds that make you think the next one will burn you alive. The sounds of mortars and rockets, machine guns and cannon all around. The monster of war, Moloch, devouring its children, that makes you want, more than anything, for the rear gate to be lowered, for hatches to be opened, so you can escape into... Into what? The machine gun-fire that will rip you to shreds? So you sit in the rumbling beast, in the dark, smelling sweat and diesel and grease and gunpowder and fear, jostling inside, like Jonah in an iron, earthbound whale, doing penance for defying a vengeful God.

Leading the way, just in front of them, was a D9 bulldozer, meant to detonate mines and widen the alleyway. Coming up behind them were two Merkava IV tanks, each with their 120mm cannon and 12.7mm machine guns.

As they roared up the Street of the Martyr, twenty-six-year-old Abdul Hakim Ashrawi popped up and watched them rip their way up to waypoint twenty-seven, which corresponded to node twenty-seven on his control board. He knew about the underbelly armor of the Nagmachon, and knew how heavy the D9 bulldozer was, and how formidable the steel on the Merkava IV.

Then he saw a juicy piece of low-hanging fruit.

The distance between the D9 and Nagmachon carrying the American and Givati raiding party had widened, when, suddenly out of a side street named for Leila Khaled, an M113 Armored Personal Carrier appeared.

Its crew was lost.

In the smoke, and fire, and thunder, and ash of battle, they had gotten separated from the rest of their unit. They had sped through the alleyway, knowing they were well and truly screwed, alone in Hamastan, cut off from the protection of their own armor in a fifty year old piece of crap APC that the Israeli army should never have allowed to go into battle. And the truth was, it wasn't supposed to go into battle. It was just there for them to train on. They were supposed to get the newer and heavier Achzarit, which was supposed to be delivered tomorrow. This was just there for the training exercises, not the real thing!

And then the tunnel attack happened, and suddenly this was the real thing, and they sent them into battle in a fifty-year-old sardine can on wheels, with Vietnam-era armor, facing 2014 anti-tank weaponry.

Their commander, twenty-one-year-old Ziv Harari, felt the same horrific panic every soldier knows at least some time in their combat career... "I don't know where the hell we are! Where the hell are we, man?!" Of course, as commander of the eight-man crew, he couldn't say that. He couldn't show fear, lest it spread like SARS through his men, so he said to his driver, Aviv Abutbul, "Go! Go, Aviv! Full gas! Get us out of here."

Thus, when he saw the reassuring sight of the giant D9, and the Nagmachon, and two big nasty Merkava IV's, it was like a little kid finding his big brothers after being separated from his mother. He saw the space between the D9 and the Nagmachon, and told Aviv, "Go! Go!" and squeezed in between the big boys, safe once again amongst his own.

And then his engine stalled.

And the fifty-year-old junker M113 chugged to a halt, blocking the way of the Nagmachon, and separating it from the D9.

Because Dani and his force were on a separate radio channel, they couldn't communicate. And now they were stuck on the Street of the Martyr, and all of them were sitting ducks... Right there at waypoint twenty-seven. Right where Abdul Hakim Ashrawi wanted them.

Aviv was a good mechanic, as well as driver. They had already experienced a stalled engine tonight, and Aviv had gotten them back up and running, so Ziv said, "*Yallah*, let's go! I'll cover you." And he and Aviv popped the hatch and scrambled down to the engine compartment. Aviv had his Micro-Tavor at the ready, pointing all around.

In the Nagmachon, Dani was going nuts. "What is this kid doing? He's going to get us all killed!"

He motioned frantically for Aviv and Ziv to get out of the way, and turned to Allon, the young Givati Lieutenant, commander of the Nagmachon force, and pulled rank.

"Ram 'em!" he said. "Push them out of the way!"

And that's when Abdul Hakim Ashrawi touched node number twenty-seven on his control board. The explosion ripped up through the Street of the Martyr, and threw the M113 into the air, and that's when the RPG team led by twenty-two-year-old Adnan Fakhoury fired the RPG2 into the side of the M113 Armored Personnel Carrier, finishing it off, as it burst into flames.

Dani saw him, and fired the MAG machine gun that literally ripped Adnan in two, left his torso dangling outside of the tunnel. They could hear the men screaming in the M113, as they burned to death, and Aviv and Ziv were on fire now, too.

Allon gave the order to two of his men, Eytan and Davidi, to go out and rescue the two men in flames. They popped the top hatch and scrambled down the side of the Nagmachon, as Dani covered them with the MAG.

Dani watched as Aviv ran. His clothes were now burned off him. He was naked, except for his boots and belt, and his skin was charred and hung in black strips from his arms.

Ziv took his own weapon and shot himself through the head to end his agony.

Eytan and Davidi tackled Aviv and threw him to the ground, extinguishing his body that smoked like something foul which had fallen into a cook fire. He was screaming for them to kill him.

Davidi, who was a medic, shot Aviv full of morphine, but he continued to scream.

Dani got on the radio with the D9, and told him to throw it into reverse and push the burning APC out of the way. There was nothing to be done for the men burning to death, or already dead inside.

And then the Hamasniks poured out of one of the buildings, two houses down, on the Street of the Martyr.

Like jackals, they were after body parts to kidnap, and later bargain for. Others were readying RPGs to fire at the Nagmachon, and trying to cut down the two Givati kids who were carrying the charred, but still-living, thing that just before had been a rock star-handsome young boy, back to their Armored Personnel Carrier. Dani opened up with the MAG, and one of the Merkavas pulled out enough to open up with its 12.7mm coaxial machine gun. They cut the Hamasniks down. But more were coming down the street, smelling blood. The Merkava fired an anti-personnel shell into them, turning them into charred pieces of ripped-up meat, as well. The D9 flattened a house on the left side of the Street of the Martyr, in order to turn around and push the burning APC out of the way.

The two Givati soldiers came back in, lowering the still-smoking body of Aviv Abutbul, whose skin hung off him like charred beef jerky, who cried out for his mother, begged them to kill him, pleaded for death, and the blackened remains of Ziv Harari, who had ended his own agony with a bullet to his brain, as Allon told them to button up, closing the smell of burning flesh into their iron tomb on wheels, and Tera vomited and then so did one of the Givati boys, adding that to the smell as Allon put it in gear, and they followed the D9 out of this alley, strewn with smoking corpses, so alike one another in death.

"What was this for?" Allon said, to no one in particular.

And, as they pulled clear of the burnt-out APC and the smoking, charred, and eviscerated bodies of the Hamasniks, some of whom they simply rolled over and flattened into the asphalt, there at the next corner, they saw number thirty-seven .

"That's it!" Dani said.

Allon gave the command to stop. They were roughly fifty meters from the cinderblock structure. They pulled up short, so the noise of the tanks wouldn't warn the terrorists inside and give them a chance to escape.

Allon didn't look at Dani. He hated him and his Americans. What they were doing tonight had nothing to do with Israel's fight. This was a favor for America, and his guys were dying for it, and he hated it, and them, and Dani didn't blame him a bit.

"Let's open it up and go," Dani said, and Allon gave the command and the hatches opened, as Aviv stopped crying for his mother and died in the arms of nineteen-year-old medic Davidi Ninio, who, up until that moment, had never even seen an animal die, let alone held the still-smoking remains of the person he didn't recognize as his own grade school friend, Aviv.

They popped the hatches, and Washburn led, like the warrior he was, followed by Peña, McKeever, and Tera, and the ten-man Givati combat team, and Dani. They formed up behind the armored protection of the Nagmachon on one side and the Merkava IVs behind them. Allon's job was to get them there, but once they arrived within striking distance of 37 Street of the Martyr, it was Dani's operation.

He came out carrying a frame charge, and gave the order to advance on foot, after him. Israeli officers lead from the front. That's why a lot of them get killed. It's also why their men follow them so readily. They hugged the walls of the apartment building for protection, while dashing toward their target, each man checking the rooftops for snipers, weapons constantly turning this way and that for possible threats, until they could put the frame charge in place.

The frame charge was an explosive device you stuck on a wall. It was packed with C4 and rigged to explode inward, opening up a hole in a cinderblock wall, as neat as could be.

Their intel was so good they knew the apartment was a two room affair, one of whose walls was the exterior wall of the apartment block.

Dani divided the combat team into two five-man squads, augmented by Washburn with one squad, and himself with the other. He regarded Peña, Tera, and McKeever as obstacles, rather than augmentation.

He turned to them and said, "You three come in at the end of the stack with my team... Stay low. Do not fire, and do not get in the way. Your job starts once we have the bad guys neutralized. Understood?"

Peña, McKeever, and Tera nodded. Tera was at the end of the stack, and looked as if she were in a daze, as if she were a glue sniffer, zoned out.

"Can you function?" Dani demanded, instead of asking, "Are you all right?"

She vomited again and then nodded.

"I need to hear it," Dani said. "Do you understand what I told you? Rear of the stack."

"Rear of the stack," Tera repeated, wiping the bile away from her mouth with the back of her sleeve.

"No fire. Don't get in the way," Dani said, looking at her eyes, trying to ascertain whether or not he should send her back into the Nagmachon.

"No fire. Don't get in the way," Tera said. She nodded and swallowed, and said, "Copy."

The plan was that the D9, which was already maneuvering its way to charge the door of number thirty-seven, would, on Dani's signal, ram the front door at an angle, with the blade of the dozer. If the door was booby trapped it wouldn't even put a nick in the giant D9.

Stack A, under a young sergeant called Kooshi, or Blackie, because of his Yemenite, dark skin, would bust in with dynamic entry technique. Kooshi would toss in a flash-bang grenade to disorient whoever was in the front room.

At the same time Dani's Stack B squad leader, a Druze Arab named Rafi, would detonate the frame charge, blowing open a hole in the cinderblock wall. Dani would toss in a flash-bang grenade to disorient whoever was in the back room. Dynamic entry; first guy; left, second; right, third; left, fourth; right, and so on, until the room was cleared and the bad guys no longer posed a threat.

He had drilled into their heads that neither stack was to enter the room of the other. The biggest danger was that, with the adrenaline pumping, they would start shooting one another, mistaking them for the bad guys.

Stack A took the front room.

Stack B took the rear.

If the bad guys were in one room, and attempted to flee into the other, the second stack would neutralize them.

They needed these guys alive.

Each Stack had a marksman with tasers ready.

Only as a last resort were they to use lethal force. The point wasn't to eliminate the bad guys, but to interrogate them.

The Heron drone circled overhead, sending back live pictures of the operation to the forward command post.

Dani set the C4 frame charge on the outside wall of where he judged the second room to be.

The D9 was lined up at an angle, ready to charge and bust open the front door.

Both stacks were ready, waiting for Dani's command.

Suddenly, from the rear of the building, a veiled woman came running toward the back of the stack.

"Allahu Akhbar!" she shouted, but before she could depress the red button in her hand, Tera raised her M4 instinctively, and fired off a long burst, splitting the woman's head open, exposing and spattering her brains onto the walls of the building.

"So much for the element of surprise," Dani muttered.

He signaled the D9, and signaled Rafi to detonate the frame charge.

All his men, McKeever, Peña, and Tera flattened themselves along the wall, waiting for the explosion. Tera could not stop looking at the woman with the blown-open forehead, and brains spilling onto the recessed section of street usually intended for donkey urine.

The D9 raced forward and slammed its blade into the door, bursting it off it's hinges and then quickly jammed into reverse to let Stack A do its thing.

The frame charge, with a deafening roar, blew a hole in the cinderblock wall of the apartment house.

Kooshi tossed his flash-bang grenade through the door frame, and Dani tossed his in through the newly blown open, still smoking, hole in the wall...

Both seemed to explode at once, blinding light splashing from both entryways, jarring Tera out of her reverie.

Without the need for any order from Dani, both Stacks pushed their way into their respective rooms.

The bad guys were in the rear room.

Dani recognized Kawasme from his photos.

The other man in the room would turn out to be a Hamas operative named Daoud Abu Shukri. Kawasme had not reached his weapon, an AK 47 leaning up against the wall, but Abu Shukri had his Kalashnikov up, and, still blinded by the flash-bang grenade, he began firing wildly, spraying bullets everywhere. Dani and Rafi fired at the same time, both hitting center mass, and dropped him where he stood.

Opher, the marksman with the taser, was about to shoot the darts into Kawasme's body, when Rafi shouted at Kawasme, in Arabic, *"Arini yadaik!* Show me your hands!"

"Yallah!" Dani commanded.

Kawasme was shaking the cobwebs out, and his vision was returning to normal. He raised his hands, and opened his palms, and showed them to the Israelis, while Opher kept the taser on the ISIS terrorist.

Rafi crossed to the opening of the first room and shouted out, "Clear!"

The first Stack, per the operational plan, took up defensive positions outside, while Dani and Washburn aimed their weapons at Kawasme, red laser dots dancing on his forehead.

"Check if he's dead," Dani said to Rafi, referring to Abu Shukri. Then, he and the others began checking for booby traps. They pulled cans of Silly String out of their combat vests, and began spraying them through the room to reveal any trip-wires that had been strung to detonate booby traps upon them. The string hung in mid-air at head level. They found both trip-wires immediately.

This was work for professionals. Slow and methodical. Except, they had no time to be slow today. The jackals were out there, and, in a matter of moments, they could be facing a hundred Hamasniks springing up from tunnels all around, and, indeed, beneath, them.

Dani ordered Kawasme to strip, telling him to use his left hand to unbutton his clothes, and drop them to the floor.

Once the Givati soldiers finished clearing the room for booby traps, Washburn, Tera, Peña, and McKeever would begin searching the room for documents. Already, Tera had spotted a laptop in a rucksack against the wall.

"Don't touch it, 'til it's checked for booby traps," Dani ordered.

"Got it," Tera answered.

They had decided, back at the Givati base, that once Kawasme was naked, they would put a loose robe and a hood on him, and handcuff him. Then they would hustle him back out to the Nagmachon so they could all get out of Dodge. McKeever said that he would cuff him and hood him. "Done it a thousand times," he said.

Perhaps, in retrospect, it was because McKeever had made a career of covering things up, and now he was operational, that he immediately volunteered to cuff Kawasme and hood him. He wasn't the sleazy go-to guy protecting the Bureau's posterior any more, lying about plane crashes off Long Island. He was operational. He was in the field. He would cuff him and hood him. Done it a thousand times.

Dani had agreed. It was more important to have the Givati fighters ready to fight, than messing about with hoods and handcuffs. At least McKeever could be useful.

Kawasme dropped his clothes.

"Underwear, too," Dani said in Arabic. Something was gnawing at him. Something he had forgotten to do.

Tera didn't avert her eyes. She kept her weapon trained on Kawasme, and toyed with the idea of pulling the trigger. She wouldn't give in to the urge, but the thought of it pleased her. He reminded her of the men who had brutalized her in the fragrant orchards of Baluchistan. So she indulged the thought of squeezing off a round into his stomach for a moment. She traced with her assault rifle sight, down his torso, until she noticed the fresh scar that ran across his abdomen, as McKeever crossed over to cuff him, and Dani remembered what it was he'd forgotten. He'd told Rafi to check and make sure the other terrorist was really dead, but he hadn't actually seen him do it.

"What's that scar on his stomach?" Tera said.

Dani saw, for the first time, what he had been looking at for the past few seconds without its importance registering in his brain; the newly cut scar that ran across Khaled Kawasme's midsection. Then he glanced over at the dead terrorist on the floor.

Too late.

The dead terrorist Rafi was supposed to check was still alive, and his hand held a cell phone, and pressed send.

"Down!" Dani shouted, and threw Tera to the ground, covering her body with his, as the grenade-sized charge, which had been surgically implanted in Khaled Kawasme's stomach cavity only three weeks before, exploded, blowing Kawasme's body apart at the abdomen. It killed McKeever on the spot, and sent a piece of shrapnel straight into Rafi's neck.

Dani rolled and shot Daoud, as did Washburn.

Too late. Too late. Too late.

"*Chovesh!*" Dani called out for the medic, who came running back into the room of carnage, sprayed with intestines and blood.

Davidi, the medic, looked at McKeever and Rafi. He and Rafi had become as close as brothers. He had gone many times with Rafi to his village of Isifiyah on Mount Carmel, above Haifa. Rafi's mother treated Davidi as if he were her own son and pampered him, and made them feasts of *sinyeh*, *tabouleh*, and *sambusak*. And here his friend was, clutching his throat, his windpipe and carotid artery severed, blood spouting as if from a hose with each heartbeat that bled his life away in his friend's arms.

Washburn turned McKeever over, and saw the shrapnel that had gone through the FBI agent's eye, penetrating his brain and killing him instantly.

Dani pulled his camera out of his cargo pants' side pocket, and took pictures of Kawasme and the dead Hamas terrorist who had detonated the IED in Kawasme's stomach. Very carefully, he searched the rucksack for booby traps, and removed the laptop computer, and checked it for booby traps, too. There were notebooks, and a map showing what looked like the location and layout out of part of a tunnel network. He snatched those up, as well.

Tera and Peña, after the shock of McKeever's death were functioning, and searching the room, as Dani urged them on.

"We've got to finish up and get out of here."

"Tell me about it, *'mano*," Peña muttered. Dani had been right. This wasn't any gunfight.

They took McKeever's body, and Rafi's, the rucksack, laptop, notebooks and maps, and the Hamasnik's cell phone, and, as the Givati combat team covered them, they made their way out into the street.

At 12:50 that same morning, Abdul Aziz Al-Tikriti boarded Air Canada's flight 6511, from Cairo International Airport. He had new paperwork identifying himself as Achmed Ali Tibi, an Egyptian businessman. It would be a long journey. From Cairo International to Heathrow, and from Heathrow to Toronto, and from thence to Benito Juarez Airport in Mexico City. But he was flying first class, and they had those wonderful seats that flattened into beds.

CHAPTER 13

Failure in any endeavor leaves a bitter taste.

But nothing, save causing the death of your own child, is as bitter as failure in war. Because your troops are your brothers, and if your foul-up got them killed, you nail yourself to a cross from which there is no deliverance, and no resurrection.

Dani was mentally pounding the last of the nails through his palms, in his own private crucifixion.

He had told Rafi to check on the terrorist to make sure he was dead. But he never checked to make sure Rafi did it.

Rafi was a kid. Dani was the supposed adult. It was probably Rafi's first time in war. It was Dani's fourth. He should have watched him, asked him, demanded a verbal confirmation.

Did you check him?

Yes, I checked him.

Did you check for a pulse?

Yes.

And was there a pulse?

No.

You sure? Are you sure... Because lives are going to depend on that one act, maybe your own.

Dani had a dear friend, one of Israel's first pilots, a man who, in fact, had saved the newborn state, in 1948, by leading the first attack of the Israeli Air Force against a ten-thousand-man Egyptian armored column that was a mere hour and a half drive out of Tel Aviv. But for Lou Lenart, and his three fellow pilots, that armored column would have invaded Tel Aviv the next day. There would have been a slaughter, and the State of Israel, and the dream of two millennia, would have been dead.

Lou had been a Marine fighter pilot, in the Pacific, in WWII. Before that he had been a grunt, island-hopping with the Marines, going up against the Japanese, in some of the most vicious fighting of the war. He referred to Dani as "The Younger Brother". And he told Dani that, when it came to the Japanese, they always put "an insurance round" into the guy's brain, just to make sure.

Dani had heard that story a dozen times. So why didn't he check when he told Rafi to see if the guy was really dead? Why didn't he check? Why didn't he say, "Did you do it? Did you check for a pulse?"

And why hadn't that scar on Kawasme's stomach registered with him earlier? He was looking right at it.

And why did he leave the space between the Nagmachon and the D9, that let the kids in the M113 squeeze in between them, and get blown to pieces, and burned alive?

All his fault. Every bit of it.

It was his mission.

Get Al-Tikriti and Kawasme.

Get them alive, and interrogate them.

And bring your guys home safely... In peace. That was the Hebrew phrase, to return in peace, whole, complete and in peace. It was part of the Givati mission statement, that Moti Dagan drummed into his officers' heads.

Dani knew it. And he failed.

He had let Al-Tikriti get away and Kawasme had killed Rafi and McKeever and himself. Everything about it was a a total failure. Ten people dead, and for what? Two dead terrorists, a few notebooks, a map, a laptop, and a cell phone. Ten people dead. All his fault. Every bit of it.

Keep your mind on the job, he told himself. *It isn't over yet. Not by a long shot.*

He took three soldiers, and loaded the bodies of McKeever and Rafi into the last Merkava IV tank.

There was no room left in the Nagmachon.

Or maybe he didn't have the guts to ride with them, staring up at him, accusing with dead eyes.

Then he took what was left of his unit.

Stack A goes into the Nagmachon first, then Peña, Washburn, and Tera. Then Stack B.

He'd be second to last in, and then Kooshi, the Stack B squad leader, would button it up.

Then once he knew for certain he hadn't left anyone behind, he'd get back up into the doghouse superstructure of the Nagmachon, and get them out of here. Get them back through Gaza, through IEDs and RPGs and ambushes and booby traps, back into Israel, and maybe if they were lucky, no one else would choke to death on their own blood tonight, or be burnt alive.

Stack A was in.

He saw Allon looking down at him, asking Davidi what had happened. Saw Allon shake his head and curse at the mention of Rafi's death. Saw Allon look at him, and knew the kid wished him dead, instead of his friend, just as Dani wished himself dead, as well, but couldn't afford the luxury. Not yet. Not 'til they were all out.

Washburn, Peña, and Tera were in.

No one looked at him.

No one spoke.

No one had to.

They had failed.

Dani had failed. Again.

McKeever and Rafi and the eight kids in the M113 were dead because of it.

Stack B! Dani counted them off and walked around to the other side of the Nagmachon, just to make sure, even though he'd counted, just to make sure no one was still outside. Kooshi was up top, standing next to the hatch, and Dani was on the other side of the armored personnel carrier, when suddenly he heard Kooshi shout out in agony, *"Shema Yisrael, Adoshem Elokeinu, Adoshem Echad!"* This was the foundational prayer of Judaism. It was also what one said before one died. Dani raced around the Nagmachon, just in time to see Kooshi leap down on top of a Palestinian woman, who held a suicide vest detonator in her hand. Dani couldn't get a clear shot, because Kooshi was on top of her, pinning her hand to the ground. But the woman didn't struggle. She was trembling, crying and then she said, *"Ani Yehudia!"*

"I'm a Jew!"

"Rawini ediki!" Dani said in Arabic, "Let me see your hands!"

She showed her hands palms up and said, *"Ani Yehudia. Ani Midaberet Ivrit."*

"I'm a Jew. I speak Hebrew!"

"Tera!" Dani called out.

Tera popped up out of the hatch, as Dani brought the woman to her feet.

He asked the woman, in Arabic, what her name was, and she answered again, in Hebrew, and said, "My name is Miriam,. I'm a Jew. I'm an Israeli."

By now, Allon had popped his head out as well, and wanted to know what the hell was going on?! They were sitting ducks out here! How many more of his men did Dani intend to kill?!

Dani pushed the woman, who had said her name was Miriam back into the house of death they'd just left. Kooshi followed, and said, "I saw her with the detonator and my gun jammed. I knew I was going to die, and I started praying the *Shema*, and all of a sudden she starts trembling, you know, like she saw a ghost. She didn't fight against me."

"Tera," Dani said, "Get in here, and strip her."

Tera could see that the woman was shaking, just as she too had been shaking, after being defiled again and again in Queta.

"Shu Ismik," she asked in Arabic, "What's your name?"

"Min Fadlak," the woman who called herself Miriam answered in Arabic, "Please." That's all she said, just "please". And Tera remembered when she, too had, only been able to utter that one word, "Please... Please."

"Take the suicide vest off her. Slowly and carefully," Dani said to Tera. He and Kooshi both had their weapons trained on the failed female suicide bomber, the red dots from their laser sights slow-dancing on her forehead.

"I know how to do it," Tera said. "I've done it before."

"Yeah," said Dani. "That's what McKeever said."

Slowly and expertly, and not without a great deal of kindness, Tera removed the suicide vest from the terrified, trembling girl, while Dani kept his weapon trained on that spot right between her eyes.

"So you're Israeli?" Dani demanded in Hebrew.

"*Ken,*" she said, "Yes."

"Okay, where from in Israel?"

The girl stopped, as if trying to put together pieces of a puzzle in her mind, which had all been scattered a long time ago. Instead of answering Dani, she said, as if in a daze, "He was saying the *Shema*... My father used to have me recite the *Shema* at night when I was a little girl. I haven't heard it since..."

"I asked you a question!" Dani demanded, in Hebrew.

"She's trembling," Tera said, putting her hand on the girl's shoulder.

"She just tried to kill us. Let her tremble."

Then, Dani said again, in Hebrew, "Where from in Israel?"

Miriam tried to focus, tried to dredge up a long forgotten name, and finally said, "Afula."

"*Aht mi Afula?*" Dani asked. "You're from Afula?"

"Yes," Miriam said, almost excited that she could remember the name, excited at the memories that started to flood in on her.

"And what do they have," Dani asked, "in Afula, that they're famous for? What do they have there that's better than any other place in Israel?"

The girl who called herself Miriam looked around, almost in a panic, and then smiled and laughed as she remembered, "Sunflower seeds!" she cried out, "Sunflower seeds! The best! Everyone bought sunflower seeds, near the old bus station, and there was a falafel place, where the guy flipped the falafel balls up into the air and did tricks. I remember, when I was a little girl. It was something... Golani... Something."

"Mifgash Golani!" Kooshi said. "I know the place. Mifgash Golani!"

"Yes!" Miriam said, like a child winning a spelling bee, "Mifgash Golani, and it was near the place where they had sunflower seeds and nuts and... I remember it!" Miriam broke down crying, tears of joy, and relief, and exaltation at the memory of a home she'd long kept buried.

"What's she saying?" Tera asked, "What's going on?"

"She is Jew," Kooshi said in wonder, and began to tear up, "She hear me praying the Jewish prayer, and that what saved my life... That prayer. She recognize it."

"Praise Jesus!" Tera said, fighting back her own tears.

Inside the Nagmachon, they had covered the charred remains of the two dead Givati soldiers from the M113 with blankets. McKeever's and Rafi's bodies were in one of the Merkava IVs, but the stench in the Nagmachon was overwhelming.

Miriam gasped for breath, and Tera kept her arm around her, comforting her as if she were her sister, as if she were her child.

Dani rode up top in the doghouse, next to Allon, as the D9 led the way out of the hell that was Gaza. Dani maneuvered them out of the *Sha'jaiya* neighborhood as quickly as possible, and back out into open farm country. The streets and alleyways were the death traps.

Crossing the fields, they still had to contend with a mortar round or two being fired at them, and there were two more RPG rounds, but the armor of the Nagmachon did its job.

Miriam whimpered and jumped with every thunderous explosion that hit them, and Tera held her tighter.

Peña, who was sitting next to her, could hear Tera singing softly to the terrified girl, "Hush little baby, don't say a word, mama's gonna buy you a mockingbird, and if that mockingbird don't sing, mama's gonna buy you a diamond ring..."

Peña found himself unconsciously humming along with it.

Kooshi looked over at the hastily-covered bodies, that hid the burnt offerings, which only a few moments ago were the smiling, loving friends he loved more than any girl he had ever known.

Very softly, he began reciting the Kaddish. The mourner's prayer for the dead. "*Yitgadal, Vi Yitkadash shemei rabah...* Magnified and sanctified be His Great Name, in the world He created as He willed it to be..."

"And if that diamond ring gets broke..." Tera sang, "Mama's gonna buy you a billy goat..."

This whole thing is nuts, Peña thought.

The suicide bomber was a Jew.

He was a Jew, in a tin can full of Jews, with this holy roller singing nursery rhymes to the *puta* that was willing to blow them to bits an hour before, and now Peña was humming along with her too! And the guy they called Kooshi was praying in Hebrew, tears rolling unashamedly down his cheeks.

Peña listened to the prayer, but couldn't take his eyes off of Tera. He had, quite simply, never seen anyone so kind before in his life. As kind as his *Abuelita*.

He looked around the Nagmachon, and these tough kids who had just been fighting for their lives, and were rumbling now through hell, with the blackened remains of their friends. All of them were quiet, save for Kooshi, praying, "*Ya aseh shalom, Hu ya aseh shalom, aleinu vi all kol Israel, vi imru, Amen...* O make peace! He will make peace upon us, and upon all of Israel, and let us say, Amen." And, as Kooshi finished the prayer, all of them found themselves looking at golden-haired Tera, holding the Jewish girl suicide bomber, singing, "Hush little baby, don't say a word..." as if they were watching the Madonna and child.

Just as the sun was sending its first bloody fingertips, streaking the acrid skies, billowing black smoke from secondary explosions of Israeli air strikes hitting Hamas rocket and ammo dumps, they rolled back through the Nachal Oz Crossing, into Israel.

They had radioed ahead, and ambulances were waiting for them, together with chaplains.

The Givati soldiers crawled out through the hatches first, followed by Tera and Miriam, Washburn and Peña.

Kooshi kept his weapon on Miriam, but, by now, they all believed her.

Her father had died when she was four years old, and her mother had fallen in love with an Israeli Arab from Nazareth. They had gotten married, and been disowned by her Jewish family, and the mother converted to Islam. Then, one night, her new Arab step-father spirited her mother and Miriam away to Gaza, where the step-father, Hisham Massoud, had family.

Once in Gaza, Hisham took a second Moslem wife, and from that time on, Miriam and her mother had been treated like dogs. They lived the lives of slaves, beaten and abused. Her mother had given birth to a second daughter, Jihan. But she, too, was treated with brutality and contempt.

Then her stepfather, when the war started, had his Hamas friends come into his home, and they fitted Miriam with a suicide vest, and gave her a choice.

She was a Jewess whore, she and her mother, and little sister, as well.

But if she became a martyr, she would save her mother and sister.

That was her choice.

It didn't matter to her. She was ready to die. She wanted out of this life. It would be a blessing.

But then she heard Kooshi praying the prayer her Jewish father had taught her, so many years before, and she couldn't press the button. Her body began to quake, as if her soul had been re-awakened.

As Tera stayed with Miriam, keeping her arm around her, comforting her like an older sister, like one who knew her secret pain and suffering better than anyone else, Dani stayed down below in the Nagmachon.

Very carefully, he placed the charred remains of Aviv and Ziv into body bags. Their bodies were burnt through so badly that the feet fell off. Dani carefully placed them in the proper body bag. Each boot had, sewn into it, a metal dogtag. He checked that against the dogtags around the corpses' necks, and carefully, like a monk doing penance, for a crime for which no amount of penance could atone, he placed each charred body part in the proper body bag, and then lifted each up through the hatch to the waiting medic and chaplain who received it from the darkness, like a baby being born into the world.

Dani was scrubbing away at the blood that had pooled and coagulated at the bottom of the armored personnel carrier, when Allon looked down into the Nagmachon and said, "Leave it. You think you can wash away your sins?"

Dani climbed up through the hatch. He didn't avert his eyes from Allon's.

He picked up the intel bag containing the notebooks, map, laptop and cell phone, and looked at Tera and said, "Let's go."

He, Washburn, Peña, and Tera walked with Miriam over to Lieutenant Colonel Micha Bar Shimon, of Military Intelligence.

Dani gave him the intel bag, and explained what was in it. He said he would have a written report for Bar Shimon ASAP, but right now they needed to know what was in the notebooks, laptop, and cell phone and what the maps meant. Bar Shimon had already been briefed about the importance of this to the Americans. He also knew about the disastrous, failed mission Dani had led, and that this was all there was to show for it.

Then Dani took Tera and Miriam over to the Shin Bet, or Security Services Liaison Officer, and within an hour, the officer had not only verified Miriam's story, but had found a relative of hers in Afula, who confirmed the details of Miriam's tale on the phone, and described the distinctive purple birthmark on the upper left side of her forehead.

The girl was a Jew.

Her name was Miriam.

And she had been living in hell.

Her mother and little sister were still there.

And there was nothing anyone could do about it.

CHAPTER 14

The Givati Unit which had gone on Dani's failed mission was pulled out of the line and given a twenty-four hour leave to go to the funerals of their fallen comrades.

Dani was required, by direct order of the General Staff, to accompany the Americans, with the body of Clinton Spencer McKeever, to the American Embassy in Tel Aviv. As Dani busied himself turning in the intel packet, and handing Miriam over to Imri Pilo of the Shin Bet, Washburn, Peña, and Tera asked to phone the American Ambassador.

Moti Dagan, Commander of the Givati Brigade, had been there to meet them when their Nagmachon pulled back into Israel from Gaza. After talking with Dani briefly, he crossed over to the Americans and shook each of their hands and said, "On behalf of the Brigade, and the Israel Defense Force, please let me extend my deepest condolences to each of you. Anything you need. Anything at all. My office and my soldiers are at your disposal." And then he did something they had not seen any other Israeli soldier do. He saluted them.

He gave them use of his briefing room, so they could make a conference call to the American Ambassador. He made sure to cover all the maps first, but it was perfunctory. These were comrades in arms, and he treated them as such.

The three remaining members of their group dialed into the secure line at the Embassy, identified themselves, and asked to speak to the Ambassador.

He kept them holding for almost ten minutes. But, what the hey, there was a war going on, so, you know?

Once he came on the line, they informed the Ambassador of their colleague's death, and wanted to know what arrangements would be made to bring the body back to Washington, and how McKeever's family was to be notified. He was a hero, who had died in combat, at the behest of, and in service to, his nation, and he should be treated as such.

"Yes. Of course," said the Ambassador.

"'Yes of course' what, Sir?" Tera asked. She was, quite frankly, in no mood to be BSed, nor trifled with.

"I'm sorry?" said the Ambassador, letting a little attitude creep into his voice.

"How is Special Agent McKeever's body to be transported back to the United States, and who will notify his family?

"And, is there going to be an Honor Guard to receive him?" Washburn asked.

"I mean, the guy died a hero," Peña said.

"Uhh," said the Ambassador, "I'm sure all of you are tired, and would like a chance to rest up, so, why don't you just come back to the Embassy, and after the debriefing..."

"Ambassador," said Tera, "I don't mean to be disrespectful, but..."

"Then don't be," said the Ambassador.

"We were a team," Papa SEAL said, thinking, mistakenly, that that simple statement would make everything clear, even to some knuck-lehead, pencil-necked, pencil-pushing, geek like this clown.

"I'm sorry?" said the Ambassador, once again, as if they had a bad connection.

"I said, 'we were ...we ARE a team'." Washburn said, and looked at Peña and Tera.

Both of them nodded their approval back at him.

"Pardon me," said the Ambassador, "but with whom am I speaking?"

"With a member of that team," said Washburn.

"And what is your name?" asked the Ambassador, and they could tell he was reaching for a pen with which to write down the name of whoever it was who dared to speak to His Excellency, The Ambassador, in this fashion.

"Force Master Chief Petty Officer Darwin Washburn, NAVSPECWARCOM, United States Navy."

"Well, Chief," said the Ambassador, "how the body is to be shipped..."

"Special Agent McKeever," said Tera.

"I beg your pardon."

"We're talkin' about Special Agent McKeever," said Peña. "Not 'the body'... Sir."

"I tell you what," said the Ambassador. "This conversation came to an end around thirty seconds ago. You deliver the body. The Embassy will coordinate all the arrangements with Washington. And that's pretty much all you need to know. That, and the fact that I expect you here by four o'clock this afternoon, to be debriefed."

With that, the Ambassador hung up the phone, and Peña made a comment ill-reflecting upon the Ambassador's mother.

They picked up the ubiquitous Israeli Army tuna sandwiches, hopped into the SUV and headed north to Tel Aviv. There were three rocket attacks along the way, causing them to pull the car over and take shelter, but they were at the Embassy by 4:00 p.m.

Dani waited for them while they were debriefed by the Ambassador, who, on the instructions of the the Secretary of State, Jack O' Leary, made sure that the CIA Chief of Station was not invited to participate.

"So, let me see if I understand all of this," said the Ambassador.

He was a man in his mid-fifties, with mousy, rather than distinguished-looking, grey hair. What he lacked in a chin, he made up for in a very high forehead. His tortoiseshell granny glasses, perched on his nose, gave him an almost Dickensian look, like a middling headmaster of an impoverished school for wayward boys. "Let me see if I understand this," he said, peeking above the rims of his glasses. "The point of the exercise was to get this Al-Tikriti character, and Kawasme, the supposed ISIL terrorists, supposedly closing some sort of deal with Hamas, to do what, we do not know... Only that supposedly, it involved certain drug cartels in Mexico, and/or South America. Pretty much it?"

"Pretty much," said Papa SEAL.

"As to Al-Tikriti...?" asked the Ambassador, clearly relishing every moment of this.

"He got away," said Tera.

"He got away," The Ambassador repeated, making a note of that on his yellow legal pad. "We never actually saw him, in fact. Correct?"

"'We', sir?" Tera asked.

"You," said the Ambassador. "You never actually saw this supposed ISIL terrorist."

"Affirmative," said Papa SEAL.

"So," said the Ambassador, tapping his rather yellowed teeth with his pen, "We don't really know whether he was in Gaza or not. Correct?"

"Correct," said Tera, who was beginning to truly dislike, in a decidedly non-Christian fashion, this bureaucratic onanist.

"And Kawasme?" the Ambassador asked with that kind of undertaker's smile, the kind that seemed to ask, 'Mahogany, or simple pine for the casket?'.

"Went boom," Peña said.

"I beg your pardon?"

"Kawasme detonated an IED, which had evidently been surgically implanted into his stomach cavity," Tera said.

"Killing..." the Ambassador was looking at his notes, trying to find the name of the deceased.

"Special Agent Clint McKeever," Washburn said.

"And, as mentioned, the point of the exercise was to apprehend and interrogate the two alleged terrorists, one of whom may never have existed, and the other of whom was permitted to detonate an explosive device, which killed not only said terrorist, but Special Agent McKeever and an Israeli soldier. Thus, one could say that the mission, insofar as it was defined, was not accomplished."

"The data from the laptop, cell phone, the notes, and the maps have not yet been analyzed," Washburn said, glancing at his watch. "But, other than that, yes, I think you can safely say no one spiked the football on this one."

"Right," said the Ambassador. "Well, we'll just hope for happier news once the Israelis finish going over the various items you *did* manage to bring back. So, thank you gentlemen...and lady... That will be all. Please make yourselves comfortable. Anything we have here is yours."

"What about the arrangements for Special Agent McKeever?" Tera asked.

"I'm waiting for advice from Washington. Until then, the Israelis have been kind enough to take the remains to their morgue. Other than that, it really doesn't concern you."

"And his family?" asked Papa SEAL. "Have they been notified?"

"That doesn't concern you either, Chief."

"Will they at least be told that he died on a mission, for his country?" Tera asked.

"Ms. Dayton," said the Ambassador. "Did I stutter, or are you not wired for sound? Nothing to do with the deceased, his remains, his family, whether we throw a parade for him, or just keep him on ice for a while, is of any concern to you. To any of you. It is above your collective pay grades. Now, if you'll excuse me..." The Ambassador got up, collected his notebook, folded his granny glasses, and put them in his breast pocket, and left.

Washburn and Peña decided to go out and get blitzed.

Tera demurred, and, seeing as how the Embassy was located right on the Promenade of the beach, said she would be going for a walk.

Dani was waiting at the rear of the Embassy when she came out.

"How'd it go?" he asked.

"It sucked," she said. "Big time. Pompous, bureaucratic son of a ..."

"Can I buy you a drink? Or, maybe some dinner?"

"And, what would be the point of that?"

"To have a drink, and maybe some dinner."

The sun was golden on the horizon, and despite the threat of rocket fire, Israelis were out swimming, surfing and paddle boarding, as lovers strolled along the beachfront, holding hands.

"I've got to hand it to your people. They don't let anything stop them," Tera said looking at a couple of twenty-somethings, who strolled with their arms around each other's waists.

Dani saw her look at them, and said, "Sure you don't want to go to dinner?"

"And get laid? Is that it?"

"Well, normally, I'm not that easy, but you've talked me into it."

"Major, I killed someone today."

"Which is better than someone having killed you today."

In the distance, looking south, Tera saw the Old City of Jaffa, looking more like it belonged somewhere in Turkey, or on a Greek island, rather than fitting in with the gleaming high-rise hotels and the *Tayelet* Promenade that ran down the coastline. They were just beginning to take in the beach chairs and set out the couches for the impromptu restaurants on the shore, that would be open 'til three or four o'clock in the morning. The truth was, under normal circumstances, she would have loved to have a romantic dinner on the shore of the Mediterranean, on a velvety summer night, beneath a hazy crescent moon, pale light bathing a city in white, that seemed to love to party into the wee hours, where even the ice cream stands were open until dawn.

"How many women are you currently sleeping with?"

"Why would that have any impact on whether or not you and I go out for something to eat?"

"Because I have no intention of becoming one of them."

"Then you have nothing to worry about."

Dani thought, *Man, this is going to be a mistake.* But whether it was force of habit, or that he just didn't like the idea of being struck out before he even got up to bat, he pressed on.

"So..." he said. "What do you like? European, Middle Eastern? I mean, we did the Itzik Ha Gadol thing the other night, so, personally I'd be up for Ernesto's. A really lovely little Roman trattoria on Ben Yehuda Street. I mean if you like pasta, and they have these Carciofi alla Judea, these deep fried artichokes that..."

"So, you're seeing other women," Tera said, cutting off the culinary tour of Tel Aviv.

"Absolutely. And, sleeping with them, too. I like to call them 'The Coalition of the Willing.'"

"We killed people today. Two of our people were killed today. And you want to go out on a date after that?" Tera asked, looking him straight in the eyes.

"Actually, ten of our people were killed today. There were eight kids in that APC, and I consider their deaths my fault, as well. And, if I'm lucky, maybe in the next few days, I'll get killed, too. And, so might you. And, if you wondered why people party every night until dawn in this town, it's because, without making a big deal of it, people around here take any chance they can to grab a little bit of happiness, because none of us know what's gonna happen tomorrow."

"Please don't try to make promiscuity sound patriotic, or noble."

"Doctor Dayton, have you ever been married?"

"No," said Tera.

"Well," said Dani. "Now you know why."

Tera looked at him, for what seemed like forever. He could see tears welling up in her eyes, and was about to reach out to comfort her, when she leaned back to her right, put all her weight on her back foot, and then her front, and stepped into the most viscious, right-hook slap across the face he had ever experienced.

"You son of a bitch!" she said, and the spittle hit his face.

He watched her lean back once again, watched her right arm snake out as she lunged forward, and slapped him again. He had never met a woman who could hit harder, and, if he had stopped to think of it, he would have been hard-pressed to think of a man her size who could pack as much fury into a punch. She slapped him again.

"You don't know anything about me! ANYTHING!" Her voice was hoarse and raspy, and he recognized in it the shout of his own pain as he was told his wife and child had been blown to pieces. "You don't know anything!"

She slapped him again, and then let out a long, low moan, the most tragic and horrific sound he had ever heard since he heard it well up in his own throat at the thought of his own dead child. He pulled her in toward his chest, and held her softly, her heart racing against his.

For a moment, she allowed herself to cry, to be comforted, to find shelter in his arms. And then, the moan began anew, as if the most terrible thing in the world was happening to her, all over again.

"Nooooooooooooooooo!" she cried out, and pulled away from him, but he held her by the shoulders, and forced her to look at him.

"What happened to you in Pakistan?"

"What?" she said, in shock.

"Washburn said there was a rumor that something happened to you in Pakistan," Dani said, still forcing her to look at him, staring directly into her eyes. "What happened?"

She looked down, and then up, with a look that Dani imagined was not one of someone about to cross any particular Rubicon of the mind. Rather, he thought, it was probably the same look people had before they chose to leap to their deaths, rather than die, burning alive, in one of the Twin Towers. She stared at him, not to try to look into his soul, but to force him to look into hers.

"I was gang-raped in Pakistan. You satisfied? You happy now? Did you get what you wanted? I was gang-raped by ten men, fifteen men. I don't really know. I think I stopped counting after eight or ten."

The sun was sinking, blood-red behind them, like a violated maiden in a medieval poem.

"I'm so sorry," Dani said, not looking away.

"Blow your pity out your ass."

She tried to turn away from him now, but he held her by the shoulders, the red glow of sunset, and the blood rushing to her face, blending into what looked like a bruise.

"Did you get any help? Did you..."

"Any help?! If I go to a CIA shrink, my career is over!"

"What about your pastor?"

"My pastor?" she said, face flushing hot, tears beginning to run down her reddened, bruised-looking cheeks. "'Gee, pastor, I was raped and sodomized by fifteen men, who told me if I didn't perform oral sex on them, they'd cut my head off, and if I didn't tell them how much I liked it, they'd cut my tongue out, so I did!! I told them I loved it! I'm filth, I'm a whore! I should be dead! I envy McKeever! Do you understand that? *I envy McKeever!* I'd trade places with him in a heartbeat!"

Dani held her shoulders. Held her gaze. Held her, so she couldn't look away. Then, he said, dead-voiced, as down-and-dirty honest as could be, "So would I."

She just looked at him.

"There's not a day that goes by that I don't have an argument with myself about why I shouldn't stick my Tavor assault rifle inside my mouth, and pull the trigger, and every day, I lose the argument! And, I cannot tell you how much I long for the day when I don't."

She was no longer looking at his face. Only his eyes. She knew that he wasn't lying.

"What do you do?" he asked. "Drink vodka at night, so no one smells it on your breath? You do, don't you? You've got a flask. And, maybe some Valium, or Prozac, and maybe an upper or two, so you can get your eyes open in the morning. Don't you? ...Don't you?!" he demanded.

"Yes," she said quetly, looking away, ashamed.

Very gently, he turned her face back to his. "Me, too. Used to be, at least."

"What do you mean, 'used to be'?"

The sun had set completely now, into the Mediterranean, a ball of fire flaming out in the sea, its fury spent, its heat extinguished, its light given up to moonglow.

"I gave it up to God," Dani said. "I sure as hell couldn't carry it. This is too heavy for you, Tera."

And, as he said that, she began to cry. Not sobbing, just tears streaming down her face, perhaps more in relief than pain.

"You're a Christian, right?"

"Yes," Tera said.

And he knew there was possibly nothing as awful as being someone of faith, whose shame and heartache had estranged them from the very thing that once had been their refuge.

"Isn't there something in there about laying it down at the feet of your Savior?"

She said nothing, nor did she nod her head. He was leading her down into deep water. It was as if she could no longer feel the earth beneath her, and, quite literally, she now would either sink, or swim.

"I tell you what," said Dani. "I won't go to bed with you. But, I *will* pray with you. There's a poem. I was going through some pretty serious PTSD. And, my wife sent me a poem. I only remember the last part of it. It was written after World War II." He looked off into the distance past her, not remembering the lines of the poem, but the love of the one who had given it to him, which, now, he was giving to Tera Dayton.

"'Only we two, and yet our howling can,
Encircle the world's end.
Frightened, you are my only friend.
And frightened we are, everyone.
Someone must make a stand.
Coward, take my coward's hand.'"

He held out his hand to her. He would not take hers. She would have to reach out to him, or drown. It was her choice, and he knew it. And, so did she.

There is something so tempting about a death in warm, and quiet, waters. A return to the amniotic fluid of the womb. You don't close your eyes. You leave them open, and it all goes black. And, after a moment of panic, there is no longer any pain, nor is there any life. It was so seductive to simply sink beneath the surface of one's own sorrow, and drown there. This wasn't between her and Dani. This was between her, and her God, and Dani knew it. He waited, hand held out. He would have waited until hell had frozen over. And, then, in the growing darkness, he felt her hand take his.

They walked across Hayarkon Street, down into the sand, looking, for all the world, like early middle-aged lovers or, perhaps, a one-night hookup. A wartime romance on the edge of the Mediterranean. They walked down to the water's warm edge, and, there, they knelt, silhouetted against the moon, and together, they prayed.

Further down, by the old city of Jaffa, was the Andromeda rock, the place where, in Greek mythology, Andromeda had been chained naked, as a sacrifice to sate Ceta, the monster who lurked beneath the blackened night-time waters stretched out there before them. And tonight, other monsters screamed up through the skies from the south, searching for their sacrifices, as well.

The Code Red Siren sounded.

On the beach, people walked quickly into the various shelters at the foot of the high-rise hotels that lined the promenade.

But Dani and Tera stayed knelt in prayer along the shore. They were alive inside the 23rd Psalm, inside the Valley of the Shadow of Death, cloaked in grace, fearing no evil, as Iron Dome launched, trailing fire in a velvet sky, exploding all eight rockets above the Tel Aviv, diamond-lit skyline, like Fourth of July fireworks, celebrating in the heavens.

Along the shore, the lovers and diners, the young couples and kids and old people, cheered as the interceptors knocked the Fajr 5s and M75s out of the firmament. Then, the lovers, and kids with surfboards, the old people and the young, the revelers and the diners, went about grabbing their pieces of happiness, 'til the next rocket attack, as Tera and Dani stayed where they were, still in prayer, near the ancient Port of Jaffa, from whence Jonah had fled from the Voice of the Lord, which now they so earnestly prayed to hear within their own hearts. And, this time, Tera Dayton, as the water caressed them both along the shore, as if in baptism anew, in thanksgiving, and humble joy, began to weep.

Raul Peña and Force Master Chief Petty Officer Darwin Washburn cheered the Iron Dome interceptors as well, albeit from different locations, and with differing degrees of enthusiasm.

Peña had decided to get blitzed. The sooner and drunker the better. Thus, he perched himself on the terrace of Mike's Place, the expat pub next to the Embassy, and ordered boilermakers. Three of them lined up in a row. He had downed the third, when the Code Red siren sounded, and the patrons walked into the "Safe Room" in the bar's interior. Peña, however, stayed at his high-topped table, facing the sea, drinking.

"Cowards!" he muttered. "Deserting your posts in time of war! *¡No tengo miedo de ti!*" Peña said loudly to the rockets arcing up toward Tel Aviv from the south, slamming back his fourth Jameson, and washing it down with the local beer.

When the Iron Dome interceptors took out all eight rockets in the skies above his head Peña shouted, "All righhhhh', *'mano! ¡Los Judíos ocho*, rag-heads zip!" and when the waitresses and patrons came back out onto the terrace, he ordered two more of the same. Then, remembering his favorite McBain Schwarzenegger moment from *The Simpsons*, for no apparent reason whatsoever, he leaned back his head, and shouted out, in what he hoped was an Austrian accent, "MENDOOOOOOZAAAAAAAAAHHHHHH!!!"

For his part, Darwin Washburn had decided not to get drunk with Peña. It wasn't that he had decided not to get drunk. And it wasn't necessarily that he had anything against Peña, or drinking with him. It was that he wanted to call his wife first, and didn't want the sound of raucous drunks, doing *Simpsons*/Schwarzenegger immitations at the top of their lungs in a bar, bleeding into the conversation.

He had phoned his wife from a bar in Southeast Asia once, and the bar girl crooned, "Me love you all night long, G.I.," while Washburn was professing drunken fidelity to his long-suffering spouse, LaDonna.

She had never let go of that one.

Officially, he was not to have any communication with his family. They were not supposed to be aware of where he was. Officially, of course, he was almost never where he really was.

But tonight, today, LaDonna's time, he wanted to hear his wife's voice. She had stuck with him through thick and thin. And Lord knows they hadn't skimped on the "thin" part. Um mmm. There was plenty of that in their more than two decades of marriage.

Mama SEAL had become a bit of a legend to the wives, in her own right. She was part black and part Hawaiian, and always said, in that half black, half pidgin patois she affected, when necessary, "Mama always said, don't cook in no small pots." By which it was meant that there was always room for one more, or six more, or ten, if that's how many Frogs her husband had invited over, or how many football team-mates her son, DJ, told to drop by.

Mama SEAL didn't cook in no small pots.

And she didn't ask no questions, neither.

And that was the advice she gave to the young SEAL wives. "You didn't marry an insurance salesman," she would say.

SEALs had an unofficial motto, one amongst many: "Anything worth doing, is worth doing to excess." That was not only who they were, that was part of what enabled them to do what they did... And stay alive.

So LaDonna didn't ask any questions about whatever happened on whatever deployments, and whatever R and R's that came with those deployments. That was part of her arrangement with Darwin, Sr. She didn't ask questions.

There were two other parts of the arrangement:
1)   She was not to be made a fool of. By which she meant, what-ever he did, about which she asked no questions, he would NOT... Repeat... WOULD NOT rub her nose in it. Hence the fact that she never let go of the "Me love you all night long, G.I." phone call from, as she carefully enunciated it, syllable by syllable, Bang–kok.

2) He was not to ask any questions of her, either.

That was the deal. Take it or leave it.

And their marriage, under those auspices, had outlasted almost any other marriage of any of their contemporaries.

Tonight, with the ash taste of failure, and useless death, of governmental betrayal and bureaucratic meanness, in his mouth, Darwin Washburn wanted to hear the voice of the woman whom, despite what she sometimes accused him of, and despite their deal, he loved more than any other on earth.

The problem was, there was always that nagging fear that when he called home, after DJ had gone to school, that, perhaps, she wasn't alone.

He had voiced that fear to her once saying, "Maybe you got you another man on the side."

To which LaDonna had answered, "Only one?"

Still, his need to hear her voice, to lean on her sweet shoulder, from halfway around the world, outweighed the fear that she might be otherwise engaged. He always wondered if he would be able to tell by her voice, though he had no doubt whatsoever that she would most certainly be able to tell by his voice, were the situation reversed. She seemed to be able to read his voice like gypsies read crystal balls.

He bought one of those pay-as-you-go international cell phones, with cash, so there was no record of the transaction, and dialed her number in Dam Neck, Virginia, home to SEAL Team 6, where it was now almost two in the afternoon.

"You okay?" she asked, instead of saying hello. She had seen an unfamiliar foreign number pop up, and knew it had to be from him. There was nothing he could read in her voice to tell if she had been caught at an inopportune time or not.

"'T's all good," he said. "You alone?"

"Wouldn't you like to know," LaDonna answered.

"No. Not really. If you're not, just lie to me."

"You wouldn't know the difference if I was."

"I sure hope I wouldn't," said Papa SEAL.

"What's wrong?"

"Nah, nothin'. Just wanted to hear your voice, is all," he said, leaning into the phone, pressing it closer to his ear.

He was sitting on a bench, off a little side street, in a quiet residential district near the beach. There was a playground there for little kids, with little swings and slides and such, and grass and flowers and places for dogs to run. He didn't want anything to sound like "Me love you all night long, G.I." in the background.

"Where are you?"

"You know I can't say."

"Someplace safe."

"I'm always safe," he said, watching a grandmother push a pram in the Mediterranean-warm evening, turning slowly into night.

"Then why'd you call?"

"Like I said. Just wanted to hear your voice."

"Somethin' bad went down."

"Yeah," he said.

"But you're okay."

"Never better. How are you?"

"Never better."

"How's DJ?"

"You sittin' down."

"He got a scholarship?! " Darwin asked, suddenly brightening.

The question of how he would pay for his oldest boy's college education was never far from his mind. But DJ was an athlete, tight end, with big hands. They'd sent his reel out to over a hundred D2 schools. He wasn't quick enough for D1 ball. But he had a real shot, Darwin thought, of a full ride at a decent D2 school. But the school year had ended, without an offer. Still, Darwin held out hope, and, if not, DJ had been approached by a couple of JuCos. The Junior College route wasn't the worst way to go, and there were three or four who made it clear they wanted him.

"He's joinin' the Teams," LaDonna said.

"That's what HE thinks!" Darwin said, "He's goin to college or..."

"Darwin..." said La Donna, "He's eighteen years old. He doesn't need our permission. Not yours, and not mine. He already signed the enlistment papers, and, because he's your son, he's going to get his shot."

Darwin felt sick. This was not the life he wanted for his son. After today, he wasn't sure it was the life that he wanted for himself, anymore.

To be in some foreign country, not even in your own country's war, and get blown up and your family doesn't even know, will never know where you were or why, and they just stick you on ice 'til they can figure out what lie to tell?

"I want to talk to him," Darwin said, feeling like someone had just kicked him in his gut.

"He's not here. Out with Jamal and Scotty and them."

"This is not what we talked about."

"Well, what'd you expect, Darwin?" there was an edge to her voice. This was not what she wanted for her son either, and she blamed him, and he knew it. "Boy idolizes you, wants to be jes' like his daddy, so whatchyou expect he's gonna do?"

"I was thinkin' of quittin'," Darwin said, suddenly so very tired.

"Yeah," said LaDonna, "Well, I was thinkin of leavin' you for Denzel Washington, but that ain't gonna' happen neither. So we both stuck."

"Yeah... Guess if he's goin' in..."

"That's right... You're stayin' in to make sure he either washes out if he's not cut out for this, or gets off on the right foot, if he is. Either way, Force Master Chief, 'til he's settled, you're stayin' in, an' Denzel's goin' back to his wife. An' that's the way it's gonna be."

"I thought you were gettin' partial to Jaimie Foxx."

"Too short," said La Donna. "So, I guess I'm stuck with you."

"We could both do a lot worse," he said.

"Well YOU could, that's for sure."

"You know I love you, right?" he said.

"You know I love you, back?"

"Yeah, I do," he said, holding the phone close, and wishing it was her. "You okay?"

"I'll tell you what... There's gotta be somethin' better than government work."

Just then, there was another Code Red air raid siren. There was a bomb shelter there in the park, and Darwin got up and started toward it, as did the grandmother with the pram.

"What's that sound?" LaDonna asked.

"Just nothin', you know? Listen, I gotta go," he said moving toward the bomb shelter, and picked up one end of the pram to help the old lady negotiate the stairs.

"T'anks you," she said in heavily accented English.

He put the phone between his shoulder and his ear and said, "Let me get that for you, ma'am."

He picked up the pram, and carried it down into the darkness of the air raid shelter, and the signal on the cell phone dropped before he could hear LaDonna say, "You keep your head down, Darwin."

By his fifth boilermaker, Peña was totally blitzed. He was wandering down the Promenade, looking to pick up one of those hot Israelian *chicas*, but being as drunk as he was no one wanted anything to do with him, except this one Israeli guy who, when Peña said, "Hey '*Mano* is there someplace around here where they got, you know, a *Latino* band... So I can hear somethin' other than this *Hava Nagila* crap?" had replied, "*Ladino*?"

The guy was in his fifties. There was something in his accent that made Peña think maybe this guy spoke Spanish.

"*¡Latino, sí, música latina! ¿Sabes, donde hay algo caliente?*"

"I know," said the Israeli guy, "where you can hear *Ladino*. My father family is from Thessaloniki. He speak *Ladino*. I don't speak. But the *música*, very beautiful. You come. I show."

Peña couldn't figure out what the guy was talking about. He had never heard of Thessaloniki, and he couldn't figure out why this guy kept saying *Ladino* when he told him *Latino*. But he was too drunk to do anything but follow. He just hoped the guy wasn't gay and taking him to some kind of Israeli, *Latino* gay bar or somethin', 'cause, '*mano*, he was lookin' for one of them Israelian *chicas* with the miniskirts. *¿Tu sabes?*

The guy led him up the Promenade, and took a left at a dimly lit street. They walked up one block, and the vista changed from gleaming high-rise hotels to a slummy-looking place of old-style buildings, like a hundred years old maybe, with arched windows and those slat shutters, and there was a club, and outside it said, "*La Niña Blanca*".

Okay, thought Peña, *La Niña Blanca. ¡Sí, Se puedo!* And he went in.

It was dark and smoky, in a way you couldn't find in any city in America any more. The cigarette smoke was so thick, it was like haze in the spotlight that lit up the face of the middle-aged, olive-skinned woman on stage. She was backed up by guys playing instruments he had only seen on TV maybe, like Cuban instruments, or Arab, or somethin'. The woman had grey hair and a wrinkled face, and hands that looked like she took in washing instead of got mani-pedis with the rest of the girls. This wasn't no *chica* in a miniskirt, man. This was an ol' *vieja*, and he was ready to leave, until he heard her sing.

Her voice was dusky and plaintive, and spoke of life hard-lived, but the song and the accent, the Spanish... It wasn't Mexican Spanish. It was the Spanish of his *Abuelita*. It was fifteenth century Spanish, and that accent that spoke of Andaluz, where his *Abuelita* said their people came from, and when she said, "their people" he knew she meant *Los Judíos*.

It was a song with which she used to sing him to sleep. A *Romansa*, meant to be sung without accompaniment, sung by grandmothers, singing of loves and passions long past, as they rocked *los niños* to sleep in olive-skinned arms.

"*La rosa enflorese*," she sang...The rose blooms, "*en el mes de Mai....*" in the month of May, "*mi alma s'escurese....*" My soul darkens, "*sufriendo del amor...*" Suffering from love.

It was his *Abuelita's* voice, and the song she sang to him as a child, the song she sang to him when she took him from the bath and he still bled and cried, and she rocked him like a babe, singing, "*El bilbiliko canta, suspira del amor, y la passion me mata, muchigua di dolor...*" The nightinale sings, it sighs with love. Passion kills me, increasing my pain.

It was the song of his people. And, for the first time in his life, he was with them, not in hiding, but in this funky, smoky club in Tel Aviv, under rocket-fire.

He was, for the first time, home.

That's when his phone rang. It was Tera, telling him to meet her, and Washburn, and Dani. They had an idea.

Meanwhile, Abdul Aziz Al-Tikriti, equipped with the new identity of a Spanish businessman named Juan Carlos de Santiago y Montoya, an oil executive with close ties to PetroMex, boarded AeroMexico Flight 170 from Mexico City to Tijuana, right on the American border.

CHAPTER 15

A drunken Raul Peña met a slightly less drunken Darwin Washburn, and a sober Tera Dayton and Dani Kahan, on the terrace of one of the beachfront cafes, called Massada. When Peña asked what all this was about, Washburn said, "They're probably gonna anounce their engagement."

"Actually," said Dani, "I want to tell you a story. Then, we can all decide what we want to do about it."

Dani's mentor in Military Intelligence, he told them, was a legendary officer named Gadi Simchoni.

Gadi had participated in a clandestine operation to smuggle Ethiopian Jews out of refugee camps in Sudan. It was a combined operation of the Mossad, the Israeli Navy, Air Force, and Military Intelligence.

The whole idea was insane.

Menachem Begin, then Prime Minister, had heard about the plight of the Ethiopian Jews. If they were discovered amongst their Moslem counterparts in the Sudanese refugee camps, they would have been killed.

Begin called in the head of the Mossad and said, as only Begin could, "Bring our people home."

That was it.

That was the operational order.

"Bring our people home."

Only a quasi-mystic like Begin could have uttered such a statement. Who did he think he was, Moses?

And yet, when the Prime Minister says, "Bring our people home," you salute and, at least, go through the motions of trying to do it.

The Mossad had a few other pressing issues at the time, after all. The plight of a handful of Ethiopian Jews wasn't exactly a security issue.

So, the head of the Mossad called in one of his agents, who was a religious Jew, and said, "I'm giving you the assignment because you're religious, and you're probably stupid enough to think that God wants you to do this, and he'll find a way."

And the Mossad agent, Gadi Simchoni, who later would transfer into Military Intelligence, said, "Of course! It's in Isaiah 11:11, 'Then it will happen on that day that the Lord will recover a second time, with his hand, the remnant of His people... From Cush!' Cush is the biblical term for Ethiopia! It was all prophesied three thousand years ago!"

Well, between Isaiah's prophesy, and the Mossad operation to bring the Jews of "Cush" into the Land of Israel, there was a bit of connective tissue that had to be provided.

No problem for Gadi Simchoni.

The cover was a supposed Italian diving resort on the Red Sea, which Gadi convinced the Mossad to buy, as a front.

They would then smuggle the Ethiopian Jews out of the Sudanese camps in the middle of the night, and truck them over to Gadi's "dive resort".

Meanwhile, an Israeli naval vessel would be waiting offshore and Israeli SEALs would come ashore in rubber Zodiacs, load up the Ethiopian Jews, and take them back to the ship, smuggling out several hundred at a time.

It was the first time in history that black Africans had been taken off the continent of Africa into freedom, instead of slavery.

One night, there was a fourteen-year-old girl who had a ruptured appendix while on board the ship. The medic on board said he lacked the proper facilities and equipment to operate, and save the girl's life. She would die unless she could be medivacked back to Israel.

Gadi radioed the Kirya in Tel Aviv. The head of Military Intelligence contacted the Chief of Staff, who woke up the Prime Minister, and apprised him of the situation. A fourteen year old black Jewish girl was dying off the coast of the Sudan. Without hesitating, Begin ordered a

Sikorsky "flying surgery" chopper, with a team of doctors, a refueling plane, and a flight of F15s to provide air cover, to save the life of a fourteen-year-old black Jewish girl... And no one even knew her name. All they knew was she was a Jew, in trouble.

That girl's daughter, Irit, became the commander of the all-girl observation unit that spotted the terrorists, and averted the greatest disaster in Israel's history.

"Funny how that 'God has a plan' thing works out," Tera said.

"America must have been like that, once," Washburn said to nobody in particular. "Everybody lookin' out for each other."

"Not in my neighborhood, *hermano*," said Peña.

But, now knowing that story, and because they had the foul taste of death and failure in their mouths, and wanted desperately to do something to wash it away, they drove back to the Givati base, and met with Colonel Moti Dagan, commander of the brigade, and asked to mount an operation to go back into Gaza, and get Miriam's mother and little sister, and bring them home, to the Land of Israel.

"And how, exactly, would I justify ordering something like that?" Dagan asked.

"I wouldn't order it. But I would permit people to volunteer," Dani said.

"I volunteer," said Tera.

"Me, too," said Peña.

"Wouldn't miss it for the world," said Washburn.

"I think the kids who were with us would volunteer, as well," said Dani. "We all heard her story. Maybe there's something good that can come out of this."

"Okay. You get volunteers. Big deal. How do I justify putting lives and equipment at risk for a non-military mission, in the middle of a war? I'm a religious Jew, but we're not social workers. We're the Givati Brigade."

"I'm the Brigade Intelligence Officer. It is my considered opinion that the mother and sister are high-value informants. I'll be happy to put that in writing."

"As a representative of the CIA, I'd be happy to put that in writing, as well, Sir," said Tera.

"See if you can get any volunteers," Moti said. "Then we'll talk."

Dani found Allon in the dining hall, getting a late-night snack.

He was sitting by himself in a corner, eating a combat ration tuna sandwich.

"You feel like going back in?" Dani asked.

"With you?" Allon said, without looking up.

"To get that girl's mother and sister out of there... Yes, with me."

Allon looked up at him.

"Not to blow any tunnels up. Not to kill any terrorists, or take out any rocket launchers. To get out a Jew who married an Arab."

"Right," said Dani. "And her daughter."

"Somebody was stupid enough to order this?'

"No," Dani said. "Strictly volunteer. I'm hoping the guy who drove the D9 and the two tanks will say yes, too."

"And why should we do this? Why should I risk my guys?"

"First of all, you're not going to risk them. It's their choice, just like it's yours. Why should we do it? Because she's a Jew, in trouble, and if we don't do it, no one else will."

"This doesn't change anything between you and me."

"No," Dani said. "It doesn't."

"Okay." Allon said and took his sandwich, picked up his flack jacket, helmet and Micro-Tavor, and walked out with Dani.

They all said yes.

Shachar, the driver of the D9, all the Givati kids, including Davidi the medic, and Kooshi, the guy Miriam had tried to kill, both crews of both Merkava IV tanks, all of them, without exception, in the middle of the night, after no sleep for twenty-four hours, said yes.

Tera, Washburn, and Peña were waiting for them at the assembly point, too.

"You guys have done enough already. There's really no need for you to come along on this thing," Dani said. "I mean, I appreciate the gesture in taking the meeting with Dagan, but..."

"You think this was all an accident?" said Tera. "You think God doesn't have a say in this?"

"I ain't doin' it for God," Peña said. "I just want to get another crack at killin' some of them Hamas *maricónes*."

"You know me," said Papa, "Always up for a party."

228

And so, at 04:30 hours, two Merkava IV tanks, one Nagmachon and one D9 bulldozer pulled up in front of the house of Hisham Massoud.

Miriam got on the D9's loud speaker and spoke in a firm voice, waking the man who had beaten her, and had his Hamas friends fit her with a suicide vest.

"I'm not dead!" she said. "Do you hear that? I'm not dead! The one you called a Jew whore isn't dead! I'm here with *my* people. And we've come for my mother and sister, you son of a bitch."

Hisham, still in his pajamas, opened the curtain of his house and saw the tanks and Nagmachon and D9.

Arik, the commander of the two Merkava IVs, gave the order to swivel their turrets, and point their 120mm cannons and machine guns, right at his face.

In two minutes, the door to the house opened, and Miriam's mother Sara, and her little sister Jihan came out of the house. They carried no suitcases, nor anything else. The door closed behind them, and the cannons and machine guns stayed trained on Hisham's house, until Sara and her daughter were reunited with Miriam, in the Nagmachon.

And, for the second time in twenty-four hours, Tera Dayton said, "Praise Jesus."

CHAPTER 16

W hen they rumbled back into the Givati assembly point, Imri Pilo was waiting for them. He was the Shin Bet liason officer who had verified that Miriam was a Jew, an Israeli from Afula, whose mother had married Massoud, and who, with her daughter, had vanished years before, probably to Gaza. He would be the one to debrief both Miriam, her mother, and little sister.

There was, at least, some information to be gleaned from them.

How did the father know the Hamas recruiter who came and fitted the suicide belt on Miriam in Massoud's home?

Who was the recruiter?

What was his name?

Was there anyone else with him?

Did they have a contact number for him? A cell phone?

Anything and everything they had was of importance, if it could be pieced together.

And the truth was, it could.

Israel had a number of informants in Gaza. Some they paid. Some they blackmailed. Some they helped out. Perhaps one had a relative in prison, who could be set free in exchange for certain information. Perhaps another needed treatment in an Israeli hospital. Anything could be arranged, if the information was good.

But the most valuable informant they had was Ali Al Bahkri. He was the son of a high-ranking Hamas official, and, unbeknownst to his family and his closest friends, he had become a secret Christian, and had accepted Jesus as his Lord and Savior. Jesus came to him in a dream and held out his hand, and Al Bahkri took it.

And then it dawned on him.

Jesus was a Jew.

The Jews were here long before Islam was even born.

Seven hundred years before the birth of Islam, Jesus was a Jewish Rabbi who walked the streets of Roman-occupied, Jewish Jerusalem, and went up and chased the money changers out of the Jewish Temple, on the Temple Mount, known almost seven hundred years later to Muslims as the Noble Sanctuary, which housed the Dome of the Rock, and Al Aqsa Mosque.

These were the places where Arafat said there never was a Jewish Temple.

But how could that be, if Jesus preached there?

And so Ali Al Bahkri, son of Sheik Achmed Abu Ali Al Bahkri, one of the most important Hamas officials in Gaza, became an agent for the Israeli Shin Bet.

He did it despite his love for his father and his people. He did it to save lives. He did it because, as a Christian, he could do nothing less.

He was put on a secure phone line with Miriam and Imri.

"How did Massoud know the Hamas recruiter?"

"He didn't. But, he did jobs for Hamas, and he asked the man he did the jobs for to send a recruiter. They could use his wife's Jewish daughter. He did it to ingratiate himself with them, because he had a good job, and he wanted to keep it."

"What was his job?"

"He had a small business. Two trucks, and he hauled things for Hamas."

"What kind of things?"

"All kinds of things. He would pick them up at the smuggling tunnels, or sometimes they were from the UN humanitarian aid trucks."

"Like what?"

"Electrical cable."

"What do you mean, electrical cable? What kind?"

"Big spools."

"How big?"

"Big, big spools, maybe two meters in diameter, that's how big the spools were."

"And what else?"

"Arches."

"What kind of arches?"

"From cement."

"And, who did he deliver them to?"

"I don't know. I never went with him. But it was a good job, and he wanted to show them, you know, Hamas, here take this girl and make her a *shaheeda*, a martyr. I give her to you."

"Do you know the name of the man he worked for?"

"Yes, of course. He came to the house. Many times. My mother and I made dinner for him. Many times, because Massoud wants to be his friend, to be nice, to show respect, so he keeps getting the good jobs."

"And what was his name?"

"Al Hamdi."

"Bashar Al Hamdi?"

"Yes."

"A short man, very, very broad, with, you know, a milky kind of eye? His left eye?" the Palestinian Christian Shin Bet agent asked.

"Yes, that's him! I have his phone number, if you want."

"You do?"

"Yes. I have all Massoud's phone numbers. When he saw the tanks, and cursed my mother and my sister, and said, 'Go, go to your Jews,' and called my mother a whore, and her daughters whores, and said, 'Go... Hamas will find you and kill you!' When he said all that, my mother didn't say anything. She just took his cell phone that was sitting on the table, and hid it in her blouse. I have it here."

And, so saying, Miriam Mizrachi of Afula, daughter of Sara Mizrachi, and the Jewish step-daughter of Hisham Massoud, handed over the latter's cell phone to Imri Pilo of the Shin Bet.

Imri and Ali, Israel's most valuable agent inside Hamas, quickly realized that Massoud was hauling construction materials to this Al Hamdi. Ali knew the man, knew he had a job in Hamas, but didn't realize what it was, until now. He must have been one of, if not the, chief contractors for Hamas, and in charge of building their attack tunnels. The regular smuggling tunnels didn't have reinforced concrete arches, or miles of electrical cable. And now they had Al Hamdi's cell phone number.

Imri immediately contacted the commander of the Golani Brigade, which was operating at that moment in Sha'jaiya.

Then Ali called Bashar Al Hamdi, the contractor.

The joy here, was that few people in Hamas knew what others in Hamas actually did. They might know you were a brother, but were you in the Al Aqsa Brigades? Were you in intelligence? Were you this or that? No one knew. That way, if anyone was caught, they could not implicate the others.

Thus, when Ali called the contractor, he identified himself. "Listen," he said. "This is Ali Al Bakhri, the son of Sheik Achmed. You know me, and I know you. We are, both of us, brothers."

"Yes," said the contractor.

"Well, I saw the Israelis capture a *shaheeda*, a female suicide bomber. It was the Jew daughter of that dog, Massoud."

"What does this have to do with me?" said the contractor.

"I'm trying to help you. You don't need to know what I do. But I can tell you, this Jew whore gave herself up to the Israelis, and then they came and took her whore of a mother, and her whore of a sister from Massoud. You can check what I'm saying. People saw it. It's true."

"So, what does this have to do with me?" asked the contractor, though he already knew in his gut what it had to do with him. He had been betrayed. The Israelis knew what he did, where he was, and were coming to get him.

"You're in danger," Ali told him. "I've got a safe house where you can go . If you try to get to Shiffa, the Israelis are everywhere. They're probably coming for you already. If you want to live, you have to leave now. One of their drones is probably already on its way to kill you."

"Yes. Okay," said the contractor. "Where should I go, brother?"

Imri had already called the Golani Brigade commander, and told him to pull back away from from the area between Al Quds and Salah A Din Streets.

"There better be a good reason for this," said Colonel Salah Muadi. Muadi was the first Druze Commander of the elite Golani Brigade, a Druze Arab, commanding one of Israel's most storied combat units, and his guys were in the process of kicking some serious Hamas tail, when this clown from the Shin Bet says pull back!?

"There's a great reason!" said Imri. "All your guys out, except for the best platoon from your Recon Unit. They're going to liaise with one of my guys, and he's going to take them to Salah A Din Street 84. First floor apartment."

When the contractor asked "Brother Ali" where he should go to be safe from the Israelis, "Brother Ali", of course, told him "Salah A Din Street 84. Ground floor apartment. *Insh Allah*, our people will be waiting for you."

And because they had now locked onto the contractor's cell phone, they tracked him as he dutifully left his home, and carefully made his way to the area between Al Quds and Salah A din Streets.

True to Ali's word, there were no Israelis in the area.

Allah be praised! thought the relieved contractor. *The Brothers of Hamas and Allah il Rahman, the Merciful, are watching over me!*

When he got to number eighty-four, he found the door to the ground floor apartment open, and was immediately snatched, grabbed, cuffed and hooded by 2nd Platoon, Company A of the Golani Recon Battalion, who, together with a Shin Bet agent identified only as Tsachi, spirited him out of Gaza, and into one of those kind of rooms few people ever want to enter.

There, they persuaded Brother Al Hamdi, the contractor, to give up the location of every terrorist attack tunnel he had helped build. There might be other tunnels, built by other contractors, but the IDF now knew the precise location of the entrances and exits to at least thirteen. Over the next week, they used that information to foil a half dozen additional Hamas attempts to murder and kidnap Israeli civilians. Then they used the same information to blow the tunnels up.

And all because a would-be female suicide bomber's Jewish soul began to tremble at the sound of the holiest Jewish prayer.

Neither Dani, nor Allon, nor any of the members of the Givati unit, nor the families of the slain, nor Tera, nor Washburn, nor Peña would ever know what their rescue mission had actually accomplished. Hundreds of lives had been saved because of what they all thought of as a failed mission.

As Tera Dayton would have said, "Praise Jesus."

CHAPTER 17

W hile Imri Pilo and Ali Al Bahkri were running the operation, evidently as part of a Divine Plan, which began with a Muslim terrorist's dream of Jesus, Dani Kahan, and the remaining members of the American team, went to the funerals of the fallen Givati soldiers.

That was not the original plan, nor intent.

None of them had more than two hours sleep the night before. Indeed, Peña was still hungover from his boilermaker binge.

Later, after they had met with the Ambassador, Dani had told them it wasn't necessary for them to come. They could take the time to get some rest, take a nap, or have a swim in the ocean.

But Washburn, Peña, and Tera all said they wanted to go.

They had gone in together, and they would pay their respects together, at least to the Israelis, if not to their own.

They were in need of ceremony.

Their colleague, Clint McKeever, was lying in a cooler with an Embassy tag dangling from his toe.

That morning, upon their return from the Golani assembly point, and turning Miriam's mother and sister over to Imri Pilo of the Shin Bet, they had been told by Wilt, The Ambassador's chief of staff, to meet the Ambassador at 08:30, in the small briefing room generally used by the CIA Chief of Station.

Like all rooms of this nature, it looked like a junior high school classroom in a mediocre, middle-American school district. It was completely devoid of any personality. There was a laminated wood conference table, government issue, and plastic-backed chairs. There were no ash trays, as smoking was forbidden in the building. There was no coffee maker. No maps. No whiteboard. Nothing on which an impression could be made or retrieved. No water dispenser. Nothing, in short, in which any bug could be secreted. There was a pull-down screen, but no projector of any kind. There were no windows. The light was was compact fluorescent, CFLs, the kind that always gave Tera Dayton migraines.

The Americans had assumed they were going home with McKeever's body, and thus had hastily packed their belongings into their duffles and backpacks.

Peña, Washburn and Tera stood, dutifully assembled there, by directive of the Ambassador's silent-eyed majordomo, a ferret-faced individual, who made no sound when he or she walked.

They thought of him, or her, as he or she, because Wilt seemed to be of no determinate sex.

Indeed, Wilt, which for all they knew was an acronym, seemed somehow other than human, at least in the normal understanding of the term. It was as if he, or she, were not only conceived, but somehow birthed, in a petri dish.

Nor were any of them sure if Wilt was a first name, or last; just as they were vaguely unsure as to Wilt's gender.

He or she was overweight, but not obese.

He or she may have been a mildly pleasant-looking, pudgy, slightly effeminate guy, or an unattractive, somewhat masculine, overweight woman.

The slight mustache above his or her upper lip merely added to the uncertainty.

In addition, Wilt was the Ambassador's shadow. Indeed, even if the Ambassador was not there, Wilt appeared to be, somehow, a disconnected shadow, like a soul wandering, not yet in heaven, nor consigned, yet, to hell. Simply, somehow misplaced.

"Hey," said Peña.

"Are you addressing me?" Wilt said in the monotone voice of something electronically generated.

"Yeah," said Peña. "I'm a little hungover, so, no offense, 'cause, you know, I'm still a little messed up."

"The Ambassador will be here momentarily. He apologizes for the delay." Wilt said, and added by way of explanation, "Bookkeeping chores."

"Yeah, listen, no," said Peña, "that's not... I got a question."

"I believe I just answered it," said Wilt.

"Are you, like, a guy, or a girl?"

"He shouldn't be more than another minute or two," Wilt said, and padded noiselessly out of the room.

Tera smiled in spite of herself, and Peña caught it. "I mean, like, what do you think?" he asked. "And 'Wilt'.... Is that like 'Wilt Chamberlain', or like 'Jane Wilt', ya know? I mean, I'm a little weirded out, you know, 'cause, in Spanish you could talk to her, or him, you know, in feminine and then he'd say no, you know, and use the masculine. But English is like... You don't know who you're talkin to, ya know?"

"I think she's a woman," Tera said.

"Nah," said Washburn. "That's a guy. Adam's apple."

"That's not always a sure sign," Tera said.

"One hundred percent, sure sign," insisted Papa SEAL.

And so it went. One hungover, both, slee-deprived, they argued about whether or not a bobbing Adam's apple was a foolproof gender marker.

Tera insisted it wasn't.

Washburn insisted it was.

"Man hands," said Peña definitively, trying to end the discussion, which was making his head hurt even worse.

But none of them had their hearts in it, anymore. Whether or not Wilt was male, or female, or, somehow in transition no longer made a difference.

They had been expecting to accompany McKeever's body to the airport for the flight home.

Their mission was complete here.

The terrorists were dead, but they had gotten intel from the laptop.

They weren't sure how the mission would be classified. Success, or failure?

It didn't matter to them, any more than whether Wilt was male or female. They had come to do a job.

They had done it.

Somebody else would decide whether or not it had been worth it. That was above their pay grade. Just like somebody else would decide if Wilt was a guy or a girl.

All they knew was that now they would accompany the body to the airport.

Then they would board the long flight for Andrews Air Force base.

They would meet his family, and offer their condolences, and each would go his, or her, separate way. And, in all likelihood, they would never see one another again.

But despite the uncertain outcome of their mission, as androgynous as Wilt, the Ambassador's shadow, they expected certain things.

They expected that there would be a Marine honor guard. McKeever had been a Marine. Once a Marine, always a Marine. They expected a flag-draped coffin for him, as well.

Even though they hadn't known him longer than a fortnight, they had forged a bond with him, unknown to those who have never faced death together.

They had become comrades in arms.

They expected respect.

McKeever had died trying to hood and cuff a terrorist they had come to apprehend, and each of them had, somewhere in the back of his, or her, mind, the fact that perhaps a piece of shrapnel that would otherwise have killed them was lodged in McKeever's body, instead.

That was when the Ambassador came in, with Wilt standing silently behind him, and told them there would be no flight home for the late Clint McKeever today.

No Marine honor guard.

No flag-draped coffin.

No respect.

"Uh, Washington has decided," said the chinless Ambassador, "to postpone the flight 'til Friday morning."

"That doesn't make any sense," said Peña.

"Sure it does," said Tera.

"Means the body gets to Andrews Friday night," Washburn said, shaking his head. "No news coverage that way. That's when they used to fly 'em back from Afghanistan. Low profile."

"No profile," Tera said. "You want to dump documents or a body, do it late Friday. All the big time anchors are off. All the hotshot reporters are home watching ballgames."

"Whatever," said the Ambassador. "There are some forms you're to sign."

So saying, he nodded to his shadow, who stepped out into the CFL light, and wordlessly passed out a series of forms to the three Americans, and then stepped dutifully back behind the Ambassador.

"What are these?" Tera asked.

"Nothing out of the ordinary. Boilerplate, really. Just a formality. Just sign at the bottom... Wilt?" The Ambassador said, and the shadow stepped out into the light once again, and proffered government-issue, US Embassy-embossed, dime store Bic pens.

"These are secrecy forms," Tera said, skimming through the paperwork.

"Government confidentiality agreements," corrected the Ambassador.

Tera read aloud from the form, "I have been advised that any breach of this agreement may result in the termination of any security clearances I hold, removal from any position of special confidence or trust, termination of my employment... Uhhh or relationship with the Department or Agency... In addition, I have been advised that any unauthorized disclosure of classified information... What classified information?"

"Everything which has happened since you were picked for this assignment is now regarded, officially, as classified information," said the Ambassador, smiling his vague smile.

"Especially the circumstances of McKeever's death?" asked Washburn, who was an old hand at this type of government CYA exercise, which was usually used to cover friendly fire deaths, or the slaughter of innocents by American-flagged forces.

"All of it is classified," said the Ambassador, no longer smiling, and stressing the word "All".

Tera continued to read aloud, " ...Unauthorized disclosure of the facts will constitute a violation or violations of United States Criminal laws, including the provisions 641, 793, 794, 798, 952 and 1924 title 18 United States Code... Nothing in this agreement constitutes a waiver by the United States of its right to prosecute me..." Tera looked up, "So, no matter what, you can prosecute us?"

"The government of the United States of America, Ms. Dayton. Not I. I'm just the messenger. I should also advise that you are liable to prosecution, by virtue of your previous oaths, if you do not sign that form."

There was a dead silence in the windowless room.

"So, how did McKeever die?" Washburn asked, looking down at the chinless Ambassador.

"I don't believe," said the Ambassador, "that's been decided yet. When it is, you either will, or will not be informed."

"We'll be given the lies to tell, or someone will say we just weren't there," Tera said, feeling ill.

These were the forms that Clive Harriman Walker III, her mentor and friend, who loved her as if she were his daughter, had given her to sign after she'd been gang-raped in Quetta.

It would have been inconvenient for US/Pakistani relations if a female operative had been gang raped in the fragrant orchards of Baluchastan. And so, of course, it had never happened.

"Sign the forms, Ms. Dayton." the Ambassador said.

The three Americans looked at one another.

There was nothing to do.

They signed the forms, and Wilt collected them, and the government issue, US Embassy-embossed, dime store pens.

Then the Ambassador and Wilt left.

Peña shouted after them, "Hey! Is he a guy or a girl?"

But the Ambassador and his shadow had already disappeared down the energy-efficient CFL-lit hallway.

CHAPTER 18

D ani was waiting for them at the beachside rear entrance to the Embassy. He had expected to take them to the airport.

The working assumption, that all of them had, was that the Tel Aviv Municipal Coroner's Office would transfer the remains of Special Agent McKeever to the Marine Corps guards, who would, then, following their own proud tradition, treat those remains with the utmost respect, as if he were one of their own.

A government-issued metal coffin, thirty of which were stored in the Embassy basement for those American Nationals unlucky enough to have their lives upon the planet cut short by a Hamas-fired Fajr 5, or M75 rocket, would have been brought up, via the rear freight elevator, to the Embassy loading dock.

There, a detachment of Marines would have transferred the body, lovingly, and with military precision, into the metal coffin.

They would have draped his coffin with the American flag, securing it with a Bungee-like cord that wrapped around the casing.

Then, eight Marines, marching in lockstep, carrying the casket at shoulder-height, dressed in US Marine Corps Combat Utility Uniform, Desert MarPat, would transmit the coffin to the Embassy's Suburban.

A Marine Corps driver and escort would then have driven the Suburban, followed by another Suburban filled with the eight Marines, who would then transmit Special Agent Clint McKeever's remains, in the flag-draped coffin, marching in lockstep, coffin held shoulder-high, to the waiting military transport plane that would bring Special Agent McKeever's remains to Andrews Air Force Base, where another detachment of eight Marines would, lovingly, slowly, and with the utmost respect, transmit the flag-draped coffin onto a waiting caisson, to be met by McKeever's family, as befits a returning hero.

Dani had volunteered to take Washburn, Peña, and Tera, in the third vehicle of the procession, to that area of Ben Gurion Airport reserved for foreign military transport planes. He was dressed, not in fatigues, but in his Class-A uniform, as a sign of respect both for his American colleagues, and the Israeli fallen, whose funerals he would attend that day, as well.

Israeli soldiers and officers rarely wear their unit's berets. In the field, unlike their British counterparts, their berets are not even counted as part of their uniform. Instead, they wear their unit's baseball cap, or the ubiquitous Israeli military *kovah temble*.

The only time Israeli soldiers wear their unit's berets are at official parades or ceremonies, when they are being court-martialed, or at the funerals of their fallen comrades in arms. Otherwise, even when wearing their Class-A uniforms, the berets are neatly folded, and tucked underneath the left epaulette.

As a sign of respect, Dani Kahan showed up in his "A" uniform, with his purple Givati Brigade beret, with red-backed insignia, firmly planted on his head, with the black leather piping at eyebrow level.

He had expected to see Washburn, Peña, and Tera standing at the curb, with their duffels, and two Embassy Suburbans loaded with Marines and a flag-draped coffin.

Instead, he saw a dejected-looking trio of Tera, Washburn, and Peña standing at the curb, looking like forlorn third-graders who had missed the schoolbus on a class field trip.

He stopped his SUV, got out, and crossed over toward them.

"What's up?" he said.

"Ever hear of a document dump?" said Tera.

"You mean, the Friday Night Special?" Dani asked.

"Right," said Washburn. "Except, this was a body dump. They're flying McKeever's remains home when it'll get the least coverage. My guess is, the family won't even meet it at Andrews, because, of course, he was never out of the country to begin with."

"They'll be lucky if they don't FedEx his ass," said Peña.

"I'm sorry," Dani said, removing his beret, folding it, and tucking it under his left epaulette.

"Yeah, well," said Washburn, "don't make no nevermind. He's dead."

"His family isn't," Tera said, softly.

They were all quiet for a beat.

The morning joggers and bicyclists were out on the *Tayelet* beach promenade. The surfers were carrying their boards down to water's edge, as the cabana boys were placing the beach chairs out on the sand, and grandmothers strolled their grandchildren in prams along the seashore. It was, considering the number of funerals that would be held today, an almost sickeningly perfect day for the beach.

"What about you guys?" Dani asked.

"Waiting for orders," Washburn said.

"Yeah, man," said Peña. "Guess we got us the day off."

Dani nodded his head.

Next to the Embassy, they were sweeping up Mike's Place, the expat and official Marine Corps bar, from the previous night's wartime debauch. The smell of stale beer and cigarette butts wafted toward the four of them.

"Well, maybe, you know, just catch up on some sleep," said Dani. "You know, get some sack time, or..." He looked out across the sand, to the Mediterranean, blue-green and foaming, as it lapped up against the shore. "Perfect day for the beach."

"What about you?" Tera asked, looking up at him, eyes meeting his.

"Decent day for funerals, too."

"We thought we'd go along with ya, if that's okay," Washburn said.

Dani looked at them, quizzically. "You don't need to, you know?"

"Sure we do." Tera said, eyes looking straight at him.

"Absolutely," said Dani. "My bad. Absolutely."

"I wanted to wear my Dress Whites," said Washburn. "As a sign of respect. But, you know, officially... We're not even here."

"Not that the sight of a six foot, five inch black man in US Navy Dress Whites would draw attention, or anything," Dani said.

"Right," said Washburn, and they climbed into the SUV, Washburn riding shotgun, Peña and Tera in the back.

Dani pulled out onto Ha Yarkon Street. They drove down toward the ancient city of Jaffa, looking like a Greek island, or medieval Crusader movie set plopped down along the coastline, amidst the high-rise glass and steel hotels, gleaming white in the morning sun.

Dani turned left, and they went up just one street, into turn-of-the-century architecture: romantic archways with slatted shutters, to guard against the harsh light of the Levant. One neighborhood nudged up against the other, like crowded passengers in some crazy, Middle Eastern subway car. Open-air markets, Ottoman train stations, the Vineyard of the Yemenites, the neighborhood of the Lovers of Zion. Cobblestoned, Tuscan-like streets, and alleyways that smelled of donkey urine nudging up against luxury, five-star hotels. And the unbelievably savory smell of Zachariah's Soup Restaurant. Oriental spices, and boiling onions, garlic and crushed chickpeas, and creamy sesame *techina* all competed with one another to make the mouth water, and Dani thought about how crazy in love with this place he truly was. He headed North, toward the old port of Tel Aviv, turned right along the green belt of the Yarkon Park, with early morning rowers sculling along the river, until the air raid siren sounded, and the CODE RED ALERT was intoned by the radio announcer.

By now, Tera, Washburn and Peña all knew the drill.

Dani pulled over. They huddled up for shelter, and looked toward the sky.

Arcing up toward them, from the South, they saw the white trails of Hamas rockets streaking toward Tel Aviv. And then, the Iron Dome interceptors taking them out, exploding white, in clouds above their heads, as they ducked, and shrapnel rained like hailstones on the beachfront city down below.

Then, as if they had simply pulled over in keeping with some bizarre new ritual, they, and the other morning drivers, simply got back in their vehicles, ignored the war, perhaps said private prayers of thanksgiving, and went on about their business as if nothing at all out of the ordinary had happened.

Dani pulled onto the freeway.

There would be a dozen funerals across the country, throughout the day. The music playing on the radio was neither martial, nor somber dirges, nor was it Mozart's *Lacrimosa*.

They were playing Israeli folk songs.

Sweet, simple melodies, perhaps as nostalgic as they were sad. But, never maudlin. They were peasant songs, the kind young soldiers sing, and have sung, forever.

The one that was playing, on the normally pop station, was called *Anachnu Shneinu Me'oto Hakfar.*

Unconsciously, or, perhaps, because he couldn't help himself, Dani sang softly along with it.

Tera sat behind and to the right of Dani. From where she sat, she could see a kind of grimace on Dani's face, his lips pressed in against his teeth, shaking his head slightly, as if to ward off something evil which had this way, come.

The melody was minor-keyed, and a Marine honor guard could have carried a casket, shoulder high, in lockstep to its rhythm.

They were on their way to the funeral of Aviv Abutbul, of Blessed Memory, twenty-one years of age when he had burned to death outside the wreckage of the piece of crap, fifty-year-old M113 APC that had broken down in an alleyway of *Sha'jaiya,* and offered a perfect target to the Hamasnik who set off the IED.

Aviv had lived just long enough to die in the arms of his friend, Davidi Ninio, inside the Nagmachon Troop Carrier, with the smell of his burning flesh filling all their nostrils, and seared forever into their souls.

And, somehow, the melody of that song seemed, to Tera, to capture all the sadness and heartbreak of young lives lost in fiery deaths, in the arms of lifelong friends.

"What is that?" she asked softly, almost inaudibly, almost against her will.

"What?" Dani asked.

And, beneath the Oakleys that hid his eyes from the glare of the Middle Eastern sun, she saw the tear streak down his cheek.

He looked away, and brushed his sleeve across his face, as if, perhaps, there were an itch, or a pesky mosquito, which he had just brushed away.

For his part, Washburn stared straight ahead, not looking once at his friend. Not wanting to embarrass him.

When Dani spoke, his voice was hoarse, as if from too much smoke inhaled.

"It's called," he said, and cleared his throat. "It's called *Anachnu Shneinu Me'oto Hakfar.*"

"What do the words mean?" Tera asked.

And, as Dani spoke, Washburn and even Peña, leaned in, because they were affected by the melody, as well. It was as if Tera had asked the question for all of them.

"It means," Dani said, "'We are both from the same village'. It's from my step-father's generation, from the Yom Kippur war. True story. About these two guys, Yosef Regev and Ze'ev Amit."

Dani translated along with the song. "It says, 'We're both from the same village. We used to walk through the high grass of the fields. And, in the evening, came back together, both of us, from the same village. In the orange groves, and in the pathways between the trees, we loved the same girls. We ran away to the same places. We went to the same wars. We crawled through the same thorns. And', what do you call them, not stickers, but..."

"Brambles?" Tera said.

"Yeah, probably. 'We crawled through the same thorns and brambles, and returned to the same village. And, on Friday evenings, the Sabbath, when a soft breeze passes through the black treetops, you are the one I remember'."

The song changed from chorus, to melody, and Dani's voice grew hoarse once more, as he translated. "'I remember that in the battle that did not end, how, all of a sudden, I saw that you were broken. And, when dawn came up across the hills, I brought you back to the village, where everything has remained the same. I pass through green fields, and there you are, lying on the other side of the fence, both of us, forever, from the same village.'"

The funeral of Staff Sergeant Aviv Abutbul, of Blessed Memory, was scheduled to begin in the military cemetery of Kfar Saba, at eleven thirty. Normally, it took just under half an hour to drive the distance. Dani had picked up Washburn, Tera and Peña at around 08:30, and it was now almost 11:00 hours, and they were stuck in a traffic jam, still miles away from the cemetery.

Dani muttered to himself about Israeli drivers.

"It never takes this long," he said to no one in particular. "There must have been an accident up ahead, somewhere."

"Man, this is worse than DC," said Papa SEAL.

"Israeli drivers... They're the worst. I told you, that's what you really have to be afraid of, here. Not the rockets, the drivers."

But, as they inched toward the exit for the military cemetery, in the small town of Kfar Saba, they saw that there was no accident. No tow trucks, no ambulances, though there were police.

They were there to direct the hundreds, upon hundreds, of cars that streamed into the cemetery.

"This doesn't make any sense," Dani said.

"What?" asked Tera.

"That there would be this many people. I mean, Aviv was a twenty-one year old kid, from some hole in the wall town. If you take all his friends, and all his relatives, and everyone he ever knew in his life, that might add up to a couple hundred people, at most. There's gotta be thousands here. There's no *way* he could have known that many people."

Indeed, later, the report on the radio said that police estimated at least five thousand people attended the funeral of Staff Sergeant Aviv Abutbul, of Blessed Memory, twenty-one years old at the time of his death.

Dani pushed in, along with Washburn, Peña and Tera, to get as close to the grave as possible. Soldiers of Aviv's unit in the Golani Brigade had been given a twenty-four hour pass to go to the funerals of their fallen comrades in arms, and console the bereaved families. They leaned upon each other's shoulders, these nineteen and twenty-year old boys and girls, their brown berets perched atop their heads, and wept, openly, and un-ashamedly, in each other's arms.

It was, after all, the Middle East. The Mediterranean. They were not stoic Marines. They were Middle Eastern Jewish kids, all of them from the same village, weeping together, as the military chaplain intoned the prayer, "God, Full of Compassion".

The honor guard fired its volley of shots in salute to the fallen warrior, and the plain wooden casket was lowered by ropes into the open grave. And then, there was the awful sound of shovelsful of earth thrown in against the hollow-sounding wood, the weeping of his mother and father, his sisters and brothers, his fellow soldiers who would have died in his place, and, literally, the thousands of others, who knew neither Aviv, nor his family, nor his fellow soldiers, nor his friends. They were simply Israelis, five thousand of them, who had come to bury one of their own. To walk with him on his final journey, in the green fields of the village.

And, later that day, in Isifiyah, in the mountains of Carmel, police estimated that fifteen thousand mourners came to the funeral of the Druz Arab soldier, First Sergeant Rafi Alamuddin, of Blessed Memory, twenty years of age at his death.

Fifteen thousand people of the Jewish state, for the Israeli-Druz soldier, who also, evidently, was from the same village.

The last funeral would be in Jerusalem, in the military cemetery on Mount Herzl. It was for Max Steinberg, a kid from LA, who had joined the Israeli Army, and served in the Golani Brigade. He was, what was known in Israel, as a "Lone Soldier", meaning he had no family of any kind in the country.

Even though he was not from Dani's unit, nor his brigade, Dani wanted to be at his funeral, because he, too, was a "Lone Soldier", with no family left alive in the country.

Unlike Aviv and Rafi, Max Steinberg had been in Israel barely more than a year.

Barely enough time to make any friends, outside of the guys in his own platoon.

Dani turned to Washburn, Peña, and Tera, and said, "if you guys want, I can drop you where you can get a taxi back to the Embassy. But, I really want to go to the funeral for this kid. There's not gonna be anybody there, and, I just feel like it's important."

"We'll go with you," Washburn said.

"You sure?" Dani said. "I mean, it's all the way up in Jerusalem. You guys could still get a little beach time."

"We'll go with you," said Tera.

"Yeah, man, why not?" Peña said. "You guys know how to throw a funeral, I'll say that for you."

Dani was ready to take offense, when Peña continued. "I mean, I ain't ever seen nothin' like it. You know, *Latino* funerals, they break your heart, man, but... I never seen nothin' like this. Soldiers. I mean, guys we were in combat with yesterday, tough guys, leanin' on each other's shoulders, cryin' their eyes out. And, like, fifteen thousand people show up for that one guy, and he wasn't even a Jew!"

And, though he didn't say it, Dani knew that all three of the Americans were comparing the way the Israelis had treated their fallen, with the image of McKeever, lying cold and alone, in a metal drawer, with a family who probably still didn't even know he was dead, and would never know he had died a hero.

Dani pushed it as hard as he could, all the way to Jerusalem, but there was no way he could get there in time.

Israel was a small country, and they had literally traversed from north to south, and then inland. The funeral was scheduled for 3:00 p.m., and they didn't arrive until past five.

And then, they realized that the funeral had still not yet begun.

They had to park miles away from the gravesite, and there were buses taking people up from the parking lots.

Later, on the radio, they heard that *thirty thousand* people had turned out for the funeral of a twenty-year-old boy, whom none of them had known.

None of them were blood relations.

None of them were friends.

None of them were friends of family, or family of friends.

Thirty thousand people.

It turns out, thought Tera, *that in this land, no soldier is alone*.

As they drove from the funeral, a song that had just been written during the war played on the radio.

It was called "Absent Friends". Dani translated the words, his voice, once again, hoarse. He stopped sometimes, to choke down tears.

"In the twilight's light I see their faces beaming.

I hear their laughter ring out once again.

Then I wake and sadly realize that I was only dreaming.

And wish I could sleep and dream them all again.

So let's drink another round,

To batlles fought, and lost and won!

To the ones we loved,

Who'll never come again.

To the birth of a new moon,
And the rising of the sun!
Let's drink another round,
Let's drink another round,
Let's drink another round,
To Absent Friends
Ten times a day the rockets rained above us,
Through battles raging night, and day, and noon.
And they ran through lead and fire,
And with a brother's love, they loved us,
And bought the lives we live,
And then, were gone, too soon.
So let's drink another round,
To battles fought, and lost, and won!
Let's drink another round,
And one again!
Let's drink another round
To fathers, brothers, and our sons.
Let's drink another round,
Let's drink another round,
Let's drink another round,
To Absent Friends

The next day, Thursday, in McLean, Virginia, Nancy McKeever, wife of Special Agent Clint McKeever, was informed that her husband had died in a training accident.

She was told that he was killed when a weapon he was using at the training range misfired, exploded, and lodged a shell fragment in his brain.

Supposedly, the accident had occurred at the LAPD Police Academy, where McKeever had been on temporary assignment.

Clint McKeever's body would be flown back in the cargo hold of a United Airlines commercial flight.

There would be no honor guard to meet it. No songs playing on the radio about absent friends all from the same village.

Instead, the FBI would see to it that the remains were transferred to the mortuary of her choice.

And, that night in Israel, Dani Kahan, needing to hide in the arms of a woman, drove down to see the widow in the south.

CHAPTER 19

G oing to see the widow was never a joyful event.
It wasn't sad either, as far as that went.
They were like two comrades in arms, combat veterans, the sole survivors of a platoon that had been wiped out.

Their bond was shared tragedy.

They took what comfort they could from each other, expecting nothing, asking nothing, accepting what moments of joy they sometimes had, and always grateful that there was this other person who understood their particular brand of pain.

They could not always give to one another. And both of them respected that as well. There were times when pain was too great, or, in Lea's case, life too overwhelming. She dealt not only with the death of her husband, but the fact that now she was raising their autistic son, Shai, alone.

Neither she, nor her late husband, had any family in Israel. Her parents immigrated from Turkey, and both had died young, without leaving any other family in the country. Her late husband had quarreled with his parents, and the breach had been irreparable. They had been embarrassed by their autistic grandson, and Lea, therefore, wanted nothing to do with them.

Her husband had been a friend of Dani's. They had gone into the army together. But her husband wasn't killed in combat, nor felled by some grim disease. He was killed in a car accident, driving drunk, from an assignation with his mistress, and killed a father and child in an oncoming car in the process.

The wife, who had gone not a little crazy after the death of her husband and only child, actually accosted Lea, and said it was her fault for not being able to hold onto her man!

How did one, in the parlance of our times, "process" that?

There was no nobility to her husband's death. Just humiliation and disgrace.

Part of the bond Dani shared with Lea was that, before her husband was killed, he'd had an affair with Dani's wife while they were still married. The affair had not been the cause of the divorce. But, still, it provided the bond of having suffered mutual betrayal. Not that Dani and his ex-wife ceased to be friends after the divorce. Their marriage had, with the benefit of hindsight, ended before her affair, and their friendship outlasted both that, and the divorce, and they were bound together by their love for their child.

Mutual betrayal, however, had been the basis of the first time Dani and Lea slept together.

Revenge.

Except it wasn't sweet, and when it was over, Lea had wept, and Dani couldn't wait to leave.

He came back the next night with flowers and champagne, and said, "Listen, we're doing it right this time." And they both broke up laughing, and wound up drinking the champagne and eating omelets, watching a DVD of *The Big Lebowski*, and quoting the dialogue to each other at the top of their lungs, "Shomer Shabbas!", and the more obscure throwaway lines only Hebrew speakers could get, "*Etz Chaim He*, as the ex used to say," though Dani accused her of going lowbrow when she put on *Caddyshack*.

They fell asleep in each other's arms, watching *Borat*.

It was, Dani thought of the betrayal, so mundane. So petty. So lacking in anything with even a shred of dignity. His best friend had *schtupped* his wife. Or the other way around.

What a cliche.

Like a Sondheim lyric: "Send in the clowns. There ought to be clowns".

And then he was dead.

And then so was she.

And so was Dani's son.

Lea was, in truth, his sister in sorrow, with whom he occasionally slept.

They loved each other, like brother and sister. Would always be there for each other, were fiercely protective of each other. They might even have fallen in love and married one another, but for the fact that each, ultimately, reminded the other of inescapable tragedy.

They could only be in each other's presence for so long, though they were always in each other's lives.

Dani had helped Lea move from Tel Aviv to Beer Sheva, so she could be nearer a village for special needs children and adults, called Aleh Negev-Nahalat Eran.

It was founded by one of Dani's former commanders; one of the most famous, and respected, soldiers in Israel's history, Major General Doron Almog.

Almog was a war criminal.

He was indicted by a left wing British Magistrate when a law firm, sympathetic to those who always brand Israelis as war criminals, filed a warrant for Almog's arrest while he was on an official visit to London. Luckily, the Israeli Embassy had been tipped off, and Almog never got off the plane, and the Brits decided, there being Israeli sky marshals aboard the plane, whom, it was intimated, would be less than willing to hand over a national hero to a Brit Magistrate, for supposed war crimes, without a fight, wisely, not to storm the aircraft, and let it fly back to Israel instead.

And what was the alleged war crime for which Almog had been indicted?

Amongst other things, while he was General of Southern Command, he was in charge of an operation which killed one of the most wanted terrorists in the world; a man who had murdered ninety-four Israelis.

Almog was not just in line to become Chief of Staff of the IDF, he was regarded by one and all as a shoo-in.

He had been the first Commando off the plane in the raid on Entebbe, which rescued 102 hostages, in one of Israel's most daring and famous Commando operations.

He'd helped rescue thousands of Ethiopian Jews from the camps in Sudan.

He was one of Israel's most decorated heroes and respected commanders.

Chief of Staff of the Israel Defense Forces, in Israel, is on a par with being Prime Minister. In some ways, it is an even more exalted position, above party politics, with the fate of the nation squarely on one's shoulders. Indeed, ex-chiefs of Staff go on to become Prime Ministers, as did Ehud Barak and Yitzhak Rabin, or they become legends, like Moshe Dayan. And at the height of his career, just as he was assured of following in those august footsteps, Doron Almog resigned from the military.

Doron's son, Eran, had been born with severe brain damage. He lacked the connective tissue between the left and right sides of his brain. He never learned to utter one word; not *Abba* (Daddy), nor *Imma* (Mommy). He never learned to look anyone in the eye. And yet, Almog told Dani, "Eran was my greatest teacher. He taught me more than anyone else in my life. He taught me that all my medals and accomplishments meant nothing, if I could not be the best father I could to my son."

Dani was with him when Almog decided to resign.

"Let me get this straight," Dani had said. "You're going to retire at the pinnacle of your career, in order to dream up and build a village for special needs kids?"

"And adults," Almog had said.

"Why?"

General Almog was quiet for a bit, and then said the most unlikely thing for a man who had spent his life perfecting his war skills. "Because, there isn't one... And I decided to listen to my heart."

"Yeah?" said Dani, in shock. "And what did your heart say?"

"That there are a lot of smart guys who can be Chief of Staff. But if I don't build this village, no one will do it. And I know I can. So I will. It's not just going to be for special needs, autism, what have you," Doron said, and Dani could hear the passion in his voice. "It's going to be for stroke rehabilitation, too, and for traumatic brain injury. For Arabs, for Jews, for Muslims, Christians, for Druze, or Baha'i, or whatever. You know tragedy is an equal opportunity employer. It has no prejudice. It picks you, no matter what your race, or religion, or politics. And we'll mix the populations, between stroke and brain injury and special needs, because these aren't people to be hidden away. To be ashamed of. These are the purest people in the world. They've never lied to anyone, never stolen anything. Never hurt anyone. And we, as a society, will be judged not by how great we are, but by how we are to the most vulnerable. The most innocent. And it won't be a warehouse. We will never give up on anyone. As long they they try to learn, we'll teach. We'll rehabilitate, and, more than anything, we will love them."

And that's what he created.

The War Criminal.

Almog's son, Eran, got to see the village that bore his name open, before he, himself, died, at the age of twenty-two.

It was one of the reasons Almog and Dani were so close. Even though Dani was, at the time, a pissant Captain, and Almog a Major General, they called each other "My Brother".

Dani told Lea about the place, and she moved from Tel Aviv to Beer Sheva to be near the village, and her son, Shai, thrived there.

He loved his mother.

But his friends were at the village.

He would come home on the weekends, but, always, he couldn't wait to get back, and it both broke Lea's heart and filled her with gratitude at the same time.

Except now, ever since the beginning of the war, the village was under rocket attack.

It had been hit twice.

All the residents had been moved into the bomb shelters, and, instead of living two to a room, they were living thirty to a room. The worst thing you can do with a special needs individual was alter their routine. And now, they had to learn that the Code Red Siren meant they had seconds to take shelter, and they were terrified by the sounds of the explosions of the rockets and mortars with which, night and day, Hamas pounded the area... Lea, who volunteered there, was falling apart. She hadn't slept in three days, but when she saw Dani, she said, "Something bad happened, didn't it?"

Dani nodded, and she took him into her arms.

They didn't make love that night. That was one comfort Lea was in no condition to give, and Dani knew it immediately.

So they held each other all night long, like brother and sister.

Like comrades in arms.

Dani hated the thought of going back to his apartment, his empty apartment, when the war was over. When the cease-fire took effect, and he had time to think about the ten lives he had lost, about the sights he had seen, the charred flesh he had smelled, the near misses, and ones he wished hadn't missed. He hated almost nothing so much as the thought of "coming home".

And so, every day, as he'd told Tera, he had an argument with himself, about whether to chamber a 5.56x45mm round, and put the barrel of his Micro-Tavor into his mouth, and pull the trigger.

And, always, he lost the argument, because, the truth was, he could not bring himself to add more sorrow to Lea's pain. He could not stick another layer of tragedy on those frail, brave shoulders.

So, he lost the argument each day, and waited for the one that would start the next day, and the day after that.

He joked with her that he was Don Quixote to her Dulcinea, and indeed she called him her Devoted Q, and he referred to her as Lady D.

They spooned, and he kept his hand on her stomach, waiting to feel her breathing go slower, softer, shallow, waited for the little purr she made always in his arms, just before she succumbed to sleep, smelled the fresh soap smell of her skin and whispered, when he knew she could no longer hear him, "I love you".

Then, he too fell asleep, and dreamt of Tera Dayton, who, ensconced in the embassy's dorm-like guest room, slept, for the first time in a long time, without the aid of either vodka or valium.

Washburn fell asleep in one of those same embassy dorm rooms, doing mental calculations about how much he had saved, versus how much they owed on the condo and credit cards and car, wondering if he could afford to retire on his Navy pension and whatever he could make doing.... What? What on earth could he do, outside of lead SEALs?

He was too old to become a cop. He had no other skills. And what would he be if he wasn't Force Master Chief Petty Officer, Papa SEAL? Who was he kidding? Nothing in his life scared him as much as the day when he would have to take off his uniform and be, not an elite warrior, but a has-been, married to a woman who had never had to live with him for more than six months at a single go, in all their twenty plus years of marriage. Who was he kidding?

Peña had fallen asleep on the sand, on the beach, half-way down to the waterline, humming *Romansas*, and remembering his *Abuelita*, and wondering where, exactly, it was that he fit in, in life. Was it here with these people, whose language he didn't speak, whose religion he didn't believe in? He was a Catholic, man, raised in the Church, talked to Jesus and the Saints! I mean, his *Abuelita* could say they were Jews all day long, and these clowns could sing all the *Romansas* in the world, but he was an American, '*mano*! Big Macs and Burger King! He didn't even score with one of those Israelian *chicas* in the miniskirts, and here he was, hugging the sand on the beach, instead of with a wife an' kids, back home. And where was that exactly? Was it the place where they'd shoved a pencil up his penis when he was a kid? Was that home? Or was it with the low riders, or in some fleabag hotel in Mexico, surveilling some druglord who lived like a king, while Peña ate stale sandwiches and drank day-old coffee? I mean, what did he have in life, anyway? He had a DEA badge and a 9mm. That was it. *Hey, great life,* '*mano*! *Way to go, bro!* Look at you! And with that thought, he puked, and fell asleep on the shore.

At 03:45 hours, Dani's phone rang.

He slid his arm out from under Lea's neck, hating to wake her, and picked up the phone, and walked into the other room, silencing the ringer as he did.

"Yeah?" he said into the phone.

"Dani?" said the voice on the other end.

"Yeah," Dani said trying to wake up.

"This is Micha Bar Shimon."

Dani couldn't clear the cobwebs. Micha Bar Shimon...

"Dani?" he heard the guy say again.

Micha Bar Shimon... Oh yeah, Dani remembered, the Intel guy Dani had given the bag, with the laptop and map and notes from the failed op in *Sha'jaiya*, that had gotten ten kids killed because of Dani's foul ups. THAT Micha Bar Shimon.

"Yeah," said Dani. "Micha... What's up?"

"We've got those items analyzed. You need to assemble your people, and I'll brief you."

"Okay," Dani said. "Listen. I'm about an hour away from Tel Aviv."

"At 05:45, have your people in my office."

"Find anything good?" Dani asked.

"Like I'm going to tell you on a cell phone. Where's your head at?"

"Right..."

"Also... Depends on what your definition of 'good' is."

"Interesting?"

"You won't be bored," said Bar Shimon, and hung up.

He heard Lea slipping on a robe, and padding over toward him in her slippers.

"What is it?" she asked, putting her arms around him.

She was beautiful.

Tiny, dark haired, dark eyed, beautiful.

Not like Tera, not blond and blue eyed, and midwest American farm girl beautiful.

Lea was a beautiful Jewish woman, and when she ran her hand through her dark hair, and looked up at him at an angle, heartbreakingly beautiful, familiarly beautiful, one of his people beautiful.

He put his arms around her, and she rested her head on his shoulder.

"I've got to go," he said.

"Something happen?" there was concern in her voice.

He was like a news station for her, now.

Was the war taking a turn for the worse, or for the better?

Would there be a cease-fire?

More rockets?

Was her son safer, or in more danger?

"I just have to go. There's a briefing. That's all."

"I'll make you some coffee."

"No, go back to sleep."

She pulled away from him and kissed his cheek.

"I can't go back to sleep, now. I'll make you some coffee."

"Okay," Dani said. He reached for his phone, and speed-dialed Washburn's number.

"Do you want something to eat?" Lea asked. "I can make you an omelet."

"No," said Dani. "Just coffee is fine."

"I'll make you some toast," she said, "with melted cheese, and I've got some pastries you can take."

"Come on!" Dani said, as Washburn's phone continued to ring. "Pick up."

"What?" said Lea.

"Yeah," Washburn said finally into his phone.

"Papa, it's Dani. Get your people together. I'll pick you up at 05:30."

"What time is it?" Washburn asked, still half asleep.

"Time to get up," Dani said. "05:30."

"All right. All right," Washburn said, and hung up.

Lea came in with a travel cup of coffee, sweet and with milk, the way he liked it, and for a moment, he thought, *it's almost like being her husband*, and the thought pleased him.

"Here's the toast," she said, and gave him the toast with butter and melted yellow cheese on top. "And, take these pastries."

"I don't need the pastries, sweet girl. This is perfect."

"For your soldiers. Someone will eat them." she said.

"Okay," he said, taking the brown bag of pastries that soaked through the bag, leaving a brown stain on it.

"By the way," said Lea. "Who's Tera?"

"Huh?" Dani asked, doubling the bag of pastries, and putting them into his backpack.

"You said her name in your sleep," Lea said.

Dani zipped up the backpack, cleared his weapon and put in the magazine that he had taken out the night before. He smacked it with his palm to make sure it was securely in the receiver, then slung the Tavor over his neck and shoulder and picked up the backpack.

"Tera's a Christian girl who I'm not sleeping with," he said.

"How do the Christians say..." said Lea, "Thank you, Jesus!"

"Amen," said Dani.

"When will I see you?" she asked, walking with him toward the door of her small apartment.

"I don't know," he said.

"You know where you're going to be?"

"Not a clue," he said.

"But you'll call me."

"If I can."

"You will call me," Lea said. "Whether you can or you can't, you will call me. You understand?"

"Yes, my Commander."

"Don't 'Yes, my Commander' me," Lea said. She put her arms around him. "My Officer and Gentleman. My Don Quixote, at war with windmills. I need you to stay alive."

"That's always the plan, Lady D," he lied.

He went to kiss her on the mouth and she turned her head, and said, "I haven't brushed my teeth."

He kissed her on the cheek instead, and held her closer and longer than he had intended. For some reason, he had the horrible feeling this was the last time he would ever hold her. He wanted to tell her he loved her, but he knew it would frighten her, like maybe he thought he'd never live to see her again. Which of course was true.

"I'll see you later," he said, and turned, opened the door, and walked down the stairs, waving without looking back, knowing she was watching him leave.

Outside the apartment building, the air was still warm, mid-summer desert warm. He walked down to the SUV, pushed the unlock button, heard the chirp, opened the door, tossed in his backpack, and put the Micro-Tavor in the well next to the seat, put the coffee in the cup holder, finished the toast in a bite, started the engine, and drove north to Tel Aviv.

He turned on the radio, and heard the end of the four a.m. news. There was the litany of rocket and mortar attacks that had happened the night before. Then there were the casualties. Four killed in a mortar attack. They didn't say if they were civilians, or soldiers. Two wounded here, a half a dozen there, four more somewhere else. And then, the announcements for the funerals.

The announcements were somber, simple, and heartbreaking.

And so it went.

He passed the turnoff that led to Aleh Negev-Nahalat Eran Rehabilitative Village, and thought of Doron and his boy, Eran. Then he thought of the kid at the roadblock. What was it now? Ten years before? Twelve? Maybe more. It was during the second Intifada, and Dani was an intel officer attached to Central Command, which was where most of the suicide bombers came from, if they didn't come from Gaza. It was at a roadblock outside of Jerusalem. The whole idea was to try to stop them before they got into densely populated areas, like Tel Aviv, or Jerusalem... Or Haifa.

Five members of Doron Almog's family had been killed in the suicide bombing of the Maxim restaurant in Haifa in 2003. They were at a family dinner, three generations; grandparents, parents and grandchildren all killed, one boy blinded.

And still, Doron didn't hate.

Remarkable, Dani thought. *The war criminal who didn't hate.* And then he thought of the boy at the roadblock.

When was it? Probably 2003. He couldn't keep track. More than a thousand Israelis had been killed in the suicide bombings in those years. There was a kid, maybe fourteen or fifteen. He approached the roadblock on foot, and he had on a coat, even though it was summertime. So the reservist soldier in charge of the roadblock chambered a round, and pointed his weapon at the boy's head, and ordered him to stop.

The boy looked around, confused and frightened, and Dani saw at once he was mentally disabled; retarded, autistic, slow-witted, whatever you wanted to call it. He was a poor kid, who began peeing in his pants as he raised his arms, and said in Arabic that same phrase Dani had heard from the would-be female suicide bomber the day before, "*Min Fadlak...*" Please.

That's all the kid could say, "Please."

They shouted at him to unbutton his coat with one hand... Slowly.

By now, every soldier at the road block had their M16s pointing at the kid's head. They could all see the urine running down his pant leg, and the tears streaming down his face.

This kid wasn't exactly Usama bin Laden.

He was a fourteen or fifteen-year-old, slow-witted child, peeing in his pants, about to get his head blown off if he made a wrong move.

He opened up the coat with one hand and they saw the suicide vest on him.

They told him to keep his hands in the air.

They could have just shot the vest and blown the kid up, and problem solved, ya know?

There were no cameras around.

It was before the invention of the smartphone. No press. No cameras. And one of the guys had said it. "Just shoot him! He's a suicide bomber, wearing a suicide vest. We've got a right to. It's legal!"

But, before Dani could say anything, the kid in command of the roadblock, just a first sergeant at the beginning of his reserve career, maybe twenty-three or twenty-four said, "He's retarded. Can't you see?"

"So?"

"So he's retarded. You can't just shoot him."

And the kid went out, and Dani and a sapper from the bomb disposal unit went out with them and, slowly, carefully, they cut away the coat, looking for trip wires. They saw the red detonator button, which hung by the kid's side. Whoever had rigged the boy up had put the vest on backward, so it fastened from behind. There was no way the kid could have taken it off.

It took them over an hour, but they got the kid out of the suicide vest.

Then, one guy draped a blanket around him, because he was shivering, even in the heat, and was embarrassed about peeing in his pants. They took him to a shelter.

Doron Almog, who had five members of his family killed in a suicide bombing, had created a village for special needs kids and adults, open to Moslem Arabs and Jews, alike.

And Hamas put a suicide vest on one of their special needs kids, and sent him to an Israeli checkpoint, to blow himself up.

Because whatever happened would be a victory for them. Either the kid would kill some Jews, or the Jews would kill him, and maybe in detonating his vest one of them might be blinded, or lose and arm. Either way it was a win for Hamas. Because they thought of both the Jews, and the kid, as subhuman.

There was a Palestinian Moslem stroke victim, at the village Doron had created.

Dani had seen him there. Very handsome guy in his early thirties, and his wife was with him in the rehab room. Doron came up and kissed the guy and put his arms around him, encouraging him. There had been another soldier from Dani's unit who had come along with him to see the village, because he had a special needs nephew. This guy was a competitive power lifter, who had won a world championship in Las Vegas, for Israel, and wore a ring that looked like a Super Bowl ring. It had his name, his event, the date, and the words "World Champion" on it.

The power lifter watched as a former Israeli General kissed the cheek of the Palestinian Moslem stroke victim, and was so overcome that he took off his world championship ring and gave it to the Palestinian guy and said, "This is a loan. When you can walk again, you have to give it back to me. But it's a world championship ring. And that's what you are. From now on, you're a champion, and you're going to walk again. And every time you see that ring on your finger, it's going to remind you of that." And the guy walked away. Just like that. An Israeli soldier gave this Moslem Palestinian his world championship ring, and walked away.

Doron caught up to him, and asked why he did that and the guy said, "I guess goodness is catching."

And we're the ones they called war criminals, Dani thought.

He hit Derech Hashalom, "The Way of Peace" exit, off the Ayalon Freeway, and turned left, toward the beach.

Washburn had, upon receiving Dani's call, gone to Tera's dorm room, and pounded on the door.

"Wha?" she said, through a sleepy haze.

"Rise an' shine, Doc," Papa SEAL said. "Dani's pickin' us up at 05:30. They got the intel."

Tera wanted to say, "What intel? What Dani? Dani who?" but she knew, from force of habit, it was wiser to say nothing until she was finally awake and in the shower.

"Yeah," she said. "Right".

She stumbled toward the shower, kept it cold, and stepped in.

She uttered some un-Christianlike things, and shivered in the freezing water.

Peña, on the other hand, fought Papa SEAL every step of the way. Bad idea.

When Washburn hadn't found him in the Embassy dorm, he called his cell phone. Peña informed him he was, he thought, on the beach.

Washburn jogged out onto the sand in front of the Embassy, and found the DEA agent halfway down to the waterline.

"Let's go, *hermano*," he said.

"Oh, man," said Peña, "I am so messed up. You, go without me, ya know?"

"I said let's go. That means let's go. Let's *vámonos*."

That's when Peña fought back at Washburn's less than gentle assistance in helping him rise to his feet.

And that's when Peña learned what a bad idea that had been.

Washburn threw Peña over his shoulder in a "rescue carry", and said the words every potential SEAL in BUD/S class learns to fear and loathe, "Let's get wet and sandy!"

So saying, Washburn carried Peña down to the surf, and threw him in.

Peña said bad things in Spanish.

Then, Washburn grabbed him by the collar and drug him through the sand, scraping the skin half off Peña's face, before the latter got to his feet.

"Okay, okay... I'm up!" Peña said, in agony.

Washburn threw his wayward Hispanic brother into a shower, just as cold as the one Tera Dayton had inflicted upon herself.

Thus, like medieval monks rising for morning prayers, Tera and Peña afflicted their flesh, and met the day.

Washburn had them outside the Embassy, as Dani pulled up at 05:30.

He looked at Peña and Tera, and said, "Well, good morning to you! We're all in our places, with bright, shiny faces!"

Dani had them at the Kirya by 05:45, and in Bar Shimon's office at 05:50 hours.

Bar Shimon looked at his watch, and at the very least, two out of three, obviously hungover Americans with Dani, and said in English, "Good afternoon."

The briefing room was like all intel briefing rooms; completely sterile. There were chairs, a conference table, Bar Shimon's computer, for his PowerPoint presentation, a carafe of coffee, some bottles of water, and a paper plate with some day-old, chocolate covered, waffle–like cookies. There was, in short, only what was necessary for this particular briefing, and nothing more.

Bar Shimon turned to the Americans, and said, "May I offer you some coffee?"

"Oh, yeah," said Peña.

"Definitely," Tera answered, smiling weakly.

"I'll take it in an IV drip, if you got it," Papa SEAL said.

Bar Shimon passed around the coffee, and the paper plate of day-old, chocolate covered waffle cookies. Peña looked green. But Washburn wolfed down half a dozen. When you're six foot five, and weigh two seventy-five, you need a calorie or two. Tera was still trying to wake up from the first good night's sleep she'd had in weeks.

"Well, gentlemen, and lady..." Bar Shimon said, "We have analyzed the contents from the laptop computer, and we've translated the notebook, and analyzed the map you gave to us from your operation in *Sha'jaiya*."

Washburn and Dani and Tera immediately took out pocket notebooks. Peña patted his pockets, and obviously came up empty.

"Uh... You got a piece of paper I could have, bro?" he asked.

"Be my guest," Bar Shimon said, and slid a note tablet across the table to him.

"Uhh.... And a pen or pencil... I think... You know... I musta... Maybe misplaced mine."

"Please," said Bar Shimon, and slid a ball-point pen across the table as well, which Peña missed. The pen slid onto the floor, and Peña crawled under the table to get it. He banged his head on the table coming back up, and almost threw up from the pain.

"I'm good," he said.

"Also," said Bar Shimon, "we have positively identified the two terrorists who were killed.... As opposed to being captured alive, and interrogated, which I gather was the objective of the mission?" he said this looking at Dani.

"It was," Dani said. "And I take full responsibility."

Bar Shimon ignored the last comment and went on. "The terrorist who blew himself up was Khaled Kawasme, known as the Engineer. He was a senior ISIS terrorist, with a good deal of experience in both Iraq and Afghanistan. He was a seasoned military planner. His presence indicates that ISIS put the highest importance on this mission."

He let that sink in to the Americans, who were all taking notes, as was Dani.

"The second terrorist was a senior Hamas operative, Daoud Abu Shukri. He was responsible for engineering, what we now know is, a vast network of Hamas tunnels which run under the border from Gaza into Israel. In addition, he helped plan the command and control tunnels that interlink all the Hamas fighting positions in Gaza, and make up what is virtually a subterranean fortress."

"Any notion about Abdul Aziz Al-Tikriti? The one they called The Sword of Islam?" Tera asked. She was fully awake now, and functioning completely as a highly proficient intelligence officer.

"From what we've been able to ascertain, he smuggled himself out of Gaza, and into Sinai. There is a very competent Bedouin smuggler, Sheikh Abu Ali, whom the Egyptians believe spirited Al-Tikriti out of Sinai, into Egypt. They also believe that he is no longer in Egypt. He left Cairo on a flight to Heathrow with a new identity, that of an Egyptian businessman. For reasons I'll explain later, we don't believe that London's Heathrow Airport was his final destination."

"What was his final destination?" Washburn asked.

"We don't know," said Bar Shimon. "Neither do the Egyptians. But, we believe he landed in Mexico. We haven't been able to verify that yet. But that's what we believe."

The Americans all looked at one another. One of the most dangerous ISIS terrorists in the world, was now in North America.

"Five years ago," Bar Shimon continued, "Israel fought its first war with Hamas. Operation Cast Lead. That's where we first ran into their really extensive use of tunnel warfare in El Atatra. You were there, weren't you, Dani?"

Dani nodded.

"One third, to one half, the houses in Al Atatra were booby trapped with these tunnels, which were going to be used to kidnap wounded Israeli soldiers. But the Lord was compassionate, and we captured a Hamasnik and found a map on him that had every single booby trap, and every single tunnel on it. So they didn't succeed even to kidnap one soldier. We were very lucky. But someone smart in Hamas, maybe Yasser Darwish, maybe Daoud Abu Shoukri, said, 'Look, the baby shouldn't be thrown away with the bath water you know? The tunnels are a good idea. But not just defensive tunnels. What if we made them offensive tunnels... Not in our villages, but tunnels that would run under the border into Israeli villages! Then, we could kidnap not soldiers, but women and children and, you can imagine, you will get a much bigger price for the life of a mother and child. And if the object is terror, then nothing is as terrible as the death of a child.'"

He looked at Dani, and regretted having said it the moment the words came out of his mouth. He hurried on to change the subject.

"Anyway," said Bar Shimon. "We found their map, and all their tunnels, and we gave them a good... Ehh what is the expression... Varnish?"

The Americans all looked at one another.

"A good shellacking," Dani said.

"'Shellacking'?" Bar Shimon asked.

"Right."

"What is 'shellacking'?"

"The same thing as varnishing," Dani said.

"So, why I can't say 'varnishing'?" Bar Shimon asked, like a typical Israeli.

"You can say it. It's just not the expression," said Dani, and added in Hebrew. "The expression is 'shellacking'."

"Okay," said Bar Shimon. "So we hit the Hamas, and they got the shellac, and the varnish, and we hit them very hard. Okay? So now, at the end of this war in 2009, Hamas says, 'Oh! The Israeli genocidal war criminals! Look what they have done! They have destroyed our homes and hospitals and baby clinics. So, we need cement and steel to rebuild them.' Because, somebody very smart in Hamas must have said, you know, like I told you, 'Let's make the tunnels again, but this time as an OFFENSIVE weapon'. So they said, 'We need cement and steel'."

"And when Israel objected," Dani broke in, "they said, 'What are you afraid of? You think we can make rockets out of cement and steel?'"

"Exactly," said Bar Shimon. "And so, your government, and your taxpayers, paid for the cement and steel, like good compassionate Americans, and we good and compassionate Israelis said, 'Sure! Let them bring it in.'"

Bar Shimon flashed pictures in his PowerPoint presentation of hundreds of UN trucks bringing cement and steel across the border into Gaza.

"But they didn't use this cement and steel for baby clinics. They used it to dig the terrorist attack tunnels that I believe you saw first-hand at *Kibbutz Kfar Shimshon*. And now, we think they may have as many as forty such attack tunnels under our border. Though their map doesn't correspond to the tunnels we've found. So, maybe there are more we don't know about, heaven forbid."

Bar Shimon clicked his PowerPoint presentation to a picture of the Ayatollah.

"Now, you have to remember that, at this time, in 2009, Hamas was part of the military projection of Iran. And Iran says to Israel, 'If you think of bombing our nuclear facilities, we will unleash Hezbollah on your northern border, and Hamas on your southern border.' Maybe that would deter Israel, maybe not. But the Ayatollah at that time is still afraid of the Americans. What can he do to deter them from attacking his nuclear program? And that's where what we found on the laptop, and in the notes, comes in."

Bar Shimon popped up a new picture in his PowerPoint presentation, one which neither Dani, nor any of the Americans except Peña recognized. Peña put down his pen and stared up in amazement.

"That's Oscar Grandi Félix!" he said, all but jumping out of his seat.

"Precisely," said Bar Shimon. "My congratulations."

"Who's Oscar Félix?" Dani asked.

"He was head of the Tijuana cartel. One of the most powerful drug cartels in Mexico," said Peña. "What's he got to do with..."

"I shall tell you what he's got to do with," said Bar Shimon. "the Ayatollah had a very good idea. They instructed the Hamas leadership, probably Yasser Darwish, himself, to approach Señor Félix, and say, 'Look my friend, we in Hamas are experts in building smuggling tunnels. We will provide the expertise for you to build a series of tunnels beneath the border of Mexico and the United States. These tunnels will have their entrances in Tijuana, and their exits all throughout San Diego. And you can use these tunnels to smuggle all the drugs you like. Because these will be high quality, with electricity, air conditioning, phone lines, railway tracks, if you like, for large shipments. And we'll do it at a very nominal price. And, why will we do this? Because, there may come a time when we wish to use these tunnels ourselves... For something other than smuggling drugs."

"Iran was going to use the tunnels to attack the United States?" Washburn asked.

"Exactly!" said Tera. "They had Hezbollah operatives in South America, who were, and are, for that matter, under Tehran's command."

"My compliments again," Bar Shimon said.

"We estimate there are almost five thousand Hezbollah operatives trading drugs, diamonds and weapons in the Argentina-Peru-Paraguay triangle," Bar Shimon said.

"And," said Peña, "Ain't no problem for them to get from there to Mexico. They just need enough heads-up time."

"Also true," said Bar Shimon. "But the Middle East is a complex place. Hamas built the tunnels for the Félix cartel. That is Hamas' leverage. Hezbollah doesn't know where are the tunnels, and neither, we think, does the Ayatollah. Then, The Ayatollah backs Assad in Syria. Assad, like the Iranians and Hezbollah, is a Shi'ite. Hamas is Sunni. Assad is slaughtering Sunnis, by the hundreds of thousands, and Hamas says, 'We cannot support this.' So, Iran says, 'Oh, you cannot support our ally Assad? Then we will no longer support you.'"

"They cut off Hamas' money?" Peña asked.

"All of it," said Bar Shimon. "So, Hamas turns to Qatar and says, you know, 'You are Sunni, we are Sunni. You would like to have a terrorist army to give you power, and we need money. Will you become our backer?' And Qatar says, 'Yes'."

"But," said Dani, "they don't start paying the money right away."

"Which," said Bar Shimon, "is a big problem for Hamas, because what do they make in Gaza, besides rockets and terrorist tunnels and suicide bombers? So they have no real gross national product. They have the smuggling tunnels, and they tax them. And the Palestinian Authority owes them money, because they say 'We are going to make a unity government with them'. But then Egypt cuts off the smuggling tunnels, and the unity government falls through, and the Palestine Authority doesn't give them any money."

"All of a sudden," said Dani, "Hamas finds itself unable to pay forty thousand of their own bureaucrats and, more importantly, their fighters."

"In a word," Bar Shimon said, "Hamas was broke. Which was why they started this war. They lose a war to Israel, and the world will give them money to rebuild Gaza, which they'll steal. But all that takes time. They haven't lost the war yet. And Qatar wasn't paying yet. The Palestinians had said no deal. Iran had abandoned them, so what did they do? They turned to ISIS."

Bar Shimon popped up a table showing ISIS's sources of income.

"ISIS has become the richest terrorist organization, or terrorist army, if you will, in the history of the world. They captured oil wells in Iraq, which bring in millions per day. They sell it on the black market, through Turkey. They sell at discount prices, so they have plenty of customers. Maybe five million a day, they make from their oil wells. Then, they have a very lucrative kidnapping business. They kidnapped maybe a thousand foreign nationals, and most of the countries are paying them ransom. A million here for this one, two million for that, three million for a French executive we know about. It adds up. Maybe another four million a day. Then they robbed every bank they could find in Iraq and Syria. They stole dollars, gold bullion, dinars, rubles, yen, and pounds sterling. Not to mention euros. All in all, we believe they have in excess of two billion dollars, and more on the way. So what does Hamas do? They come to ISIS, and say, 'you wish to displace Al Qaeda as the greatest terrorist group in the world?' You know this is bragging rights. What you call street crud."

"Cred," said Washburn.

"What did I say?" Bar Shimon asked.

"You said 'crud'," Dani said.

"And it's cred," said Washburn. "Street cred."

"Okay," said Bar Shimon, and popped up a picture of Abu Bakr Al Baghdadi.

"So," he said. "They go to this man, Abu Bakr Al Baghdadi, the new Caliph of ISIS, or *DAEESH*, the Islamic State, whatever you want to call it. He is the head man. And they say to Al Baghdadi, 'we can give you the ability to carry out the largest terrorist attack in the history of the world. Something that will dwarf the 9/11, and the Mumbai Massacre, and everything else combined. And, for one hundred million dollars, what your laptop tells us, Hamas sold to ISIS, their terrorist attack tunnels, that run from Tijuana to San Diego. And what it also tell us, is that two months ago, they began sending ISIS terrorists to South America."

"How many?" Tera asked.

It was the exact same question that Washburn hand on his mind.

"One hundred, in advance of an additional four hundred, to nine hundred more," Bar Shimon said. "And that's what's going to pop up in downtown San Diego, from the tunnels that begin in Tijuana, Mexico. Five hundred to one thousand ISIS terrorists, with anti-tank missiles, machine guns, hand grenades, thousands of pairs of plastic handcuffs and tranquilizers. What you saw almost take place in *Kfar Shimshon* was a very small-scale dress rehearsal for what is about to take place in America. The worst terrorist attack in history."

"Is there a date, when this is supposed to happen?" Tera asked.

"Not that we could find. But if Al-Tikriti went to Mexico, it wasn't to buy a *sombrero*. It was to put the finishing touches on the plan."

He let that sink into Dani and the Americans.

"There is one other piece of intelligence we have," said Bar Shimon. "The name of the new owner of the tunnels."

"Alejandro Reyes," Peña said.

"How did you know?" Bar Shimon asked.

"Because he's the one who murdered Félix, and took over the Tijuana cartel."

"And, do you know where Reyes is?"

"We've never been able to find his hideout," Peña said.

"Well, we know, perhaps not where his ultimate hideout is. But, we do know where he will be meeting Abdul Aziz Al-Tikriti, and when. And that, my friends," said Micha Bar Shimon, "is actionable intelligence, and it's the only thing standing between your country, and the worst terrorist attack ever to take place on American soil."

"Has our government been briefed about all of this?" asked Washburn.

"Of course," said Bar Shimon. "Your President was briefed yesterday. You are, I'm afraid, the last to know."

CHAPTER 20

T   he day before, during which time Dani had gone to seek the comfort of the widow in the south, the President of the United States
was scheduled to be briefed on the intel Bar Shimon would soon
share with the Joint American/Israeli team. The President, however,
had missed over half of his Presidential Daily Briefings. This fact had
been leaked to the press by VPOTUS Bo Fitzgerald, in retribution for
POTUS' consistently embarrassing the older man.

When queried on whether or not this was true, by the Fox News
White House correspondent, Press Secretary Josh Kirkus had parried
the question, by saying that the President received the PDBs on his iPad,
and thus was always fully up to date on all matters of national security.

VPOTUS found that particularly irksome.

So did Jack O'Leary.

Both of them secretly affirmed to themselves that, had either of
THEM been elected, THEY most certainly would never have missed
a Presidential Daily Briefing.

VPOTUS thus made it a point to check in personally with Mallory
Mohsen's office to make sure that he was properly informed as to the
place and time of the upcoming briefing, which POTUS did, in fact,
intend to attend. Today, he was assured, that the briefing would take
place in the situation room at 13:00 hours.

He was there at 12:45.

General Matt Tunney was already there.

"Tunney Time", as it was known to his subordinates, was always
twenty minutes early. And if you were on his staff and showed up
only fifteen minutes early for a meeting with the Chairman of the

Joint Chiefs, he would simply say, without looking up, "For a second, I thought you were on vacation."

And it would never happen again.

Secretary of State Jack O'Leary, Secretary of Defense Dick Gaynor and CIA Director Doherty were there at 12:50 hours.

Acting FBI Director Jack Profitt was there two minutes later, as was Acting DEA Director Graciel Esteves.

13:00 hours came and went.

VPOTUS Fitzgerald conferred with Jack O'Leary as to whether this was the scheduled time and place for the meeting. O'Leary confirmed that it was, and muttered under his breath about having a few other things to do today.

Finally at 13:22 hours, POTUS, National Security Advisor Deborah Wheatley, Mallory Mohsen and Attorney General Steadman all came in, laughing at some private joke.

Like they're the cool kids in class... thought Bo Fitzgerald. *Like they've been out in the quad joking around, and finally remembered to come to class, except in this instance there isn't any teacher to call anyone to account.*

There was just POTUS, who slipped into the high-backed leather chair at the head of the rich mahogany table, slung his right leg langourously over the armchair, and said, "'Kay... What do we got?"

"Well," said National Security Advisor Wheatley. "We already talked about the Yezidis."

"Right," said POTUS. "What else we got?"

"Well..." puffed VPOTUS, "what about the Yezidis?" He was busy scanning through his paper briefing book. Bo didn't like iPads. His favorite saying was, "I never had a piece of paper crash on me once in my life." He was furiously looking through the hardcopy PDB for mention of the Yezidis.

"The Yezidis," said POTUS, "are pretty well screwed."

"What are the Yezidis, again?" a bleary-eyed Dick Gaynor asked.

Gaynor desperately wanted to do a good job as SecDef. Whatever other, many, failings he had, he had been a soldier once, and proud. He had served with brave men who were, in retrospect, barely more than boys. He had held some while they died. He had saved some and some had saved him. In all his compromising, drunken political life, he felt he had never done anything to dishonor the trust put in him to lead the nation's fighting men and women. It's just that he had been such a quisling, and a drunk, for so long....

The man's a complete embarrassment, thought POTUS. The only reason he ever appointed him was because he needed a Republican fig leaf on the Defense Department budget cuts that returned the US Military to the size it was in 1938, but the man was an idiot, in addition to being a hopeless alcoholic. "Oh, and uhh, one other thing, Dick, I'm still waiting for you to sign off on those detainees from Gitmo. I ordered those weeks ago, and I was just informed that you haven't signed them."

Gaynor's head was exploding from the hangover. He wanted an aspirin, or a drink, or an aspirin and a drink. "Mr. President," he said, "the recidivism rate for Gitmo detainees returning to the battlefield, and fighting our troops, is between thirty and forty percent, and these detainees in particular..."

"Was I unclear, Dick?" asked POTUS. "I didn't ask about somebody's guess about recidivism rates. I asked why you hadn't signed off on something that I've ordered."

Gaynor gulped at a glass of water. "Mr. President, those things will be signed in.... Uhh... I just feel I owe it to the troops to do all of the due diligence in order to..."

"Dick," said POTUS, "I admire loyalty. And your loyalty to the troops is certainly praiseworthy. Your first loyalty, however, is to your Commander in Chief. If you have any doubts about that..."

"No, Sir," said Gaynor. "No doubts."

"I want to see those signed releases. I pledged to close Gitmo, and I'm going to do it! Even if it has to be a dozen detainees at a time... We clear on that?"

"Yes, Sir," said Gaynor.

"Where were we?" POTUS asked, looking at Wheately.

"The Yezidis," she said.

"Right," said POTUS. He couldn't remember what about the Yezidis they were discussing, but he just wanted to move this thing along.

"The Yezidis," said Wheatley, looking at SecDef Gaynor, "are a religious minority in Iraqi Kurdistan for the most part, and ISIL are threatening to wipe them out. We have reports that they've gone up on their holy mountain, Mt. Sinjar. I'm not sure what we can do for them that won't leave more of a military footprint than we feel is desirable."

"It's all over CNN," said O'Leary. "It's all Wolf's been talking about."

General Tunney looked up from his briefing book. "ISIS is threatening to..."

"ISIL," Wheatley corrected him, but he paid her no mind. It was bad enough he had to take crap from Dick Gaynor.

"...They're threatening to annihilate them, kill all the men, rape the women, and sell their daughters as sex slaves. It's doubtful that the Kurds will be able to protect them. They're starving up on that mountain of theirs. ISIS seems content just to surround the thing and let them die without risking any casualties. We could air-drop supplies, bring in some special ops guys, or we might even see this as an opportunity."

"An opportunity to do what exactly, Matt?" asked President Kabila, with a bit of an edge in his voice.

He had this habit of calling people by their first names instead of using their titles. He insisted that it was a friendly informality, though he also insisted on being called Mr. President, even by Mallory Mohsen.

General Tunney wanted to say, "Well, I'll tell you what the opportunity is, Ralphie." He used to fantasize about that. About calling him Ralphie, or "Hey, Ralphie boy", just like Norton on *The Honeymooners*. But Kabila was too young for that show. Probably didn't even know who Gleason was.

"To bomb the sons of bitches!" General Tunney said, burying his inner Ralph Kramden, and resurrecting his hidden George C. Scott. How he longed to say, 'We're not going to just shoot the sons-of-bitches, we're going to rip out their living goddamned guts and use them to grease the treads of our tanks!' But, he sufficed, by saying, "Mr. President, there are about five thousand of them surrounding Mt. Sinjar. That makes the base of that mountain a very target-rich environment. We could put a real dent in their day, Sir. We could take them down a notch. We're going to need to, sooner or later. We should have done so, already. With all due respect."

"Well," said POTUS, "when, and if, this country decides to become a military dictatorship, then I guess the Joint Chiefs will be able to make that assessment and carry it out. But until then, my read of the Constitution is that I still have that job."

"No one was suggesting, Sir, that..." General Tunney quickly put in. He was a career military man, and when it came to mouthing off, he had long since decided he was no Georgie Patton. He knew when to salute, and say, "Yessir, three bags full!"

"No, of course not," said POTUS, "I'm just a little teed off this morning. But... Just to be clear, I didn't pull our troops out of Iraq, just so we could start bombing there all over again. I mean, that wasn't the point of the exercise, Matt, in case you missed that particular memo."

Even when he's attempting to apologize he can't help being snarky about it, O'Leary thought.

POTUS was, indeed, teed off this morning, but not because of the Yezidis or ISIL.

Mickey Jay, arguably the greatest basketball player who had ever played the game, had called POTUS a crappy golfer on ESPN.

I mean, the President of the United States had invited this bozo to the White House, had flown him on Marine One to Camp David, taken him to hear Al Green at the Kennedy Center, and then had offered to play golf with him at the Grand Oaks Golf Club in Florida. I mean they filmed *Caddyshack* there! MOST people in the United States might have thought of that as an honor, but Mickey Jay said, "I'm not sayin' he's not a good politician. I'm just sayin' he's a crappy golfer."

POLITICIAN?! Thought POTUS, *That low-life doesn't even think to call me a great President, he says, "I'm not sayin' he's not a good politician?!"*

The problem was, he had a foursome scheduled with Mickey Jay this weekend at Grand Oaks, and if he cancelled now, Mickey Jay would trash-talk him on ESPN, and say he chickened out of the game.

Of course, the fact that they were scheduled to play this weekend, after POTUS' Florida fundraiser, was PRECISELY why Mickey Jay HAD trash talked him on ESPN.

He did it to rattle him, to get under his skin, make him choke when he got out on the green. Mickey Jay didn't get to be the greatest basketball player in the history of the game because he WASN'T competitive. Mickey Jay was the most competitive man on the face of the earth! And he didn't care if he was shooting backyard hoops, or if you were President of the United States of America, playing for a box of Cuban cigars, or Kobe Bryant, playing for the world title.

He'd do anything to get into your head and screw up your game. He woulda trash-talked POTUS' ol' lady, if he had to. In fact, Mickey Jay was probably laughing about it right now on the phone with Charles Barkley, and POTUS knew it!

"Mister President," said Jack O'Leary, "we're going to have to do something about this Yezidi thing. They've got a CNN crew up on top of that mountain and an NBC crew is on the way. You've got women dying up there. People are comparing it to a modern day Massada."

"Who's comparing it to a modern day Massada?" POTUS demanded. "The Israelis?!"

"No, Sir," said Jack O'Leary. "The Kurds are. We've got to at least drop them some food and water up there."

"We could land some choppers up there, with enough food and water to..." offered General Tunney.

"We're not landing any choppers up there, and risk ISIL shooting them down! Doesn't anybody get it? We're through with Iraq!"

"Obviously ISIS hasn't gotten that memo, Sir," said General Tunney.

"Air drop," said POTUS. "That's it. Parachutes. From whatever altitude is out of their rocket range. That's all. And Jack, I want you to get the French in on this, and the Brits, and the Germans, too. We shouldn't be the only ones with exposure on this, and we shouldn't be out front on this thing, because if we are, then that's where the French and the Brits will make sure we stay! What else we got?" POTUS said, looking at his watch. "I've got to be in Florida for that fundraiser."

"We have the report from your joint team that was sent into Gaza with the Israelis," said CIA Director Doherty.

"The Israelis screwed the pooch on that one!" POTUS said. "They were supposed to interrogate those two ISIL guys, not blow 'em up! Kivi Natanel! Big Commando!"

"Wasn't exactly a precision operation." said Jack O'Leary.

"One of our agents was killed in the firefight. Clint McKeever," said Profitt. "We're flying his body back today."

"Actually, I think it would be wiser to bring his body back late Friday evening. Slowest news day of the week. We keep a low profile, that way," said Mohsen.

"We wanted an honor guard for his family," Profitt said. "His twin brother and he have been in the Bureau for thirty years."

"Low-profile, Jack," Mallory Mohsen said and glanced at POTUS. "His family isn't to know he was in Gaza. They're not to know he was out of the country. You put something together, a drug bust that went wrong, or something."

"No one's saying be disrespectful," said POTUS. "Good funeral. Give me a letter to sign, for the family... But, uhh, Mallory's right. Low profile. Killed in the line of duty... Maybe... You know, a weapon misfire on the range or something... But uhh... Low profile, Jack. Got it?"

"Yes sir," said Jack Profitt. He glanced at no one. Simply pretended to make a note on his yellow legal pad.

"I think a weapon misfire is probably the way to go on this thing," Mallory said. "Otherwise, some reporter can always check, and say, you know, what drug bust? What bank robbery, or whatever? You know. Low profile."

"The uhh, terrorists's computer and notebook have been analyzed," CIA director Doherty continued.

"I read it it on my iPad," said POTUS.

"If the information is correct, we could be looking at a potential disaster here, Sir. If we have a thousand ISIS... ISIL terrorists popping up in San Diego, the way they did on the Israeli border with Gaza..."

"Y'o, I just want to say something here, Francis. We haven't analyzed that computer yet have we?"

"No, Sir," said Doherty. "The Israelis have."

"The Israelis have," POTUS said derisively. "Well, until *we've* analyzed that computer independently, and even then, my natural inclination is to err on the side of caution here."

"Exactly," said Deborah Wheatley.

Mallory Mohsen nodded her head vehemently.

"You mean, take some kind of preemptive step against ISIL?" The Vice President asked.

POTUS all but sighed audibly. "No, Bo. I mean the exact opposite. What do you want me to do? Invade Mexico?"

"No, of course not," said VPOTUS, "But..."

"I mean, I said caution," said President Kabila. "Not shoot first and aim later. For all we know, this is just a bunch of Israeli BS that Kivi Natanel is pulling, to show us how valuable they are to us, and why we should speed up that shipment of hellfire missiles which they requested, and you okayed without my knowledge, Matt," POTUS said, looking at the Chairman of the Joint Chiefs.

"It was a normal request, Sir, and in light of the kind of warfare the Israelis are engaged in..."

"You want to talk about CNN's dead baby coverage?" said POTUS. "What do you think is on a loop over at CNN? And NBC and ABC and CBS? Huh? And in Europe, in every capital, there are marches denouncing not just Kivi Natanel, but ME! They burned ME in effigy in the streets of Paris, because we're supplying Kivi Natanel with the missiles and bombs they're using to kill all those children! So, it's not 'normal' at all, Matt! And nothing goes out to the Israelis from now on without my written approval. We clear on that?"

"Crystal, Sir," said Tunney.

"Well," said Bo Fitzgerald, in his best Vice Presidential tones, "maybe we ought to get the Mexicans involved in this. Let them do some of the heavy lifting, if the terrorists are in their country, and planing to attack us!"

"With all due respect, Sir," said CIA Director Doherty, "the Mexican government is the LAST body on earth we should inform on actionable intelligence regarding ANYTHING that could POSSIBLY have ANYTHING to do with a drug cartel! I mean, Judas Priest!"

"I think it's very wise to be skeptical of the intel the Israelis are feeding us," said Jack O'Leary. "But, at the same time, I think it would be imprudent to ignore it, Sir."

"Perhaps," said Deborah Wheatley, "we should simply continue with the same plan the President has very wisely put in motion."

Matt Tunney looked around the room, as if he were listening to people on hallucinogens. "I'm sorry. Honestly... I... Is there a plan in place to deal with this, of which I'm unaware?"

He looked at POTUS.

POTUS looked at Wheatley.

Wheatley looked back at Tunney, and said, as if speaking to a slow-witted child, "Well, yes, General. We have a team in place, appointed by the President, who went in with the Israelis. They are the ones most intimately familiar with this supposed intelligence, and the ones best positioned to evaluate its veracity, or lack thereof."

"Exactly," said POTUS. "They should be dispatched immediately to ... Uhh... Mexico... And, uhh..."

"And," said Wheatley, "they can liaise with the DEA agents already stationed there, to see where this intel does or does not lead..."

"Which would mean, our Agent Peña would take a lead position," said Acting Director of the DEA Graciel Esteves.

Everyone ignored her.

"It will not require any additional findings or personnel," said POTUS. "We simply stay the course, General."

"Uhh," said FBI director Profitt, "we're one man short on the team now, with the death of Special Agent McKeever. If you give me an hour, I'll have someone on a plane to Mexico to hook up with the others and take his place."

"Mister President," said the Director of the CIA, not wanting to miss a chance to gain a bit of ground in the ongoing turf war with the FBI, "I think we're probably better off adding that Israeli Intelligence officer to the team. He's the one with real field experience with these tunnels, if the threat turns out to be real. I think that would be the most prudent thing to do, rather than sticking in another domestic counter-terrorism guy. I mean, I think that's just redundant. Tera Dayton can pull that oar just fine. What we need is someone who can recognize Middle Eastern fingerprints, if there are any. Especially Hamas' fingerprints."

"The FBI is perfectly capable of ..." broke in Profitt, but POTUS cut him off.

"Francis is right, Jack," he said, pointing his finger at the CIA director. "This isn't about closing the barn door after the horse has escaped, like Boston."

That last was an incredibly thinly-veiled reference to the fact that the FBI's record at actually PREVENTING terrorist attacks wasn't exactly the gold standard. The FBI hadn't caught the Underwear Bomber. They hadn't caught the Times Square Bomber, or the Shoe Bomber or the knuckle-headed pressure-cooker bomber who they INTERVIEWED AND THEN LET GO so he could bomb the Boston Marathon!

And despite his personal antipathy for Kivi Natanel, POTUS did have a healthy respect for Israeli Military Intelligence. "If this guy knows the tunnels," POTUS said, "I want him on the team."

With that, POTUS looked at his watch once again, and brought the meeting to an end, or almost to an end.

"One last thing, Matt," he said to General Tunney. "Work up a plan for that parachute drop to the Yezidis. Food, water, medical supplies only. No weapons. Strictly humanitarian aid. Mallory, I want a statement that I can make about how we can't sit idly by. Jack, you get the Brits in on this thing, and the French too."

"Yes Sir, Mister President," said Jack O'Leary.

"Oh," said the President to Mallory Mohsen. "Cancel that golf game in Florida. I'll come back right after the fundraiser, and just say, you know, that the President felt it would be inappropriate to be playing golf while the Yezidis are starving on Mt. Sinjar, that sort of thing, blah, blah, blah."

He smiled at the thought of sticking it to Mickey Jay, and left.

Meanwhile, Abdul Aziz Al-Tikriti, now carrying an EU passport, which identified him as Señor Juan Carlos de Santiago Y Montoya, ensconced in the Presidential suite at the legendary Rosarito Beach Hotel, just south of Tijuana, Mexico, sent off a fax to his supposed Venezuelan counterpart, Señor Miguel Ángel Machaca, which read as follows, "Arrived. Deal proceeding per previous conversations. Shipments of goods authorized, per memorandum of understanding. Juan Carlos de Santiago Y Montoya."

Upon receipt of the fax sent by Fabio, the capable concierge at the Rosarito Beach Hotel, which was thought less likely to be intercepted by the NSA than an email or text, Zaid Abu Zuheri, otherwise known as Miguel Ángel Machaca, head of the Islamic Caliphate Martyrs Brigades in South America, authorized an advance team of one hundred IS terrorists, all with fake South American identities and paperwork, to begin moving, in cells of no more than ten members each, toward their rendezvous points in Tijuana. The Caliphate, praise be to Allah, was going to strike at the heart of the Crusader homeland, in an attack that Abu Zuheri knew would eclipse both 9/11 and Pearl Harbor... Combined.

Two days later, in Israel, Washburn, Tera, and Peña were told to pack their belongings. They would be leaving on a direct flight to Los Angeles, and, from thence, would travel by car to Tijuana, Mexico.

In addition, Major Dani Kahan would now be a part of their team.

"No way," Dani Kahan said to Moti Dagan, when the Colonel informed him that he would accompany Washburn, Dayton, and Peña to Mexico, in pursuit of the contact identified on Kawasme's laptop. "Absolutely no way."

"Yes, way," said Colonel Dagan. "They think you're the expert on terrorist attack tunnels."

"So, let them get another expert." Dani said.

Outside Dagan's tent at the Givati forward assembly point, Dani's soldiers, who had returned from their twenty-four hour pass to console the families of the bereaved, were suiting up once again, and loading their gear into Achzarit Troop Carriers, getting ready to go back into Gaza.

"They want *you*," Moti said.

Dani looked out the tent flap at his troops. As always, his Micro-Tavor assault rifle was slung around his neck and shoulder. An Israeli soldier is never separated from his weapon. What he should be doing right now, he thought, is loading his gear, along with all the others, and getting ready to go back into *Sha'jaiya*.

"Did you hear?" Moti said. "The Americans want you."

"Well, I don't want them."

"You want that little Tera whatsername," said Colonel Dagan, smiling at Dani.

"That's beside the point," Dani said.

"Well, what isn't beside the point is that the government of the United States has made an official request of the government of Israel, which has made an official request of the Chief of Staff of the Israel Defense Force, who has made an official request of the General of Southern Command, who made an official request of me, to supply them, with the services of Major Dani Kahan. And that's what I'm doing. So, turn in your weapon. Get out of your uniform. And report to the American Embassy."

"Turn in your weapon, and get out of your uniform" are probably the two most awful phrases an Israeli soldier can hear. You immediately become less than what you were the second before those words were uttered.

"Are you gonna tell me," Dani said, "that the United States of America, the most powerful country on earth, with the greatest military the world has ever seen, with fourteen years of combat experience in Afghanistan and Iraq, can't manage without some middle-aged, know-nothing, previously court-martialed--and demoted, I might add--Israeli officer? I don't believe it!"

"Who cares?"

"*I* do!" Dani said. "I'm not going!"

"You're going," Moti said.

"No, I'm not! Moti, I'm not going! Period. End of story!"

Colonel Dagan looked at Dani for what seemed like an inordinately long time. And then, finally, he said, simply, "Dani... It wasn't a request."

Dani grabbed one of the ever-present Israeli Army tuna sandwiches, and headed over to the Brigade Armorer.

"Hey," Dani said to Avi Shitrit, the warrant officer in charge of the entire brigade's armaments.

"What's up?" Avi said. "Whatever you want, I don't have it. Everybody else has already checked it out. It's all going inside," he said, nodding his head in the direction of Gaza.

"I'm not here to check anything out," Dani said.

"So, *nu,* what are you here for?"

"To check everything in," Dani said, and began piling his gear on the counter in front of him. The Micro-Tavor assault rifle, eight mags, plus the one that was in the gun, his ceramic body armor, weapons vest, helmet, comm gear, Camelbak, everything but his underwear.

The armorer pulled out his file, and signed on each piece of equipment returned. Then, Avi looked up at him. "Did they court martial you again?"

"Something like that," Dani said.

"In truth?" Avi asked. "Are you gonna have to go to jail?"

"Worse," said Dani, and he turned around, walked out, and waved without looking back.

He drove back to the main Givati Base, went to his Bachelor Officers Quarters room, and packed his gear into his duffel.

Then, he pulled out his jeans, a t-shirt, and a sweatshirt, took off his dogtag, and put it in his uniform pocket, and stripped down, making sure that none of his civilian clothes had a "MADE IN ISRAEL" label anywhere in them.

He caught sight of himself in the mirror.

Where just a moment before, there had stood a Major in the Israel Defense Force, there now stood some middle-aged guy in a pair of Levi's and a t-shirt, and some sneakers.

He pulled out his cell phone, and speed-dialed Lea's number.

The phone rang once, twice, three times, and then went to voicemail.

"Hi, this is Lea," her voice said on the recording.

Dani loved the sound of her voice. There was no word for it in Hebrew. It was mellifluous. Calming, feminine, sexy, without even trying. It was the voice of a woman, not a girl.

"Hi, this is Lea. Please leave your message after the beep. *Ciao*. Bye!"

"Hi, my Sweet Lady D," Dani said. "I'm fine, I'm alive, I'm wonderful, in good health, eating tuna sandwiches, but you're not going to hear from me for a while. It doesn't mean anything's happened to me. It's just Army stuff. So, when I can call you, I'll call you, but I don't want you getting crazy. I'm fine. Give Shai a big kiss, and a hug, from Uncle Dani. Bye."

He pushed "END", then put the Israeli cell phone into the duffel with the rest of his gear.

And, as much as he tried not to, he remembered the feeling the last time he had seen Lea.

That he wouldn't live to see her again.

Then, he shouldered the duffel, locked the door behind him, and went off to meet the Americans.